Hannah's Revenge

a Novel

Matthew Waller

HANNAH'S REVENGE

Third Edition

This is a work of fiction. All characters and events portrayed in this book are fictional, and any resemblance to real people, places, or incidents is purely coincidental.

Cover and interior design by Matthew Waller.
Set in Book Antiqua.

ISBN: 9798709848610

To Caspian

TABLE OF CONTENTS

"I deny everything but what I have all along admitted —
the design on my part to free the slaves."

John Brown

Chapter 1 - Fencer

Later, when she was under suspicion of being a murderess by the police and her very liberty depended on the use of her wits, Hannah would recall, as if from an earlier age, how she had been feeling particularly smart that night — the night the football players decided to rape her.

It was 6:00 pm and the windows of the Enleike Center gym were already dark when she strode out clean from the shower, her mask tucked under her arm so the épée in her hand slanted back from her hip. The clack and ping of fencing blades, a sound she loved, mingled with the squeak of sneakers as the other girls of the Hills College fencing team finished their last practice matches, making little white advances and retreats away into the shadows of the big space. As the winner of the mock tournament she had been liberated early. She hung her mask and sword on the pegs and, fumbling with the zipper of her white down parka, headed for the big double door to the night.

"Hannah! A quick word."

Across the gym she saw Coach Bailey come upright from his crouch and step off the strip. The student he was teaching slumped, hands on knees and blade akimbo, catching her breath. Hannah angled over as Bailey pulled off his old grey mask. His round yet gaunt face, that always reminded Hannah somehow of an elderly jockey's face, wore a look of discomfort.

Hannah first addressed the student. "You know, when he gets

you in circles like that he's trying to tire you out. Look how much effort you have to make to counter the tiny movements of his wrist. Don't fall for it. When you're trapped, feint and lunge."

The student, who was a Senior, two grades ahead of Hannah, gave a loopy roll of her mask. "I know, I know," came her muffled voice. "I can't feint."

"Sure you can. Try it."

"Listen to Raider, Margaret," said Coach Bailey. "But don't listen too hard. Radhe's the only one of you punks who can beat me and I want to keep it that way."

"What kind of coaching is that?" laughed Margaret.

"It's called job security," said Bailey. "Go do one more match with Anne. And practice feinting and lunging."

"What's the matter?" Hannah asked when they had moved to the wall.

"Oh, it's Dean Haughton. He asked me to talk to you about maybe writing a retraction for the paper. I don't want to get in the middle of it."

"A retraction? Me? And what specific part of my article, pray tell, does he say is inaccurate?"

"I'm not getting in the middle. Before you go home for Christmas he wants you to stop by his office."

"I'm sure he does. Just like last time. Well, no thank you. And I can't believe he asked *you* to talk to me — he thinks I'll listen to it coming from you. That's low."

Bailey sighed. He looked more uncomfortable, and lowered his voice under the echoing female gasps and grunts. "Your article is getting noticed. School paper or not, some media picked up on it and I guess they've been calling him. He says he doesn't have anything against the general points you make about rape in society. He just wants you retract what you said about the college having a history."

"The college *does* have a history," said Hannah, "as do others. I didn't call special attention—"

"*I* know—trust me, I know all too well about this school." He met her eyes, and for a moment their look went deeper than a coach-student relationship. "But you went and mentioned the Kingfishers. Roarter from the football alum office bent my ear about it too."

She looked down. "Sorry, Coach. I didn't mean to put you in the hot seat. But you can tell Haughton I'm not changing a word of my article."

Bailey gave another sigh, short and shallow, that translated to, "Well, I tried." His grey fencing gauntlet slapped her parka arm. "Tomorrow night you should come by the house at seven. Kate says not to bring anything."

"You sure? Sounds good."

"What's this? Christmas party at Coach's house and I'm not invited?" Susan Kinsler, loser of the mock tournament final and her best friend on the team, breezed up to them in a floral waft of shampoo from her damp feathered hair.

"Nope," said Bailey. She stuck out her tongue at him.

"Susan," said Hannah. "Let's meet at the cafeteria at seven, then after dinner we can go straight to Stokes for the Jawbone concert."

"I can't believe you're dragging me to see that radical dyke band. I'll get a reputation. I'll watch from the shadows, but I am *not* going backstage with you afterwards to interview a bunch of angry sweaty feminists."

"Oh, you'll love them. They're awesome."

"I'd rather go to Coach's Christmas party," Susan said to Coach Bailey with a hinting smile.

"You wouldn't enjoy it," said Bailey. "It's going to be nothing but feminist talk, all night long."

"They're having W— as a dinner guest," said Hannah, mentioning the name of a star of the contemporary women's movement, whose book on the culture of beauty was a best-seller.

"Old friend of Kate's," Bailey explained to wide, reappraising eyes from Susan. Even Susan had read her book. "She's in Boston for the holidays. Kate's filled her ear about you, Raider; she's looking forward to meeting you."

"I'm looking forward to arguing with her," said Hannah.

"You would argue with W—?" said Susan. "About what?"

"I think she's wasting her talent. Today's feminists are writing from the standpoint of already liberated women, battling with leftover cultural minutiae. I suppose it's a necessary phase. But in Burma women are still stoned for adultery. In Saudi Arabia they're not allowed to walk in public unescorted. In Southeast Asia there's a twenty billion dollar trade in underage sex slavery. The first fight is not yet won, and it requires real fighting. That's my fight. It's why I don't like to call myself a feminist. I'm more like an abolitionist, of bad laws that need to be overthrown. Maybe an action feminist."

"Like I say, all night long," said Bailey.

"Watch out world," said Susan. "Now I'm even more worried about this Jawbone concert."

"See you at dinner at seven," said Hannah, smiling. "And I'll see *you* tomorrow at practice."

Bailey nodded. "Haughton's office—think about it."

"I have. No."

"I'm not getting in the middle," he said, turning back to the gym with a gloved hand upraised. With a smile she pushed open the doors and exited into the cold air of the night. She and Susan separated and she walked alone across the empty campus toward her dorm. It was 6:31 pm.

An observer would have seen a slim girl, 5'8", with a boyish stride emphasizing the strong legs of a fencer, lightbrown hair bouncing in a ponytail, whose white coat gleamed and vanished under the successive pools of the lamps. Hannah didn't consider herself a militant, really, and the closest she had ever come to fighting was what took place on a fencing strip. At 19 she was energetic, idealistic, and too ambitious in her role models for her own good, as she herself would have admitted. Later she would have cause to wonder about the little speech she had just made. Her own encounter with male violence was just minutes away.

Peripherally she was aware of how deserted the school had become. With the end of exams yesterday the place had been all but evacuated, save for the sports teams lingering for a five-day Athletics Week and the small flotsam of long-distance castaways stuck in Boston over Christmas. Fields of cratered snow extended lunar shadows from the lamps. The campus seemed even bigger, closed-up buildings creaking in the cold, and she could hear traffic from the city outside. She saw no one as she crossed the salt-whitened road and trotted up the cement stairs. A strange quiet reigned as she approached her dorm.

"Hey, Hannah." A figure emerged from the shadows, large and casual.

"Steve," said Hannah, and braced herself for the inevitable crude remark.

She knew him only peripherally, from when she had spent

some time hanging out with the football team the previous year; he was one of the linebackers. But Steve Badenhut made a point of distinguishing himself in every gathering by making the loudest and dirtiest comments. His favored T-shirt read "Life is too short to talk to fat girls." To Hannah he used to say, "Hey, I like feminism. It's a club for ugly bitches who can't get laid. It keeps them all in one place." Then laugh uproariously. For a while when their paths crossed on campus he would stoop a little to give her a leer and a wink.

However, all he said now was, "Hey, Chris has your book and he wants to return it. He's hanging out down in my room if you want to come get it."

"Oh, right." She had loaned Chris, another footballer, her copy of "The Second Sex" earlier that semester; she'd almost forgotten about it. She looked at her dorm; she had been planning to go through her emails that had piled up during exams. But Steve's dorm, Hunter, was right next door. She debated for an instant, then said "Sure."

And just like that she followed him back to his room. Where they were all waiting for her.

Chapter 2 - Prey

In her formal sexual assault statement, given three days later in a lime-green room at the 14th Precinct in New York City to an impassive female officer and a tape recorder, while her anguished mother waited in the lounge, the question that unexpectedly aggravated her the most was whether she had ever dated any of the five players. She emitted an impatient sigh. "And if I had, what does that mean? That I was actually consenting to it? Or am somehow making a mistake identifying it as gang rape?"

"Of course not, Hannah. I'm just trying to get all the details here. Because you know the boys you're accusing will get to tell their side too."

She drew a long breath. She was, it occurred to her, a fiercer sort of person now—though what she would finally become was very much up to her—and she would have to be more careful. Behind her agenda of reporting the most horrible event of her life to the police, as a good feminist should, her primary object was to conceal from the practiced eyes of Detective Laniya Wilson the extent to which her own revenge was already under way, and this very statement part of her cover story. She foresaw a long dialogue ahead with the cops, rather more than an ordinary rape victim would have, so if step one was simply to be *believed* about the assault she would bloody well dredge up for the police record the sordid details of her affair with fullback Chris Kelly the year before.

"We met back when I was going to football team parties. At that point I was into visiting male subcultures, trying to preach the gospel, you know, make friends, talk to them about women's rights, I suppose it was a fool's errand—maybe worse than that. Anyway Chris and I only dated for about two weeks, until I found out that he did it to win a bet with the team. Like, who could date the feminist, ha ha. It wasn't a fun experience, and it's been over a year since it happened. So I didn't have any lingering *feelings* for him, Detective, if that's what you're implying, and in fact I hadn't seen Chris in months until he showed up in that room." She ran her hands through her hair. "Sorry. I'm guess I'm just upset about the whole thing."

"I understand," said Detective Wilson. "Why don't you go ahead and tell me what happened."

Steve was uncharacteristically quiet as he led her to his first-floor room in Hunter. There was no one else on the long hall whose dun-colored walls had a light woven texture, and she felt the silence of the empty dorm around them. It made her a little nervous. *It'll be easier to get my book back from Chris in company*, she was thinking; it was still awkward to have to encounter him. Since their breakup last year he had taken to mooning around her, pestering her to get back together; she had finally loaned him the book as a way to fend him off. It had worked, but she did want her book back.

"Here, come on in," Steve said, opening his unlocked door on the left and walking straight in himself, straight to the back of the room. That was odd behavior too, but Hannah followed him in. There was Chris, sitting back there in a red tee-shirt with his floppy blond hair and big chest, and she had a brief impression of a couple of other guys in a narrow space —

Then the door slammed behind her.

She jumped and whirled. Two tall guys who had been hiding against the wall had closed it and now stood blocking it. She whirled again, to Steve and Chris facing her, Chris now standing, and a fifth, even bigger guy stepped out from the side to join them.

"And here's the party girl," said one of the guys at the door.

"Right on schedule," Steve said happily.

Her heart, which had leapt into her throat at the bang of the door, wasn't slowing down, it was racing furiously as she looked rapidly around. "What is this?" she said, struggling to sound normal. "I just came for my book —"

"Nonsense!" said Steve Badenhut. "You came to have a good time tonight. Isn't that right, Hannah? A good time? I'm sure that's what she said to me." He smiled around at the group, then leaned forward and waggled an open green beer bottle at her. "Well you're in luck, 'cause that's what we're here to have."

"I don't *have* your book," Chris said, with a sullen, triumphant thrust of his chin.

It's a trap. I've walked right into — She was caught in a narrow space, with a wall of shelves on her right and a bed on her left; with the people behind and in front of her she had room to turn but nowhere to go. Hard male breathing was all around her; the room was stuffy. She stared stupidly. Her body was screaming the reality of what was happening at her but it still wouldn't add up in her mind.

"Take off your coat and stay awhile! Here, have a beer, relax!" Steve offered the open bottle to her.

Was it a joke? A taunt? Was it — sincere? She turned away from his strange pale-eyed smile, facing the blocked door again, and saw that the others had beer bottles too—all capped. "Yeah, have a drink," said the thin one, whom she recognized as Andrew Keith, another football player.

In fact she knew all of them slightly, from her time with the football team. Alongside Andrew at the door was Davey Coleman, the Freshman quarterback, by far the biggest in the room, slab-faced with a confused expression under an almost-white buzz cut. Andrew himself was slim—*that's why they put him next to Davey, to fit*—and normally good-looking, though now a sly smirk had come forward to distort his features. The very muscular guy with Steve and Chris at the back, in a tight grey tee-shirt, was—*what?—Reggie!—Reggie Mathis*—he stood with his huge arms folded and an emotionless glower.

"If it's all the same to you I'll leave," she said to Andrew, breathing shallowly. She could only keep pretending it was normal. "If, if you don't have my book."

He and Davey didn't move, though Davey looked at Steve, and she turned back, mainly to avoid seeing Andrew's smiling little shake of the head.

"All the same to us?" Steve cried to her. "Oh, it's *hardly* all the same to us. Don't make us *force* you to have fun, now." He held out the beer.

There was a pause. *What should I do? Should I take it? To buy time?* She was scrambling to think of a way to get out. The room was a Hunter triple and they were all in the small side; across the shelves lay the bigger side of the room, accessible from the wider space in back. Her epicritical senses told her there was no one back there. But she couldn't get there, and anyway she knew that the other side had no door; the only one was the one that was blocked.

She sensed immediately that Steve was the one in charge; the others were glancing at him, waiting on him to give the lead. Even Reggie Mathis, whose bouncer pose radiated the menace of the stereotypical black guy, looked to Hannah somehow — soldierly. Awaiting orders.

As for Chris, her former boyfriend, he was the only other one whose beer bottle was open, and in fact almost empty. He stared with lifted chin and unfocused eyes above a little smile. He looked drunk.

None of the others did.

"And just to be clear, who are the five boys you're accusing again?" In New York Detective Wilson's pencil poised over her spiral notepad.

"Steve Badenhut, Chris Kelly, Davey Coleman, Andrew Keith, and Reggie Mathis," she repeated.

A flip back to an earlier sheet and now an open hint of skepticism in the professional neutrality. "And you say you're pressing charges for *attempted* rape against some — ?"

"I told you. One of them raped me, and it's attempted rape for the others. But it was only attempted because I *myself* — "

"The rape charge is against Steve Badenhut?" the detective said. She looked up from her notes.

Hannah met her eyes and nodded, her mouth firm.

Steve was still extending his opened, full beer bottle to her with raised eyebrows. "Come on, why are you always so anti-social? Have a swig, party a little. Exams are over! I promise you'll enjoy it." The last phrase in a gentle sing-song; his pale blue eyes were ice-cold.

"We're going to make you forget that comic book jerk," Chris blurted.

Immediately Steve stepped partly in front of him. "You see, Hannah, Chris has a bit of a grievance with you. We don't think it was cool, the way you dumped him, and how you've been treating him like a fool. When you betray one person on the team, you betray us all. But you probably didn't understand that about us. Just like there's stuff you wrote about without understanding." Reggie Mathis gave a grunt. "But that's all right! We're going to have a great big party and become great friends again."

This – was about her newspaper article! She saw it in a flash and the whole strange ambush dynamic suddenly made sense. It had nothing to do with her affair with Chris Kelly: this was *vengeance*, some sort of team honor thing, and they had used a line on Chris to get him to be the bait. *Poor, stupid Chris*, she thought in horror, staring between him and Steve. And when she realized what they were here to do, her brain finally caught up to her body and she took an involuntary step back from Steve's bottle.

"Aw, I guess we do have to force you. Davey, take her arms." Steve spoke without a change in his mild voice.

Then everything happened too fast. Before she could make sense of his words she felt a touch behind her; by the time she had gasped and turned her head her arms were seized and pinned behind her back, hard. She was immobilized, still in her parka, pulled close to Davey Coleman's huge form above her. His back remained against the door, facing her forwards into the room.

Her heart was hammering in her ears; she was filled with a tragic sense of her own idiocy and slowness. She looked wildly around at the shelves on her right—they held a football trophy, stacked textbooks, a pile of winter gloves—but she couldn't move her arms at all. Meanwhile the eyes were all on Steve, who stepped close, still holding the beer bottle. "Last chance to have fun. I told you if you had a drink you'd enjoy yourself."

Another, even worse layer clicked into place. In fact it was so ludicrously bald that it cleared her head. "A date rape drug?" she said incredulously. "*That's* your idea of a party?" His eyes fastened to hers didn't deny it. But through the absurdity she saw its deadly effectiveness—because it *was*, for the others, their idea of a party. This vengeance rape scenario bore no relation to the usual pattern of Hills College rapes, where in big dark roaring parties girls are fed the drug in a slippery milieu of general drinking. It was what had confused her at first; this was different, almost like a street attack. And the half-conscious or fully unconscious girl here would *half normalize* it for them; it would at least give them the plausible denial they needed afterward: "We all partied, she got drunk, she was into it." That was the party line, to use the grim joke, they all used, every time, to gain impunity from a cooperating athletics program. It was the prevailing system. *That's* what the drink was for—and it would work.

For the others. Because in the same instant she saw more: that for Steve, the leader, *this* kind of rape—the ambush, the street attack—was *his* kind of rape. A bolt of communication passed silently between their eyes (*last chance to have fun*) and he didn't deny that either.

She seized the simple and immediate solution. Putting all her sarcasm into her voice she said, "And what if I don't drink?"

That gave her the moment she wanted, an instant of confusion in the room as the guys all exchanged glances. But she couldn't move or take advantage of it, and she would pay dearly for it. With a smile Steve took a half step back and set the bottle down, then two steps forward and was upon her. He pulled down the zipper of her parka. "The drink was for *your* sake, not mine," he breathed in her face. "Keep holding her up, Davey. Don't let go." His hands ran over her body inside her coat and his fingers opened the button of her jeans.

No – no no no –

"Did any of you *read* my article?" she said desperately, looking from face to face at the others, Chris, Reggie. "I didn't say anything about the Kingfishers other than –"

"We know what you said," Reggie Mathis stated. "The Coach read it to all of us. You can't unsay it."

Later she would learn that Coach Pruecastle had paraphrased a small section of her article as a motivational clubhouse speech to stir the team up before a game.

And that's when her choked, groping silence blended into the worst moments of her life. She heard voices – "Dude," and Davey Coleman's high "Oh man" – and she tried not to hear, not to feel, tried as hard as she ever had not to think.

In New York she came out of an actual sweating horror at the station to realize that Detective Wilson was looking at her with sympathy and, more importantly, finally belief. *The power of truth.* "Take a moment, Hannah. You don't have to go and relive all the details of that."

"I honestly blacked out most of them," she said.

"That's normal. But, so, I don't see – you said the other four *didn't*, ah, penetrate you?"

"That's right. They – I – I –"

"That's okay, take a moment. But go on, because I want to hear how the hell you got yourself out of that."

"I'm next," said Chris Kelly.

"You'll get your turn, Chris." Steve said. "Davey next." She came back to the room to find Chris closer, Steve a few steps away pulling a sticky condom off himself, and the whole room smaller and tighter around her. Her arms were still pinned; her pants and panties were around her ankles. Smells hit her: not just the immediate rubbery stink but a heightened reek of male arousal. It was started now; everyone was closing in; Steve had erased the last pretense. It had begun, and it was going to continue and continue and —

"But she didn't drink," came Davey's high voice above her; she felt the vibrations through her back.

Humorless chuckles circled the room, and Hannah again saw the promises given of the drug, perhaps mainly to Davey (the Freshman superstar who needed to be "brought in"), now made meaningless through Davey's culpability though he didn't get it yet. Not that her insight could help her, or was anything she could later to explain to Detective Wilson, despite the officer's presumed familiarity with the different psychological categories of rapists, but from two steps away Steve's cold smile as his eyes met hers told her everything that would now be done to her *his way*, through them, and probably by himself again, and again.

He picked up the beer bottle and held it up with the same smile. "How 'bout it bitch?" he said. "You *suuuure* you don't want to drink?"

And for a terrible moment that Hannah would remember for the rest of her life, she was tempted. The room waited.

Not on your life, came a clear voice in her head.

She looked down. "Okay," she said. "I'll drink."

Surprised guffaws all around her. Steve stepped closer with the bottle. "All of it?"

Rapid nods, head down. Completely defeated and limp. A rag doll awaiting dismemberment.

Steve extended the beer bottle, and Hannah made the slightest movement of her right shoulder as if to accept it with her hand. And Davey Coleman responded automatically; he let go of her right arm.

Before he had fully released it, working entirely behind her back, she spun her free hand around, grabbed the first two fingers of his, and bent them backwards with all her strength, breaking them at the root.

"Whoa!" Detective Wilson said. "No shit. You go, girl."

There was an appalling soft crack that maybe not everyone heard, but she did, and behind her Davey spasmed against the door, sucked in a gasp and let out a sustained high-pitched shriek. What happened had been invisible to most people in the room. Before anyone else could react, she put her shoulder against Davey's side and, pulling by his broken fingers, *rotated* the two of them in place, putting her back against the door. The move pulled her coat off and it went with him. Then with free arms she pushed Davey into Steve.

She was hoping they would both go down but Steve merely staggered back, the bottle spilling over his shirt and falling to the carpet. "What the hell—?" he said. Davey slumped at his feet, in a fetal curl with his back upward, drew a second breath and screamed again. In a flash Hannah pulled her pants up with her left hand and shot a look at the door: Andrew Keith was still standing in front of the knob, staring at her — *he* had seen what she had done. "Hey — " he started to say.

She had less than a second to act. Reaching across him with her right hand, she grabbed Steve's football trophy off the shelf alongside her and raised it high over her head.

"Let me out of the room right now or I'm smashing this to the floor!" she yelled.

It wasn't what you would call a conscious guess, but if she had thought that his Biletnikoff trophy might be Steve Badenhut's prize possession she was correct. It was a fragile item, with a sculpted gold football player in an action pose attached by only its toes to the base. She was holding it by the player and even the motion of throwing it would wreck it.

"Don't! Everybody stop!" yelled Steve.

"I mean it! Let me out *now!*" Her eyes were locked on Steve's. "Here it goes!"

"Andrew open the fucking door!" yelled Steve.

Andrew opened the door and Hannah was out into the hall and gone like a greyhound from the gate.

Steve followed, running at high speed. Her night of terror wasn't over.

Steve's dorm, Hunter, was connected indoors to hers, Fitz-henry, and if she had thought about it she probably could have made it to her room, but she blindly seized the first exit she came to and ran outdoors. She had the trophy under one arm and was holding her pants up with the other hand, and she had never run faster in her life. Steve was close behind her. She looked wildly for people out on the campus; there were none; she looked for shadows; the snowy fields were well-lit by bright lamps to all sides. So she simply ran, blanking out the strange stinging friction between her legs; she had no legs; she was just speed. She heard Steve screaming behind her: "You fucking bitch! You fucking cunt! I'm going to rip you the fuck open you bitch!"

She half flew down the icy cement steps to the lower campus without a misstep—and gained a few paces when Steve stumbled on them—and crossed the frost-white road. There were no cars in either direction. She aimed straight for the nearest building: the student union, at an angle in front of her. The metal double doors were around the corner to the right and she gained an instant where she wasn't in his line of sight. She pulled open a door; the building was deserted, the lights dimmed; the hallway ran in both directions. She hesitated a fraction of a second, then ducked back from the door, threw herself over the small hedge, and cowered in the shadow as the door swung slowly closed.

Before it finished swinging Steve was upon it, and with a hard pull he was inside the building. "You bitch!" came his amplified echoing voice, and then the door shut behind him.

She didn't move. Immediately above her was a big window and she huddled against the wall underneath it. She finally did up her pants, feeling for the first time only now strange sorenesses and a kind of swimming nausea as the cold air clamped around her. She fought against a wave of shivering and held the trophy against her belly. For a terribly long time she stayed motionless, listening to his ongoing voice travel weirdly back and forth inside the student union, not knowing where he was or if he was near a window. Sometimes the voice dropped low and sing-song—"I'm going to *fiiiind* you"—and other times it roared out: "You do *not* do this to me! No fucking bitch—no fucking bitch—you're not leaving this building, you cunt! You got no way out! You hear me?" But what finally propelled her into stumbling motion was a sudden glassy smash upstairs followed a long series of crashes and tinkles, and a sobbing falsetto scream: "Nobody — nobody — nobody ever — *I'm going to kill you, I'm going to kill you!*" The echoes followed her as she fled crookedly from shadow to shadow across the dark college back to her dorm, still holding the trophy.

"Well, Hannah, I think you probably have an actionable case," Detective Wilson said. "Unlike a lot of college assault situations there's nothing remotely ambiguous here. And this happened three days ago?"

"Yes. Uh, Tuesday night. I came home yesterday, Thursday. I, I know I let a lot of time pass — "

"No no, that's all right. You're reporting this event very quickly. But, so you spent Wednesday up at Hills College, another day?"

She hesitated. Now came the hard part. Up until now she had told only the truth; now there were several events she would have to skip over. "Yeah. I did. I guess it was probably stupid of me, I mean it definitely was. I knew that it wasn't over, that I was still in danger, but I was too freaked out to think straight. And I wanted to report the sexual assault to the school, which I did."

"You did? Okay. Why don't you tell me about that. And when you say you were still in danger, did anything happen to make you think that? Did you encounter any of those players again?"

"Well, yes. But I did that on purpose." Hannah suppressed a smile.

"Okay, you should definitely go ahead and tell me about what happened Wednesday. And if you yourself did anything, even something illegal, like slash someone's tires or something, I want you to tell me. There's no judgement; I just need to know all the details."

Hannah nodded, her lips tight. She took a deep breath and told her about Wednesday.

Chapter 3 - Victim

Wednesday was, in a different and more serious sense, a worse day. It was on that long, difficult day on the Hills College campus that Hannah learned what it is to be a rape victim, and observed her antagonist change from five demented and overprivileged rapists to the school that protected them.

So it's finally happened to you. Join the club, kiddo. Don't lose your head.

Those were the appropriately feminist thoughts that greeted her with the morning light. Hannah had certainly spent enough time studying the campus rape issue, working in the rape crisis center, sympathizing with other girls including friends, and writing about the cause that she of all people should have known the drill. But come the morning after she discovered there *was* no drill—and as for her head, it wasn't so easy to find.

For one thing, with the first opening of her eyes she had seen with a bolt of stark terror Steve's trophy, still sitting on her floor amid the pile of her sodden clothes like part of a nightmare dragged into reality. The taste of vomit in her nostrils brought the rest of the memory piling in: how she had barely reached her room before she had to run back down the hall to throw up in the bathroom, then had squatted under a hot shower fully clothed, for so long that she had startled out of a doze to find the water cold. Now, staring at the trophy, she had the palpable conviction that her terror wasn't over, that at any moment Steve would come smashing through her door for it, and her. She jumped out of bed and shoved the thing into the back of her wardrobe closet. But even then she felt its presence like a screaming beacon in her room.

What do I do?

Moving with a strange jerky jumpiness she pulled off the two layers of sweatshirts she had needed to sleep warmly – the bureau drawer was still open – and clumsily got dressed, trying to think rationally. In the process she made discoveries: a stinging tear where there had never been one before, deep purple bruises on her thighs from Steve's hands. He had been less gentle even than she remembered.

It could have been worse, she told herself with a shudder. But any self-congratulation on that score was replaced by the blur of close pursuit that ended her night, and the sense that she was still a hunted rabbit. Meanwhile, under her rebounding thoughts her body was slowly starting to feel achy, disturbed inside, sick.

I was raped, by Steve. I'm a rape victim. She wrapped her arms around herself and with a push of effort willed herself not to cry. *No. I have to act. I have to do something.*

What she did was dress, hiding her bruises under clean clothes, as if from herself. Together with a clinic rape test they might have provided evidence, but she knew there was no point seeking a test: he had used a condom. And without one she also knew, with despairing certitude, how little point there would be in reporting the assault to the school. She knew from the statistics, and firsthand from several of the girls (Margaret, on her team, was one) how many assaults were reported at Hills versus how many resulted in *any* disciplinary action for the boy, never mind expulsion, or God forbid arrest. The ratio nationwide was over 50 to 1 and Hills was no exception. The administration bent over backward to present the college as a bastion of Boston probity. She had always felt an outraged desire to fight those numbers, but now when it was she herself she felt only deflation. What did she have? Her word only, against theirs — the classic losing game.

Couldn't she think of a way to make her story stick, find evidence? She thought hard, but kept coming up blank, or maybe just blanking out.

With a start she realized she had been just standing in the middle of her room for an unknown time. She carefully hung her wet clothes on the back of her desk chair. A minute later she gathered them up and shoved them in her wastebasket. Then she continued to stand there.

Hannah's single in Fitzhenry was a tiny room with a bed, desk and second-floor window; the angled wardrobe filled one corner. She turned to gaze at her inspiration wall alongside the desk, hung with framed historical photos of suffragettes and abolitionists. Its centerpiece and by far the largest image held the stern, fiery gaze of the young John Brown: her particular hero of fearless direct action in a good cause.

What would you *do?* she asked him silently, then turned away. Don't give up, was his ready answer, but that told her nothing.

Yet.

There were messages on her cellphone. "So where were you?" Susan Kinsler's put-out voice blared in her ear. "I even went to the stupid concert and waited for you there. Don't tell me — you were backstage interviewing gross roadies the whole time, weren't you? I'm pissed at you, Raider. See you at practice."

Practice! She was due at 10:00. The little red digits of her bedside clock were rushing through the morning while she stood there doing nothing; it was 9:40. Would she go? Just—return to her life? If not she would have to make up some excuse. Today was Wednesday; Athletics Week ran through Saturday: four more days. She discovered an extreme reluctance for any plan that involved leaving her room.

Her second voice message turned her paralysis to a mournful groan, almost a sob. "Hey, it's Randall. Us non-athletic types get to make the obligatory gloat call about being on vacation already. I'm here in New Jersey; my first day back I watched I think five stupid movies, are you jealous? I spoke to my parents; they're fine with me coming up to New York after Christmas. Should I wear a tie for your folks? I look like a scary religious proselytizer when I do. Happy fencing."

She sat on her bed, cellphone upside down on the coverlet, face in her hands, though what she was feeling now was an anger so broad it had no name. Would she tell Randall? Probably not, how could she? And with that Hannah felt the filthy taint of rape altering her life.

She had never had much of a love life; her physical strength and political opinions tended to intimidate boys; at 19 her romantic history partook mainly of the bizarre, like guys who dated her to win bets or secret high school affairs with math faculty with Special Forces backgrounds (*that* had gone well; she had gotten the teacher fired). Now, just in the last semester, she had *finally* found something like a normal boyfriend—and this, this *thing,* comes roaring in to wreck it.

"It's not fair," she said into her palms, and she was helplessly intelligent enough to see herself beginning the typical downward spiral of girls who *didn't* tell, who kept it locked inside for months or years: the gained weight, the falling grades, the retreat into solitude, depression, sometimes self-harm.

"All right, enough," she said aloud. She remembered that she had unread emails to check and threw herself into her desk chair and turned on her laptop. If she was staying in her room she could return to this much of her life at least. Indeed, these emails were immensely important: they were from June Anders at the State Department, relating to her internship next summer. She had qualified for a Women's Studies research tour of Saudi Arabia sponsored by the Global Women's Initiative; she had been ambitiously requesting supplemental information; June Anders was impressed with her engagement and the State Department had been sending her zip files full of background material. She saw the internship as the first step of her real career in women's liberation; it was her life; it was her dream.

But opening June Anders' documents she couldn't absorb a single word. She tried to read the same paragraph ten times and it made no sense.

Back on the bed — *What do I do — ?*

At 10:05 am she was suddenly able to pull on shoes and a sweatshirt (her parka was gone) and leave the room — because, she realized, the football team would now be at practice. *Oh, brava, subconscious.* But she didn't go to the Enleike Center gym to join Coach Bailey and her teammates for her own practice. Instead she headed the opposite direction, and did what she knew would be the least effective thing of all.

She went to the office of Alistair Haughton, Dean of Students, at Balarkey Hall, to report the sexual assault.

I can't just do nothing. I can't pretend it didn't happen.

Reporting the assault was after all school protocol. It was what students were supposed to do. And such was the measure of her desperation that when she stood looking up at the castle-like stone front of Balarkey Hall she felt a yearning reassurance. *I'm a Hills College student too. I was raped, and almost much worse, on campus. My school will be there for me — it has to be.*

The Dean of Students' office was large, walled with calfbound books to the ceiling and outfitted with dark leather couches; a latticed window spread white light upward from the snowy lawn three floors below. From the shade of a recess the seventeenth-century founder frowned in gilt over the large mahogany desk. Dean Haughton's jowly face set in long, wig-like dark curls arose in front of him as Hannah entered by the oaken door.

"*Hannah,*" he intoned in a lowered, drawn-out voice, as if greeting a long-absent daughter. "I'm glad you're here. Did the intervention work? Are you come at last to talk about a retraction?" His words rode a genial chuckle.

She stopped halfway across the tapestry rug. "Intervention?" She had forgotten all about his request for a retraction. *Did he mean Coach Bailey — ?*

He made a hooking gesture with two fingers for her to come forward. "Don't be alarmed. But I know all about what the boys tried to do last night, and how it got out of hand, and I know you made off with Steve Badenhut's Biletnikoff trophy. Don't *worry!* I'm not going to pin you with a theft demerit. Come closer, have a seat, I won't bite. Here, I have your coat." He reached for a coatrack alongside and lifted the arm of her white parka. "You know, I told those boys they should have spoken to me first; I could have warned them about your famous touchiness on the subject of your articles." He shook his head with a paternal smile; the curls moved in fixed relation, as if waxed.

Hannah stood where she was. *They got their story in first. How?*

When? But of course they had. They'd had all morning; she had dawdled. *Idiot!* "What, exactly," she asked, "did they say happened? And who, exactly, said it?"

"Well, the word 'theft' was used, which I am choosing to set aside, as serious as that word is here at Hills. You and I must first have a conversation yet more serious, though hopefully brief, about the retraction. And trust me, my dear" — he chuckled again — "I can picture the scene. When four football players ambush a small girl like yourself in a room, and try to talk you into writing the retraction themselves" — he smiled — "oh my. Well-meaning as they might have been, I can appreciate the end result of your getting hysterical and over-reacting. As you have before. But again, I am setting, I have set, all that aside. The important thing is — "

"There were *five* football players in that room," said Hannah, "and what happened was gang rape. Actual rape in the case of Steve Badenhut, and all but in the case of the others, and when I escaped Steve chased me with declared intent to harm. Clearly declared."

Here we go. My word against theirs. Let's see.

Her words hung in a heavy silence between the rug and the thick curtains. After a moment Dean Haughton gestured to the handsome leather armchair in front of the desk, and in a low-pitched voice said, "Sit down."

Hannah sat.

"You are making a rape accusation?"

"Yes. Last night I was raped. And I would have been gang-raped or worse if I hadn't escaped."

"And why did you say there were five?" he asked. "Whom are you accusing? Names, please."

"The attackers were Steve Badenhut, Chris Kelly, Andrew Keith, Davey Coleman, and Reggie Mathis."

The Dean emitted a long breath, looking at her sidelong with an expression that mingled condemnation and relief. "Hannah, before you go any further with this, stop. Your over-reaction continues, I see, and you've decided to jump on the modern feminist trend of rape accusation. Alas, your story has a fatal flaw. *Davey Coleman* wasn't in the room with you. He couldn't have been, because he spent last night in the hospital. I was there with him myself. He had a fall on the stairs earlier that day and injured his hand. In fact he's out for the year."

The last sentence had a gravity that eloquently conveyed how the combination of this football emergency and the crisis over her article was wearying the Dean enough without having to deal with some fabricated rape claim.

Hannah studied him carefully. *Does he really not believe me, or does he not* want *to believe me?* What had the players told him? How much did he actually know about Davey's injury?

Haughton's face was a well-trained mask, currently set to an expression of lofty disapproving checkmate; it was hard to tell what he really thought. His first move, at any rate, had expertly tilted the board, put the burden of proof on her; even to begin she would now have to engage in a debate rather than make a report. Hannah suddenly felt like she was in a fencing match with a highly skilled opponent.

But even a skilled player has to play by the rules. "Dean, I'm telling the truth. Those five players sexually assaulted me last night, and I've come to your office to report it, as I believe students are supposed to do. I know how Davey Coleman's fingers were broken because I broke them myself to escape his holding me against my will. May I report what really happened?"

"So you're not here about writing the retraction?" The Dean assumed a sad, long-suffering tone. But he did have to play by the rules. "Very well, tell your story," he sighed.

And the rape victim told the authority what had happened to her.

Of the many times Hannah would have to retell her assault, from parents to Detective Wilson in New York through multiple police interrogations, this was the only one in which her every word felt like an invasion of privacy. Haughton listened with his jowled lower face bisected by steepled fingers held to his lips, elbows on desk, unimpeachably impassive while still managing to convey skepticism. Nevertheless she watched that face hard. And once, just for a fraction of a second, she saw the mask drop.

It was when she was describing breaking Davey's fingers. In the slightest flicker of his eyes up and to the right, the slightest intake of breath, a covering micro-shuffle on the chair, she saw that her description of the injury chimed against something — *something from the doctor?* — and in a flash she seemed to see a long night of emergency hospital consultations with coaches and administration figures in which *no one* believed Davey's story of falling down the stairs, with the boy too scared of Steve to be anything but stubborn, and that *this*, this right here, was the explanation, presumably matching medical data to which the Dean had been privy. In the space of that fraction of a second she saw, first, that Haughton accepted *her whole story* over the players' — and, second, that *he pretended not to*. The mask was back almost before it had gone. But she had seen.

"That is what happened," she finished. "And I heard him breaking something in the student union, that should still be broken, if you're looking for *other* proof." She crossed her arms.

My word against theirs. This was flat-out unambiguous rape by a third of your precious football team and you know it. Do the right thing. Or else I'll —

She had no idea what she would do.

Yet.

Haughton stared at her with wide eyes that communicated nothing, then drew and released a breath. "Were you, then, in fact, gang raped?"

"No. But only because at the last possible second I myself — "

"No. You weren't. So this isn't a gang rape accusation. And as far as you're accusing a single student of rape, do you have any medical evidence, any injury, or any witness who can vouch for your version of events?" His tone was overly rhetorical — *of course you don't* — but behind it she glimpsed a check just to make sure.

"I...don't." She knew perfectly well that the bruises on her hips could have come from anything; there was no point mentioning them. "I'm still reporting it," she said. "You have to, to investigate it. There's a school policy — "

"Yes there is. At Hills College we take every sexual assault allegation seriously and our priority is to make sure our campus is safe for all students. You know that. But you should also know, Miss Radhe, that this office is the first line of defense against false accusations, of which there are many, more than you are aware, and especially, for some reason, against famous athletes where dragging the boy through the mud would gain the girl notoriety. Miss Radhe, let's be honest. This started with you writing an unjustified attack on the Kingfishers in the Vista, based on no facts, solely to win credit in feminist circles. We have had this same conversation before, you and I, when you wrote that article accusing our founder"— hand waved behind his head at the painting—"of having children with his slaves."

"It, it's not the same conversation. That has nothing to do with—"

"It's exactly the same! You have ambitions of making a name for yourself in the women's movement, do you deny it? And you don't mind crawling over your school to do it. Are you in possession of Steve Badenhut's trophy? Are you? That's the only 'proof' I have here of anything. First you come in talking about gang rape and then admit there was no gang rape, that the others *intended* it—how do you know what they *intended* to say or do? Because they're football players?" Hannah watched in horror as Dean Haughton gathered momentum, improvising his line of defense as he went along. "You, you people on the left—do you have the slightest consideration for what the boys on the Kingfishers go through on a daily basis, the pressures that someone like Steve Badenhut might be dealing with right now? Do you, Miss Radhe? Do you think about Steve Badenhut the person?"

"I might," she said, "if he hadn't raped me."

"And you continue." He leaned forward again. "Hannah, as your dean I must urge you, very seriously, not to go around repeating any part of what you just told me. Now listen. I understand that something went wrong last night. I said that at the start. I will speak to Coach Pruecastle myself to make sure that…whatever happened, ends here. Okay? Let's none of us escalate this in public, and you can trust the school to handle it. Will you do that for me, Hannah? Will you just stand down and not make any public accusations while we work to sort this thing out? Will you do that for Hills?"

This is it. The famous wall, the unwritten rape protection program for athletes. It's real. I'm looking at it. It's my word against their multi-million-dollar football program and I can prove nothing.

"What about the fact that Steve chased me and threatened me, and that he might still be after me? What do I do about that?"

"I already told you I'd speak to Coach Pruecastle." Still, she saw a faint flicker of conscience cross Dean Haughton's face. *Does he actually know — what Steve is?* "I tell you what. When you first entered this room I thought you were here to talk about the retraction. I still intend to have that conversation. Return Steve's stolen trophy to me, and write out a simple one-paragraph denial of the part of your article that names Hills College and the Kingfishers. You can do that right here; I have a suggested text. Then I myself will return the trophy to Steve, and we'll send him home early from Athletics Week. Come next semester cooler heads will prevail. How does that strike you?" He put a piece of paper and a fountain pen onto the desk.

Too fucking unbelievable for words, she didn't say.

She stood up straight from the chair, feeling every inch like John Brown. "Dean, I am not changing a word of my article."

"No retraction. Very well. In that case, Miss Radhe, there's nothing more I can do for you. If you feel unsafe on campus, then I suggest *you* go home early. Your exams are done; go enjoy Christmas. *Fencing* will survive." He stood up too, and handed her coat, in a manner that almost physically opened the door behind her.

She was about to say *How dare you?* But something hijacked her voice and she heard herself saying instead, without knowing why, "You know what? That's a good idea. I think I *will* go home early."

— And press charges with the police? her mind continued, as if on

the trail of itself.

They faced each other that way, eye to eye, in a moment that was obscurely like a salute. Then she left the office carrying her coat.

"So you feel you went through the proper channels at your college, and nothing will come of it," Detective Wilson said, when Hannah related the interview to her in New York.

"As I suspected it wouldn't. I'm not naive. I just didn't think he would state it so baldly."

"And so you decided to step it up and report it to the police." Then Hannah saw how Dean Haughton's dismissal carried an authority that made itself felt across state lines at the 14th Precinct. The sex crimes detective shifted on her chair. "Hannah, I've got to tell you, in cases like yours, if the college refuses to act, there's very little chance of a prosecution. It can be hard for officers even to talk to the accused players. And going through the legal process can be a very public, upsetting thing for the girl. Let me ask you, realistically, what do you expect to see happen to Steve Badenhut as a result of you pressing rape charges? Do you expect him to go to jail?"

"Honestly, I don't expect his situation to change much," Hannah said, smiling.

"Then—"

"Then why am I here?" she returned readily. "Because it's the right thing to do. Trust me, detective, I ran through all the options open to me. Believe it or not I am trying to do the right thing for the next girl like me, and all the girls like me." *I'm merely doing it outside the law*, she didn't add.

"Well that's good, ah, that's fine, if that's what you want." She looked down a little wearily at her notes. "And you're right, of course we encourage all sexual assault victims to make a report."

"I'm not a victim," Hannah said before she could help it.

That earned a long look from the officer. "That's a good attitude. But you said you had a further encounter with some of the players that day. Did you?"

"Oh yes," Hannah said. "For one thing, that night Steve tried to break into my room."

"He did. Okaaay. Tell me about that."

It was 9:00 pm and Hannah sat on the edge of her dormitory bed, fully dressed with the lights out. Over and over she was trying to master her sense of helpless outrage and think through her options, and over and over she was coming up zero.

From Haughton's office she had gone straight to the Enleike Center, arriving an hour late to practice and in the mood to take out her aggression on the strip. Without a word she had suited up and grabbed her épée—and proceeded to have the worst practice of her life. Everyone and everything hit her, gleefully; she was blinded by sweat behind her mask, three beats behind everyone's blade, and so frustrated she could have screamed. Afterward the coach gave a single sideways jerk of his head and, with all eyes on her, she had followed into his office, a tiny ground-floor room with exposed pipes, a metal desk, and big Olympic fencing posters on the walls. She had thought up an excuse for being late, having to do with a medical emergency with her parents, but the problem was Coach Bailey *knew* her parents, and the complications—

"What's the matter, Raider?" he had said, his perceptive eyes in a face of sudden alarm.

And she told him everything.

"Oh shit Hannah." He listened with neither sympathy nor anger, but the full, pursed-lip belief of someone hearing a familiar tale, brought too close to home.

"Uh-huh. I've seen that crap from Haughton before, but I never thought I'd see it come down on you. The bastard. If there's anything I can do, I'll do it. If you wanna go home early, I'll make excuses to the team, tell 'em you had a family emergency."

She smiled wryly. "I'm thinking of going to the police," she said. "Maybe when I'm in New York."

He gave a long sigh, shaking his head sadly. "Hannah. I've seen that approach too. It don't work, you know that. Some ways it's even worse. The minute you send cops onto campus the total wall goes up. The boys'll have lawyers and nobody talks, and the college won't lift a finger to help. As it drags on you'll get dragged through the mud, *by* the college. Plus, Jesus, you gotta understand, what you did to Davey"—he chuckled ruefully—"it's gonna cost the college potentially millions of dollars. As it is they've got reason to keep it secret, but if you go make it public they'll turn around and make your life here *miserable*. They will drive you out. And even if you got the bastard into court, unless you got evidence or witnesses it'll still be just your word against his. Think about it. You got better things to live for, Raider—your summer program thing—the Olympics! You can *make* it." He spread his hands.

She would have tactical reasons for not mentioning this conversation to Detective Wilson in New York—it would beg the question of why she *was* pressing charges—but she was also ashamed at how she had suddenly leapt up from the chair with a tearful scream of rage: "So, what, then? You think I should do *nothing*? Just shut up and *take* it? Is *that* your advice?"

Bailey didn't flinch. He shook his round, crinkly-skinned head slowly. "Whatever you do decide to do, I'll back you up. If you wanna go ahead and press charges, hell, I'll testify. But I think you should look at the most important thing."

"Which is?"

"You got yourself out of the room, Hannah. Before the worst came down you got yourself out of the goddamn room."

Yeah, but for what?

Her bedside clock read 10:30. The more she sat on her bed thinking the more her mind went round and round in circles.

Report it to the college. No go. Report it to the police. Almost certainly the same result. Do nothing and try to return to normal life? That wasn't an option either.

Besides the moral repulsiveness of it, there was Steve. She still had the back-of-the-neck feeling that this wasn't over. She glanced at her wardrobe closet, where she could almost feel the presence of the Biletnikoff trophy. Coach Bailey had been right: her injuring Davey wasn't small potatoes. *They* knew she had done it. *He* knew. There were still three more days of Athletics Week.

Go home early? She had told Dean Haughton she would, though she didn't know why. In fact that was the worst option of all: it was a recipe for spending her Christmas vacation in a state of fear, and there was no guarantee that things would "blow over" next semester.

Other options?

Her eyes pulled focus to her spare épée, on her desk behind her laptop. "Well," she said aloud, "there's always *one* thing I could do." For the first time since the rape she chuckled, and for

a long time lost herself in a happy fantasy of how to murder Steve
Badenhut.

At length she drooped her head, hair hanging between her
knees. Maybe it *would* blow over. Nothing bad from Steve or the
football team had happened that day. Maybe Dean Haughton
had even intervened through the coach. She glanced sidelong at
her wardrobe. She should probably think about how to return
Steve's trophy to him.

And at that moment she heard Steve's footsteps in the hall outside.

Her breath stopped in her throat. From the instant the sound
reached her ears she knew it was him: heavy tiptoes trying to be
quiet. Her hall had been perfectly silent; most of the students on
it were gone; she didn't know who if anyone was left. For a second she sat paralyzed, thinking wildly of bolting out of her room
in the other direction down the hall — and in that second it was too
late. The shadow of feet appeared in the strip of light under her
door, and she heard the heavy rasp of his breathing. The locked
knob jiggled.

No no no —

She was profoundly grateful that her light was off. *Maybe he'll
think I'm not here.* She tried not to breathe, scanning around the
dark room for a weapon. There was nothing. The knob jiggled
again, more forcefully, and there came a panted "Fucking bitch"
under his breath: it was him all right. She heard a shuffle, and
then, amazingly amplified, a rat scratch at her lock mechanism,
something sliding back and forth.

Her lock had no deadbolt, just a turn button on the knob.
Those could be opened.

Time seemed to have stopped with her heart. The knob jiggled back and forth and the sliding thing scratched, thunked, scratched.

She did the only thing she could think of. Moving fast and silently she opened her wardrobe, took out the trophy and set it down on the floor exactly where it had been that morning. Then without a sound she crawled into the closet and pulled the door closed.

Her heartbeat sounded deafening, but she could still hear the scratching at her door. Abruptly the noise stopped with a loudly-whispered "Fuck!" For a moment all she could hear was her heart. Then Steve said aloud, "The hell with this, a green light is a green light." The next instant there was a wall-shaking thud as he shouldered the door.

Hannah bit her lip and tried to be as soundless as possible. The thud came again, together with a small crack of wood as she felt the walls shake. She thought wildly of what in the closet could work as a weapon; she wished she had at least grabbed her épée.

"Hey, hey, what are you doing?" Another voice sounded in the hall. "Is that your room?" Hannah recognized the voice: it was Phillippe, the old Cuban janitor. She knew him; she had interviewed him once for the Vista. He had migrated to the U.S. thirty years ago, and when his family tried to follow on a raft they had all been killed.

"You keep your nose out of this, spic," Steve's voice said. "There's been a theft. This girl has my fucking trophy, and —"

"That's no excuse for banging on doors. If there's been a theft, why don't we walk over to Security and tell them about it?"

There was a silence. Then she heard Steve step back, and his voice got lower. "You don't breathe a word of this, understand, or you're out of a job. All it takes from me is one complaint. And *you*"—his voice rose again—"if you're in there, you're marked, ho. You got no protection, and that's official. When it comes to you we got free rein and no questions. I *will* get my goddamn trophy back." His footsteps burst into a run and faded down the hall.

"I guess he didn't want to go Security," Philippe said. There was a gentle tap on the door. "Everything okay in there?" Hannah said nothing, and after a moment the janitor's footsteps followed in the same direction as Steve's.

By that point she was standing bolt upright in the center of the room, her epée in her hand, staring after the footsteps. After a long moment she turned and looked at her photo of John Brown in the half-light. Then with a lick of her lips she gave a single nod.

Yep, she said to herself. There was indeed one thing she could do.

"And you say that encounter cleared your head?"

"Like a charm," Hannah told Detective Wilson. "All the fog and indecision I'd been in were gone. I mean, clearly I couldn't spend another day on that campus. So," she continued brightly, "the next morning as soon as I woke up—which was late, 'cause it took me a long time to fall asleep, it was like ten or ten-thirty— I went straight to the Enleike Center, made my apologies to the team and got the hell out of there. I took the train straight home. That was yesterday. And, well, here I am this morning."

Hannah had told the truth that her head was, for the first time since the assault, perfectly clear. And her statement could later be verified to the extent that she did, that Thursday, make her apologies and leave campus at midday, as witnesses would attest. But whether she had taken the train straight from Boston to New York would become a matter of some controversy. And in fact she hadn't slept a wink the night before.

She was too busy working out the details of how to kill Steve Badenhut.

Chapter 4 - Early Bird

The more she looked at it, the more it showed itself as not only the most personally satisfying option but the one with potentially the farthest-reaching consequences. Because while murdering Steve might solve a lot of immediate problems, the feminist in her wouldn't stop there: the plan she was putting together would, provided a lot of things went right, serve also to expose the whole rotten collegiate system that protected and permitted the likes of him.

After a while she noticed that she had turned on her room light and was clicking loudly at her laptop. She didn't care. As if finally liberated her mind was in high gear and ideas were coming on top of ideas.

So far, Steve Badenhut, you've tricked me, raped me, chased me, terrified me, had me continuously at a disadvantage, and are apparently backed by a school that will defend you from the consequences of anything you do. But I can bloody well outthink you.

Hannah had never committed a crime in her life, much less plotted a murder, and her joy of thinking clearly again would not have been complete without a pause over the moral dimension. She didn't linger long. In a quick glance she found herself capable, and every ounce as justified as a girl would be who had indeed been gang-raped to within an inch of her sanity. But in fact vengeance was not her game. It was not she who was operating by the law of the jungle here; she had been face to face with the jungle that morning in Dean Haughton's office and it was hers to bring the light, and if they hadn't bothered to check that she was the kind of girl who had a framed photo of John Brown on her wall (her extended finger called it to attention) then it was their look-out.

The actual act of killing a man almost half a foot taller and some 150 pounds heavier didn't worry her in the least. It merely required surprise and a weapon, and she had very good blade control. The difficulty was elsewhere. To pull off the murder she needed, first, an airtight cover story — she already had some ideas in that line — and, more importantly, evidence of the rape.

To dispatch Steve without the latter would accomplish nothing; it wouldn't even prove he was a rapist. She had heard of women painting "RAPIST" on the body and such, but she considered that gauche as well as inconclusive. No, for the effect she intended only hard proof would do. But where hours earlier she had been despairing of her lack of evidence, now the perfect solution sprang up to her fully formed.

From her desk drawer she took out the little digital audio recorder she used to conduct interviews for the Vista, and fitted two new AA batteries into it. She contemplated the unassuming black plastic rectangle small enough to fit in her palm. *For hard evidence, how would a confession from the source do?* She had an idea for how to trick Steve into making it. And with luck, she could get him to incriminate a whole lot more than himself — perhaps even Dean Haughton.

She didn't fully buy Steve's claim of a "green light" from the college to molest and abuse her — though if he believed it, that was dangerous enough — but there was nevertheless no doubt in her mind that the *system*, and Dean Haughton in particular, was her real enemy. The willful, profit-driven silencing of rape from on high was, in the end, the *creator* of people like Steve, demented predators engorged with carnal animality in a circus world of fame and blanket license. Under John Brown's eyes she was aiming her blow at nothing less than that system.

The combination of a recorded confession from a rapist and a murder that looked like a college vengeance killing would, Hannah foresaw, light up the headlines, shining its blaze into the dark corners of the campus rape epidemic and by the very nature of its polarizing controversy raising the stakes for all concerned. In a pause of thought she stared at the vision with uplifted eyes. She was out to *start a conversation*, kickstart a process of needed change, and if she was using bloodshed as the kick, well, the level eyes of John Brown from the photo seemed to meet hers with approval.

The recording trick obviously had to happen first, and she had missed her window to do it today, which meant spending at least part of Thursday on campus, a prospect that made her stomach squirm. But it couldn't be helped, and in the meantime she still had a lot of work to do on her cover story.

If her murder successfully proved Steve a rapist and looked like revenge then she was headed straight to the top of the list of suspects, and her alibi had better be damn good. She had an idea for that, too, but the devil was in the details here, and she spent the next several hours at her laptop scanning through Google Maps, Amtrak train schedules, electrical substation charts, recipes for remotely-triggered bombs, fire prevention systems, and more. A good cover story can't be small, she reckoned, but deliberately causing a train delay on Amtrak's Northeast Corridor presented a daunting obelisk of self-education. The digits of her bedside clock flickered through the night.

For the electronic aspects she fleetingly wished she could call Randall; he was good with computers and that sort of thing. But of course she couldn't, and Randall as such was a problem for another day.

In a bleary, wired pause of eye-rubbing frustration she suddenly became aware of John Brown again, who seemed to be regarding her now with slightly lifted nose. *What sort of reformer*, he seemed to say, *is so concerned with their own skin?* She leveled an exasperated 21st Century teenage gaze at him in return, and suddenly realized that *he didn't know*. Her photo was of the *young* John Brown, perhaps not so very much older than herself now. It was up to her to tell him, silently in a strange dazed state, about the great law decreeing that they who use violence as a means to a better world can never live to see it. He was destined to fall victim to it.

Well, I won't, she told him. Again she pointed her finger at him, this time with a challenging smile. *I bet you*, she said silently, *that I can plan this out better than you did. I bet I can get away with it*.

She returned to her alibi.

Her clock read 4:35 am when she leaned back, stretching in the chair, her final math on the screen. *It should work.* When Steve was murdered in his dorm room in Hunter tomorrow night—no, *tonight*—she would be snugly aboard the Amtrak en route to New York City, heading home early from Athletics Week just as the dean had urged, over a hundred miles from campus and getting father away every minute. Or at least she would be able to prove it.

She stood up. Her alibi required getting started *now*—she had a lot of pieces to set up, some of them in Rhode Island—and the latest she could plausibly claim she slept in was 10:30. That meant doing the whole setup before her trick to record Steve. Ideally she would have liked to have her evidence in hand first. But there was nothing for it; she would get the recording when she returned. Hurriedly she set about the room collecting the clothes she would need, running over her scheme in her head and finding no holes—and it was with a shock that the next, obvious question presented itself.

She had just spent hours ensuring that she wouldn't be a suspect in the murder—so whom should she frame for it? And suddenly the fastest, most creative thinking she had ever done in her life came grinding to a halt. Because the appalling thought hit her that if her alibi *worked*, and she *didn't* frame someone, the police would likely wind up arresting someone close to her for the murder, someone they would say had taken vengeance *for* her: Coach Bailey, Randall, maybe Susan Kinsler or other members of the team—

She could not, under any circumstance, allow that to happen.

Could she frame Chris? But no, that wouldn't work. A vague scheme of making it look like a falling-out among the rapists dissolved into smoke as she looked at it...

As she pondered she continued to move around the room, tossing clothes onto her bed. On one pass she opened her desk drawer, found her little blue-and-white USB thumb drive, put it in her pocket, and went back to thinking and sorting clothes.

Another queer thought hit her, criminal that she had become. From this moment on, she realized, her adversary was no longer Steve, nor anyone at Hills College. It was a man she didn't know yet, a police detective out to solve the murder, a figure still in the shadows of her life but who would come forward with the clear

eyes of a hunter, seeing everything. He would stand in this very
room; his eyes would scan her books, her shelves, her desk, everything here. She almost saw him: a notepad, a necktie, a busy
pencil. She had to not only baffle that man but, assuming she
could, also deflect him from a misguided stoop upon her friends.

"Oh, bloody hell," she sighed aloud. There was only one possible way to do it.

She would have to frame herself.

Well, it makes one thing easy, she thought. *I can kill Steve with a
fencing sword after all.*

It was 4:49 am when Hannah pulled on her black hooded
sweatshirt and a black knit hat and left the dorm. As she stepped
into the cold air she forced all emotion from herself — *game face*.
Starting now she was on an exact and fast clock that led to 11:30
pm that night. Her first task was to make a round trip to Rhode
Island, touching a lot of bases en route, and be back by 10:30 at the
latest. She had timed her morning as precisely as she could.

The pre-dawn hours of Thursday, December 15, 2013 were
frigid under a clear sky as she crossed the campus lawns, walking
fast, a black knit hat on her head and hands thrust into her sweatshirt pocket. A few stars penetrated the diffusion of Boston city
light. The distant sounds of traffic were just beginning, percussions of the big trucks on the potholed roads. The snow was cal-
cified into a cement mold of a thousand shoeprints, almost
soundless under her tread.

The first thing she needed was money, and money that
couldn't be traced to a withdrawal from her own account. With
her key she let herself into the deserted offices of the Vista, where
at the back of the room she took a hidden key from under a book

and opened the safe that contained the cash kitty for the end-of-year party. It came to $2,500. With luck she would replace it at the beginning of next semester before it was missed.

Without luck? Well, she would be in jail.

With the money in her pants pocket she walked off the Hills College campus to its local Green Line stop, where she stood with her hood pulled over her face for the security cameras until 5:01 am, when she caught the first T of the day. Her disguises would get better along the way. The T clanked and squealed, and at 5:58 am she was in Alewife. From the station it was a quick walk, still through icy darkness, to the Neville Place Assisted Living home, where she picked up the car.

Hannah didn't have a car of her own, but her 85-year-old uncle, Jacob Wheeler, lived here, and several years ago her Aunt Betsy from Florida had purchased a used car for him. He no longer drove, but it still sat in the Home's parkinglot and was used by the extended Wheeler clan whenever they came to visit. Hannah walked the edge of the back parking loop under the trees to the old blue Buick sedan, knelt, and fished the keys from the top of the right rear tire. A moment later she was warming up the engine. There were crumpled napkins on the floor and a smell of stale coffee in the cold air that traced to a shiny stain on the passenger seat. "Fred," she muttered. For a moment she looked at the prim two-story building, asleep with its windows dark. "I'm sorry I didn't visit more, Uncle Jake," she whispered.

Then she shifted with a clunk into reverse, backed out of the spot, and hit the road. Her watch said 6:10 am.

Her next two stops were local, a good warmup for her driving skills. She knew how to drive, of course, and had once driven most of the way to Maine with her parents, but her plan called for the longest solo driving of her young life. *Piece of cake.* She might wish for a newer and more anonymous car, or at least one with a working radio, but this is what she had.

The first stop was just down the street, a 24-hour Walmart, where with her hoodie down at the register she bought a package of rubber kitchen gloves, a pair of oversize galoshes, a pair of flip-flops, a bag of hairnets, a small bottle of alcohol, a screwdriver, and a pair of cheap sunglasses. She could thank her secret high school boyfriend Dan, he of the Special Forces background, for lessons on how to avoid leaving DNA at a crime scene, secrets that he had related in the pine grotto behind the boarding school dorms. Of course he had then been caught and fired, which didn't, she think, reflect on the particular expertise in question. He had been quite cheerful about the firing as he faded back off the grid. *If only he could see me now.* She paid cash.

She wore the sunglasses with her knit hat pulled low at the next stop, a Goodwill thrift store, from which she emerged with a giant crinkly bag full of more clothing and other items. The plan she had worked out called for no fewer than six disguises for multiple Amtrak security cameras, if one counted the hoodie/knit cap combo as Disguise #1.

Half a block from the Goodwill she saw a good target for the screwdriver in an alley, and when the Buick pulled onto the street again it had new license plates. She would be going through toll booths.

Now she drove home, or at least to what had once been: the small private boarding school in a rural suburb just off Route 128 near Waltham. Hannah had attended the Mayden School for two years before college, drawn by their fencing program which was considered one of the best in the country. She nosed the Buick down the familiar curved, unpainted roads through snowy woods, past the well-spaced expensive homes, and remembered midnight walks she and Dan had taken here. She looked to her right through a flicker of slim trunks until she saw the gloaming snow of the school's lower fields; the main entrance was a quarter mile ahead. No one was around as she parked on the side of the road and turned off the headlights. Her watch read 6:28. She pulled on a pair of the rubber gloves and three hairnets, slid the galoshes over her shoes and tucked her pant legs into them, following Dan's lessons. Thus armored against exfoliation she got out, opened the trunk of the car and took out the tire iron. Then she walked quickly through the thin belt of woods, leaving wide featureless prints in the snow, to the bottom of the field where the Shop, a small shed-like house, sat alone. Here she could get her sword.

If she was killing Steve with a fencing sword she obviously couldn't use her own épée, or one from the college at all. This should be hard to trace.

It was still well before sunrise, but with the blue pre-dawn light on the snowfield it was easy to see. The little wooden building was locked, but it was a thousand feet to the upper campus where the dorms were; plus, she knew that the Mayden School was on winter break. With a quick swing of the tire iron she broke the shed's window, then reached in and unlatched the door. As she came in she turned on the light.

In the cluttered space full of tools and the cold smell of sawdust she went straight to the workbench under the toolboard and lifted the scarred wooden lid. From the pile of broken, discarded fencing blades inside, used for metalwork practice, she selected a saber intact save for a broken tip. She made a couple of test lunges with it in the small space. She would only need the hilt and bottom part.

A fencing sword, in its natural state, is specifically designed to make injury unlikely and death all but impossible. It's a highly flexible piece of steel, more like a wand than a sword. But the flexible part, the foible, comprises only the final two thirds of the blade; the lower part, the forte, is good solid metal rooted in the hilt.

She took the sword to the belt sander. Now she would have to hurry; this was the riskiest part. Pressing the switch she activated the machine, which roared to life with a screaming whine. Hannah grabbed a pair of cutters off the wall, snapped off the foible and held the end of the forte to the belt. Working as fast as she could but with perfect steadiness, deafened in the spray of sparks and silver fragments, she filed the forte to a razor-sharp, balanced, diamond-shaped point. She had learned this skill right here in this room. She made two test lunges with her now poignard-sized saber, then, satisfied, hit the power switch.

The whine of the machinery declined and died. She looked at the tell-tale silver shavings fanned across the wooden floor. The dustpan hung on the wall within reach. But her ears were still ringing, and the one broken window offered her no visibility to what was happening uphill at the campus. She licked her lip, her hand halfway to the dustpan.

It struck her all of a sudden that leaving the shavings might not be a bad move, provided none of her DNA was among them. *Talk about framing myself.*

Her goal in using a fencing sword was to eliminate others as possible suspects. The idea was that when she was cleared by her alibi (assuming it worked) the cops would have to go looking for someone *else* who would use a sharpened fencing sword. That alone didn't deflect them from enough of her friends, though. She had been racking her brains for how to frame herself more. This — the tell-tale shavings at the little, obscure Mayden School, assuming the cops found it — would do the trick. It wouldn't *prove* she was here — unless she left DNA — but it would eliminate pretty much everyone else.

And it would *really* point the finger at her. Should she? She had no time to weigh it. *My own alibi had better bloody work*, she thought, turning off the light on her way out. No one was in sight. With her heart pounding, the tire iron in one hand and her murder weapon in the other, she walked quickly back through the woods. She tossed both items into the trunk of the car and drove off. A minute later when the ramp put her onto 128 South her watch said 7:00 am exactly.

She had gotten the sword for free. But the rest of her alibi would cost money. A white winter sun was rising over the grey garages, motels, and chain stores of Attleboro at 7:42 am when she pulled into the parkinglot of the big Sears. The shopping went faster than expected; at that early hour the store was mostly empty. In less than twenty minutes she was hefting into the back seat the thousand-dollar portable fire pump in its roll cage. It came with separate boxes for its starter battery and hose extensions, that went on the floor of the back seat. The last box, the long cardboard one with the fluorescent ceiling bulb in it, she set carefully onto the passenger seat.

From behind the wheel she looked back at the shiny red pump, sitting at an angle on the saggy rear bench of the Buick.

Her alibi would go like this: as publicly as possible she would leave Hills College later that day and take the Amtrak to New

York. She would be recorded by the security cameras at both ends of the trip, boarding in Boston and disembarking at Penn Station. Her cellphone GPS would show her phone aboard the train for the whole southbound route. In that span Steve would be killed. Now, a cynical person might argue that one could get off the train, say at Providence, pick up a pre-positioned car, drive north to Boston and commit the murder, then drive south again to meet and re-board the train, say at New Haven, before it reached New York. But such an argument would be absurd. The train is too fast. There simply isn't enough time for anyone to make such a round trip in time to meet it.

Not unless it was delayed.

Hannah had traced the Amtrak Northeast Corridor on Google Maps, scrolling her computer screen to follow the frail double line on a light grey background, and noted that it runs hard by several large bodies of water. A gas-powered fire pump projecting a 100-foot stream, drawing from the water source, could easily hit the exposed catenary high-voltage wires running above the tracks, and short out the system at the closest transformer. Hannah had taken the time to read through several old newspaper reports of train delays from blown transformers, and the standard time to restore service was between one and two hours. That would give her the delay she needed.

She figured the ruse of being on the train would be enough to clear her of suspicion. *It should work. It should be enough proof.* Staring at the pump she tried to convince herself. *Well, there's nothing for it but to try*, she thought as she started the car and drove off.

In fact what Hannah didn't appreciate, being an amateur at the criminal game, was that the mere act of staging a clockwork interstate rendezvous with a moving train would be miles beyond the scope of what most police would even consider, and *sabotaging Amtrak for the purpose* so disproportionate to the requirements of an alibi as to render her scheme, when later glimpsed in outline, almost legendary in the annals of law enforcement.

The pump ran on a gasoline motor. At a Shell station nearby she filled its little tank.

Now came what for her was the trickiest part. The pump had to fire ahead of the train during the ride; in other words she had to trigger it remotely. Most of her midnight Internet research had centered around clandestine means of triggering devices, usually bombs, at a distance. She had printed out a list of what she would need. But to assemble it she would need help.

It was 8:07 am when she reached the stripmall Radio Shack outlet off Route 1 in Providence. For a moment she sat in the car looking at the tiny electronics store, wedged between a liquor store and a dry cleaners in the Chuck-Jones-Palladian mallfront. The car softly ticked. She took a deep breath.

"I'm sorry, you want to do what again?" The Radio Shack clerk was a balding, beanpole-skinny man in his forties, whose stoop betrayed an impatience to return to his newspaper open on the countertop. The store was otherwise empty.

"I want you to alter the electric starter of this fire pump" — she pointed to it on the floor — "so it can be remotely triggered by an incoming cellphone call. I've printed out the instructions to do it, and I'll buy whichever of these prepaid phones you recommend, but *you* need to do the wiring."

The clerk emitted a wobbly exhalation that passed for a laugh, shaking his head. "Miss, we can't do anything like that here. You have to go to an electrician or something. I mean, I can sell you a—"

"You can. You have the necessary equipment and I'm willing to pay. If you yourself can't do it, please call your manager, or someone who can."

"Well, *I'm* the manager...I dunno...y'know, you should have come in when Eric was here. He might be able to help you. He's more your age; he likes doing stuff like this. Too much so, in my opinion. He'll be in again on Saturday if you want to come back then."

"Call him."

"What, at home? At this hour? Miss, I, I can't—"

She handed him a hundred-dollar bill. "Call him and pass me the phone."

The manager dialed a number on the desk phone and passed her the receiver. Hannah spoke briefly to a middle-aged woman, waited a moment, and then heard a snide, sleepy, bewildered, "Hello?"

"Eric? I am a nineteen-year-old college girl standing in your shop with a thousand dollars cash. I need the starter on a fire pump rigged to a remote trigger from an anonymous cellphone, and an off switch based on a fluorescent light bulb. I need it in the next hour, and your manager isn't able to help me."

"Don't move! I'll be right there. Mom! I'm taking the car!"

"*You*," said Eric, not without appreciation, fifteen minutes later, "are planning to short out a high voltage transmission line with the spray from a fire pump. Activated by a telephone call from a remote location."

"College prank," said Hannah.

They were standing in the dim workroom in back of the store, by themselves, with the pieces laid out on a worktable cleared of a tangle of cables, old motherboards, voltage testers, and the like. "That's a pretty damn illegal prank," said Eric.

"Can you do it?"

"Shouldn't you ask first *if* I'll do it?"

She smiled. "I haven't told you my name. I haven't told you *what* college. I haven't told you *when* we're doing it."

Eric looked at her across the worktable. He was short, perhaps 17, with dark hair cut to fall over one eye, wore a black leather jacket over a threadbare black concert T-shirt, had tattooed words in bad handwriting partially visible on his neck, and held her in a stern gaze for the transparent purpose of continuing to stare at her.

"Please continue not revealing that information. Now. Your cell-phone trigger is easy. You got these bomb-trigger instructions from the web; I know the forum. I can improve on this, since I'm not wiring the ringer to an actual bomb fuse. You'll place a phone call to this phone, whose motherboard here will be wired to the starter, and the voltage from the ring will start the pump. But this fluorescent bulb…"

The most crucial aspect of Hannah's alibi was to conceal the fire pump, not only before it fired but afterwards from the repair crews that came along. The delay had to look like a natural accident. She could physically hide it near the tracks, but the problem that had given her fits last night concerned shutting the water stream *off*. It obviously couldn't still be firing when the repair crews arrived. Plus, it was winter. As long as the water was hitting live wires it would presumably vaporize, but if the pump continued for even a few seconds after the lines were cold, crews would find the wires draped in icicles, which would literally point them to the pump. A timer wouldn't work. The pump had to shut off exactly simultaneous with the system's line voltage, and there was certainly no way to connect a direct switch between them.

"Nice idea," said Eric, holding the fluorescent bulb. "These things glow under high-voltage wires." He gave her another look that this time was lifted about two-thirds from her breasts.

"Can you use that to make an off switch? I couldn't find anything on the web —"

"Pff. Easy. I'll encase it in an opaque tube and put a light sensor in with it. When the line goes dead, the bulb will go dark, the sensor will activate and trigger an interrupt to shut off the pump."

"Nice idea," said Hannah.

An icy fog huddled over Greenwich Bay and no one was out walking as she pulled into the parkinglot of the bayside condominium a little north of the town of East Greenwich, Rhode Island, at 9:34 am, a little behind schedule. It was just as the satellite view on Google Maps had portrayed it to her when she selected it as the best of the Northeast Corridor's close approaches to water. The condominium consisted of two long three-story buildings of grey brick at an angle to each other, with a foggy blank space beyond. The Amtrak line could be seen running just behind the buildings, with its accompanying flight of wires on metal struts; beyond that was the Bay. She wore no disguise, because what she was doing was suspicious enough, as she lugged the modified fire pump, wrapped in old tarps she had collected on the way, down the little access road to the water.

Six minutes later she returned to the parkinglot empty-handed. In some ways the setup was better than she had hoped: the condo buildings and tracks were some twenty feet above the waterline, with the pump concealed below on a narrow strip of land at the water's edge, at a point exactly between the angled buildings. Its rubber hose snaked into the slurping salt water; its black nozzle, firmly braced in heavy rocks, was aimed up within a stone's throw at the catenary wires. There had even been thorny bushes in which, with a judicious arranging of the tarps, she had been able to conceal the thing's shiny red surface. It was certainly invisible from up here, and would be even from the third-floor windows, none of which actually pointed that way anyway.

More worrisome was the dark, trashy pile of tarps down below as seen from the Bay. It wasn't a particularly ritzy part of the shoreline but it was clean and well-tended. Still, at this time of year there weren't too many boats about—she had seen none—and the narrow strip of land was safely obscure; no one was likely to clamber out there to clean up litter. She looked at her watch: 9:40 am. She had done her best; she had to head back to school.

It doesn't need to be there for long, she told herself. *It will be used tonight.*

At 10:11 am an unrecognizable woman in shades, scarf, knit hat and a long heavy wool coat locked the Buick's doors behind her in the parkinglot of the Providence, Rhode Island Amtrak station, put the keys in a voluminous pocket, and carrying a big Goodwill bag entered the station and bought a northbound ticket for Boston with cash. The Buick's parking was good through tonight; on the floor of its back seat, buried under a loose pile of the Goodwill clothes, lay the sharpened saber. Disguise #2 came off in the restroom at Boston's South Station. And at 11:17 am Hannah Radhe was back on the Hills College campus, looking like herself again with the hood of her black sweatshirt thrown back and her ponytail free. She was a little late, but it should be all right; the sports teams, including her own, were all at practice, and there weren't too many people about. In her dorm room with the shade pulled she quickly transferred the makings of her next disguises from the Goodwill bag into a green duffel bag, and zipped it closed. Then she took a deep breath.

The preparations for her alibi were complete. Now came the key to it all, that alone would give the murder meaning: the trick to get Steve to confess.

She picked up the little digital audio recorder from the center of her desk.

She now needed to talk to a rapist.

Fighting her heart down from her throat she left the room.

Chapter 5 - Provocateur

In contrast with the many things she had concealed from Detective Laniya Wilson, it was imperative that Hannah *mention* these next events in her statement. The problem was she wasn't sure how to bring it up. The interview was coming naturally to a close, the detective squaring her note papers and starting in on how they would forward the rape and attempted rape charges to the Boston police who would conduct the investigation. Hannah was forced to baldly interject:

"Actually, Detective, there's something I didn't tell you, that maybe the Boston police should know about. See, I did something on campus yesterday morning, before I left, that might have been illegal."

Detective Wilson was immediately all attention, and had a smile and practiced line at the ready. "Uh-huh. Why don't you tell me about that? I'll say again, there's no judgement here, okay? If you got high and there's dope in your room, or if you slashed someone's tires, whatever it is, tell me. Because if you withhold it now and it comes out later, that's when they can say look, she's not trustworthy. Okay? It's important that you tell me everything you did."

"Right," said Hannah steadily. "Well, when I woke up I was thinking, you know, about my case, and how if I was going to press charges it would be just my word against theirs. So I came up with this plan to maybe get evidence of what they did. To maybe have Steve confess."

"Uh-huh." The detective looked dubious.

"I have a little digital audio recorder. And I thought, you know, every time Steve comes after me he's swearing up a storm, 'You bitch, you ho,' stuff like that. What if I could get some of that on tape? I knew he still wanted his trophy back. So I concocted this plan, and for all I know it worked. I'm not sure. What I did was, I set up a time and place that evening where I'd give Steve back his trophy, and I hid my recorder there in advance. My plan was that he'd show up but I wouldn't; I'd stand him up; I'd be long gone for New York. Ideally he'd curse me out, rant and rave, and with luck he'd mention the rape, like he wanted to rape me again, fuck me up, stuff like that. I figured he might bring other guys and have an audience, you know, so he'd be more likely to mouth off. I arranged it for this little place down near the reservoir, kind of this remote little park where he'd be free to really, ah, show his true colors. So, I know, it's illegal to record someone without their permission, right?

"No, not at all, not if it's a recording made in a public place like a park."

Hannah had to pretend surprise. "Really? Great! Because I was going to say, I did leave the recorder running there when I left for New York. Assuming he came down there at six o'clock, it might have something on it."

"I will pass that information on to the Boston police, and they'll go collect that recorder and see what's on it. So I want you to draw me a map of exactly where that recorder is hidden."

And Hannah would draw the most exact map she could to the place where, after leaving her room again, she had hidden her recorder. It was the triangular green made by two roads down by

Edwards dorm near the reservoir, a park so tiny, remote and open that anyone meeting there would gravitate naturally to its solitary bench. Behind the bench the land rose up a wooded hill, and her recorder was hidden a few feet up, slightly behind a tree, half-buried in snow in an open baggie insulated with white cloth. It was 11:28 am when she started it recording; the file had an eight-hour limit, enough to cover her 6:00 pm appointment.

She explained all this with what she hoped was appropriate girl-sleuth enthusiasm to the detective as she drew her map. But she didn't mention that the recorder would no longer be there when the Boston Police went to find it, nor where it would turn up. And she didn't mention the second microphone.

Per her plan she would, in fact, be long gone from Hills by 6:00 pm to catch her train, and it would be intolerable to put her scheme into motion and drive all the way back to campus to find what, if anything, Steve had said, or if he had even come. Thus she had also hidden, twenty feet down from the bench and higher up the hill, a second sound device. This one she called her "Skype baby monitor" after its intended use according to the website: it consisted of a second pre-paid cellphone she had bought at Radio Shack, on which she had attached a miniature directional mic and installed the Skype Internet communication app, with the latter set to automatically connect audio on an incoming call. By placing a call to her "baby monitor" from her laptop, she would be able to hear audio live from a safe position off campus before boarding the train. With luck, her "baby" would be Steve's confession.

As she drew her map to the precise tree of the first digital audio recorder, the missing piece of Hannah's plan finally occurred to Detective Wilson.

"But, so, how did you—what did you do to set up the six

o'clock appointment with Steve?" she asked. "Did you talk with him?"

"Not Steve. Chris Kelly."

Of course it had to be Chris, Hannah thought. But she knew that he ate lunch apart from the other football players, in the little Eyrie Room cafeteria alongside the bookstore, where he was desperately studying for a makeup exam to avoid repeating Psychology. When she entered the cafeteria she saw him on line for food, his big body towering between a few other bookish students and some faculty in tweeds. He hadn't seen her and for a moment she stood, contemplating her blond ex-boyfriend and trying to calm her thudding heart.

Their two-week affair had been kind of a disaster even before the day a cheerleader, Debbie Ackerman, told her that he had only dated her to win a bet. In bed Chris had had performances issues that often led to tears; she wound up comforting him most of the time. When she broke up with him, telling him she knew about the bet, he didn't deny it, even sneering and laughing at her, but then afterward he inexplicably kept approaching her on campus, mumbling about their getting back together. It was as if he didn't want to admit to being the one who got dumped. He suddenly developed an interest in women's issues, or pretended to, always wanting to talk about them; it was why she had finally loaned him her Simone de Beauvoir. That at last had seemed to get rid of him – until the night before last, when he had been eager to gang rape her.

Well, let's see how he handles this. There was no point donning a game face now, and she couldn't if she tried. She took a trembling breath and approached him on line.

He saw her coming and for an instant looked as terrified as she felt. "Yo. I've got something to say to you," she opened.

The cafeteria was small, and though the kitchen was loud with clattering plates they were in earshot of several people. Chris immediately put on a blustering smile.

"Hey, Hannah! Listen, you know, about the other night, you know that was all a misunderstanding, right? We were just going to talk to you about the retraction, maybe scare you, it wasn't going to go farther than that. Steve feels bad about getting out of line. All he wants is his Biletnikoff back, and everything will be cool."

She stared at him. She felt like laughing, but the point was to be sarcastic and cold. "Thank you for parroting Dean Haughton's line," she said. "Everything will be cool? Does that include Davey Coleman?"

"Oh yeah, totally. I mean, he's out for the season, it sucks, but, like, stuff happens, you know? I'm telling you, just give Steve's Biletnikoff back and bygones and will be bygones."

Then they're all out to get me. Behind Chris' obvious script — *"Now if any of you run into Hannah"* — she could see wheels turning, plans being laid, and even discern the distinct absence of any intervention from the Dean. Her stomach flipped with the idea of a plan to make Steve *madder*, and for a second she couldn't speak, but she held herself straight. At any rate Chris was trying to fence with her, and he was a very poor fencer.

Feint then. "I'm happy to give the Biletnikoff back, but bygones are never going to be bygones," she said. "I'm going home to New York tonight and I'm going to press rape charges against all five of you."

That drew a few discreet head movements from around them

in line, but if Chris noticed they seemed to have nothing to do with his eye-roll of minor annoyance. "Oh come on, Hannah. Don't keep overreacting. Steve wants to apologize, all right? Look, if you want you can give the trophy to me, I can bring it to him."

Too easy. *And thrust.* "I'll give the Biletnikoff to Steve and Steve alone. Tell him to meet me at six p.m. tonight at the bench in the little triangular park down by Edwards. I'll give him his trophy back there. Tell him to come alone."

"Naw, don't be ridiculous, Hannah. Come on, there's no need to make a —"

"That's the message. See you." She started to turn away.

"Wait, wait, stop. Are you fucking serious?" he said, lowering his voice to an exasperated stage whisper.

She had him on a very risky line, but he was a poor messenger and she had to make sure he knew the message. "Six pm tonight. The bench at the little triangular park. Tell him it's his one and only chance to get the damn thing back because afterwards I'm going home to New York."

He stared at her, and she could almost see the gears turning in his head. *A setup?* he was thinking. Then: *Who does she have lined up?* Derailed suddenly by: *I'm not your goddamn errand boy!*

The last won out. "Look, Hannah, don't screw around, all right? Just give the trophy to me, and I'll give it to Steve. Don't be such a, a —"

He was thrashing on the line, ready to turn dangerous. But it was a public place and all he could do was thrash. "Steve and Steve only," she said steadily. "At six p.m. precisely, *alone*, otherwise he doesn't get it back." She was hoping the reiteration, and the suggestion of a setup, would encourage him to bring other guys.

The queue was approaching the servers, and Chris was out of options. "Fine!" he said, shaking his head as if to clear flies. "Fine, if that's the way you want it. What *park* is it again?"

She made sure he understood exactly where the meeting point was, and then she went out on limb and tried for a little extra. "And tell him not to try anything, because I spoke with Dean Haughton and I have Haughton's personal promise of protection."

She very much hoped that name of Haughton, communicated through Chris to Steve, would come out in some form if Steve threw a fit. What Hannah *really* wanted a berserk Steve to mention on tape was not only the rape but his so-called "green light." Ideally he would finger the dean by name.

"Haughton's protection," she said again. Be sure to tell Steve that."

"Oh, don't worry. I'll tell him," said Chris coldly, looking at her with a transparent secret vow to be there himself and show her how much protection she had.

She left him to furiously scoop fried chicken pieces onto his tray, and left the cafeteria.

That's it, she thought, weak-kneed as she walked out into the cold sunlight, trying to see with her back if he was rushing after her. After a moment she allowed herself to look at her watch. It was 11:55 am. *Everything's in place. It's all set up.*

It was time for her to leave the Hills College campus for New York.

And not a minute too soon.

Chapter 6 - Avenger

Coach Bailey was not surprised, given her second late arrival to practice, to hear that she was leaving Athletics Week early after all, and nodded slowly when she told him in his office that she *was* going to press charges, back home in New York.

"I'll make your excuses with the team," Bailey said. "And if you need me for anything over the break, call me."

"Well," she said, "Can you do something for me now? I just ran into Chris at lunch and I'm, like, totally freaked out about being on campus. Can you walk me back to my dorm so I can pack for the train? I'm going to leave for New York, like, right now."

The reason she didn't like lying to Coach Bailey was that he knew her too well. He gave her teenage grammar a sidelong look, but she was able to coast by on the strength of being a traumatized assault victim, plus the unlikelihood of her actually needing to be witnessed as continuously as possible from here until she boarded the Amtrak.

"Sure, sure, I'll walk you to your room. I'll walk you to the goddamn T station."

He stood by while she threw the clothes she had already set out into a small roller suitcase. They made awkward conversation about missing his party that night, filled with pauses even more awkward. "And these are my winter clothes!" she joked, hefting the green duffel bag.

"Here, I'll get that," he said, taking it.

Together they walked to the campus T stop—her for the second time that day—and he stood with her until a train came. "See you in the New Year," he said, and there was a quick hug, in which to her surprise Hannah could feel a hesitation, caused, she realized, by the presence of rape. For some reason that, of all things, triggered an eruption of anger in her. *Those bastards*, she thought. *Look what they*— She shook it off. She had no room for anger now.

The T windows moved Coach Bailey and the platform backwards. She looked at her watch: the time was 12:45 pm.

Here we go. Game face again, kiddo.

It was a little before 1:30 pm when she carried her two bags into the echoing hubbub of Boston's South Station. At the ticket counter she used her credit card for the first time that day, buying a ticket for the 6:45 pm train to New York. Everything now was Hannah Radhe on the record for all to see, going home to New York. Then she crossed the station and entered the dim, polished alcove of Eastern's Tavern, a franchise sports bar, where she took a booth in plain view of the crowds.

Now came the part of her alibi that she knew to be the weakest: she had to sit here at the station for several hours, and take a later train when there were plenty of earlier ones. There was no help for it. For one thing, it had to be dark when she slipped back onto campus, not to mention when the pump fired. More importantly, she didn't yet know whether she *would* be slipping back to campus. Her whole plan hung fire on whether or not her trick worked, whether or not she had evidence, which she wouldn't learn until the setup time for Steve in the park—6:00 pm. Chris might not deliver the message, and even if he did Steve might not show up. If the trick fell through, there would be no point killing

Steve at all. She would then simply take the train home, and fall into exactly the Christmas vacation of fear that she dreaded, made worse by her own setup that would infuriate the rapists further.

Under those circumstances she doubted she would return to Hills. And where would her life go from there?

Hannah looked at her watch. Four and half hours until 6:00.

She could at least start with a perfectly accountable move for her alibi—she was starving. She had eaten very little at dinner the previous night and nothing whatsoever at Chris' cafeteria. So she quite legitimately ordered a bacon cheeseburger and iced tea from the stout, mid-thirties waitress with a nice sweaty face and blonde hair in a stubby ponytail. She made a point of asking the woman if the bar had wi-fi, though she had researched it in advance. But when she opened her laptop on the table and put on her headphones, what she was actually doing was dialing the Skype number of her "baby monitor." She was thinking that it wouldn't hurt to test the system ahead of time.

There were already rapists talking in the park.

The audio was crystal clear.

> "And you're sure she meant this fucking park. You're a hundred percent sure. 'Cause if we have the wrong fucking place—"
>
> "Dude, I told you exactly what she said. This is the park, those are the two roads she mentioned. That's the bench. Edwards over there, the hill, the reservoir…we're just here first, man."
>
> "Maybe we are Chris. Maybe we fucking are. *Don't*—don't fucking look around like a moron! The whole point of this is who scopes the ground first. That's the whole game.

He who scopes first breaks heads first. He who gets scoped loses out on sweet vengeance pussy. That is not going to be us. OK, so I want Andrew there, and Tumpus with binoculars on the roof…"

Steve Badenhut's unmistakable voice faded away. But it, and others, would return at well-spaced intervals, arising in Hannah's ears as she ate her burger, drank iced teas, and idled away the hours with a legal-advice web page up on her laptop to hide the Skype screen. At first she smiled to realize that Steve had taken the bait, indeed gone one better. Expecting a setup, he had laid an ambush. And he had assembled at least a small squad of footballers. Different individuals were dispatched regularly to stroll the park, apparently posing as if talking on their cellphone while really scouting the woods for Hannah's hidden forces and reporting back. The directional mic clearly picked up the various voices:

"…Nothing—nothing—wait! A car! Hang on—okay. Nothing. No, dude, I can see *all* the way up the hill, there's no one in there..."

But as the hours wore on, her smile faded. So far she hadn't gotten a direct confession. Steve had spread his people out and very few of them were walking past the bench; when they did she got snatches only. And at the same time what they did say was draining the blood from her face:

"…Naw, nothing happened, man, I just had to come down. It was too fucking cold on that goddamn roof. My cellphone hand was a block of ice. I couldn't even fucking dial."

"Dude, I need you back up there. I need your eyes. We're counting down now, something's gonna happen soon. Don't worry about your hand, you can warm it up in Hannah Radhe's pussy, before or after I put my fist into it a few times myself. That will happen before this day is out, my friend, and you have the privilege of being in on it. Remember, this is for Davey."

"Yeah."

"So finish this patrol with me, then get the fuck back…"

"What you're reading must be intense," the blonde waitress said. "You look kinda white."

"Uh, yeah," said Hannah. "It's, ah, true crime stuff."

A little later came the familiar voice of Chris Kelly, apparently walking alone:

"…call you back then. Bye. Ahhh….La de da, la de da, what a lovely park, I'm just out for a stroll, la la de da, I like to stroll. I was strolling through the park one day, in the merry merry month of December. I was looking for a girl to rape, in the merry merry month of whenever. Hannah Hannah Hannah. Don't worry, I'll keep you warm, with my big body in the snow as I rape the shit out of you, la de da. Yes, right in those lovely woods, and to any poncy fencer boys hiding in there, guess what, I'm here to rape a girl. Rape a girl, rape a girl, merrily merrily merrily—God, this is fucking cold. This is fucking cold and fucking stupid. (long pause) Hannah, I promise you this: you will see that I'm a man. You will see that I'm a man. See, I know you've never seen one before. It'll be all right between us. I understand, I understand, I'm the one who understands...hello snow, whaddaya know? (Laughter) Fuck…"

That one prompted the waitress to set down a fresh cup of hot tea unasked.

And at 6:28 pm on December 15, when Steve Badenhut finally accepted that he'd been stood up, when from what she could gather his gang had mostly melted away, when he stood with Andrew Keith directly in line of her microphone, in what must have been the freezing cold, dark and empty park between the woods and the reservoir, and delivered the one-minute-thirty-three-second speech that came to be known in court as the "Torture Rant," her triumph came together with a wave of ice seeping into her bones as if forever.

"—So what if we have to wait through winter break to get ahold of her? That just runs up her taxi fare, man. Andrew, my friend, when she gets back she's going to have a bill the likes of which no cunt has ever seen, and her cunt is the only way she can pay it. You know what? Listen to me. The first time, in my room, when I was the only one who got to do her, it was going to be what I call a gentle rape, she was even going to be unconscious for the rest of you. Well, she fucked us over then. For breaking Davey's fingers she got tonight, where we were gonna do it the old-fashioned way in the woods with the whole blue crew. So now? She goes and fucks us over *again*? *All* of us? *Again*? *The bitch*? Well, *next* time, Andrew, we're gonna grab her on her first day back and take that bitch out to some cabin in Vermont, and she'll be missing for six months. And every so often we'll drive up there together, and bring some hoses and garden rakes and baseball bats, and we will make it last so long that she begs us to kill her. She will offer to marry us and have ten babies with each of us and be our sex slave for life if only we'll untie her. And when there's nothing left of her but drool and cum rolling down from her every ripped-open orifice, we'll toss her body in the fucking woods and take a piss on it. Hannah Radhe just wrote out her own future tonight, and it's a very short one. Come on, man, I need to get fucking warm, I need a…

As the voices faded out Hannah closed her eyes and took the headphones out of her ears.

That's it. That's the confession. He said it. It's not everything – it's well short – but it will do. I believe it will bloody well do.

She hadn't counted on it leaving her trembling all over.

The waitress sat down across from her. "Honey, are you okay? You look sick. Are you sure you should be looking at that crime stuff?"

"Oh – sorry. It – well, it's material about rape."

"Oh honey," said the waitress in a tone that revealed much. Hannah ordered hot tea and they started talking. By 6:44 pm, when she had to pretend to miss her train, she and Kimberly Atkins were close friends.

Another witness.

Missing the train was her one trick for justifying her hours at the station. Acting like she had lost track of time, she bid Kimberly Atkins a sudden harried goodbye and hastened with her bags across South Station, where she "discovered" that she had just missed the 6:45 to New York. At the ticket booth she put another $25.00 on her credit card to switch to the next train, then

slogged her bags back to Eastern's and a surprised Kimberly Atkins to wait it out. She picked a bad one to miss, Kimberly told
her; the next one to New York wasn't until 9:30, the last train of
the night. Hannah nodded: she knew.

The 9:30 Southbound was *her* train, and had been from the
start.

At 9:26 pm, bags in hand outdoors on the night platform in the
shuffling herd of winter coats, she paused, turned around, and
stared back at the glass doors to the terminal as if she'd forgotten
something. She looked around until she located the security
camera. She gazed straight at it for a few seconds — a lone hatless
face in a sea of backs — then turned forward again and, ponytail
bouncing, boarded the train.

Amtrak 67, the 9:30 Regional Southbound, departed Boston's
South Station precisely on time, due at Penn Station, New York at
2:15 am, an ordinary five hours and fifteen minutes later. In the
clicking, gently rocking car Hannah took an empty seat next to a
portly lady in a pink coat, first putting her two bags, the suitcase
and the green duffel, on the rack overhead.

Ten minutes later she finally called her parents to tell them of
her sudden trip home. She had waited until she knew they were
out — they were at a friend's Christmas party — so she could get
their voice mail. This way her phone record would show a call
from the train, backed up by her parents' voice message. She spoke
in a low voice, her face averted from the lady in pink, but clearly,
and expended the last tremors of Steve's speech into the effect she
wanted:

"Mom, Dad, I waited till you were out to call because I didn't
want to spoil your night. I'm on the train home now, tonight,

early. Something happened at school...well, I was raped. By a football player. I'm not *hurt*, okay, I mean not physically, and I'll, I'll *be* okay, all right? But right now I'm really shook up, so I'm just coming home. I'll be in the city about two-fifteen a.m.; I'll take a cab to the apartment and let myself in. *Please* don't wait up; I'll tell you all about it in the morning. I do want to press charges. I love you."

When she ended the call she was calm as stone. Calmly she pulled her suitcase down from the rack and tucked her cellphone into an outer pocket. Its battery was fully charged for its GPS run to New York. She put the suitcase back on the rack.

At 9:56 she told the lady in pink that a college friend of hers was supposed to be on the same train, and she was going to look for her. The lady seemed politely happy to have the empty seat back. Hannah took her green duffel bag down from the rack and walked off through the car. No one noticed that she left her suitcase behind.

In the rest room of the next car she pulled Disguise #3 from the green duffel. Exiting at Providence would be a woman in a long wide-shouldered white coat, which would have trailed on the floor without the eight-inch platform boots thus concealed; white gloves; a voluminous floral scarf tugged up over the chin and mouth against the winter cold; and a wide-brimmed, feathered, white hat that hid her hair and shadowed her face. Her regular clothes went into the duffel. No one in the night-darkened, dozing car paid any attention as the altered woman emerged from the rest room and took an empty row, putting her duffel bag on the rack overhead.

At 10:22 pm Amtrak 67 glided to its stop at Providence, Rhode Island, and the elegant lady got off the train, minus bag. With firm clacks of her heels she crossed the mostly empty Providence station in company with six other disembarking passengers, but stopped at the bank of pay phones by the front doors. She waited until, with a pneumatic hiss audible through the windows behind her, the doors of Amtrak 67 closed and the train slid into motion, accelerated down the pier, and disappeared into the night.

Then she dialed the fire pump.

Hannah heard a ring tone, a click, and, to her surprise, the recorded voice of Eric in her ear: "Have fun with your prank!" There was a final click and the line went dead. She hung up, left the station, and walked fast to her Buick waiting in the dark parkinglot. It was 10:28 pm when the blue sedan, exhaust pipe steaming, nosed off through the deserted late-night streets of Providence and got on the highway northwards toward Boston.

Twenty-one miles ahead of the train in the other direction, a roaring, buzzing conflagration of blue sparks lit up the maritime nightscape of Greenwich Bay as a high-pressure jet of seawater fired upward into the electric catenary lines above the tracks. The big rocks held the nozzle firm against the vicious thrust and the source of the jet could not quite be seen from any direction. Indeed the dark seawater itself was almost invisible, transmuted on contact into clouds of steam lit by staggered flares of leaping lightning. Even the loud growl of the fire pump's gas-powered motor was all but drowned by the high-decibel crackle and explosive percussions of the wounded 25,000-volt circuit. Lights went on in the neighboring condominium, but no window offered a direct view, though residents with their noses to the glass saw the bursting flares; neither of the two cars that stopped abruptly on Route 1, including the one that deployed a cellphone out the window, saw more than an unexplained blue catastrophe aloft behind the condos.

It was the salt steam, finally, in its constantly-regenerating accumulation, that forged the final short circuit. A crescendo of bolts volleyed rapidly between the wires in a night-shredding sizzle, then everything stopped. The Northeast Corridor was dead. In the sudden darkness of green-blinking afterimages, none of the distant observers noticed the drooping spew of water behind the hill, from the pump that had silenced itself at the exact same instant.

No icicle hung from anything.

Hannah drove through the night at a steady 65 miles per hour. She didn't know whether the pump had fired or the train was successfully stalled. If it was, her research told her it would be roughly one and a half hours until it got moving again. She simply had to trust, as she had known she would and worried she could, but to her surprise she did. She didn't sweat; she didn't speed. The Buick's engine hummed and she drove steadily, relentlessly, into the night. Traffic on Interstate 95 was sparse; she crossed the Massachusetts state line at 10:39 pm. In Boston the city streets were empty. Exactly forty minutes after leaving Providence she pulled onto the Hills College campus. She parked at the extreme far end of the lowest parkinglot, under the shadow of a stand of evergreens, and in the darkness of the car changed into Disguise #4 from the clothes left in the back seat.

This disguise was the most important. It involved a huge blue parka as a fat suit, with extra belts under it holding two five-pound dumbbell weights to her body; over it was a man's shapeless tweed coat, with men's slacks and an old pair of extra-large hiking boots below, in the latter of which were two inches of foam inserts. On her head, over the hairnets, she wore a tall baggy striped knit hat that flopped to one side. She pulled on two pairs of rubber kitchen gloves, and put her pair of brand-new flip-flops into the coat pocket. Then she reached around to the floor of the back seat, picked up her sword, and tucked it carefully, point down, inside the big coat. She buttoned the coat.

She had parked close to the little triangular park by the reservoir, and not a soul was in sight as she crossed behind the bench and found her digital audio recorder right where she had left it, in its baggie at the foot of the tree. She stepped as gently she could on the hard snow, and reached long to pick it up, though the false shoes and weights would disguise her footprints and later, after she drew her map to this location for Detective Wilson, there would be policemen tramping around here searching in vain for the device.

She also gathered up her Skype baby monitor, minding her footprints with similar care. She tucked that cellphone into another pocket of the big coat. Then she began the long walk up campus to Hunter dorm.

Now she was beyond the area of blind trust, and onto the fencing strip of the unplanned. She didn't know whether Steve would be asleep, awake in his room, out at a party, alone or with company. There was no way to plan and she hadn't bothered to; if she came upon him in company with others she might have to kill them too; she left that decision uncharted to the instinct of the moment. Then again, he might be spending the night in some girl's room, which would save him. Even out at a party upped his odds, because she was on a tight clock and couldn't afford a stakeout. It was a 132-mile drive to intercept her train at New Haven. Estimating conservatively for the train delay, she had calculated that 11:45 pm was the absolute latest she could safely leave campus.

Anything later and she would have to speed dangerously.

It was 11:19 pm when she reached the cement stairs to the upper dorms, the same ones down which she had fled in terror two nights before. She had still seen no one.

Hunter dorm loomed above her.

Steve was at a party. He was in his own dorm, in Andrew Keith's suite two floors above his room.

He had been drinking hard since dinner and he was in the worst mood of his life. His Biletnikoff trophy was gone, the bitch was in New York, Davey Coleman was out for the season with his broken hand and Coach Pruecastle had launched a screaming tirade at them that morning that still rang in his ears. You could tell he hadn't believed the story about Davey tripping on the stairs, and though he excoriated the whole team the tirade was largely directed at *him*. Somehow the bastard *knew*. The rest of their season was fucked and a lot of his own chances with it, because on some level he knew that his stats were largely built by riding on Davey's play. Then, when he'd tried to pick the guys' spirits up by leading them against the whore's transparent setup, it had all gone to hell. No guys had been waiting to jump them, the cunt herself had gone home to New York — at *noon*, they later learned, in other words just to fuck with them — and everyone had left cold and sore at him.

Andrew Keith perched his rangy body on the arm of the old couch next to him. He didn't look drunk, and wore his usual little smile.

"So, we lost out tonight big time, didn't we?" he said.

"Don't remind me. Tonight I'm going back to that slut's door and bust it down. I'm getting my fucking Biletnikoff back. You wanna come?"

"What if she took it to New York with her?"

"Then we'll take a piss in her fucking room."

"I think there's a smarter play. In fact, I've been thinking that maybe what happened tonight was for the best. Pruecastle already has his eyes on us, and if we'd had a big brawl, or actually caught her with all those guys, we couldn't have hid it. I have something else in mind."

"Oh yeah? Like what?"

"Well, it depends." He leaned closer, and lowered his voice as much as possible in the thudding music. "What you said earlier, you know, in the park, about first thing next semester. How serious were you?"

"I was fucking serious, Andrew. And you know what else? With every single drink tonight I'm getting more serious."

"Well, if you are, I'm in. I know someone who has the cabin. And maybe some of the stuff. But I think it should be just the two of us. Don't involve the others, especially Chris."

"Yeah. Chris. You're right about that. He—shit, we can't really rely on him. He's a bit weird when it comes to that girl. He really did want to fuck her up, though."

"And the others, you know, they were into it mostly because of what Coach said about the newspaper article. They thought they were shielded. Something like this, I think the fewer people in on it the better. You're the one with the experience."

Steve looked at him. "Yeah, but you, Andrew? Are you seriously into that shit?"

Andrew shrugged. "It's my last year in college. I don't have a football career beyond it like you guys. My Dad will get me a good job and I'll lead a boring life. It's my one chance. I've always been curious about it, and if you're into it, yeah, I'd like to try it. Like I say, I'm in a position to contribute a few things and I think we can do it right. I have some ideas."

Steve gave him a measuring gaze. Andrew was quiet and smart—he was the one who had suggested using Chris' borrowed book to lure Hannah to the room—but there was something about him that Steve didn't trust. He always wore that little smile. Still— "We'll talk further," he said.

"So don't go break into her room tonight. Save it. In fact, go to bed, I'm about to close up shop here anyway. It's almost eleven-thirty."

"Yeah, you've got a point." Steve hauled himself upright. "Christ I feel like shit."

"Hasta mañana," said Andrew.

Steve left the room.

The heavy metal soundtrack accompanied him in muffled echoes as he made his way down the stairs of the dorm. His hall was empty, though he thought he heard someone in the restroom. Fumbling with his key he let himself into his room. "Worst Christmas ever," he muttered to himself, and without turning on the light he started stripping for bed.

Suddenly he yelped. His door, which he hadn't locked, was opening. A straight line of light angled onto his carpet. He drew breath for a furious profanity, but the breath stopped in his throat.

In the ray of light a bare feminine hand appeared, holding the hilt of a glinting sword.

He thought it was very pretty.

At 3:45 am on the morning of December 16, Amtrak 67 pulled into Penn Station and opened its doors, an hour and a half late. In the slow-moving spill of slouched, exhausted, stiff, cold, disgruntled passengers onto the platform, one, a young woman in a white down parka with a bare head and a bouncing ponytail, stepped out with a straight back and a brisk step.

A few feet shy of the bright doors to the terminal she stopped briefly, set down her suitcase and green duffel bag, and smiled into the security camera.

Chapter 7 - Renegade

"Cowley!"

"Where is it?"

A pair of sunken eyes rose from the most cluttered desk in the homicide department. Chief Koontz of the Boston Police threaded his blue-suited bulk toward them through the maze of desks and low cubicle walls.

"You're gonna love this," he said. "We got a Hills student killed in his dorm room, football star. Campus is on break but it's Athletics Week for the teams. Solly found him. He was there because a girl filed a rape charge against him and four others. Solly goes up this morning, he talks to administration, they were trying to find the students, not very hard, one of 'em was missing, Steve Badenhut. They think, maybe he'd run. So they open up his room and, boom, there's the corpse."

"How was he killed?" Detective Alan Cowley was halfway to his feet, one arm lifting his coat from the back of the chair.

"First look is knife wound to the heart, small, like a letter opener or something, single entry. But get this. Corpse is on its back on the bed, shirtless, and sitting on the chest is a digital audio recorder identified as belonging to the girl, that according to Solly the girl mentioned in her statement as possibly having rape evidence on it and was supposed to be in a park. Her name on the back. Placed right next to the wound, on the corpse."

"Have Solly hold the other four for their own protection. She

might be going after all of them. Solly touched the goddamn recorder? To see the name?"

"It's Solly." Chief Koontz spread his hands. "He's up there
alone, with one officer. Cowley, wait, you think the girl –?"

"Do we have time of death on the student?"

"All we have is a corpse, Cowley. CSI's on the way, they'll
meet you there. Meanwhile all *I* have is a phone lit up with calls
from Dean Haughton. This is gonna get crazy fast. Cowley, the
girl was the one who filed the rape charge against him. With the
NYPD. Why would she do that and then go kill him?"

"She filed in New York?" Cowley paused with the jacket on
one arm and shot Koontz a look from his sunken eyes. He was
forty, his unkempt hair and indefatigable stubble still dark, and
his grey eyes were clear and piercing with sudden interest.

"Yeah. Yesterday."

"Then it depends on time of death. She might have killed him
first. What do we have on her? Who is she?"

"Ah, her name is Hannah Raid, spelled R-A-D-H-E, she's a
sophomore, nineteen...Cowley, I would appreciate it if for once
you wouldn't leap –"

"Where is she now? Do we know?"

"New York. But, ah, believe it or not she's on her way here."

"Boston?"

"Here!" the chief said. "The station. To see us."

"What?" The jacket hung from one arm.

Chief Koontz exhaled noisily, his usual response when multiple things happened at once. "Solly called her yesterday before
any of this happened, about her rape charges. Since she gave her
statement in New York, to a Detective Wilson, Solly told her she'd
have to give a repeat statement to us. Apparently she knew this

would be the case and agreed to come in person. She'll be here at four o'clock. Probably on the train now."

"Huh." Cowley reached down with his free arm, took a sip of cold coffee and reset the mug on the stack of manila folders, then slung his jacket fully on over his harness and grabbed his hat, an old fedora, from the rack. "Call New York and see if she really left. If she does show up here, hold her for questioning." He started across the room.

"On what basis?" Chief Koontz yelled after him.

"I'll call you from the scene and let you know," Cowley's hat shouted at the fluorescent ceiling.

But at the doorway he stopped and turned back to face the chief.

"Supposed to be in a park?"

"Told you you'd love it," said Koontz.

At that moment Hannah was, in fact, en route to Boston for her appointment with the police. She had known, when she "pressed charges" in New York, that the Boston police would be handling the sexual assault case and that she would have to repeat her statement to them.

It was an integral part of her plan. She had left a lot of pieces scattered between New York and Boston that had to be cleaned up, first and foremost of which was the fire pump, still sitting under its dark tarps on the shores of Greenwich Bay.

The thought of that pump hung at the back of her mind throughout the emotional, exhausting day she spent in New York with her parents. To begin with, she was actually exhausted. She had *told* her parents not to stay up for her, on her voice message from the train, and yet, when she let herself into their 11th floor apartment on East 88th Street as quietly as she could, a little after 4:00 in the morning, on the heels of two sleepless nights, the cries of "Hannah!" "*There* she is!" burst from the brightly-lit living-room, and an instant later her mother and father came toppling into the foyer with wide arms and faces deformed with sympathy. For the next two hours she had to sit in the livingroom on the long red couch narrating her night of terror and receiving, even through an expurgated version, one mingled loving reaction after another of shock, grief, gratitude at her escape, anger, intellectual bias confirmation against sports, gentle remonstration for getting herself even partially involved with "that group," and an infinite home-and-safe welcome that presumably ended some minutes after she had fallen asleep on the couch.

But only until sunrise, when with the first touch of conscious-ness she threw off the tan wool blanket and flew to the little kitchen TV (the apartment was at that point quiet), where she zig-zagged between news channels with the sound off until she had reassured herself that the body hadn't been found. She didn't ex-pect it yet; indeed she was counting down a rough timeline in her mind — she had locked Steve's door on her way out; in an hour he would miss football practice; there would be knocks; calls; mys-teries; waiting until dinner; speculation; worry — and she figured she probably had until tomorrow morning before anyone forced open his door. But anything could happen, and there were things she *must* do first, before the big show began. Top priority was pressing charges, which she had to get securely on the record as a cover story while Steve was still pressable.

But here she ran into unexpected resistance. Over breakfast in the large diningroom, around the squeaky oval table of dark wood amid the houseplants, her sympathetic parents *now* wanted her to sleep on it, think it over, make sure that pressing charges was *really* what she wanted to do. "It's a big process, honey, there'll be *publicity*," her mother said. "This Coach Bailey," said her father, "can you count on him? Won't he side with the school in a pinch?" "You're too *agitated* to talk to police now, sweetheart." "Do you want more eggs? Honey, get her some more eggs."

And slowly through her adamant counter-arguments and the food and the familiarity (there was *always* an argument over breakfast), Hannah felt a terrible new reality rise into place overlaying the scene: the reality that she, her parents' only child, had brought murder into the house. She almost felt it dripping from her just-showered hands. As if in a double vision, she saw their apartment soon to be crawling with cops, because her decision to frame herself meant that she *would* be a suspect, if only until she could present her alibi. And even if the alibi worked, the new reality would remain: she had introduced a thread of lies into their life that could never be pulled out, that could only be lived with.

Or perhaps lived up to.

This is the price for what I'm trying to do. I'm still willing to pay it — I must be willing — but it's steep. Steeper than I thought.

"Mom, Athletics Week only runs through Saturday. If the police want to question the players and maybe the school administrators I *have* to report it today, and I *want* to report it today, that's what I came home early *for*."

That finally got her and her mother, through a ridiculous attention to hair and nice clothes, out the door.

Her mother, a high school English teacher and minor poet, thus sat fiddling with her hands in the lounge of the 14th Precinct while, in the lime-green interview room, Hannah made her sexual assault statement to Laniya Wilson. It was thankfully in her presence, then, that Detective Wilson, shaking her hand after the interview, explained that her daughter would have to give a second statement to the Boston P.D., and probably soon, since Boston's goal would likely be to question the accused students while they were still on campus.

"Oh no—back to Boston *before* Christmas?" her mother groaned, while Hannah nodded, suppressing a sigh of relief.

She permitted herself the full sigh when, over dinner that evening, a Detective Solsberger from Boston P.D. called and she arranged to give her statement in Boston the very next day. It had spared her faking a call to generate the same result. Her parents threw up a double-barreled moan of sympathy, but in a few moments they had rushed into action to help her pack and, since a return to campus was out of the question, arrange for her to sleep with their friends the Peabodys in Newton. Her father, a television producer at NBC, was in high organization mode. "When you're done at the police station, go straight to Newton, and the next day Mike will drive you to the college and accompany you to collect whatever you left in your room that you'll need here. He has an SUV, it will fit a lot."

"Okay Daddy," she said.

And finally she had slept a full night through.

Now it was with a nervous, troubled impatience that she sat on the Amtrak out of Penn Station with a ticket back to Boston and her appointment with the police. One could have wished for another excuse to return north, but this was the only one she had been able think of. She looked at her watch: 10:05 am. Her appointment wasn't until 4:00 pm. On the news that morning there was still no sign of the body being found, but her radar told her that it could happen at any moment, and it would have a rather large influence on how her meeting might go.

Of course at some point she would be told that Steve was dead, and she would have to display wide-eyed, off-balance surprise. She looked ahead at her questioning by the cops, should it begin today, as a strange fencing match in which their winning move would be to catch her at the ready.

Either way, by then she *had* to have her trail cleaned up.

Between her ankles was her green duffel bag, which she had told her parents contained her overnight things for the Peabodys. Instead, what came out of it in the train's rest room at 11:20 am was Disguise #6, the last of them: a red curly wig, big babushka, and blue-and-orange coat. It was in this outfit, with the empty green duffel squirreled beneath her coat, that she disembarked early at the New Haven stop.

There, across the parkinglot under the dull grey overcast, was her first loose end to collect: the blue Buick, parked where she had left it the night before last, still tucked between the same eighteen-wheeler and RV. She marveled at how close to the station it was. At that point, 1:45 am, fresh from the achingly steady, 65 mph, 132-mile drive from Hills, she still hadn't known whether her fire pump had even fired. Her train might have been long past, sailing on to Washington DC on its normal schedule with her cellphone and suitcase on the rack. She had forced herself to walk, not run, in Disguise #5's multiple scratchy sweaters, over what had seemed acres to the station doors. It was only when she reached the ticket booth that she learned ("Honey, you're in luck") that she was a full fifteen minutes ahead of the delayed train to New

York, and handed over her cash with gloves only then trembling.

Now it was a warm morning, the formless overcast blending with the slush to envelop the world in a colorless smear. After each overpass she had to use her wipers to clear nuggets of falling snow from the windshield. As Route 95 to Rhode Island unrolled monotonously before her, Hannah finally had liberty to think of other things—including what came next when the body was found.

She *wished* the car radio worked. Admittedly the constant dialing would have made it harder to drive. But one way or another, they would find him eventually. Her message to the world would be loosed, and at the same time she would be receiving a *lot* of attention from the cops.

She actually didn't think she would be a suspect at first. Yes, she had left as garish a rape-and-revenge scene as she could, with the rapist's confession placed on his barechested body and her recorder even helpfully advanced to the right spot (despite her desperate clock she hadn't missed a detail), but the police would quickly verify that the raped party had left campus and gone to New York hours before the deed, and even pressed sexual assault charges against him afterward. Initially she expected mere questioning. It would be later when, bereft of other suspects, the spotlight would narrow in on her. That was the whole point of framing herself, of eliminating others from suspicion one by one: the killer used a sword; the killer probably got it by breaking into the Mayden School shop (if they found that); above all the killer picked her hidden recorder up from behind the tree, when only she knew it was there. Someone else *might* have done any of those things, but it would look like only she fit the bill. And it was then, with the spotlight shrunk to her only, that she would present her own alibi proofs and step out, leaving the stage empty, the case forever unsolved.

It had occurred to her in New York that to *get* her alibi proofs—the Amtrak station platform footage, her straight-arrow cellphone track—she would probably need a lawyer.

But *meanwhile*—other things would start to move. As the car engine hummed and the wet grey highway unrolled before her, Hannah allowed herself to look ahead to the coming social explosion: Steve's vicious tirade and rape confession broadcast to the world. What would happen?

Well, for one thing she was about to receive more "publicity" than her worried mother could have imagined. She was *named* in that dire recording, and it was *her* setup that had caught the rapist on tape, as the press would soon discover. Assuming her alibi worked—and she wasn't out of the woods yet—she was about to become as notorious as her hero framed on her dorm room wall. *Good.* Because she intended to take full advantage of it. She would have to.

In truth she hadn't been completely happy with what Steve had put on her recorder, for more than the obvious reasons that made her, remembering them, turn up the Buick's heater. He hadn't mentioned Dean Haughton, or his "green light," his sense of protection. *That's what I get for being greedy.* Indeed what he *hadn't* said had been almost enough to save his life. But what he *did* say was, in its own way, so very much worse, and would play so particularly well in her chosen venue, the tabloid press (and they were all tabloid, when it came to this stuff), that she had put her plan into motion on that basis without looking back.

But if *she* was in the public eye then *she* could fill in the missing blanks. She might be asked for interviews. She could *tell* the press about Steve's "green light," about how she had reported the rape to the college and the college had told her to shut up. She could *tell* them about Dean Haughton. In the controversy she expected to erupt she would be in a position to become — spokeswoman for the aroused cause.

Her focus returned to the lines of the highway strafing at her. First, though, she had to make sure she wasn't given the death penalty for murder.

Everything depended on the fire pump. The thing had to have stayed concealed, not only from the crews that had repaired the transformer that night *right next to it*, but all through yesterday as well. If it had been found, if the train delay was exposed as deliberate, then her days were numbered: it was as simple as that.

At Greenwich Bay there was no barricade of police cars at the condo parkinglot. Down at the tiny strip of land under the steep railroad bank the water lapped at the rocks, the shoreline was deserted, there were no boats in the offing — and there was the ragged black dot among the rocks and bushes. "*Yes!*" she breathed as she hastened down the strip. The protecting tarps were windblown but the pump was undisturbed, and looking up the black gravel slope at the catenary lines she saw no sign of ice, searching footprints, or the slightest disturbance.

She disconnected the hoses and conscientiously removed the starter battery (to be discarded elsewhere), then she hefted the heavy pump by its roll cage, spun it around once and hurled it, trailing its wired extras, out to sea. She rarely had a real-world use for her strong legs, and she watched the big plopping splash fizz clear twenty feet offshore with satisfaction, hands on hips.

That's it. The coast is clear. And the murderess permitted herself a giggle of relief.

Her modified saber was buried under soggy leaves a hundred feet into the woods somewhere between Hills College and New Haven. Her six disguises were scattered in garbage bins across three states. Her "baby monitor" cellphone with directional mic had come with her to New York and gone into her parents' kitchen trash, which had been wrapped up and set out in the back hall and by morning had vanished. Her laptop, which she had in her overnight bag, had been reformatted, erasing all records of the Skype application.

By 3:50 pm Aunt Betsy's Buick, with its proper Florida license plates reattached, was sitting in its selfsame parkingspace at the Neville Place Assisted Living Home in Cambridge. And on the bright afternoon of December 17 Hannah Radhe mounted the steps of the 9th Precinct building in Boston.

Where they were all waiting for her.

Chapter 8 - Prime Suspect

Cowley burst into the lounge, wet coattails open and flapping. "Am I hearing right that you let her walk out of here?"

"I let her walk out of here," Detective Scavelli said from the couch.

"Goddamn it, I told you to hold her!"

Scavelli spread big hands. "We tried! Racona and I together. She's innocent, Cowley."

"The hell she is!"

"Cowley, calm down," Chief Koontz struggled up from the end of the black vinyl couch, sweat stains in the armpits of his open-necked blue shirt. Scavelli scrambled to his feet after him, a tall, rangy man in his mid-thirties with a boyish grin and crew cut, in slacks and a white shirt with sleeves rolled back over long wrists. It was after 9:00 pm and the upstairs review lounge was close with stale sweat and old cigarette smoke. On the big wall TV Hannah's face, in an overhead camera angle showing the corner of a small room, was suddenly still as Lieutenant Racona, still seated, pressed the Pause button and looked up. She was in full uniform, crisply ironed and buttoned to the neck, dark hair pulled severely back over pebble eyes in a face with high cheekbones. She evinced no perspiration. "What's happening at the scene?" Koontz said. "No luck with Bailey, huh?"

Cowley stood in the doorway, his tie loose, his sunken eyes glaring. "No, no luck with Bailey. And you know why? Because

Bailey's digital audio recorder wasn't set out on top of the god-damn corpse, that's why! Hannah Radhe is the *prime suspect*. We've got six channels crawling all over HC and you let her just walk out of here? Is that her?" He aimed his gaze at the TV.

"We couldn't hold her, Cowley! Now will you calm down and let Scavelli —"

"I don't think she did it!" Scavelli said. "We pulled her in like you wanted and Racona and I grilled her hard for over three hours. We —"

"Like *I* wanted? All *I* said was hold her for questioning. You mean you went ahead and —"

"I thought it was you who said —"

"I told him to do it," Koontz interrupted, "based on *your* call from the scene in which you said, quote, she's the killer. Is she? Because she sure as hell doesn't look like it on this."

"We gave her the works," Scavelli said, backing up the chief in an accusing tone. "Direct accusation of the crime, we told her we had evidence, fingerprints, I invented a witness of her on campus, everything. She insisted she was innocent all the way through. When we told her Badenhut was dead she was properly shocked. Sorry, man, but you miscalled it big-time —"

"And what the hell did you accuse her *of*, Scavelli, machine-gunning him with a Gatling gun? You can't interrogate someone before we even know the CSI findings, or what's on her recorder, or anything —"

"*I* know what's on that recorder," Koontz said, "so get off Scavelli's back, Cowley. This case is hotter than any of you know, okay, and it was *my* call to scare her into a confession and wrap it up fast. I did that because I've learned to trust *your* instinct. *You* said she's guilty. And she's innocent! Unless you brought something from HC to tie her. Did you?"

Cowley continued to stare at the screen. "Right height," he muttered. After a beat he blinked and looked back. "And so the two of you say she's innocent, do you? What about you?"

Lieutenant Racona didn't move from her legs-crossed sitting position in the hard chair. "I'm not as easy on her."

"Not as easy! What did you bozos do, assign her a fucking essay question?"

"I don't need to listen to this," said Racona.

"Racona's pissed because her bad cop routine didn't work," Scavelli said.

"I'm not pissed, and I want to know why it didn't. Even innocent people crack under what she got. I'm...suspicious."

"Suspicious!" Cowley's hands went to his head. "Did either of you *read* her New York statement? She practically boasts about killing him! *'I don't think it will change his situation much.'* Come on guys!"

"Cowley we had nothing to hold her with!" Koontz shouted. "Eventually after three fucking hours she asked if she was free to go and what could we do? The girl was in New York when Badenhut was killed. This whole thing—"

"She *didn't blink*, Cowley," Scavelli said. "And for the record, I did read her statement and what the fuck are you talking about? I didn't see any boasting, and neither did the NYPD. And the reason she didn't *crack*, Racona, is that she knew she was innocent."

"She knew something, I'll give her that," said Racona.

"Where is she now? Do any of you know? Or did you drive her to the fucking airport and buy her a ticket for South America?"

"Cowley stand down!" Koontz shouted, loud enough to make the walls ring. There was a beat of panting silence. "Now I know you've had a long day, but get off your high horse and make your goddamn report. What the hell is going on at the scene? And for your information Hannah Radhe is in Newton and we have the address. We also took her laptop and cellphone on warrant and they're with CSI now. And we did all this because *you* called from the field and said you could tie her to the murder. "

"What I *said* was, she's the only one who *could* have done it."

"Well, given the situation, I told Scavelli to go for the quick kill. He hit her as hard as he could hit. She didn't break."

"What situation?" Cowley looked at the chief.

"Tell you later," Koontz muttered, rolling his eyes. He flumped heavily back down on the vinyl couch, and Scavelli followed suit alongside him.

Cowley was staring at the TV again, his eyes narrowed. "She weathered it?"

"I am telling you," said Racona, "she was a bit too cool all the way through. Why didn't she clam up and ask for a lawyer, like educated perps do? Why wasn't she more scared about going to jail? To me it was like she had something up her sleeve and was playing us to see what *we* knew."

"Really?" Cowley's eyes narrowed further.

"Needless to say that was not my impression," said Scavelli.

"Oh, you were smitten with her, John, admit it."

"I was not! That's not fair! I—"

"HC, dammit!" said Koontz. "I want to know what the hell we *do* have on this case."

"Wait, Chief," said Racona, "I want Cowley to see this. Alan, you have to see her response to the Reid question." She lifted the remote control and the image on the TV blurred in a backwards jitter under digital green numbers.

"Oh yeah, the Reid," muttered Koontz, with a strange chortle. "Dammit Scavelli —"

"Which question?" Cowley asked.

Scavelli rolled his eyes. "Sorry, that was my fault...you know the one where you ask what do you think is appropriate punishment for the person who did the crime?"

"She downplay the penalty? Or did she go opposite and beef it up?"

"You'll see," said Racona. "Here we go." She pressed play. Hannah's face sprang to life, intent, worried, and clear-eyed under her lightbrown bangs. Scavelli's voice filled the lounge.

> "—your recorder there in what looks like cold blood, and even locked the door on the way out so the body wouldn't be found. Now let me ask you this: when the police catch such a person, who murders someone like that, what do you think should happen to them?"
>
> "Well *I'm* rooting for the person not to be caught at all. My hope is that they get away scot free."
>
> "Well, ah, I mean, that's not—"

A bark of laughter had come from Cowley, who swiftly put his hand over his own mouth. Racona hit the button and the video froze again.

"I came in late with that one," Scavelli said. "But it makes sense for her to say! She hated the bastard's guts, and she hopes her protector, whoever it is, gets away with it. It's probably someone she knows."

"Maybe," said Cowley, staring with a strange intensity at the screen.

"At any rate that's a new one," said Racona. "'I hope they get away scot free?' You should send it into Reid. Cowley, there's one more at the end you should hear; it's when Scavelli was really threatening her with jail. Chief, you haven't heard this one either." The video danced in translucent expressions overlaid too fast to register, then came live on the girl looking sweatier, fiercer, more alarmed but somehow also more assured. Scavelli's amplified voice was louder:

> "Enough denials! You're just digging yourself deeper. We know it was you who picked up your recorder from behind the tree—you said yourself no one else even knew it was there—and we know you took it to his room, and only you know what happened then. Hannah, I'm trying to help you! You're a smart girl who made a mistake and I don't want to see you suffer for it. I have a version you can sign right now that says you tried to blackmail him with the audio, and a struggle broke out, and what happened was complete self-defense. Sign this and you get a *very* reduced penalty, hell, you might even walk free. Otherwise, with the evidence we have, you'll be sent to jail for life as a cold-blooded—
>
> "Detectives, I can tell you this much. *If* I had decided to kill Steve—*if.*"
>
> "Go on—get it off your chest. It will feel good."
>
> "I most certainly wouldn't do it in a way that would land me here two days later, facing those two alternatives."

The playback froze with Hannah looking directly at the camera. Cowley let out a long whistle.

"So?" said Scavelli. "That's not a confession. She didn't do it, and she's smart and angry and trying to put it to us stupid cops. Maintaining innocence isn't an indicator of guilt, Racona."

"Well, she's gonna be an even bigger headache now," Koontz said, his fingers at his forehead as he slowly shook his head. The others looked at him with raised eyebrows. Without looking up he pointed at the screen: "Cowley, do you or do you not bring any evidence to tie *that girl* to the crime?"

Cowley gave a tight sigh, his eyes still on the screen. "I don't," he said.

"Well, fuck me," said Koontz. He looked up. "You want to tell us what the fuck's going on at Hills?"

"He's on the news again!" Lieutenant Sanders popped his head around the open door of the lounge. "They've got the fencing sword angle. Channel 4 just showed video of a fencing sword bending double trying to kill someone. It's not pretty."

"And here we go," said the chief. "Sanders, for that you get to go stand in the line of fire. Tell me how bad it gets."

"*That's* what's going on at Hills." Cowley tore his gaze from the screen. "It's a circus." He leaned against the doorway, adjusting his holster strap against his shirt. "There was no containing it. Within an hour everyone still left on campus knew that Steve Badenhut was murdered in his dorm room with a fencing sword, and —

"Really?" said Racona, her eyes wide. "They're sure on that fencing sword?"

"Because *that* made no sense whatsoever when it came in," Scavelli said. "And I did *not* accuse her of killing Badenhut with a fencing sword."

"Shut up Scavelli. Do we have the weapon?" Koontz said.

"No, Chief, we don't have it, and yes, Racona, CSI says fencing sword. One hundred percent. It's a clean wound, exactly the shape and diameter of a fencing saber. Seriously, you can't ask for a cleaner wound. Which is—"

"What, did it go under a rib?" Racona asked. "'Cause all we heard was heart."

"Okay, get this." Cowley took a step in from the doorway and raised both pointer fingers. "Single strike, as you heard, directly *through* the sternum, slight upward angle, point of the blade goes exactly into the middle of the heart. Autopsy will confirm but Bannister's pretty sure. Subject was standing up at the time. Someone knows exactly where to hit, exactly how long their blade is, walks straight at this guy twice their size and hits their spot dead on, with significant force."

"With a *fencing* sword?" said Scavelli. "How is that possible?"

"Sharpened, I assume," said Racona.

"Two points to Lieutenant Racona. It was an altered blade. I listened to CSI talking this one over for an hour. It was not only sharpened, but shortened down to the forte, the lower third or so, making it good and sturdy. Someone took the time and trouble to whittle an ordinary fencing saber into a nice little murder weapon."

Scavelli frowned. "So someone wanted it to look like a fencing blade? Set her up?"

"It's still a *saber*, Scavelli, with a weird hilt, has to be held just right in the fingers, with strength, and a small killer against Badenhut has to *lunge*, lightning fast, with a damn hard kick, probably the second she enters the room, to put it through bone. No one makes that hit who doesn't know how to fence."

"Clean wound, you said?" said Racona.

"Yep. Not a lot of blood: a little spray on the ceiling, probably some on her, that's it. Another tell for a shortened blade. It means that the killer, having thrust the sword directly into Badenhut's bad little heart, *leaves it in there*. Plugs the wound. Now Badenhut dies on the spot, instantaneous. The killer lets go the blade and uses the momentum to guide him down onto the bed alongside. Sheet wrinkles tell the tale. The blade stays wedged in the bone, sticking out of him, and she doesn't pull it free until *after* she's arranged him on his back and set the audio recorder on the chest. By then the blood's settled."

"Oh Cowley, you're in love," said Koontz.

Scavelli shook his head. "So it *is* a cold-blooded killer. That doesn't sound like the girl who was in here."

"Oh, to me it does," said Racona.

"Well, Racona, that's where we differ."

"And *I'm* still waiting on something to tie her," said Chief Koontz. "So she arranges Badenhut on the bed, fine. Tell me CSI's working the forensics."

Cowley slowly shook his head, glancing again at the screen. "Nothing yet," he said, and found he couldn't keep a smile from playing at the corners of his lips.

The general misunderstanding in the department was that Detective Cowley preferred his homicides gruesome and savage. The truth was he liked them complicated. In this he was often disappointed, and had been known to complain about the inveterate stupidity with which criminals went about ruining the lives of people and families. That attribute was perhaps relative, since in twenty years his instincts had been honed to the point where a single look at a scene often sufficed to jump him to the right conclusion, well ahead of his superiors, irking them but earning their grudging respect. In all his time on the force, however, Cowley had never sought promotion or played department politics, apparently content to reside at his age-old desk and solve murders. He was thus tolerated, but as almost an outsider in the department, dispatched to "the weird ones" but also, when it came to it, the high-profile ones.

This case was both. And from the moment he stepped into the late Steve Badenhut's dorm room he had known exactly who the killer was. It was more than the obvious "message" setup, the rape victim's digital audio recorder atop her rapist's corpse (and Cowley had never seen a clearer message homicide). It was something in the air itself, a gestalt. Badenhut's position, his distance from the door, the lack of signs of a struggle, the athlete's half-second hesitation allowing the small killer to get close, the angle of the strike: it could only be a girl; in fact it could only be *that* girl. Cowley, who had then not yet viewed even a picture of the suspect, could practically see her.

It was when CSI started coming up empty that his interest began to be piqued, elevated to derisive snorts as he flipped through the printout of her New York statement, and it was with an expression almost of admiration that he took Koontz' bellow of "Nothing *yet? What the fuck does that mean?" and began to speak.

"First of all it means she was smart to kill Badenhut in his room, because of course her DNA was already in there from the rape just two nights before—"

"Skip that," grunted Koontz, and Cowley saw his quick glance at the open door.

There was a pause, then Cowley resumed. "Well, here's where she gets better. No fingerprints on the door. No fingerprints on the bed. A little alcohol rub on Badenhut's chest but nowhere else, suggesting she needed to hold her sword bare-handed for the strike, but put her gloves back on straight after and cleaned the only suspect spot, and knew how. CSI took carpet prints: she was wearing straight flat shoes, and brand-new ones that she stops and puts on inside the dorm, so as not to track anything in. Basically, chief, for a college girl without even a shoplifting record she was damn good. Better than she has a right to be."

"Do you have to keep saying *she?*" said Scavelli. "I'm telling you, none of this sounds like the girl who was just in here."

"It also means this was no simple vengeance killing, despite the setup. I'm not sure yet what it *was*—"

"Evidence, dammit," said Koontz. "Come on. They have nothing on *anyone?*"

"Nothing at all. On anyone."

"So what about Bailey? The fencing coach?"

"Bailey? All right. Bailey—"

"Because no forensics of *anyone* doesn't make me goddamn happy, Cowley. And no confession from *you* makes me even less happy." The last was addressed to Scavelli.

"Hey, Chief, that's not fair. I—"

"Shut up Scavelli. I gave you a job. And don't you start in, Cowley. What about Bailey?"

Cowley glared, but professionally. It was an open secret that he hated sandbag interrogations designed to bully and scare a suspect into a confession. The cops used them when they needed a quick arrest in a high-profile case and didn't have time for the facts. Koontz had gone behind his back to do it, and now it hadn't worked and he was upset. Too upset. Granted the chief never liked media circus cases, but Cowley felt something else going on. He glanced at the screen again. It was rare that a sandbag didn't work.

"No go on Bailey," he said at length. "Bailey knew about the rape, but he knew nothing about any audio recorder or plan to record anyone. He confirmed her statement that he escorted Hannah to her room to pack, he escorts Hannah to the T to go to New York and press charges, the times and details all match up — "

"Jesus, you too," said Racona.

"What?"

"*Hannah*," mimicked Racona. "John's smitten 'cause she's innocent, you're smitten because she's a cold-blooded demon."

"Fine, *Radhe*. Radhe." Cowley twisted his shoulders. "*He* called her Hannah. I'm telling you people, she's the only person who could have possibly — "

"Bailey, dammit!" said Koontz. "Finish your report. At this point *he's* looking like my prime suspect, and you're the one who let *him* go, Cowley."

"No dice, chief. On the night of December fifteenth he hosted a Christmas party at his house, and at the time of death, which we have exactly, eleven-thirty p.m., he was in bed with his wife and had guests sleeping in the house. And, to me the clincher, they had put away five bottles of good wine between them that night. No way he makes that hit."

"You don't know that. You don't know that. He's the goddamn fencing coach."

"It ain't him, chief. Though if you tell him Hannah's going down for it, you can get him to confess. He's ready to take the fall for her."

"He's that tight with Radhe?"

"Father-daughter tight."

"Hey, how good a fencer is Radhe?" asked Racona.

"Bailey says she's going to the Olympics."

Racona whistled softly.

Koontz sighed. "Well, I hate to ask, but what about the other four guys from her statement? The football players?"

"Went through it. No go on any of them."

"You got nothing?" Scavelli asked. "It wasn't a falling out, or one of them acting secretly to protect Radhe?"

"What, by staging a crime scene that points to her?" Cowley chuckled. "OK, to be fair, the last two, Reggie Mathis and Chris Kelly, dug themselves deeper with everything they said. As soon as they were connected to a murder they confessed separately everything about the gang rape setup. It's nasty enough stuff, what they did. But they aren't our boys."

"Fuck me," said Koontz again, and rolled his big head in his stained collar. "Here I thought this would be the easiest revenge killing in the world. You're saying we got *nobody* for it?"

"I don't get you guys," said Cowley. "She's the one. You're saying she didn't give away anything in there? Did you at least throw my theory at her, ask about the car?"

"We did!" Scavelli said. "And for the record it was a goddamn kooky theory."

"It's not kooky," said Cowley. "Look at the timeline. She leaves HC at noon and at that point drops off the grid and no one sees her until she reappears at her parents' apartment in New York at four a.m. the next morning. She tells everyone she took the late train home but that would have gotten her in *hours* earlier; it reaches New York at two-fifteen. But it's the right time for someone who drives it, after sneaking back to kill Badenhut at eleven-thirty."

Scavelli was shaking his crew-cut head, eyes closed. "Ran it past her. And all she did was pull out facts to back up her story."

"Yeah, there is that," sighed Racona. "She kept coming out with all these checkable details. First, she doesn't have a car, and that was true. We challenged her on the bit in her statement where she claims she spent like seven hours at South Station, and she I.D.'d a waitress at Eastern's by name, and said she bought her ticket *at* South Station, with a credit card. She said she called her parents from aboard the train, which will be on the phone record…hell, she said her train was delayed, and we checked, and it was."

"Delayed…" Cowley frowned, and shook his head. "Huh. Well, I guess we need to look at that phone record, and get the security footage from South Station and Penn to see if she's on it."

"I'm not sure we do," said Chief Koontz. He exhaled noisily. "Close the door." He struggled to his feet again as Cowley pulled the door closed, and stood with a certain authority that kept Scavelli from rising too. They all looked at him. "Folks, we've got a situation, and what I'm gonna tell you doesn't leave this room. Earlier today I had a visit from Dean Haughton, came down from HC. He wanted to hear what was on that audio recorder and I let him."

"You pulled it from CSI?" Cowley said, his eyes wide.

"*We* haven't even heard it yet," said Scavelli.

"All we were told was she got him to confess to the rape. Does he really?" asked Racona.

"Hoo boy does he. And Cowley, Bannister was with us and played the whole thing with gloves and all, very clean. I guess Haughton had gotten wind from the boys about what *might* be on it, and he was right to check. Thing is, what Hannah Radhe did there with her little recorder and her setup, it worked pretty

goddamn well. The shit Steve Badenhut says at the play point —
you'll hear. He was a piece a work. And going back, he's not the
only voice on there. They stalk her for hours; there's at least —
long and short, this audio comes out and Hills College is looking
at rape charges against half the fucking football team. Needless
to say, no one wants that. So our job is to solve this fucking murder while keeping the rape side of it under wraps. Understood?
The one rape and attempted gang thing in Badenhut's room, her
little setup and all those boys out there — none of that happened.
We keep that recorder audio under wraps."

The three detectives looked at Koontz and each other. "The
recorder was on the corpse," Scavelli said. "It's already public."

"But no one has to know what's on the recorder. Would have
been easy if *you* got the confession today. That's why I sent you
in there."

"What about motive?" Racona said. "Without rape, it's not
rape-and-revenge, but the whole scene is — "

"So he's killed for something else, okay? People, this comes
from high up, this is no joke. This is the whole HC football program on the line. You know what the country's like, what could
happen. Cowley, your statements from Reggie Mathis and Chris
Kelley have been sealed by the college lawyers. No one else gets
to see them. Radhe's NYPD statement is sealed by us pursuant to
the homicide investigation; the lawyers can get it but that's it. All
we know about a rape in this department is what Hannah Radhe
said in New York, which may well have been a murderer's cover
story. Understood?" He turned a slow, sweating stare from face
to face. The gaze held on Cowley. "Because it would be very nice
if she *was* the murderer. Now, I went ahead and told Haughton
that this case would be a slam dunk, based on *you*. But if it's *not*,

then the South Station cams — "

"Prove nothing," Cowley said flatly. "If she's not on them, as I think she won't be, it's just a negative, it doesn't prove she killed Badenhut."

"Uh-huh. The only thing they can do is show her, in which case it proves she's innocent. If I don't have another suspect, and all I can do is lose her, then let's not grab them just yet."

"What, you're thinking of sending her down anyway, innocent or not?" Scavelli's close-cropped head recoiled on its neck with an expression of smelling something nasty. "To, to shut her up?"

"That's not it," said Racona. "He's saying to Cowley that if he really thinks she's guilty, it's up to him to prove it positively. And he's putting him on the clock."

There was a silence in the stuffy lounge. Cowley looked at the screen.

"She did it," he said. "The station tapes don't matter; I know she never got on that train. She doubles back to campus and kills him and then drives herself to New York."

"With what car?" said Racona.

"We'll find the one she used. She's surprisingly good, and she's arranged a nice little alibi about taking the train, but come on, she's a college girl. She slipped up somewhere. I'll get her."

"If it *is* her," Scavelli muttered.

"Scavelli, she's the only person it *could* be."

Racona sighed briskly. "That's what you said before the interrogation began. If we're not farther along than that, we're in trouble."

Chapter 9 - Allies and Opponents

Hannah opened her eyes under the pillowy white comforter of the guest bed at the Peabodys' house in West Newton, Massachusetts. *It wasn't a dream*, she thought. *They didn't arrest me. I'm not in jail.*

She looked at the angled ceiling and the dormer window whose panes showed a sky well whitened with morning. The Peabodys were old family friends and Hannah knew this house from childhood. She hadn't been at all sure she would see it again, and she permitted herself a moment of sheer relief. Her green duffel was open on the floral armchair, mostly empty but holding one clean shirt—about the only thing the police *hadn't* taken on a warrant. It reminded her that her cellphone was *not* on the nightstand, nor her laptop in her bag: before letting her go the detectives had requisitioned both those items, copied her driver's license and credit card, and ordered her to remain in the state.

But they did let me go. Almost disbelievingly she got out of bed and pulled forth the shirt to match with yesterday's jeans.

It hadn't taken long, once the door closed on her in that off-white, windowless room, for the "questioning" she expected to turn into a full-bore interrogation and accusation. Somewhere she had miscalculated; the police, or someone on the police, had *immediately* zeroed in on her. She had a newfound respect for how interrogators corner suspects into confession; she almost believed she *had* left DNA or a fatal clue in the dorm, as Detective Scavelli kept claiming. And that scary Lieutenant Racona seemed to stare straight through her at every point. She was conditionally proud of how she had handled herself—she hadn't been too sorry Steve was dead—but her fixed, stubborn insistence on total innocence was less a tribute to her acting skills, she thought, than the knowledge that even if the jig was up her message had been launched regardless.

And it seemed they *didn't* have DNA or hard evidence, at least not yet, because when she finally asked sardonically if she was free to go, to her great surprise they said yes.

The rest of the night was a blur: in the taxi she had slumped unseeing until the Peabodys' three-story colonial home with candles in the windows hove into view. She remembered an interlude in the white-carpeted livingroom where she tried to describe—around and through a long call to her parents—the police's half-baked theory of her involvement in murder, with rather more emphasis on her audio recorder than was necessary, until Pam thankfully intervened and postponed the family council until the next day. Mike assured her she could stay with them for as long as needed. She had gotten upstairs via some sort of pulley system of avuncular kindness, with a hot shower attached, and then she was asleep.

Well, framing herself had sure worked, she thought as she twisted the elastic into place around her ponytail. She was a suspect, all right; the spotlight was on her, and she could probably look forward to more such conversations until she could put her alibi to the test. But in the meantime—

Her recorder was out there. What was happening with it?

She padded downstairs.

"We have the news running in the den," Mike said. "The

lawyer will be here in an hour. Your parents called again half an hour ago and you should call them back. They're taking the shuttle up this morning."

Pam set a plate of hot eggs, bacon and waffles onto the yellow tablecloth alongside the glass of orange juice. "It's the top story," she said, perhaps in response to Hannah's eyes straining at the stentorian murmurs from the other room. "So far they haven't mentioned you, or any names. But they keep saying 'fencing sword' like they're leading up to it." She shook her head. "How would they even *know* something like that?"

Mike Peabody, bald with a frontal ridge in the rough shape of a Superman logo and bright blue eyes, was a retired Massachusetts Congressman; his wife Pam was a former Washington health care lobbyist whose slim frame and sculpture of white-blonde hair were like an upheld torch in a broad-shouldered blue dress. Their household had been on high alert already, standing by to receive the brave rape survivor pressing charges, and this new development had brought it to DefCon 1. She looked at her old friends feeling like she was having breakfast in a war room under the Rockies.

"I'm so sorry about this," she said.

"Don't apologize for the idiocy of the police," said Pam. "You pressed charges against him! How could they possibly think you're the killer?"

"I was on the train when he was killed," she said with her mouth full. She had a feeling she would be saying that a lot.

"They've gone crazy with the media pressure. Hopefully they questioned you along with three hundred other people and now it's over and done with."

Mike shook his head. "If they think she's a suspect they'll

want to question her again. That's why we need to move fast. I've pulled strings to get a top lawyer — he's one of the best. I cashed in some favors; normally they don't come to you."

"Do you think he'll want breakfast?" said Pam.

"I should call my folks," Hannah said, pushing back her plate and making a beeline for the phone in the den, with its ceiling-high bookshelves, leather furniture, and running TV. As she talked to her parents — this call was mercifully brief; they were dashing out the door to LaGuardia — she had one ear and both eyes on the news. The murder at Hills was indeed the top story ("College football fans are in shock today over the slaying of — ") but though they did repeat with delicate skepticism ("Police are still claiming") that the murder weapon was a sharpened fencing sword (Hannah again noted the fast work, with both approval and trepidation), it was with growing concern that she watched the cycle through without seeing the slightest mention of her digital audio recorder.

Maybe it's still to come…

Her fingers still rested on the phone receiver in its cradle. She glanced at the door of the den, almost closed: she had an island of discreet privacy; she might not get another. Forcing herself to turn her back on the TV, she picked up the receiver, took a deep breath and called Randall. She got his voicemail. So she left what was probably the most alarming two-minute voice message of his life, beginning with, "Randall, I know your voicemail has a timeout so listen close," and ending with, "So, to sum up, I've been raped, I broke the quarterback's fingers, I'm under suspicion of murder, I'm physically okay, I already have a lawyer, my cell-phone's gone, don't call me back here, I still hope to see you over Christmas if you still want to be my boyfriend. Bye!"

Then she and the Peabodys together settled into the den to watch the news. For Hannah, staring from the firm leather couch, it was another exercise in concealment, this time of her mounting worry. *Was Steve too profane? But they can at least summarize it!* She almost didn't dare leave the den even to pee, for fear of missing the moment when the announcer's voice would turn suddenly grave.

She had told the Peabodys last night about her audio recorder ambush of Steve, by way of explaining why she was under suspicion, and now she had to endure their speculations alongside her own.

"The police told you it was found with the body?" Mike said.

"That's what they said, that someone moved it there from the park. But I guess they could have been lying."

"Well I'm glad they're not mentioning it," said Pam. "The last thing you want is your name to come up in all this."

"Maybe there was nothing on it," Mike suggested.

"Right, I still have no idea," Hannah said with gritted teeth.

And so the hours ticked by and the moment wouldn't come.

"Police are denying that a religious cult was involved in the Hills College murder," entered the cycle at a certain point, which had to be discussed as possibly an oblique reference to it. Then, and more alarmingly, came a cobbled-together, rose-tinted half-hour special on the life of "Steve Badenhut, football star and American hero, cut down in his prime," complete with minor-key music, zoom-ins on childhood photos, and slo-mo clips of grid-iron action in amber light. Interspersed were interview snippets in which suddenly appeared Dean Haughton, well-lit, his jowls deepened under his dark curls, speaking gravely about possibly re-naming the stadium in Steve's honor, followed by a pig-eyed, spiky-haired, florid gentleman whom Hannah recognized as Coach Pruecastle and who spoke in a high voice about the "blow" of losing Badenhut on the heels of star quarterback Davey Coleman's hand injury, sustained in a fall, but how "the boys' fighting spirit would prevail."

But it was what came after that, around 11:00 am, that pushed Hannah into outspoken fury. A breaking development was suddenly announced—Pam rushed back from the kitchen—and the "religious cult" placeholder was dropped in favor of something new:

"Police are now saying that Badenhut's killer was likely a woman, acting on a radical feminist agenda. A recorded message left with Badenhut's body has not been released, but police say it contains references to a controversial recent article in the Hills College Vista, the student newspaper, that accused the Kingfishers of being a bastion of so-called 'rape culture.' Campus officials have denied the accusations in the article and stress that the Kingfishers have no record of any misconduct; however, it seems the killer feminist may have seen the football team as a symbol—with tragic results. More on this story as it develops."

"The—bloody—bastards," Hannah said, her face white, leaning forward with her fists crushing the sofa cushion between her thighs.

"Oh, what distortion!" cried Pam from the doorway, her whole body arched backwards from her lifted nose. "Is *that* your recording, the one to catch the, the bad boy talking? Here because he's dead the news is free to turn it around and make it sound like some sort of terrorist thing. They'll stoop to *anything!*"

"It also sounds like groundwork for going after you," Mike said. "That was your article, right?"

"Egregiously misquoted as usual," spat Hannah. "My article *didn't* single out our football team and I would *never* use the simplistic term 'rape culture,' it was a *general article* on rape theory comparing rape to lynching as private illegal continuations of what had previously been public law in the aftermath of the broader society moving on and the *specific* role played by closed, top-down, hierarchical male societies in the preservation of *all* such outdated attitudes, *such as* the military, the church, fraternities and, yes, *also* amateur and professional male sports teams *including but not limited to* college football teams, *including but not limited to*, ours. *Dean bloody Haughton!*"

"Well, now that the media has spun it their way, no one will bother to read it," said Pam.

"And it *is* aimed at me," Hannah continued. "They're trying to silence the rape story. They know it's a race because I —" She closed her mouth hurriedly on a barrage of rapid strategic recalculation that continued uninterrupted in her appalled mind.

She had underestimated Dean Haughton. He had parried her attack, and when he appeared on-screen again, seemingly staring straight at her as he defended the Kingfisher boys' blue-eyed humble decency one and all, she suddenly understood that what actually endangered him, what in fact *really* endangered him, was not Steve's psychopathic boast but all the *other* voices on her eight-hour audio, *all* of whom would be, if not exposed outright by their own sayings, then tarred to blackness by Steve's. *He is desperate to keep that recording out of the news*, she realized, *and maybe he can.* She was stunned by the discovery of her opponent's reach and power when it came to protecting the school against a rape taint. And her anger was swiftly turning to fear. Because if she *was*, in fact, the feminist author of the article, and there were, *thanks to her*, no other suspects for the murder —

Then I'm in deep trouble. Then Mike was right: the next tick of the media cycle would likely name her, but in a way Mike didn't understand. She was now being set up and targeted as the potential truthteller of a truth they were trying to hide. She felt the seismic shift behind the newscaster's corporate backdrop, from police trying to solve a murder to direct persecution for her feminist cause by an outraged social force, for the sting she had almost inflicted on them and maybe still could. *But how can I, now?* Without Steve's vicious threats against her, without her evidence of being raped, there would be no calls for interviews. Was there anything she could still do? Call the Globe herself? But why would they listen to her? Even her setup with the recorder, which she had hoped to be of journalistic interest when it came out, had been concealed.

And I'm going to need my alibi sooner rather than later, because —

She realized that Pam and Mike were both looking at her, and because she had to say something, she diverted the energy of her fear and outrage into: "There are still four of those rapists out there and I swear I'm going to press charges against every damn one of them!"

The doorbell rang.

Daniel McFarrel, representing Sleater, Pekoinnen & Glausfarb, was a tall, balding, gymnasium-fit man in a dark-blue pinstriped suit, wearing wire-framed glasses and a ready smile. He detached an Armani briefcase to the livingroom carpet to shake hands firmly all around. To Hannah he said, "Did they take your cellphone at the station?" and when she nodded he produced a brand-new boxed iPhone from his coat pocket. "The first month is on the firm's account; your phone number is on the card."

Hannah took the box and card, sizing him up.

"I also have—" the next item came out of his briefcase, swung to the coffee table—"a printout of the transcript of your statement in New York about the sexual assault, which I've thoroughly read. I'm very sorry for what you underwent; congratulations, however, on getting yourself out of what could have been a nastier situation. Between the two of us we'll get you out of another one. I also understand you had a conversation with the police yesterday. Did you confess?"

"No." *Too smooth by half,* she thought. *But I'm in a hurry.* "Of course I didn't."

"Nice. That makes things easier. If you had, it would have presented certain difficulties, not too hard. Well! Mike, if you have a room we can use, I'd like to have my client bring me the rest of the way up to speed in a private environment."

"Would you like anything? Coffee, sandwiches?" asked Pam.

"Oh a coffee would be lovely."

Back in the den, with the television off and the door closed, McFarrel leaned over the hardwood back of the desk chair and said, "So, did you do it?" Before she could answer he said, "Whether you did it or not, I will defend you. Whether you did it or not, I can keep you out of prison. Whether you did it or not, I personally don't care in the least. So you can lie to me if you want, but be aware that if you lie to me, the prosecution will catch *me* in your lie, and when *I* look bad, *your* chances in court go down. It's a much better bet to tell me the truth, and let me do the lying."

"I didn't do it," Hannah told him, still standing, "and I can prove it. I was on the train halfway to New York when Steve was killed. Now the first thing we need to do is get the security camera footage from South Station and Penn Station, to show me boarding and disembarking. Also, the police have my cellphone. Won't the GPS signal show that I was on the train?"

"Those are excellent first thoughts," McFarrel said. "We will absolutely look into both those things. As for the cellphone GPS data, to get that requires a special kind of warrant that the police will certainly seek, but it's more difficult to get because of strict privacy legislation around that kind of thing."

"Can we voluntarily give it? Can you arrange that?"

"Well, that would involve filing a Federal counter-suit, odd as it sounds. Like I say, the legislation around cellphone privacy is very strong and thorny — and in my opinion that's a good thing. But why don't we start at the beginning! You are accused of being an avenging rape victim. So, well, one reason I asked for privacy is I'd like to ask you to go through *this* again." He flapped the transcript of the sexual assault statement with a heavy sigh, then laughed. "Where were you on the night of December fifteenth? I need to hear *everything*."

For the next hour and a half Hannah retailed her story yet again, physically restraining herself throughout from the urge to turn the TV back on and hear what they were saying. But there was nothing she could do about it anyway, and with the lawyer here she focused on the one part she could control, getting her alibi into place. Finally they were back in the white-carpeted livingroom with Mike and Pam, arranged on various seats and sofas around McFarrel, who bent forward from his armchair to scoop some nuts from the crystal bowl on the coffee table. He chewed deliberately.

"I think we have a very good chance," he said at last.

"You'll get the station footage," Hannah prompted.

He held up a hand. "Evidence is of course important in any

court case. But the nature of defense is that the prosecution starts out ahead in the evidence game. We won't know until discovery what evidence they have. The police certainly aren't going to tell us! To be honest, at this point it sounds like they don't have much, otherwise, pardon my French, she would already have been arrested. Right now she's still just a suspect. A person of interest. That's good for us. Let's keep it that way. Let's not jump in and start a preemptive evidence war. *The root of our defense* – " He paused dramatically to chew another handful of nuts. "The root of our defense is that Hannah is a model student, top of her class in Women's Studies, an Olympic hopeful, a sweet, clean, American girl who has never committed a crime in her life. In contrast, this guy, Steve Badenhut, well, he has a bit of a history with the law."

"He does?" said Hannah, who had opened her mouth to say something else. Mike and Pam leaned forward.

"Yes ma'am. In high school Mr. Badenhut was arrested for stealing a car, and he also has a juvie record of shoplifting arrests that I can unseal. It's *his* world, his friends, his contacts, where a killer is likely to come from. Not hers." He pointed at Hannah, looking back and forth from Mike to Pam. "Now, their argument is going to be that she had motive, because of the rape. You know what? So did a lot of people against a lot of people. In court, that argument is going to shatter against the rock of Hannah's character. Ladies and gentlemen of the jury, could that event drive a perfectly ordinary, clean, upper echelon college girl, who never did anything wrong in her life – to commit murder? Does that make sense? Particularly in a case where, you know, pardon my French, she already rescued herself? We can play that card – "

Hannah was on her feet. "Mr. McFarrel, I don't care what use or misuse you make of all that garbage," she said. "That's your area of expertise and I bow to it. Just tell me that you will go right away to get the security camera footage from South and Penn stations, and do what you can to release my cellphone record."

"I understand!" said McFarrel at large. "The courtroom world is a strange and ugly world. To those who — again I'll say it — have no experience whatsoever there, thank God, what passes for legal logic can seem very foreign. But in that world of judges and juries, which I know, which is my world, I promise you that this *is* logic, and it's the best logic."

"Fine. But—"

"Now, let's say I run and ask for security camera footage. You think that would be the logical thing to do. But it isn't. To do that my office would have to issue a subpoena, enclosed in what Massachusetts law defines as an 'alibi defense.' The rules of an alibi defense, in turn, state that any subpoenaed records must be turned over to the prosecution; it's called reciprocal discovery. Hannah, it's the middle of winter. Everyone getting on and off trains are wearing big heavy coats, and you're a small girl. Security cameras have notoriously bad resolution to start with, and we're talking about a train platform in the middle of the night, in a sea of heavy coats. The lens might be frosty. Hannah, you could well *be* on there, and no one would see you. But the minute I subpoena that footage, it goes under reciprocal discovery, which means there's a high risk that I'd be handing the prosecution a videotape that doesn't show you at all. Do you understand?"

"Well, what about her cellphone record?" asked Pam. "Isn't that a better proof?"

"Ma'am, yes, it would be. But as I was telling Hannah in private, there are strong, hard, legal protections against releasing those records. It's more than that: a winning defense is one that starts with the right strategy from the beginning. Our winning strategy is character. Hannah Radhe is the kind of citizen whose cellphone record is not to be examined. It's sacrosanct. How dare they question it. Isn't one violation of her personal space enough? *That's* our strategy. I have already put a legal block on the police department's attempt to get Hannah's cellphone record."

Pam nodded. "I guess that makes —"

"*You are fired,*" Hannah said, on her feet. "Get out of this house, and please undo whatever —"

"Now, Hannah, hold on," said Mike, getting up as well. "Daniel, just a moment. Honey, you ought —"

"Mike, I'm sorry. This, this one won't do. The *proof* —"

"Honey, slow down. I thought he made very good points. Think of this like a fencing game, okay? What's wrong with his points? What if he pulls the tapes and you're not on them?"

The words stuck in Hannah's throat. The one thing she couldn't say was that she had gone out of her way to make sure she was supremely visible on camera at both stations. And regarding the cellphone track, how could she point out what a ridiculous, self-sabotaging argument that was, when, when —

Hannah, you could well be *on there, and no one would see you.*

It hit her all at once. *He thinks I did it.* At the very least he thought it was possible. And — *so does Mike.* She stared around the livingroom from one to the other, and, as if solving a fencing opponent's strategy per Mike's suggestion, she saw what was going on.

They think I was never on the train. The bloody idiots are trying to protect me.

McFarrel stood up with a grin. "Mike, she doesn't have to say a word. If there's anything worse than a lawyer in a suit, it's an overenthusiastic lawyer in a suit. Miss Radhe, everything I just outlined as a winning strategy is only my idea. The strategy you use in your defense is one *you* will pick, hopefully in consultation with a good and experienced lawyer, and of course with your parents. That's the way *I* work, and the only way a legal partnership *can* work." He extended his hand. "Why don't you keep my card, and the cellphone, until—"

The doorbell rang.

"That'll be her parents now," cried Pam, in evident relief, and went to the door. Hannah suppressed a roll of her eyes.

A strange man in a trench coat and fedora stood in the doorway holding up a badge.

"Mrs. Peabody? I'm Detective Alan Cowley with the Boston Police. I see everyone's at home. May I come in?"

There was an initial bustle of somewhat sensationalized introductions in the livingroom, Pam leaping back while McFarrel leapt forward, Mike admitting the guest to names and territory with the aplomb of a castellan, during which Hannah, standing her ground, evaluated the new arrival. He looked no older than forty, with a full head of dark hair revealed by the hat, but with a face that bore the mark of its trade in layers of indelible sorrow. He seemed ill at ease in their carpeted livingroom as he shook hands, an effect compounded by the hat, which had found neither rack nor relief and so was crushed temporarily under his left coat arm whose hand held a small notebook with a chewed pencil tucked into the spirals.

In the time it took to establish that he didn't want coffee, thanks, nor rolls or danish, and to receive the mighty pedigree of the legal representative present, the first syllables of which had to be echoed back in a nodding mutter, he didn't look at Hannah once, and yet she was sure he had been watching nobody but her since the moment he had walked in. It gave her a funny feeling.

Finally, of course, the introductions concluded upon her, furthest back in the livingroom, but to her he didn't offer his hand. *Good*, thought Hannah obscurely. He merely said, "Miss Radhe, it's a pleasure to meet you," with a nod, and a straight glance of perfectly clear grey eyes from within their dark sockets. She returned the glance with a nod of her own.

"I'd just like to ask Miss Radhe a few extra questions that got missed yesterday, if that's all right with you, sir," he said, turning to McFarrel. "It's nothing to be worried about, everyone's welcome to sit in, Mr. McFarrel has to of course, but the rest of you can as well. It won't take long. It's just we were caught a little flat-footed at the station yesterday and I need to dot some i's and cross some t's, clarify a few things. Is that all right?"

While he was addressing Pam and Mike, McFarrel shot Hannah a theatrically inquisitive glance, complete with lifted eyebrows and spread hands: *Well? Am I aboard?* With a sigh Hannah rolled her eyes and gave him a tiny nod back.

"Do *you* think she did it?" Pam Peabody demanded loudly of Detective Cowley.

A silence fell in the livingroom. Cowley turned that direct, piercing gaze on Hannah again. "Ma'am," he said without breaking his stare, "that's not for a detective like me to say. But I've been in the homicide business for twenty years, and if you ask me personally? I don't '*think*' she did it."

The emphasis was audible only to her, as witnessed by the plaudits of relief and renewed welcome that arose from Mike and

Pam, but to her it might as well have been double-underlined. She smiled.

"I'm glad there's one member of the police force who can think clearly," she said.

They held each other's gaze for a long beat.

"I'm definitely getting you some coffee," said Pam. "Let me take your coat and hat." She turned toward the kitchen with her burden.

"Hang on," laughed McFarrel genially. "We haven't decided yet that *I'm* going to let her answer questions. You said this isn't a full interview, but it's still part of the police record, right?"

"Yes sir, it will be," Cowley explained, with the slightest over-articulation that Hannah noticed, but McFarrel did not.

"Then why should I let her talk to you? Will talking to you help my client in any way?"

"I'd like to answer his questions," said Hannah. "Mr. McFarrel, if you sit alongside and vet the questions as they come, it should be all right, won't it?"

Cowley interrupted. "Before I ask *any* questions, let me just explain the situation a little bit, and this is something I want to explain to all of you. Thanks ma'am." He took the cup of coffee but didn't drink. "First, I want to apologize to Miss Radhe for the way yesterday's interview went. The boys at the station subjected you to what's called the confrontational style of questioning, where the goal is to frighten a guilty person into confessing. I don't agree with that style and I don't like it. There's a better way to do it that's based on facts and evidence, and that's my style, but I wasn't there. I don't mind telling *you*—" he looked at McFarrel—"that Miss Radhe did not confess or incriminate herself in any way. We were all impressed by the way she handled herself."

"That's because she had nothing *to* confess," said Pam.

"Well, Mr. McFarrel will tell you that the confrontational style sometimes produces false confessions out of innocent people. One of the problems with it. Isn't that right?" McFarrel nodded, a little purse-lipped as if he'd been caught with a card up his sleeve.

"I found Detective Scavelli very sweet," said Hannah. *What's gotten into me?* she said to herself.

Cowley looked at her. "I'll relay the message," he said. "I'm not. *My* problem with forced confessions is that it shortcuts the process of nailing the perpetrator on hard evidence, of *solving the case.* I *will* find the evidence. Given enough time, I *will* get the person who murdered Steve Badenhut."

"I'll say to you what I said to Detective Scavelli," Hannah said. "Given what Steve Badenhut was—I hope you won't."

"Hannah—" McFarrel said warningly.

"Motive!" said Cowley, pointing a finger at her. He smiled around the room. "Mr. McFarrel, it's no secret to anyone, at least in this room, how Hannah felt about Steve and why. It's the reason we questioned her in the first place. That doesn't mean she killed him."

"Still," Mike muttered with a stern sidelong look at Hannah.

"Now folks, I said I'd explain the situation and I will." Cowley sipped his coffee. "Right now, Miss Radhe *is* considered a person of interest, actually a suspect, in this case, because of three things: her motive, like we said; her little audio recorder that she hid in the park and that wound up at the scene of the crime; and the fact that Steve Badenhut was killed with a fencing sword."

"Oh, the news keeps saying that," said Pam. "Are they sure?"

"How is that even possible?" Mike demanded.

"Well, Mr. Peabody, it was a fencing weapon that had been clipped down to about a third of its size and re-sharpened. It was a modified weapon. And for Miss Radhe, that's actually good news."

"How's that?" said Hannah. She tried to sound skeptical, but what came out was genuine curiosity.

He seemed to respond directly on that level. "Well, see, your alibi for that night is you were on the train, right? So, to me, first thing I thought was, okay, a hired killer. Ninety percent of the time—anyway, no go. No killer in the world could be hired to make or use this specific weird weapon."

"Right," said Hannah. "I didn't think of that." *Will you rein yourself in —!*

"And in a case like this," Cowley explained at large, "where the suspect is a rich college student, well connected, and she even has friendly email contacts at the State Department, thanks to the summer program she's on, trust me, it's very good to be able to take a hired killer off the table. It means that whoever it was killed Badenhut, she cut and sharpened the sword herself. Miss Radhe, do you have any metal-working experience?"

Beat—beat—*then* McFarrel jumped in. "Hannah, you don't have to answer that question and I advise that you don't."

"Okay, I won't." She shrugged at Cowley.

"Are you implying that they know the killer is a woman?" Mike asked sternly, more to emphasize the sovereignty of his house following the attack than to elicit information. *He set that up*, Hannah saw. *He's playing the room like a musical instrument.* She smiled challengingly at Cowley. *Here comes your lunge — let's see it.*

"Yes, in fact we have a photograph of the killer," said Cowley.

From the back pocket of his slacks he pulled a sheet of paper that had been folded in quarters, and spread it open it on the coffee table.

They all gathered around, Pam and McFarrel sitting to get a clearer view.

The photo was a security camera grab showing the Hills College lower parkinglot at night. There, in the distance, mostly blacked out under the pine trees but with a large corner of its fender and one front wheel extending white into the electric light, was her Buick. And in the center of the photo, fully illuminated, was herself, dressed in Disguise #4, walking across the parkinglot. That was the one with the shapeless overcoat, extra weight, hiking boots, and absurd knit hat flopping to one side.

She was entirely unrecognizable. There was no sign of the sword hidden under the coat.

"That's a woman?" said Pam skeptically.

"Yep," said Cowley. "This is from a moving video, and we have computer models that analyze walking and other movement patterns. Even with this disguise, it told us it was a woman. But for myself I didn't need any of that. I knew at the first glance. See this big, shapeless coat?"

"Mm-hm."

"Well, the only people who care about disguising their body shape are women. A man concentrates on disguising his face, maybe his girth, but he never thinks about concealing his gender outline, because there's no way he can look like a woman. You see a big, shapeless, sexless hulk like that—that's a woman. Oh, by the way, do any of you know this car? It's a 1994 Buick Skylark sedan; it's kind of hard to see but its color is blue."

Hannah had been waiting for that. She was profoundly

grateful that the Peabodys were friends of the family from her father's side, not relatives from her mother's.

They shook their heads, mesmerized together with McFarrel in contemplation of the photo. None of them were challenging his blanket assertion that the person in the photo was the killer, and she understood that it would be pointless for her to do so. She looked at across the table at Cowley, and found him looking at her.

All right, your lunge missed. Let's try one of my own.

She had no idea what was happening to her state of mind; events that morning had been moving too fast to keep up. But from the moment he had entered the house her emotions had reached a certain sum. At some level below thought she understood that if the patriarchy was out to frame her (for her own murder) they still had to prove it the old-fashioned way, and so everything boiled down to *this*, to *him*. Her body had taken over: for *this* she was more than ready.

She smiled. "Detective Cowley, all this is well and good, but the whole theory you're working on has a fatal flaw. I was on the train to New York the night Steve was killed. All I need to do is prove that, and I'll be cleared, right?"

"Yes," said Cowley.

Got you, thought Hannah.

He hadn't broken eye contact. "Unfortunately, because of all this other stuff, the department figures you've got to be lying about that, and, unfortunately again, it's a hard thing to prove. How would you do it?"

"We're working on getting the security camera footage from the train stations," she said, with a flick of her eyes at McFarrel.

"Well, in lieu of a witness, that *would* be the next best thing.

Just a tip to the unwary, but you'd better hurry. The stations cycle the tapes after a few days and the footage is overwritten. I think it's five days? Maybe four at Penn."

Hannah had the mirror image of her sensation from when Cowley was making his introductions, and she had felt him nevertheless focused on her. Though he was staring directly into her eyes, she was sure he was addressing someone else. *A tip to the unwary?* With a sudden flush she realized that he was teasing her, *because he considered her intelligent.* So intelligent that—

He was talking to McFarrel. He had picked up on her phrase "we're working on it" and he understood that McFarrel believed her to be guilty, and therefore had no intention of going for the tapes. He was assuming that Hannah was *aboard* with that decision (why wouldn't she be?) and so what she had just uttered was a feint of innocence *for the benefit of the Peabodys.* He was going along with it. He was *covering* for her, with a verbal wink that McFarrel was meant to share.

Goddamn it! she thought, her flush helplessly deepening. And the reason he could safely assume that guilty partnership was that McFarrel *had already blocked her cellphone track.* Surely she had asked him to do so! She was tongue-tied in horror, not least because she didn't know whether he was serious or joking about the tapes being overwritten, which had a potentially enormous influence on her fate, but the angry flush on her cheeks derived mostly from her furious inward comment: *He thinks I'm guilty for the wrong reasons!*

Well, that's how I'm *going to get* you.

She stood erect. "Thank you for the information," she said coldly, into his surprised, uplifted eyes. "We can move fast when we have to."

The doorbell rang.

"Oh, now *that* will be Hannah's parents," said Pam, rising from the couch.

The photograph of the Buick was still open on the table.

Hannah stood stock still.

"Good," said Detective Cowley, turning as with a weary effort. "I'd like to speak to them too."

As he turned he scooped up the photograph, re-folded it, and returned it to his back pocket.

"Hannah!" "Darling!" "Mike — bless you!" "Oh Pam thank you!" "You're all right?" "And this is — ?" "May I present — " "A pleasure, Mr. and — " "Oh Hannah!" "The news has been nothing but — " "No the flight was fine — " For several minutes there was such a tornado in the foyer of hugs and handshakes and more hugs and cold coats bearing the smell of airports that Pam couldn't reach the open street door to close it again. It was perhaps appropriate that the temperature of the house had dropped several degrees by the time attention focused again on the police detective, who had been standing in the livingroom the while with his slightly open tie and his hands in his pockets.

"This is Detective Cowley," Mike said. "He's been explaining why Hannah's currently in trouble."

"But he himself believes she's innocent," added Pam.

"Well, on that basis let me shake your hand!" said Hannah's father.

"I should clarify that everyone is innocent until proven guilty," Cowley said over the handshake. "But I think you should have a high level of confidence in your daughter's ability to avoid that fate."

Hannah blushed again, this time to the roots of her hair.

"What's going on?" wailed her mother, looking back and forth from Cowley to McFarrel. "How can they even think —"

"Mom, I can explain," Hannah said. "Mike and Pam and I have been all through it. Detective, those questions you had — can we get to them another time?" She gave him a politely pleading smile that encompassed her parents' coats, bags, love, etc., together with McFarrel's waiting veto. *Just don't show them the photograph*, she thought.

Cowley looked at his watch. "Yes, I should get going. Mrs. Peabody, could I trouble you for my coat and hat." As she went to the closet he looked at McFarrel. "I will certainly be wanting to question your client again, in a — more controlled environment."

"I understand," said McFarrel.

Hannah's father was about to speak. She interrupted. "Mr. McFarrel and I have just been discussing the best way to clear my name — isn't that right?"

"Don't listen to her," her father enjoined McFarrel, who laughed. Her father rounded on Cowley with an arm on McFarrel's sleeve. "He gets to be present for any questioning, right? You'll let us know ahead of time?"

"Yes, he does — ah, yes, I will," Cowley stammered. He received and donned his coat and hat, and Pam advanced into the foyer and opened the door.

"And when do you think I'll have the pleasure of your company again?" Hannah said sweetly.

Cowley chuckled with a quick glance at McFarrel. "Oh, you'll have that, such as it is, for a little longer. You'll be coming with me. Mr. and Mrs. Radhe, folks, I'm sorry to say I was sent down here with a task. As of now, Hannah Radhe, I am putting you under arrest for the murder of Steve Badenhut."

In the hullaballoo that erupted, which came mostly from Hannah's parents and Pam and encountered businesslike tamping and reassurances from Mike and McFarrel, to whom, Hannah saw, this outcome was not unexpected, while Pam went through an ecstasy of confusion over whether or not Hannah should have her coat—the verdict was best not—and Cowley quite delicately, she thought, applied the cuffs, her main thought was: *at least he didn't show them the photograph.* And on that Pyrrhic basis the two of them were out the door into the harsh slanted sunlight of the winter afternoon.

"Get the tapes!" she shouted back at McFarrel from the walkway to the squad car at the curb.

In the pillared doorway McFarrel nodded with a smile. "I'll explain to your parents why that's not a good idea."

Chapter 10 · Jailbird

This girl — Cowley thought.

He had driven suspects to jail many times, out of every conceivable circumstance and social background, and he was used to the various reactions in his back seat. Some huddled in a sobbing ball or stared balefully out the window; some raged in bursts of defiant profanities; others peppered him with desperately polite questions about what awaited them in the mysterious process to come. He had had silver-haired businessmen fresh from brokerage offices attain to perfect dignity as they sat there, but in the manner of putting on a good face in a tumbrel. But Hannah Radhe, a slim, ponytailed little brunette who had just been pulled from the bosom of her weeping family, sat straightbacked on the seat with her arms behind her, leaning a little forward, bangs loose, eyes focused forward as if calculating how to take on whatever system lay ahead. Cowley, who knew all too well why that system was arresting her, and was more and more sure that she was the murderess, felt oddly like he was conveying a rogue gladiator to the arena to face the lions, one who was perhaps equal to the fight.

He had learned to drive with one eye on the rear-view mirror whenever he had a custodee in the car. There was nothing unusual in his taking another glance.

While still at the curb he had quickly Mirandized her, and she had just as quickly volleyed back her consents, but since then she hadn't said a word. He hadn't really expected her to, and he allowed himself to think of other things. He was worried about this case. Chief Koontz had ordered the preemptive arrest, and though he agreed she was guilty he wanted time to do the necessary legwork. Meanwhile he had Karen still sick with the flu, three weeks now, and he had to remember to do the grocery shop again on his way home because Ricky was arriving for Christmas — when? Tomorrow? Today was the 18th — tomorrow. What would he want to eat that you can't get on a carrier — ?

Hannah shifted and leaned toward the gap in the wired glass; he saw the movement. She was going to talk. They were on Storrow Drive in light traffic, almost at the station. Of course he had the car recorder running.

"Detective Cowley, do you believe I was raped by Steve Badenhut and almost gang-raped by four others, as I described in my statement?"

And of course she would ask the one question Koontz wouldn't want him to answer. "It shouldn't matter to you what I think," he said.

"Don't flatter yourself," Hannah said coldly. "Unlike Pam Peabody, I have a point. Listen. All this garbage on the news means the college is trying to cover up the rape. But *you* need the rape to use as motive. My audio recorder has evidence of the rape on it, and you said that it was found at — "

"How do you know what's on that recording? Have you listened to it?" Per her statements she had gone to New York without having seen her hidden recorder again. *This could lead to a confession*, Cowley thought. He slowed down as he made the turn onto Cambridge Street.

"No," she said, with a quick roll of the eyes. "But poor

Detective Scavelli revealed as much during the interrogation. He kept throwing ridiculous hypotheticals at me on the basis of the recorder being overripe with rape confessions that prompted me into blackmail or whatever, sent me to Steve's room. My *point* is, assuming what's on the recording is part of the case against me, it has to come out in a trial, right?"

Cowley eyes were narrowed to slits and he almost side-swiped a double-parked Hummer as he resisted laughing at her sheer audacity. He would *have* to play this car recording for Scavelli. *And yet she does have a point,* he thought.

"You want to be put on trial?" he asked, looking at her in the rear-view mirror.

"I'm not afraid of it. I haven't been since I pressed charges against the five men for attempted gang rape."

"Do you understand that you are charged with murder, and if you go to trial, it will be as the defendant on that basis?" That was for the recorder: Cowley could get in trouble if she didn't know why she was being arrested.

"Yes thank you, I'm aware that I'm being arrested for a crime I didn't commit," she returned, with the same mechanical swat as her Miranda answers. *What — were they both speaking for the recorder?* She paused, fixing his eyes in the mirror. "Look. If I *am* to be brought down for this — *thing*, then I am damn sure going to bring Steve Badenhut down with me, and hopefully more than him. So if you want to send me to court, fine: send me with that audio to prove motive. *I* want the rape publicized. *You* want it publicized. The college doesn't. That's all."

She sat back. *This — is a potentially dangerous woman,* Cowley thought. They drove the rest of the way in silence. When they got to the station ramp Cowley reached for the radio. "Car fifteen,

one in custody, cooperative," he said. The steel door at the bottom
of the ramp rose open and he drove down.

"Oh, I wouldn't say that," the girl murmured.

Over the next few hours Hannah was booked into jail at the
Boston police station.

The process was a combination of orderly boredom, mob
chaos, and ritualized dehumanization. It began in an underground booking room with a cement ceiling that was crowded,
loud and stifling, where she sat, still cuffed, in a green plastic chair
against the wall in a row of the same overflowing with a melting
pot of metropolitan refuse in various stages of inebriation, sick-
ness and terror. Cops shouldered back and forth filling out paperwork at a soiled counter under greenish fluorescent light. The
stench of sweat, urine, and fresh vomit was only partially tracea-
ble to a propped-open restroom door at the far end. Hannah was
almost the only female present, and her writhing maneuvers to
stay clear of the belched attentions of her neighbor ended with her
on her feet and the neighbor's dreadlocks asleep on her chair.

From that room she was led, still by Cowley, down a long hall
to a smaller room, really just a wider part of the hall with a halting
place and a desk, like a cheap version of airport security. Here
she gave formal agreement to the list of personal property stolen
from her (there went McFarrel's iPhone, still in its box), was stood
up against a greasy height board for her mug shots (full-face and
profile), and had her hands freed only to be ordered into a blood-
stained sink to wash with coarse pink soap before being rolled,
one pinched finger at a time, across an electronic scanner whose
screen added ghostly topographies of her suspect identity into a
nationwide law-enforcement database forever.

Then, in an even smaller room, came the strip search, at the hands of two large female guards. It took a long time. Afterward she was permitted to re-clothe herself without assistance, though her trembling hands were clumsy with the flimsy orange uniform. She was glad that by this point Cowley had disappeared without a word.

Finally a burly female officer with a nightstick at her hip ushered her down a narrow staircase, into a bright echoing corridor whose lingering estrogen fog was partially sliced by ammonia, and to a clean white cell. The cell had white cinderblock walls, a long bench with a dark blue pad, and a steel toilet in the corner. "In ya go, darlin'," and the white-painted bars were rolled shut with a hard electric *clack* that reverberated in the hall. Hannah heard the officer's boots rap back up the stairs.

She heard no voices or sounds of other people; after a moment it was apparent that she was the Boston jail's only female prisoner. The cell block was silent save for a hum of ventilation machinery.

She sat on the blue pad, her forearms on her knees, wrists sticking out of the too-short orange sleeves, and tried to take stock.

Okay kiddo, what now?

Her plan to change the problem of campus rape for the better lay in ruins. Hills College was apparently working hand in glove with the Boston police and even the media to blank her recorded rape confession out of the news, while Steve Badenhut was being industrially haloed in gold; meanwhile if the news was any indication an entirely false narrative was being spun to pin the murder on her, which might actually succeed because she had, after all, committed it and her own lawyer was refusing to get the proofs that would clear her. Instead of being a known rape victim and spokeswoman for the cause her name would now be in the papers as a blindly deranged feminist targeting the innocent, and the final result of her gambit, if Dean Haughton had his way, would be to taint the feminist left, set the movement back years, and confirm in power everyone associated with the ongoing abuse of college girls.

But they have to send me to trial to do it.

It was Detective Cowley who had given her the idea.

It was in the squad car at the curb, almost her first calm moment of the day, when he turned to read her her rights. Something in the *way* he did it, cold and mechanical, told her that this arrest wasn't his triumph — oddly, she knew what his triumph would sound like — that he was just a cop doing his job. It meant that this arrest was political, maybe premature, and that somehow he didn't like it any more than she did. What had he said in the house? That his goal was *solving the crime.*

And all at once the solution had come to her. *Let them send me to trial.* They were on a false trail: they believed she was never on the train. At a trial, she knew, her recording would *have* to come out. It was basic evidence; she had put it on Steve's dead chest; you couldn't even describe the scene without it, never mind present motive, not when *that recording* offered all the motive a prosecuting attorney could ever want. They were probably hoping to *avoid* a trial, scare her with prison time into plea bargaining —

For a moment all thought stopped, and the cold, underground silence of the cellblock with its uneven ventilator hum subsumed her awareness. The walls stood thick, solid and unchanging, as they had for years and would for years: this was a place with no days and nights, no time, where after a brief stir of law business above people were put to be forgotten. To live forgotten and die forgotten and along the way be forgotten even by themselves. The walls didn't care. The sound of her breaths was the only change.

Prison was very, very frightening.

But what if I don't plea bargain? What if I maintain innocence and force a trial? What could they do?

And she had an ace up her sleeve. They were on the wrong trail. It was risky, but if they *didn't* have hard evidence when they went to court, while *she did* —

Suddenly she stood up. All her cards depended on McFarrel. She *had* to talk to him.

But what could she tell him?

For a while she stood, nervously tapping her fingernails against her teeth.

She had a desperate idea.

When the female guard returned, she stood at the bars. "Excuse me. I haven't yet had a chance to make a phone call. I'd like to make one now, if I can."

"*Now* you wanna phone call?" Hannah nodded. The guard sighed. "I'll put in a request. It's party central up there tonight, might be a while."

Two hours later Hannah stood alongside a different, male, guard, at a bank of wall phones in a narrow hall just off the station lobby, from which echoing shouts and fresh cold air periodically burst.

Three officers were dragging a shouting, resisting man through the lobby and past her down the hall, and she had to hold a finger in her other ear as she dialed the number.

"Randall? It's me."

"Hannah? Where are you? What's going on?"

"I'm in jail. I've been arrested. This is my one phone call, so listen closely. There's something I need you to do."

"You used your one phone call to call *me?* Are you insane?"

She had to smile. She had no idea whether prisoners got only one phone call; she had used the line in the hope it would streamline things; naturally the exact opposite had occurred. "No, I already have a lawyer and I've talked with him," she said, "but there's something he's refusing to do that I very much need done."

"And again I say, you're calling *me?* Do you want me to find you another lawyer?"

"No. Something a little more difficult."

There was silence on the line. "Whyyyy don't I like the sound of that? I thought we agreed that *you* would break *me* out of prison if this ever happened, not the other way around."

Her smile widened. It was a joke between them that Randall considered her a superhero in disguise, ever since the day he had taken her to a comic book convention with some friends, and she had scaled a 50-foot cement pillar with a megaphone to announce an impromptu lecture in a vacant room on violence against women in comics. It had been very well attended. Well, she did have strong legs.

"Before you tell me," he said, "do you mind telling me what the hell is happening in the background? What sort of jail are you in? Are you safe?"

"Jail is everything it's cracked up to be. Apparently it's a wild night in Boston. My cell is quieter."

"Good, because it sounds like you're in jail in Colorado in 1872, and if that was the case there wouldn't be much I could do. So tell me. What do you need?"

She took a deep breath. *He's still my boyfriend.* That's what he'd been saying and it made her feel better than she had a right to.

"Okay. I need you to go to New York and Boston, and get the security camera footage from Penn Station and South Station for the night of December fifteenth. I then need you to bring the tapes to my lawyer, Daniel McFarrel. I'll tell you the exact train platforms and the exact times that you must get, but it wouldn't hurt to grab a whole bunch of other times and areas around it. I don't know McFarrel's office address, but you can look it up."

Again there was silence on the line. She waited tensely.

When he spoke again his voice was quieter. "Your lawyer's refusing to get the tapes?"

Ooh he's smart. That's why Hannah liked him. She glanced at her escort out of the corner of her eye; the officer was not even pretending to be inattentive. She had to be very careful with what she said next.

"Their whole stupid theory, Randall, is that I wasn't on the train the night Steve Badenhut was killed. *I was.* My lawyer's trying to play it safe with an alternate defense because he doesn't know whether I'll be visible on the tapes, but I myself am pretty damn positive that I'll be visible on them."

That was another old joke, this time between Randall and his friends: they used to go around making faces into security cameras. *Figure it out*, she thought.

"Got it. Your lawyer's clearly an idiot, and I'm afraid to tell you he's likely to charge extra for that. I'll start tomorrow morning."

She laughed, smiling. "Wait, wait. You sweet thing. You can't just walk into train stations and demand their security tapes."

"I, I have my ways."

"I'll give you a little extra ammunition. I need you to

conference in a third person to this call. Her name is June Anders and she's at the State Department. She's been helping me with background material for my Saudi Arabia trip. When you get her on, stay quiet and let me talk to her."

Hannah directed him to a webpage for her number, and Randall put through the call. There was a scary moment when the line went dead as he put her on hold, then she heard a phone ring and an adult woman answer: "June Anders."

"June, we haven't spoken before but this is Hannah Radhe, we've been in email contact regarding the—"

"Hannah, yes, of course. How are you? The Caller ID said something different."

"Yes, sorry about that. I'm actually calling you on a conference call with my boyfriend Randall, because I'm under arrest in Boston and I'm calling from jail. I wonder if you could do me a huge favor."

There was the slightest pause. "I'm ready. Go ahead," she said.

Hannah ran through the whole situation, and within minutes June had emailed Randall a Federal Authorization of Release to present at the stations, and had an associate call ahead to make sure the stations were preserving the tapes. She even gave Randall the Central Square address of Sleater, Pekoinnen & Glausfarb. Her attitude implied that it went entirely without saying that the arrest was a ridiculous mistake and Hannah would be released on bail at any moment, but whatever could be done to shorten the intervening annoyance should be.

When all the information was communicated June laughed lightly. "We've been very impressed here by your emails regarding Saudi Arabia; we can't wait to see what comes out of the

GWI trip. But I will add to your office legend by saying that only Hannah Radhe would think to make her one phone call from jail a conference call. Marvelous! Let me know how it turns out."

My one phone call? So that is *true?*

Before she could ask, Washington signed off.

"My conviction that you have freaky superpowers has only increased," said Randall.

Cowley knocked on the black-painted door of #25. It was one of seven along the tenement hallway whose stained grey walls somehow made the winter air colder. A ceiling fixture of yellowed plastic and a single window at the far end illuminated the stairway he had just come up.

From behind the door he heard a clatter of pots and a woman's husky voice say, "Just a minute." There were heavy footsteps, the deadbolt drew back, and a stout middle-aged woman with intelligent eyes and a Beatle-bowl of silvering dark hair appeared behind the chain. "Yes?"

"Detective Alan Cowley, Boston P.D.," he said, showing his badge through the narrow space. "Is Tom Corcoran home?"

The woman's eyes flicked once between the badge and Cowley's face and, with a look as of middle-class rectitude winning out over Somerville circumstances, the chain was drawn back and the door opened. "What'd he do?" she said wearily.

"I'd actually like Tom's help, ma'am, with—" he began, but at that moment there was a thundering confusion from the back of the apartment. A window was slammed, furniture violently scraped, a voice said "Holy shit!" and another said "Back door!" and down a short hall lined in piled books Cowley saw a bedroom door burst outward and two teenage bodies fly laterally into the kitchen where he heard a heavy back door wrenched open.

"Oh hell," he muttered. "Excuse me, ma'am." And with that Cowley was running through the apartment. He nimbly dodged the book piles, passed through a scrim of marijuana odor into a squeaky-floored kitchen with a 1960s stove, made a skidding turn, followed through the still-open fire door batting a returning screen door out of the way, and found himself in the cold air on the second floor of an outdoor wooden frame staircase. The two boys were just rabbiting out from the bottom into an alley. "Stop!" he yelled. His call went unheeded by the boys, but drew a gasp from the woman of the house in the kitchen behind him, and in the next instant Cowley was flying down the stairs himself. Through the rushing four-by-fours he saw the boys beating it down the alley between a brick wall on their left and a chainlink fence, heading for a gap in the fence —

And the next thing he knew there was a ripping sound, a torqueing jerk on his coatflap, and he was sprawled at the bottom of the stairs with his right wrist skinned and a singing impact lighting up his left shinbone, watching his gun skitter from his popped holster across the alley to settle on the ice under the exact center of a parked Jeep Grand Cherokee. The boys disappeared through the gap with a flash of sneakerpads.

Cowley sighed, limped to the Jeep and lay down in the dirt to fish out his piece and replace it in his holster. He examined his torn coatflap ruefully, and on his way back up the stairs found the protruding nail. He spent a few moments offering apologies and explanations to the woman, and was able to wash out his wrist, then he limped down the front stairway, got gingerly into his squad car in front of the building, and drove off.

Fifteen minutes later, when Tom Corcoran let himself into his apartment, shivering in his tee-shirt, Cowley was standing inside the doorway, while Mrs. Corcoran watched with a teacup from the couch. His right hand seized the back of the incoming boy's collar with a half twist and lift that brought Tom to his tip-toes, while his left hand closed the door behind him.

"Son, I could bring you into the station right now for both possession and resisting arrest," Cowley said. This speech had better effect. After a dramatic pause he let the scared boy go. "But I'm willing to look the other way if you'll answer a question for me."

"Wh-what?" said Tom.

"You're a day student at the Mayden School, a member of the fencing team, and last semester you took Shop," he said.

"Uh, uh-huh?" Tom nodded.

"I need you to come out to the school with me, and tell me if any fencing blades are missing from the Shop footlocker," Cowley said.

He had almost missed it. On Friday morning, the day after the Badenhut murder, an English teacher at the Mayden School named Ellen Morely, who lived in the immediate neighborhood, was crossing the lower fields on a shortcut to campus when she noticed footprints in the snow coming from the woods by the road. The footprints led to the Shop, where she saw the broken window, the door ajar, and glass on the floor. Ms. Morely looked inside, but didn't notice anything missing. She reported it to the school president, who decided to confront the students first; though the school was on winter break, there were nine kids staying over in the dorms. By Saturday afternoon he was satisfied that none of those were to blame, and contacted the Weston police. A local cop came out, poked around, and left. The next day, Sunday, was when Lieutenant Sanders visited Mayden School asking about missing fencing weapons, part of Cowley's sweep for the source of the killer's weapon. But he spoke to different people and no one made the connection with the break-in: he drove away empty-handed. It was only last night, Monday, at 9:00 pm, when Cowley was sitting at his computer clicking through Hills College parkinglot footage from the preceding six months, looking for a recurrence of the blue Buick, that his phone rang and he found himself talking to Ellen Morely. She had heard about Sanders' visit, and was asking rather pointedly whether, since Boston police were interested in their break-in, they should be worried for their kids.

"What break-in?" Cowley asked.

His squad car scrunched into the gravel parking area at the lower fields and he walked with Tom Corcoran, now in a blue down coat and knit hat, across the bristly grass to the Shop shed. The ambering sun sent long shadows of the bare trees and soccer-net goalposts across the fields in a frosty wind, but the shed was lit up in a white pool from the high portable arc lamps. Two of the white-suited CSI agents were still inside, but the other two were kneeling around a large white cooler on the grass, putting in small containers and closing it up. Cowley approached.

"Bannister. Tell me you have better news," he said.

"Well, the best news would have been the footprints, but we lost those on Saturday when the snow melted."

"What the fuck does that mean? You have nothing?"

"We have the shavings and the belt from the sander." The white-robed figure stood and spread white-gloved hands; Bannister was a tall man with dark hair and a slightly schoolmarmish face behind narrow glasses; he wore a plastic bathing cap. "When we get back we'll be able to give you an exact match on what was sanded and how long it took. But otherwise, no. No prints on anything. No blood on the broken window. No hair fibers. Nothing on the road where the prints originated, no snags on trees, no oil drips, no tire treads at the curb, those would have been on the snow."

"Goddamn it," Cowley growled.

For a moment he glared at the spotlit little building with its one gaptoothed window pane. *It's the scene all over again. It's Badenhut's dorm room – identical. It's her.*

Though they had "her" in custody, for two days now, during which the media had gleefully made Hannah Radhe a household name as the radical feminist Dorm Killer, he had to yet to turn up a speck of forensic evidence or a single witness actually tying "her" to the crime. McFarrel had blocked her cellphone record and forbidden a second interrogation; her laptop proved to have been recently reformatted, which, though suspicious, left it clean of any incriminating evidence. All they had was a computer model of the disguised figure from the Buick (Cowley had told the truth about that) whose data admitted that it *could* have been Hannah Radhe – with ten pounds of extra weight and two inches of extra height. Useless, in other words, despite Gomez of Cyber's vehement defense of the software. The Buick itself was refusing to be found, at Hills College or anywhere else, and Chief Koontz was going purple with frustration and taking it out on Cowley.

Meanwhile tensions at the office around the rape cover-up were getting worse. He, along with Scavelli and Racona, had heard the audio from Hannah's hidden recorder, capped by Steve Badenhut's bellowed vow to kidnap, rape, torture, and kill her. *What the hell are we helping protect here?* he had to not ask. Cowley had long been adept at steering wide of this kind of political crap;

now he was caught in the middle, the pressure coming down on him to nail Radhe for the murder even as he was starting to realize that this *girl* might be the kind of expert criminal he hadn't seen in years.

He felt that he could pack all the crap neatly away if only he could find *proof*. He had felt an unwonted jubilation at the Mayden School breakthrough; he had been *sure* he would finally get forensics.

"I've got one more thing to try," he told Bannister grimly. "Tom, come here."

He peeled the fascinated boy away from the open door and led him around to the side of the shed, where the contents of the footlocker were spread out on a white cloth on the grass under the arc lights. The various fencing blades, pieces of blades, and other metal tubes and pipes were all neatly aligned like an anthropological display of bones. He stood Tom at the edge of the cloth. "Do you see anything missing?" he asked.

"Where's my sabre with the broken tip?" Tom asked.

Chapter 11 - FemiNazi Fatale

FEMINAZI FATALE TOYED WITH VICTIM was the headline on the day's Globe, pressed up at an angle against the glass so that Hannah could only see part of the subhead: RADHE'S THEFT OF TROPHY, FAILED PLOT TO RECORD ANGER, PRECEDED MURDER. "See this, honey?" her father's voice came over the phone as his serious eyes peeked over the paper. "See how they —"

"I've read it," said Hannah. "So that's what they're calling me. Charming."

She was unhappy and impatient. It was her fourth evening in jail and she was meeting with her parents for the first time, in a room set up like a bank for germophobic tellers; she sat behind a sealed window holding a pink phone in a row of prisoners doing the same. Her mother and father were crowded on two stools on the other side of the bulletproof glass and traded their pink receiver erratically back and forth between them, so that Hannah missed a third of what was said. But her whole attention was on McFarrel, standing behind them in his pinstriped suit with a patient smile.

Had he received the tapes? Had the train stations given them to Randall, had Randall gotten them to him? She had seen her lawyer yesterday morning, very briefly, for the arraignment, a loud, chaotic conga line of lawyers and defendants past the judge in which they had only been able to speak about six words (two of which comprised her plea); nevertheless she had established that, as of that point, he had received nothing. After seeing her parents she and McFarrel were to have a private meeting; she could barely be polite to her parents.

"They're making your intelligence work against you," her father declared, trying simultaneously to hold her eyes and aim a long finger under the paper at the subhead, in the process chasing it half off the window. "You see? Turns out your idea to record the rapists maybe wasn't a good one, and now the goddamn media — well, you're in a tight spot, honey, but —"

"Dad, I know. Listen, I really need to talk with McFarrel."

"Okay honey. We love you. They'll post bail soon, and the minute they do — here, your mother wants to say a —"

"We *believe* you honey. Remember that. We never for a minute —"

They both think I'm guilty now, Hannah thought, as the disarranged Globe made way for her mother's hand pressed against the glass. She held her own up to the half inch of separation. *That they know about the rape makes it worse: for them it* is *a rape-and-revenge case, easier to swallow....*

Her meeting with McFarrel was in a small battleship-grey room alongside the visiting room, accessed on her side through a caged corridor. As she and the lawyer made their way to it on separate sides she had time to think about the Globe's story, and the strange way she had read it.

For the first two days she saw nothing of the news, and when she caught up she found the Badenhut murder still the top story, herself headlined by name exactly as she feared, and the media dutifully expanding on the notion of the radical feminist killer who left a recorded manifesto behind. They had happily settled on "The FemiNazi Fatale" as her universal sobriquet. But today's

Globe article had added a new twist; they had discovered her setup with the recorder, and were using it to illustrate the Femi-Nazi's wiles:

> Radhe then stole Badenhut's Biletnikoff trophy—police later found it in her room—and according to campus sources orchestrated a complicated plot to record the footballer throwing a temper tantrum. She arranged a meeting where the young linebacker could recover the trophy, with her recorder hidden nearby to catch his reaction when she failed to appear.
>
> "Apparently she was trying to capture his angry side, and thus paint him as a person capable of rape," surmised Dean of Students Alistair Haughton. "Her fixation to smear the football team was out of control, and we knew it, but of course we never suspected how far it would go."
>
> Police have revealed that the recording captured mainly wind noise, with some boys in the background dimly audible mouthing mild profanities. The voices aren't identifiable, and police said specifically that there are no mentions of rape. But that didn't stop the obsessed feminist from going through with her midnight murder of Steve Badenhut, collecting her recording to plant on the body as a demented manifesto to the world. It is unclear whether Radhe even listened to it.

It was presumably the mention of the police that was responsible for Hannah's being able to read the article. She was eating breakfast in the mess hall—a long room with ranks of tables and a sparse enough population of female prisoners so that she had a table to herself—when Detective Cowley walked in through the swinging doors at one end. He was dressed in the same trench coat as when he had entered the Peabodys' house, though slightly torn, and carried the Globe under his arm. All eyes in the room followed him as he made his way to her table and tossed the paper down.

"You were right," he said. He stared at the paper, and though his nose wasn't wrinkled, his hard, haunted face had something of that quality. "So was Scavelli," he said in a lower voice, meeting her eyes. And she understood the concession he was making, that he was referring to their talk in the squad car, her hypothesis that the recorder must contain usable rape evidence. She saw he knew she would understand. For a moment they held each other's eyes. Abruptly his expression changed and he aimed his forefinger at her. "And so am I."

With that he had turned and left the mess hall, leaving her to read the article in a buzz of suppositional murmurs around her. Knowing what was on the recording, she hadn't needed Cowley's confirmation to see the lie, but she wondered at its new elaboration, the description of her setup so close to the truth. Had Haughton been forced into it? Who were the "campus sources?"

She threw a glance at the door through which Cowley had exited. And what about *him?* There was certitude in his last utterance. Had he traced the car? Had he found the Mayden School break-in? Had she left any forensic evidence there? The longer she sat in jail the more dangerous everything became.

Thus when she and her lawyer entered the bare-walled meeting room from opposite doors she practically threw herself onto the chair at the single round table. The thick doors closed, with guards' faces behind the windows at both ends. McFarrel seated himself, smiling as his balding head tilted his briefcase to the floor. "Now I'm sure you're wondering about your bail —"

"Did you get the tapes? Did Randall Skokar give you a package containing the station tapes?"

McFarrel chuckled and his smile deepened, coming upright. "You and I need to have a long talk about strategy," he said, "which we will do as soon as we get you out. Bail will be set tomorrow morning; they had to finalize the restrictions; it's been a slow—"

"Fine, whatever, we'll talk then. But did you get the package?"

"I know how tough it is, being in jail, believe me. The worst is not knowing what's happening on your behalf, isn't it? Rest assured, my office has been working round the clock on your defense. Til' three in the morning, file boxes and empty coffee cups all over the room. Now, about that package of yours. My office did receive a box from Mr. Skokar yesterday afternoon. I have not yet opened that box. The legal risk—"

"What? You—you *open it!*" she shrieked, coming half out of her chair.

"Hannah! Sit down. Or they'll come in and end this interview." His hand shot up and his eyes went to the window, and Hannah forced herself quivering back into the chair, breathing hard. "They can also cuff you to the table, which will lead to you being marked as un—"

"Mr. McFarrel. Why—why—what possible—"

"Hannah, I explained this to you before—granted, it was in circumstances that were somewhat rushed—"

"Oh I understood every word. Now you understand mine: *I was on the goddamn train!* The station tapes will *prove* it—"

"They will prove no such thing!" he hissed, leaning suddenly forward. He continued with lowered voice, and for the first time she saw a tint of pink in his polished face. "Let me tell you exactly

where you stand, young lady. I met with the DA this morning—
discovery is under way! You send me this box, which my office
didn't subpoena, which is *illegal*, and I'm now under obligation to
hand it to State. I think I know why you did it but for God's sake
the risk—the only thing my office could possibly do with the
damn thing was throw it in a closet and pretend we never got
it—"

"But just *look* at it! It, it will prove—"

"Do you know what their case against you consists of? Do
you?" He threw himself back in his chair and spread his arms.
Having bought her attention he straightened. "Let me spell it out
for you. They can prove that Badenhut was killed with a modified
fencing sword. They can prove that a fencing sword was stolen
and modified at Mayden School, your old school, the day of the
murder. So far they can't tie it to you, but consider how that looks.
And the person who killed Badenhut moved your digital audio
recorder from where it was hidden to his dorm room, and by your
own statement you didn't tell a single other person where you hid
it. Only you knew where it was! Now I can fight this. Do you
know how?"

No forensics at the Mayden School, she thought. *Yet.* She kept
her eyes steadily on his, aided by the momentary equilibrium of
rage and relief. Obviously he was taking what he considered the
most brutal way possible to call her a liar and say that she was
guilty.

"I can fight it because their case is entirely circumstantial. *Entirely circumstantial.* Now if—and I ask you to consider this very
carefully—if *for some reason* you are *not* on those tapes boarding
the goddamn train, then that's *hard proof.* Okay? That's the one
exact thing they need. That's, to hand it to them would be

tantamount to, to—" His eyes rolled, as if searching for some metaphor to convey the scale of ridicule that would tumble upon Sleater, Pekoinnen and Glausfarb forevermore.

"Jesus Christ, McFarrel," she squeaked, pushing her hair back in desperation from her forehead. "*Why* would I go to all the trouble of—"

"Because God save us from clever defendants." He took a deep breath. "Hannah, I know what you were trying to do. You'd heard that prisoners' phone calls are monitored. You decided to plead innocent by making a 'private call' requesting the tapes, which an innocent person would do, to your *boyfriend*, knowing there was very little risk of his ever actually—"

"Oh my God!" She threw her forehead onto her fists on the table. When she raised her face again she was trying as hard as she could to keep it from duplicating the one Steve Badenhut had seen. "Listen closely McFarrel," she said. "You work for me, and I *order* you to go back to your office right now, pull those tapes out of your goddamn closet, secretly if you have to, and just *watch* them. Watch them in the bathroom! I promise you, you'll have a brand new way to fight my case by dinnertime. If you don't, I swear—"

"Well, Hannah, actually, I work for your parents. I didn't want to have to mention it. But you can't order me, and for the moment you're going to have to trust me. Okay?"

She leaped to her feet. "*Get out of here!*" she shouted.

As McFarrel stood with a weary smile the door behind her opened and a guard stepped in. "Everything all right in here?"

"This interview is over," she told the guard. "Please escort this, this gentleman the fuck away from me."

"It's just one more night," the lawyer's voice chuckled soothingly. "Then we'll have you safely out of here and you'll—"

The voice ceased as she whirled, stared at him for a second, then turned her back and stalked out of the room through the prison-side door. The guard gave the lawyer a humorous glance before following her. McFarrel stood for a moment, lightly stroking his lower lip, before passing out through the other door. He had not, however, seen the face Steve Badenhut had seen.

He had seen the face of someone thinking too fast to speak.

"Okay people, it's time to put this goddamn case to bed," Chief Koontz said, slapping a thick manila folder onto the table behind which he stood. "Sorry for the hour but we caught a break and I want all hands on deck for this. Everybody fucking awake?" He roved a glare around the meeting room, his big face sweating and his neck raw under his blue collar.

Cowley watched him cautiously from his seat at the far end of the table. He had rarely seen the chief as stressed and angry. *He's caught in the middle too*, Cowley thought. And he knew who was squeezing from above, and who was about to get the brunt of it below. Koontz secretly didn't want the case to go to trial: the intent was to force McFarrel to plea bargain with clear evidence of Hannah's guilt, which *he* was supposed to get. Well, so far McFarrel had offered no plea, and Cowley had felt the desperation level rising. He drew and released a tight breath.

"The last couple days this department has been looking like goddamn idiots, okay," Koontz resumed. "A whole week in, we have exactly one suspect for killing Badenhut, a fucking teenage girl, and until today none of you goons were able to pin a fucking thing on her. But Detective Cowley did some good work up at Mayden School last night, and again this afternoon with the blue car, and, well, it's circumstantial but we got her. She fucking did it, just like Cowley said. And tonight we're gonna nail her."

"Excuse me, circumstantial?" said Detective Solsberger, rising half out of his chair close to Koontz. "Did you just drag me here at this hour on the basis of new evidence and then fucking use the word circumstantial?"

It was 11:30 pm at the station and everyone was tired. The homicide team had been ordered to stay late for the emergency conference, and many other cops had chosen to linger voluntarily; the halls were abuzz with rumors of a final confrontation with the female prisoner downstairs, amid strange hints that she had volunteered for an interrogation. With the door shut the meeting room was close, overheated on one side and too cold by the black wired window. Around the table were detectives Cowley, Racona, Scavelli, and Solsberger, as well as Bannister from CSI. Cowley had tossed stapled packets around the table, but no one dared open them while Koontz was talking. Jackets were thrown over chairbacks and shirts were stained under armpits and holster-straps, save where Lieutenant Racona sat erect in creased blue, her stockinged legs crossed, her packet squared.

"Strong circumstantial, Solly. It's her. But yes, we still don't have direct proof." The chief threw a glower in the direction of Bannister, whose shoulders and eyebrows went up. "That's exactly why in about a half hour we're going to drag Hannah Radhe's ass out of her cell and interrogate her a second time. And this time we're not gonna pull any goddamn punches."

"Oh, an interrogation! Even better!" said Solly. "Bravo." Leon Solsberger was a tall, skinny man with a head of curly lightbrown hair and a prominent Adam's apple, who came fully erect at the table now in a pink dress shirt and blue tie to clap his long hands loudly. "To put this in English, you're going to try again to break a nineteen-year-old girl who by all accounts is innocent, who was in fact the victim of a violent rape just days ago and whose only crime was to get him on tape so as to actually win her sexual assault case. You and HC threw this goddamn girl in jail on no evidence to shut her up while the media spreads lies about her and lionizes her rapist, and after all this time guess what? You still have no direct proof! Who'd have guessed! Strong circumstantial my ass. This is a fucking witch-hunt and you know it. You realize she has a lawyer."

"Solly, sit the fuck down! And can it about the rape, I swear to God I'm serious." There was enough force in Koontz's florid face and the shift of his bulk that Solly promptly sat, though he continued to glare. "This isn't the sex crimes division here, this is homicide and you're at a meeting about a goddamn murder case. I told you before, the only thing anyone here knows about any rape is a statement given to New York by this smart-ass college girl *after* she killed Badenhut, as a cover story. That's where it stays. And that goes for the rest of you jokers. Am I clear?"

Cowley's eyes went around the room as the others looked at the table. All of them understood the million-dollar whitewash game being played between the Hills College football program and Boston P.D.; most of them, though not Solly, had heard the Badenhut audio. Cowley looked at Scavelli and Racona: they were, like Cowley himself, being good soldiers and staying quiet—though for different reasons, he thought—but he nevertheless saw them squirm in their seats. Solly had recklessly voiced what many of them felt.

Solly wasn't done. "Fine, let's hear about the *evidence*," he said, glaring from his seat. "But let me just clarify this: *without* a

confession, would you have enough to even send this case to prosecution?"

"Yes. We—could," said Koontz, with a glance at Cowley.
Their eyes, holding for a fraction of a second, were highly
charged: both men knew that they *did* have enough circumstantial
for a case; neither wanted to send it. "With the new stuff Cowley
found, especially on the car, we could. But, well, she's got McFarrel and why take chances in court, better to nail her once and for
all with a confession. Thank you Solly for that clarification, and
now if you'll do us all a favor and shut the fuck up. We don't have
much time here, and Cowley has a lot to go over, so that this time
we know what the hell we're doing when we drag her in. All
right? Cowley, go ahead."

"I've said my piece," said Solly, sitting back haughtily.

"Go on, I'm curious, what did you find?" said Scavelli. "I
heard a little about the Mayden School, but you found the car
too?"

Cowley stood, holding his packet, noting the eagerness in
Scavelli's boyish face. His obedience on the sensitive matter was
clearly a bid for promotion—which given the delicacy of the situation would likely be forthcoming—and Cowley knew that it
overrode his own doubts about Hannah's guilt. Scavelli wouldn't
be at all sorry, Cowley saw, to be proved wrong.

He cleared his throat. "I'll start with the Mayden School.
Now, it's true that we don't have forensics of her there"—Solly
made a "*pfff*" sound and Bannister rolled his eyes and whole
head—"*but*, from the beginning, one of the key questions in this
case was where the killer got the blade. All fencing swords at
Hills, private and the school's, were accounted for. We hit all
sporting stores in a three-state radius where fencing weapons are

available, there actually aren't that many, and none reported any sales to suspicious persons. We were very thorough in this. The Mayden School break-in was pre-dawn on the day of the murder, in the dark, and whoever did it came by car—the footprints were from the road—and knew exactly where to park to walk through woods to get to this little shed. No one else remotely connected with this case has any familiarity with the Mayden School."

"Still no proof it was her," muttered Solly.

"Solly, that's correct. Whoever was in there was very careful. But Bannister analyzed the metal shavings on the floor and they match the metal of an AF Elite sabre, which in turn matches the entry wound and is also the weapon my student, Tom Corcoran, identified as his missing blade. He also said the tip was broken, and we found a severed foible on the floor with a clipped-off tip. This is the source of the murder weapon, people. It's her."

"Wow," said Scavelli, shaking his head. "This brings me around. It's gotta be her."

"Cowley, do me a favor when you've got her in there," Racona said, holding her packet flipped open. "Ask her why someone would leave the shavings all over the floor. I'm curious to hear what she says to that."

"Isn't it obvious?" Bannister spoke up. "She already broke the window. She can't conceal it at that point."

"But if she cleans up the metal probably no one ever makes the connection from the window to a missing piece of a fencing blade. In this photo I see a dustpan right there. To me this is like putting her own recorder on Badenhut's dead chest. I say she *left* the shavings there, left them to be found."

"Excuse me?" said Solly. "Are you out of your mind? What is she now, the goddamn Riddler?"

"She knew there'd be no forensics and she was showing off," said Racona. "I wanna see her show it."

"It's possible," said Cowley slowly. "She might have been on the clock there and didn't have time. But she's also not low on ego..."

Racona was right: a cleanup would have taken seconds, and there had been no indication that anything startled her. He added it to a growing list of questions in this case that bugged him, dating back to her ridiculous use of a fencing sword. *Was* she the Riddler, showing off? At this point Cowley didn't think so. She didn't want to be caught, yet her own signals were drawing the noose around her too tight. His gut was uneasy: if she had miscalculated, as he thought she had, what did she miscalculate from? *There's something else. She knows something I don't yet know. I'm not at the end of this.* He had his own reasons for welcoming the interrogation rather than sending circumstantial to Grand: she clearly was desperate, she was *feeling* the noose tighten, and it would be him against her in there. Whatever she had up her sleeve, he would find it. He would *know*. He and Koontz understood each other on that.

"But you said you got something on the car?" Scavelli asked, leaning into a glaring match between Racona and Solly. "Were you able to I.D. it?"

"Not exactly," Cowley said.

"Yeah, but tell Solly what you found there," said Koontz. "This *really* nails her."

"Okay, to restate, the only way Hannah's plan works is if she has a car. She tells everyone she's taking the train home, she leaves a big trail to the train, going all the way to South Station and buying her ticket there with a credit card, she sits in plain view the whole time waiting for the train—we have testimony from Kimberly Atkins, the waitress at Eastern's—she sits around for all these hours until it's good and dark and Steve will likely be in his room, then, ten minutes before the last train, the nine-thirty, the waitress sees her pick up her bags and leave Eastern's. And at that point she drops off the map until she reappears in New York early the next morning."

"Possibly because she boarded the train, said Solly into a brick wall," said Solly.

"Solly, for God's sake—!" said Koontz.

"So our working theory is that she ducks out of South Station, has her car waiting nearby, drives to HC, kills Badenhut, then drives herself to New York. Tells her folks she just got in off the train."

"And we know the killer comes to HC by car," Bannister said.

Cowley nodded and flipped pages on his packet. "We're operating under the safe assumption that this Buick, the photo on page one, is the killer's car: it appears in the Hills College parkinglot shortly before Badenhut is killed, this obviously disguised person emerges, and at eleven-thirtyseven, seven minutes after time of death, the person returns and drives off again. So, obviously, for the last several days we've been working overtime to try to track the fucking car. And I swear to God, it comes out of nowhere. I went through HC footage for months back—as far as their system went—and it's never been on campus in that time. No 1994 Buick Skylark sedans are registered to anyone in Massachusetts. Likely it's a friend's car from out of State, but where does the friend park, and how does she get it? We looked into all her friends and faculty members and those threads led nowhere. This is another case where she's just—better than she should be.

"Well, we were getting nowhere so I started at the other end. Assuming she *did* drive herself to New York after the murder, I queried the Mass Pike tollbooths Westbound starting a little after eleven-thirtyseven on December fifteenth. And there it was. The photos are on your page eight. No view of occupant —"

"Holy shit!" said Scavelli, as paper fluttered around the room. "But you got plates! So —?"

"The plates," said Cowley steadily, "are registered to a 2005 Serro Scotty Pup camper trailer, last registration 2011, owner is Mrs. Miriam P. Stouffer of Waltham. She knew she'd be driving the Interstate, and she stopped to swap the plates."

"Nice," said Racona.

"Oh come on!" Solly said, slamming his palms on the table. "Seriously, what is this?" He flapped his packet. "You have no connection whatsoever between her and that car, and you sound like lunatics trying to make her fit. The killer is someone who knows disguise, who steals cars, who swaps fucking plates — this is garbage, dangerous garbage."

"I've gotta go with Solly on that one," said Scavelli, shifting on his chair. "Swapping the plates, I dunno..."

"Whoever it is kills Badenhut then drives the fucking car to New York, you clowns!" Koontz yelled. "We have it on the Mass Pike all the way to Sturbridge! Who the fuck else would do that? *Why* would they? It's *her* — she's pretending she's on the train. It fits. Who says she can't swap plates?"

"All it takes is a screwdriver," said Bannister. "Disguises like that aren't hard either. No, I tell ya, with the car and the Mayden School, plus the fencing sword wound and the audio recorder that only she knew where to find — it's her. You could send this to prosecution right now."

"She's already good with DNA prevention, Solly," said Cowley. "The girl is—" His lips tightened into something not unlike a smile, despite the fact that he was worried about just how good she might be. He didn't mention that he had had the NYPD search back street and garage footage and scour on foot the area around Hannah's parents' apartment for the blue Buick, in vain. *If she drove home, where did she park? Where did the car go?* He also didn't mention that South Station cams showed no trace of the car planted nearby on the murder day, or of Radhe exiting the station that night as part of her "doubling back."

What part of my theory is wrong? What am I missing?

"That's why, Solly," he said grimly, "when we're handed an opportunity to question her without her lawyer we have to take advantage of it."

"Now *what, what?*" Solly cried, staring wildly around at them. "Without her *lawyer?* Are, are you bastards saying you're going to drag that girl into an interrogation room without telling—"

But Koontz was chortling deep in his belly and shaking his head. "Nah, nah, Solly, that's not what he means. It, it's legal, we think. We caught a break—"

"It's at her invitation," said Racona. "Don't worry, Solly, if it's any consolation to you it looks like three days in jail didn't soften your little princess up a whit."

"Can someone explain this?" Scavelli asked. "I never heard what happened."

"Me neither," chimed in Bannister. "Everyone's wondering."

Koontz spread his hands. "This evening Radhe met with McFarrel downstairs. It was confidential, but it looks like they had a falling out. Afterwards Radhe goes steaming back to her cell, word is she was pretty upset. So a couple hours later she writes a note and hands it through the bars, addressed to Cowley."

All eyes turned to Cowley, who made a noncommittal gesture that included rolling his eyes, shaking his head, and licking his lips, all at once.

"It's love," said Racona. "Jailhouse love."

"Whatever it is, it's useful," grunted Cowley.

Koontz pulled his spectacles from his shirt pocket, settled them, and unfolded a piece of paper close below. "Teenage girl handwriting on a thing like this," he muttered, shaking his head. "It says: 'Tell Detective Cowley not to expect a confession, but if he wants to question me without McFarrel he can.' End statement."

A wondering whistle came from Scavelli.

"So there's your princess in the tower, Solly," said Koontz. "She's chosen another prince. And since we have her invitation, we're not going to fuck around. We're hauling her out of bed in the middle of the night and, since she's in custody, we're gonna interrogate her until the cock crows."

"It won't take that long," said Cowley. "Her alibi has a dozen soft spots to hit."

"Maybe," muttered Koontz. "I'd rather hit her with something harder."

"I do it my way," said Cowley.

"I am very uncomfortable with this," said Solly. "We don't know that she fired her lawyer. You've got to at least re-Mirandize her."

"No we don't," said Koontz.

"Beside the point," said Cowley.

"*How* are you going to do it?" said Scavelli. "I mean, I threw the same theory at her last time about her not taking the train and doubling back, and she didn't blink. I mean, what do you think *she* wants to talk about?"

Everyone looked at Cowley again. A silence fell in the meeting room.

"I think she wants to talk about rape," Cowley said. He looked across the room directly at Koontz and spoke carefully. "On the police record. And if we're going to interrogate her, we have to meet her assumptions: that she was out to publicly expose Steve Badenhut as a predator and rapist, and that she had evidence of it on her recorder. We all know what's on that recorder."

There was another silence, as eyes roved heavenward and deep breaths were taken, save for Solly who looked around with his eyes narrowed. He hadn't heard the audio. The others, hardened cops all, had.

"I'll say it again: rape-and-revenge is easier," Racona said quietly. "With that audio to prove motive there'd be no question. That thing drives anyone to kill. Hell, I listen to it, I want to off the son of a bitch myself."

"But it doesn't," said Cowley. "The murder is premeditated from much earlier, from before Badenhut says a word of that stuff. Hannah doesn't let it—"

"The jury won't care," said Racona. "They hear that shit, they'll convict. Unless they applaud her."

"Go on, Cowley," said Koontz through his teeth. "Strictly in terms of the interrogation you may be right. To get the confession. What are you thinking?"

"I think she's squirming. All she's wanted from the beginning is to expose the rape. That's why she only needed to kill one of them, her message was sent. And it wasn't a dumb idea. She figured, bam, kill Badenhut, put the evidence on the corpse, the evidence goes public. Normally that's exactly — well, in this case she was wrong. All the publicity she was counting on hasn't happened. So I think she's desperate. She wants to tell her story."

"On the police record? What good does she think that will do?" Scavelli said.

"She wants a trial," Cowley sighed, looking at the window. "That's what her line means about 'no confessions.' That's her new idea for a venue of publicity and she's willing to take chances to get there. She thinks the recording will come out as evidence. Maybe she thinks the interrogation record would come out there too, with us talking about the rape."

"If that's her goal, she's going to be pretty determined not to confess," said Racona. "Just like last time. You up for this?"

"I'll go after her assumptions. I'll tell her that her audio will never be made public." Koontz made a loud affirmative grunt. "I'll play on her frustrations about the rape story not coming out. It's possible she'll want my sympathy on that." *And I have to be careful she doesn't get it.* He glanced at Koontz, and something professional and frustrated in him made him take a risk. "In fact I think she's going to ask *me* about her audio. And ideally, the best way to nail her would be for me to play that Badenhut speech for her, and see if she gives away that she's heard it before. Because I think she has." Koontz held his eyes coldly. He finished: "Anyway, I've got Mayden School and the tollbooths to taunt her with. Even if she doesn't confess I'll entangle her in so many lies and contradictions that if the interrogation *does* come out in a trial it'll convict her."

"Oh, this is going to be essential viewing," said Racona. "You've got the big room with the mirror; Scavelli and I will be in the booth."

"Yeah, and speaking of which, why don't you all go set up?" said Koontz. "I want a word with Cowley alone."

The others pulled themselves upright, the door admitted a faint breath of fresher air, then it was closed behind them. Cowley looked at Koontz down the length of the table; he knew what was coming.

The chief stood in the corner of the room; his face was still mottled with sweat. "Cowley, you know the score. You say she wants a trial? I don't. In fact nobody does. No one wants to see that girl or her recorder in court, and that comes from higher up."

"I know where it comes from," Cowley said.

"Well the whole idea was to get enough on her to make McFarrel plea bargain and she disappears that way. *You* were supposed to get it. Now he's smacking his chops to take it to trial."

"I know. She was better than I thought. But don't pin McFarrel on me — the reason he's smacking his chops is because *you* boys took plausible motive away from the prosecution."

"Yeah, and Hills is throwing more money at making it *stay* away. What I'm saying is, go ahead and play that Badenhut rant audio in the room if you like — I see the use, and hell, it's a fucking police interrogation, cops fabricate shit, if God forbid the video should ever get out. But what I want out of this is a *confession*, Cowley. You hear me? I want her to go straight from that room to sentencing. I don't care how you break her, or how long it takes, or what you offer — she seems to have a thing for you, so you're the one going in, but by God you better get that girl to *confess*. Can you tell me you can do that?"

"It's what you pay me for," said Cowley.

Chapter 12 - A Midnight Match

A lovely aspect of jail garb was to make one very conscious of the temperature of the air on one's body. Hannah's cell had a constant chill fan blowing, stronger or weaker in different corners but always on her, and she found it much worse than the constant light in terms of disrupting her sleep. She could counter it with exercise, but that raised a sweat, so that when she stopped the chill was worse. It also raised goosepimples, among other pointed effects as she contemplated with fear and desire her coming encounter with Cowley, as if to make her wear her guilty heart on her orange sleeve, as it were.

So when the big female guard led her up the stairs to her interrogation she was mostly aware of being warmer. Her very skin relaxed, and she could taste the salt on her upper lip. She was suddenly alive to the need to brush her hair. She had no idea what time it was — she hadn't been asleep when they came for her — but she noted that the halls of the upper station were dark as they passed, quiet save for a sudden burble of voices in the distance followed by the closing of a door. She saw no window, unless one counted the huge rectangular mirror dominating the right-hand side of the interrogation room into which she was directed alone.

The room was bright, larger than her first one but just as bare, with a single deal table against the mirror and two mismatched chairs between bland white walls; the dark convex eye of the video camera was in the far right corner. She saw nothing wrong with pausing to look directly into the mirror, and even smiling; she could use the moral support of checking her own reflection even as she could politely nod to her viewers. *Two points with one move?* Then she eased herself onto the metal chair with ratty red padding, facing the camera across the length of room, as Detective Cowley closed the door, went around the table and sat facing her.

"Are you all right?" he asked, referencing the way she had sat down.

She smiled wryly. "I've never done so many fencing exercises. My legs are sore."

He nodded. "Do you need anything? Rest room visit? Water?"

"I wouldn't mind some water," she said.

He got up again, and on his way out of the room she studied him. The mental image that had accompanied her otherwise solitary nights hadn't, she thought, played her false. The man didn't look the least tired, despite whatever hour it was; the inherent weariness in his face was as if tightened inward. Together with his unruly dark hair and bristly jaw it gave him a look of focused strength. He was dressed in what she thought of as his normal outfit — slacks, white shirt, a loosened dark tie — but his affect was new: the shirt was rumpled, the sleeves rolled up, and of course the holster with its straps and heavy gun handle were starkly visible. She felt she was seeing him in his element, on his turf, and he moved with his weapon an unconscious part of him, an aspect Hannah recognized from the best fencers.

When he was gone she looked at his jacket thrown over the back of his chair. *He could have worn that, to conceal the gun. Did he expose it to intimidate me?* No, she decided: if he had worn the jacket it would have emphasized his official clothing over her jail garb. He was choosing to be closer to her. *This is for rapport.* His weapon really was invisible to him.

That's all right. He hasn't seen mine either.

"Thanks," she said, taking a small sip from the mug filled with cold water. She set it on the table as he returned to his chair. There were no further introductions as he launched into an impersonal recitation of the recording technology of the room around them, the ground rules governing her power to leave (she had none, except as he granted), and of course her understanding that anything she said here could be used as evidence against her. It went quickly and this time she had nothing to sign.

"So," he said, folding his hands on the table. "You asked to be questioned by me, and without your lawyer present. Why?"

"As regards the lawyer, it's because he thinks I'm guilty," she said.

"And why does he think that?"

She made a short, exasperated sigh. "Well, I have no insight into his mental process, and bear in mind that any guess I make will be biased by my extreme desire to smear his character. But he probably has the same dumb theory that you all do, about how I killed Steve Badenhut."

Go ahead. Ask me if I in fact killed Steve. Get an innocent statement on the record.

"Why do you say it's a dumb theory?" he asked instead, and she smiled. *Good. He heard it. We understand each other.*

"Because," she said, and swept a long gaze across the mirror, "the lot of you have a complete disregard for *evidence*. Everyone has been happy to jump to the most appalling conclusions about me. What I want to get on the record here is *evidence*. And I chose you," she added, looking at Cowley, "because you left me with the impression that you're the one cop who cares about finding the truth."

Did it work? She had come out with a fast, multi-level attack. On the police transcript it would look like a declaration of innocence. To the people behind the mirror it would hopefully look like ego: no thinking person would actually submit to police interrogation to declare innocence, unless they were (a) brazenly naive, or (b) so arrogant as to want to show off before the cops. She thought she had a little of each back there. But above all she hoped that to Cowley it would signal why she was really here.

She was desperate, and she was playing absolutely her last card.

Back in her cell after her interview with McFarrel she had spent two hours in frantic fencing exercises, then, breathing hard, had summoned the guard and asked for another phone call. At the phone bank she had dialed McFarrel's office number. She reached his voicemail. This time she muffled her mouth with her hand and spoke in low tones so that the guard alongside couldn't hear, but her voice was no less levelly charged for that: "Damn it McFarrel, I thought you said you were working late. Listen up. I am going to volunteer for another interrogation, alone, tonight. I'm going to tell them I'm innocent, but you can figure out how easy they'll go on me. You have one way to stop it, and that is to open the goddamn box as soon as you get this message, pull out the tapes for Amtrak 67 on December fifteenth on both ends, watch 'em, and bring 'em here to the station to submit as new evidence. I think they'll stop the presses. Otherwise it's very likely goodbye to you and your case."

She had then asked for paper and pencil, and sent her note to Cowley.

It was a crazy gambit, especially because she had had to leave voicemail: she had no idea when McFarrel would pick up the message. But in the meantime she had an even crazier task to perform.

There was a problem with her alibi proofs.

It was McFarrel himself who had made her see it, with his revelation that she *hadn't* left forensic evidence, that *all* they had was circumstantial. The fencing sword, the Mayden School, the digital audio recorder—this was nothing but her own self-frame, the spotlight she had *intended* to narrow on herself before she stepped out. The tapes, as "hard proof" of her innocence, would likely blow the case against her out of the water. She had imagined using them *in* the trial, as some 11th hour surprise, but she *had* listened to McFarrel and that's not how trials work. She had to get her alibi proofs admitted first—*before* a trial—exactly, in fact, as she had imagined presenting them originally. As far as she could tell they would still fulfill their original function and clear her, *especially* if, as she thought, the cops were trying to *avoid* a trial. At this point they would probably be *delighted* to let her go.

But now she couldn't let that happen. Yes, *if* McFarrel showed up with the tapes she would likely be freed—but with her rape confession still suppressed, Steve Badenhut enshrined in glory, Dean Haughton smugly victorious. Indeed, her digital audio recorder would then disappear into police custody as evidence in the permanently unsolved crime she had set out to create. It would be the empty triumph of her alibi: she would walk away scot free—with the entire purpose of her act negated and perverted.

She was looking at a choice, and she looked at it through the longest fencing exercise session of her life. But in the end she *couldn't* walk away on that basis. Not after committing a murder.

And not when she was this close.

Because if the stakes had been raised for her, they had been for Dean Haughton as well. From the moment she saw this morning's Globe she understood that her enemy was vulnerable. The dean was over-extended. Her little recorder had scared him too much, tempted him too far; he had told too many lies too publicly for too long. "Wind in the trees" indeed. Publicizing Steve's vicious, perfectly clear rant now would expose Haughton not merely as a college administrator ignoring a girl's sexual assault story, but as author and spokesman of an extraordinary rape-silencing cover-up. She had wanted her digital audio recorder to start a conversation; it was now capable of bringing down an administration. A trial—*her* trial—was the way to publicize it.

So she was not here merely to wait for McFarrel. She was thinking beyond him. She wasn't giving up her goal of getting to a trial; neither was she going to let him stupidly fritter away her carefully constructed defense. She had to get to a trial, *despite* her alibi.

And she had a reckless, desperate plan to do it.

First she had to avoid confessing—stubbornly maintain innocence. Against Cowley in particular that would be by no means easy. She knew how badly the police wanted a confession, that they would maul her all night if necessary to get one. Then McFarrel had to show up with the tapes that proved she was on the train. And then—assuming all that happened and they were in fact dropping charges—she had to do something to leave the police *still suspecting her*. She knew they had no one else; she knew there were more clues to find. She had to encourage them to keep looking at her, *find* those clues, and pull her *back* into a trial. Specifically, she had to encourage Cowley.

The rest of the police could not be counted on—they were as corrupt as Haughton and would be in no hurry to restore her trial. *Cowley would keep looking.* She somehow knew that.

She looked straight at him. He *knew* she was guilty—she liked that. He wouldn't fall so easily for the train station tapes. But she had to make sure he didn't. It was an enormous risk: she had to deliberately point him down a road that led ultimately to the fire pump sitting twenty feet offshore at Greenwich Bay, and she didn't underestimate his intelligence. But that was a problem for later, and truth be told if she stood trial on *that* basis she would mind less, and would go into history alongside her hero John Brown with her blow against the system struck. Right now she just wanted to leave Cowley *suspicious*, so that when she walked— if she walked—he would pursue her.

She had an idea for that. But it wouldn't be easy. And meanwhile she had to survive him.

The echoes of her accusation were still ringing in the interrogation room. Cowley, the alleged truth-seeker, looked at her blankly across the table, as if resisting the urge to raise his eyebrows at the watchers behind the mirror. He cleared his throat. "And what elements of the truth are you hoping to get on the record?" he asked, with the faintest tinge of sarcasm.

"Oh, eventually I'd like to get to the fact that Steve Badenhut was a rapist, and the other four as well, and that Dean Haughton and HC are covering it up, and that your department is colluding in the cover-up," said Hannah. "But I suppose you want to start by talking about me."

~ Hour 1 ~
She's using me, thought Cowley. *But for what? If she's playing*

*for a trial she could get it without this. What is she here for? There's
something I'm missing.*

Her strategy, such as it was, seemed to consist of simply
repeating her same story over and over and insisting that she was
innocent. *I was on the train, Detective.* And yet her smile and her
eyes were communicating something else. The girl seemed to be
operating on the bedeviling premise that her guilt was something
tacitly understood between them, which for obvious reasons they
couldn't mention before others. Whenever he tried a direct accusation she batted it away with a roll of her eyes as if he had
committed a social gaffe: "So would you say your goal for killing
Steve has failed?" "Oh come on, I didn't kill Steve. If you want to
stumble me linguistically into a confession you'll have to make
your sentences more complex than that. Ask something else."

The result, besides an audible chuckle from behind the mirror,
was that Cowley's usual radar for how to achieve rapport with a
suspect was turned back on itself. Should he align with her in
pretending to know what he already knew? At any rate she was
as alert and focused as he was, unprecedented in a suspect interrogation; it forced him to lift his game. And this was a young girl
after three days in jail!

Jail had changed her. Maybe it was the fact that her hair was
loose and sloppy around her shoulders, or that her color was high,
but she looked smaller and fiercer, like someone who had been
caged and proved equal to the cage. He had a sudden presenti-
ment, borne of experience, that if she *did* go to prison she would
be master of the place inside a year.

He started off by having her go over her rape in the dorm room
again, detail by detail. It was good protocol—Scavelli hadn't
asked about it at all, just jumped straight to the murder, and they

could compare her story here to the one she had given Detective Wilson in New York—but it was also a subtle shot at Chief Koontz. The department cops knew she was telling the truth about the rape, and one was supposed to start an interrogation by eliciting a flock of true answers to stuff, both to put the suspect at ease and for the interrogator to measure the delivery of truth, to compare later to its opposite. He knew Koontz got the message.

It also had the benefit of making Hannah uncomfortable. He didn't let her talk at length, but kept interrupting. *What was Reggie Mathis wearing? Can you demonstrate how Davey Coleman held you? How did Chris Kelly say that?* Frequently he had her go back and repeat details, deliberately holding her over the worst part, the rape itself. He played wholly disinterested—it was easy to do, he'd listened to far worse—and watched her. Any girl would have a hard time reliving such an experience, much less before an audience. Would she show her emotion? Blush, squirm, cry, overdo it to generate sympathy? She chose not to: she swallowed her discomfort (he saw the effort) and answered everything back with the same cold precision he was using. The tactic, regarding the violent abuse of her own body, was a bit shocking; it was costing her sympathy points behind the mirror—surely she knew that?

He decided to find out. "You seem very detached and unemotional about this experience. Is that really how you feel?"

She smiled. "Lord, I figure we're in for the long haul tonight, you and I. I don't want to use all my emotion up at the beginning." Was she—trying to gain rapport with *him?* She shrugged. "To be honest, it *is* easier to talk about this experience—knowing Steve is dead."

Deliberately provocative. And yet that had the ring of artless truth. "Are you glad Steve is dead?"

"Well, I'm not going to pretend I'm sorry, despite how all this is turning out for me. *My* plan, as you know, was to expose him as a rapist in court before the law."

There it is again. On the surface she was playing innocent, talking about the charges she had pressed in New York, but she was also referencing what she had said to him in the squad car, about what she intended to do in a trial to come. He was sure Koontz heard it too, back there.

"Let's talk about how it *is* turning out for you," he said. "You're in jail, and your name is all over the newspapers as the FemiNazi Fatale, which can't be undone, which is affecting your parents, and your uncles and aunts, and your friends at college, and the faculty members who like you, and the people who are running the GWI summer program you've been studying so hard for. Meanwhile Steve Badenhut is being eulogized in TV specials and Sports Illustrated articles, and your college is talking about naming the football stadium after him. How does that make you feel?"

Her breath was coming shorter, and something of the caged animal was a little closer to the surface. "Determined," she said.

"Determined to do what?"

"To devote whatever is left of my life, wherever it's lived, to smashing the patriarchy."

"Do you think," he pursued, "that the person who killed Steve Badenhut intended for things to turn out this way for you? Do you think they thought it through?"

"I remain convinced," she said through her teeth, "that whoever killed Steve Badenhut did so to make the world a better and safer place."

"And maybe they did! But not for you. Okay, he was a despicable scumbag, and it's quite possible that offing him saved some future girl or girls from undergoing what happened to you. Do you think that's benefit enough to justify what *you're* undergoing—to justify spending the rest of your life in prison for coldly premeditated murder?"

To his surprise she leaned back in her chair and smiled gently. "What if it was?"

"What do you mean?"

"Well—" she paused, looking upward, then looked back. "I mean, it's strange to sit in a police station having a discussion with a cop about the benefits of murder, but as long as we're into the subject, what about John Brown?"

"John Brown? John Brown is most famous for a song about his *grave*. He's not a good role model."

"On the contrary. He's an excellent role model. He started a ball rolling that led to the end of slavery in America. The same is true from a feminist perspective of Susan B. Anthony being arrested for casting a vote, or Alice Paul being thrown in prison for her suffragette demonstrations. Sometimes the law and the system are wrong and you have to fight to change them, and it's a good fight. I only mentioned John Brown because his case involved homicides, and from what I've seen of the patriarchy, especially lately, I'm really coming around to thinking that maybe his methods are appropriate—"

Cowley couldn't help a shocked laugh. "Are you suggesting that killing Steve Badenhut would lead to—"

And he caught himself up short.

That's exactly what she's suggesting—and what she has specifically threatened to do with that death—and what she perhaps has the power

*to do. And if I go there I'll be two moves from throwing in my lot with
her against my own department.*

He went cold in the pit of his stomach, and was aware of two
things in the space of an instant: first, that Koontz behind the mirror had all but slapped a hand over his, Cowley's mouth, successfully; and second — as a miniscule silence extended with Hannah's
answering eyes firmly on his — that her cause *was* a good one.

Until that moment he had thought of the murder primarily as
a *message* killing, her attempt to expose a rapist, not too far removed from straight vengeance. Suddenly he saw it, as it were,
in a new light — *as* a cause. Cowley knew how much unprose-
cuted rape went on in the country; it was one of those things no
one knew how to fix; it was just woven in. But he saw that this
girl with her recorder could get a lot of people fired and a lot of
people talking, *and by God, that's how change starts.*

But she was still a murderer. And he had to stop her.

Instinctively and almost against his will he changed his voice,
and turned the brief silence into a soft, almost intimate question.
"And is that why you killed him?"

She was silent for a bare moment. "I didn't kill him," she said,
not breaking eye contact.

After another moment he bent to his notepad, heart thumping.
"Please go on with exactly what you said to Chris Kelly at the cafeteria."

She almost said yes. He was sure of it.

~ Hour 3 ~

"How long do you think she can sit there just saying 'I was on
the train' to everything?" Scavelli asked.

"She has no idea how long this can go," murmured Racona.

The observation room was dark and they were sitting in soft chairs, mesmerized by the show in the window. Usually interrogations were boring, predictable affairs, enlivened only by the disgust quotient of what finally got revealed. What was happening now was something like a battle of wills. For hours Cowley had been attacking her alibi, up and down, at every point, and she was sticking to her story. *I slept until about ten-thirty a.m. I don't own a car. I haven't been to the Mayden School in a year and half. I took the nine-thirty train to New York. I boarded the train on Platform 12, the third carriage. The train delay happened at about 10:30 pm, somewhere in Rhode Island. The waitress at Eastern's was named Kimberly Atkins. I don't have keys to anybody's car. I spent most of the time on the train asleep. It took me about five minutes to find a taxi outside Penn Station. I slept until about ten-thirty a.m....* The fatigue of stress and boredom was showing; the girl was slumped back in her chair, her hair falling over her eyes. And yet she was hanging in there. Her young voice coming through the speakers was tired but clear, and her story hadn't varied from her previous accounts by a single detail.

"What the fuck is Cowley doing?" Chief Koontz said, pacing in the dark behind them. "This is going nowhere."

"It's all setup," Racona murmured. "Just wait."

"Maybe she *is* innocent," Scavelli said. "The Mayden School theft could be entirely unrelated...if it even was a theft..."

"Doesn't matter if she is," said Racona. "She can't last."

They were quiet for a few minutes, listening to the back and forth.

"I don't understand what the fuck Cowley is doing," muttered Koontz.

"How long do you think she can just sit there...?" said Scavelli.

~ Hour 5 ~

"I want to play a recording for you," said Cowley.

Hannah raised her eyes under her bangs. *At last*, she thought. *Here it comes.*

She had been waiting for this, and trying to stay ready. She hadn't been lying earlier when she said she was conserving her energy. And yet Cowley had waited out the perfect amount of time for it. She was exhausted — her body was too warm, craving sleep, held up by nervous energy — *and where the hell was McFarrel?* — and moreover she had been *living* in her alibi, envisioning each scene as she retold it. Could she pretend not to have heard the recording? Could she envision — hearing it for the first time? How would she react?

Don't miss a trick. He hasn't said where the recording is from.

He was gone again from the room, as he had been periodically, this time for several minutes. She seemed to feel the invisible attention from behind the mirror perk up. *They've heard it, of course. They know what's coming. Remember, I don't.*

She took a second sip from her water mug.

Cowley returned holding a little open laptop in one hand. He still looked abominably fresh. No, it wasn't fresh, exactly; his shirt was more rumpled, his tie was looser, the stubble on his chin had visibly darkened. But he was fully *here*, and swung with his laptop around the table and into his chair like someone aware of every surface in his vicinity. Hannah had been comparing the interrogation to a fencing match, her usual point of reference, but she realized she was seeing something else in Cowley, something broader-ranging, less rule-bound. *This is how he is in a firefight,* she thought. *This is how he is with a gun.*

As he plugged an audio wire into the laptop she noticed his wedding ring, a simple gold band. *Don't get distracted.* Who was she? Hannah had never thought about it. It's the middle of the night, it's the Christmas season, he's not home, okay it's a weird job, is this normal? Does she know where he is? Does she worry? What *was* his home? Was he eager to get back? Did he explain this to her by way of the media frenzy, the pressure on the case? *When he's finished with me and comes through his front door, how will he – ?*

He held his finger above the laptop and gave her a readying look. No. His focus was total. *She's not there at all, one way or the other. He's here only with me.*

The voices of Andrew Keith and Steve Badenhut emerged tinnily into the interrogation room from an overhead speaker. To Hannah they seemed to fill it. The audio was a few moments back from the point she had selected for leaving on Steve's body; the rapists were in the first flush of realizing that she wasn't coming to the park, that they had been set up.

"This is – from my audio recorder?" she said, leaning forward over the table.

She didn't even look at his response. Her body took over. She had been trying to re-envision how she had felt at Eastern's when she actually heard it for the first time, how it drained the blood from her face to the point where Kimberly Atkins had hurried to her booth to see if she was all right. All that was forgotten. Eastern's arose and dissolved around her and she was in the park itself, in the cold night at the bottom of campus between Edwards dorm and the reservoir, cars passing on the road, her digital audio recorder hidden unsuspected. As Steve started into his big rant, his confession – "So we have to wait through winter break to get ahold of her. That just runs up her taxi fare, man. When she gets back—" she was on her feet, both hands on the table, eyes darting to left and right, an amazed grin on her face.

And when, a minute and thirty seconds later, Cowley clicked the button to cut the audio, she gave him a wild, artless grin, threw a fist in the air, and cried, "It worked!"

It was the perfectly correct reaction. Long afterward, she would realize that the difference from hearing it at Eastern's was the fact that Steve was dead.

Right now she was too caught up in her triumph to think. "The stupid bastard walked right into it!" she crowed to Cowley. "Right into it! Does he go on like that? How much more does he say?"

Cowley was staring at her in surprise, horror, and—she saw it—just a tiny bit of contagious enthusiasm. He let her question hang in the air for a second, then cleared his throat. "Have you ever heard any part of that recording before?"

"No," she breathed in wonderment and satisfaction, sitting back down in her chair. "I, I guess I need to worry about Andrew Keith..."

"Can you tell me at what point in your recording, what time of day, that segment was from?"

"I, it's, I'm guessing it's from six o'clock, right around the rendezvous time. They're giving up, they know they've been had. *No, you're not getting your Biletnikoff back, you bastard!*" she shouted at the laptop. "Sorry," she said to Cowley. "That was tasteless. But that's fantastic stuff. You know, the newspapers said it didn't work, that my recorder got only wind noise, I was ready to believe that. God, no *wonder* the college is suppressing this!"

That flowed directly from her part, fingers at her mouth, but it was meant separately for Cowley and the people behind the mirror. For Cowley, who had given her the secret tip that morning in the mess hall to distrust the Globe, it was as much to say, *see me cover for you – see the act.*

"And is *that* why you killed Steve? To get this recording out past the college walls? Because you knew the college would suppress it?"

He shot that at her fast, but she was ready. "No, *my* plan was to get it out in *court*, in a gang-rape trial against all five of them. The person who killed Steve obviously found –" she sucked a breath through her teeth and shook her head slowly, in a vivid portrayal of imagining someone finding the recorder in the park and listening to the rant, then in a flash she fixed Cowley with a pointed finger. "Because I'll tell you something else, Detective Cowley. What Steve says on there, he meant every word of that. They'll try to say, oh, he's a kid, he lost his temper, he always liked saying shocking stuff. Bull crap. He meant every word. They meant to rape me if I had shown up that night, and he meant to do *all* of that to me when I showed up next semester. No one can ever prove it, but I'm telling *you*."

Why did I say that? Am I overselling it? No...I, I care that he acknowledges it...

"I agree with you," Cowley said in a low voice, holding her eyes with his own. Her breath caught.

"I would have been one of those girls," she said. Now *that* was over-selling it. But it had to be said.

Cowley looked at her levelly. "Too bad this is a recording made without the speaker's consent," he said. "You know it can never be used in court. Either in that trial or yours." And he closed the laptop lid.

~ Hour 6 ~

Detective Scavelli glanced at the observation room door. "I guess he's not coming back," he said. The chief had stepped out, for a rest room break, he had muttered, twenty minutes ago.

"He's gonna miss the moment," Racona grunted. Her eyes were sunken in her sharp profile as she leaned bonelessly back in her seat. In the other room Cowley had been hammering her steadily on her inconsistencies. *Is it believable that someone desperate to get home would sit for seven hours in a train station bar? Is it believable that someone ten steps from the gate would lose track of time and miss the six-fortyfive train? Doesn't it seem like that person wanted an excuse to keep waiting there? Why did you reformat your computer at two-fifteen a.m.? Where were you when you did it? Why do you think Steve Badenhut's killer would drive to New York? Why did you say to Detective Wilson that Steve's situation wouldn't change much? Does it seem strange to you that someone stole and sharpened a fencing sword at Mayden School the day your rapist was murdered with a sharpened fencing sword? Does that look like a coincidence? How likely do you think it is that someone found your hidden recorder in the dark, behind a tree, really? Now, do you think for a minute that your lawyer can defend or explain all that in court by saying "She's innocent, she was on the train?" Isn't it about time you woke up and realized that you're looking at conviction for premeditated murder and life in prison?*

The girl was slumped in her chair, hair over her face, murmuring her faint answers, but she hadn't cracked.

Scavelli shook his head. He was still affected by her reaction to the recording. "I think she's innocent. We're all of us barking up the wrong tree. What do you think?"

Racona tipped her head back slightly and drew a breath

through wide nostrils. "If that's true, then this whole department is fucked. You, me, Koontz at the very least. But she's not getting past Cowley. He's just warming up. There's gonna be a moment."

Scavelli glanced at the observation room door. "Do you think he went home?"

Chief Koontz was not at home. His black police car was parked in the VIP Administration parking lot at Hills College. It was 6:30 am and the campus was pitch dark, with that centuries-abandoned silence institutions have when they're deserted. Athletics Week was long over; everyone was gone; patches of gristly ice shone dully beneath the lamppost globes buzzing with a faint flicker. In all the buildings only one window was lit, at the ground floor, in slivers and shadows as if from a small desk lamp. The shadows moved within.

In the small office Chief Koontz' silhouetted bulk eclipsed the lamp. He shifted position on his feet. "I can assure you, sir, she's going down, right now as we speak. She'll be going to sentencing tomorrow. The evidence against her is solid. But you know, it really hangs or falls on that fencing sword."

"Fencing sword," echoed the man behind the desk. His arm, spreading his hand delicately over his forehead, threw his face into shadow. His voice came faintly. "That it should come to something like that."

"The important point, sir, is that the rape stuff is not gonna come out. That story is not gonna happen. We think she was kinda crazy, maybe killed him to publicize it. You know her better than us."

"I tried to talk to her," the voice said. "It was me who told her — "

"Some people won't listen. But whatever she was after, it's gonna come to nothing. The documents are sealed. Your football program's gonna continue untouched, sir. As you knew it would. The only question is what happens to her. And there you've got an option. Prison, or—"

There was a long silence. The big empty building creaked in the night. The man's face, already low to the desk, was now hidden in his hands. "And if I agree to, to what you say, you'll handle all the details?"

"I give you a script, you play along. There'll be a stir, 'cause there already is one with her, but it won't last long. In a month everybody forgets about it and life around here goes back to normal."

The man looked up and his voice was stronger. "All right, Chief Koontz. If you can promise me that, then I consent."

"Best way," said Koontz.

~ Hour 8 ~

Cowley looked at his face in the bathroom mirror. He had left Hannah alone in the room, as he had from time to time, and now he found himself reluctant to go back. Protocol gave him up to five minutes to let a prisoner stew; he had already exceeded that.

It was morning, and he was getting nowhere. The station was coming alive around them. On his way to the rest room he had passed a fresh Sanders in the hall, who threw him an incredulous stare: *You're still at it?*

Nothing was working. His system was collapsing around him. He had pointed out inconsistency after inconsistency in her statements, but they were never quite enough to throw her. She still clung stubbornly to her simple story: *I was on the train, I was on the train, I was on the train.* He had played the Badenhut audio, and the result was only to convince everyone behind the mirror of her innocence. *I was just going home, Detective. I was on the train.*

He had gone after her assumptions, as he had told Koontz he would, trying his best to warn her that her audio recorder could *not* appear in court, that she was doing all this for nothing. But Detective goddamn Wilson had said it would be admissible and the girl had armored herself in that, and Cowley could only go so far without putting evidence of Boston police corruption on the transcript.

He then hit hard on the prospect that she would *lose* in court, and go to jail for life. It had been easy to convince her that McFarrel was hopelessly overconfident, and on this front technically he had "won:" she had agreed on record to the implausibility of anyone else killing Badenhut and of her own actions at South Station, and the transcript would count against her in a trial. But she hadn't broken, and indeed had behaved *almost* in the manner of an innocent person. "I don't care how it looks, Detective. My defense will be that I was on the train—because *I was on the train!*" Here's where his gut sensed a gap, something missing, a little smiling secret behind her naivete that she almost wished him to share. *But what?*

He sighed. He was losing his ability to tell truth from lies. Just before stepping out of the room he had asked her to describe the taxi she supposedly took from Penn Station to her parents' apartment, and she had floored him by describing the driver in detail and spelling his last name. If she was resorting to bald invention then she was close to cracking—*but why did it have the ring of truth? But why would she have memorized it—?*

Could she be innocent? Scavelli and even Racona thought so now. His certainty that she wasn't came from his gut, a place that had never failed him; it had said so from the beginning and it still said so. But what if it was wrong? He was obscurely aware that interrogating this girl was becoming a crisis in his life. He had been bored with cases lately; the perps were so stupid. *What if I've made her the criminal I always wanted? What if she was just – a girl on a train?*

She was certainly as tough as he was. Even if she was innocent, the girl was the toughest innocent he had ever seen. In fact, if she *was* innocent, then afterw –

God, I've been at this too long, he thought, and poured more cold water over his face. His dripping, exhausted expression stared back at him.

No. She asked for this interrogation. Why? If all she wanted was a trial she wouldn't need this. She had asked for him in particular. What for? Why choose to undergo this? What is she playing for?

Time, came the answer. She's waiting for something.

What was it she had said, right back at the beginning? "Evidence!" "The lot of you have a complete disregard for evidence!" And a few days ago she had called her lawyer about getting the security tapes from the train stations. No! She went *behind her lawyer's back* for them. O'Brien had relayed the conversation. Then today she *fought* with her lawyer – was it over that? He, McFarrel, wouldn't want to touch the tapes because he thinks she's not on them; even if he believed she was innocent, maybe she's muddied out. So they fight about it, she loses, storms back to her cell, comes in here spitting about her stupid lawyer. She couldn't convince him. Why not?

Because there was something she couldn't tell him. That she

knows she's on those tapes. *Because she made sure she was.*

Stupid lawyer. Idiot theory. All of us insisting she never was on the train.

No area footage of her leaving South Station at 9:30 pm. None at the exits, none on the streets. Where did she go from Eastern's?

I was on the train, I was on the train, I was on the train.

What if she *did* board the train? *Could you still — if you had a car — and a day to plan it — ?*

"Holy shit," Cowley said aloud into his reflection's wide eyes.

"I have a theory," he said to Hannah, coming back into the room. For the first time in a while he noticed her water cup: it was still full. *She doesn't want to pee,* he thought. *She heard what I said about needing my permission to leave, and she didn't want to put herself in that position.* So she had gone the whole way in the hot room without either drinking or using the rest room. He felt an almost tender admiration for her.

She looked the worse for wear. He could guess that she hadn't slept well in jail, and here was another sleepless night. She pulled herself upright in her chair with an effort, as if coming out of a doze, and brushed her hair out of her face. Her voice caught, and as if reading his thoughts she permitted herself a full swallow of water. She set the mug down near the edge of the table and looked at him with clear eyes. "What theory?" she said.

Cowley remained standing, in the far corner under the camera. "That after leaving Eastern's you did board the 9:30 train."

He got a reaction: an expression of almost shocked delight on her face. What came out was: "Oh my God, is it true? Are you *finally* accepting that I was on the train that night?"

"My theory is that someone could board the train to New York and still kill Steve Badenhut. Wait! Hear me out." He had her full attention, and probably those of the two behind the mirror as well; his ejaculation was almost more for their benefit. "Now, this person would need a car, and also a head start, they would have to get started early in the morning, when you say you were asleep in your dorm. They would run a few errands first to set things up, for instance they would need disguises, big old shabby coats and whatnot, so they would go pick those up at thrift stores somewhere. Now, if this person also knew about the footlocker at Mayden School, with the metalworking equipment, and knew that the school was on winter break, well, they might swing their car by there before sun-up, and break in and prepare the murder weapon."

"This again. *Come on.* I told you, I—"

"Here's the trick. They then *leave* their car parked at a station a little ways down the line from Boston, maybe Back Bay, probably with the murder weapon in the trunk. Then they go back to school, pretend they just woke up, they hobnob around, say their goodbyes, and they're witnessed leaving for New York. Now they go to South Station and wait for the train. But not any train. Only the last train of the night will do, because this person wants to be sure to catch Steve in his bedroom. That's a long wait, but they sit it out, and they're witnessed sitting it out."

"Right, right, right—so far I've heard this theory before." Her voice was sarcastic, as it had often been, but her affect was completely different: she was wide awake and her measuring eyes were looking up at him with an extraordinary mixture of fear and encouragement.

"The killer then *boards* the nine-thirty train, and is seen by the security cameras, then once aboard puts on a disguise and gets right off again at Back Bay. They get in that pre-positioned car, drive back to Hills College, still in their disguise of shapeless clothes, the one in the photo I showed you, they take the murder weapon out of the trunk, they stop to collect the audio recorder from the park that's very close by, then they head up to the dorms and—"

"Hang on. There are children present." She gestured at the mirror without taking her eyes off him. "Is this person walking around with their cellphone in their pocket?"

Cowley paused. "No," he said, putting it together for the first time. "The killer has left their cellphone on the train."

"Oh, very clever!"

"Because *after* they—" Hannah pointed a warning finger at the mirror, and Cowley chuckled—"after *the deed*, the killer gets back in her car, drives to meet the train, probably at some stop nearest New York, like New Haven, and reboards it. Still in disguise. Then, safe in the train, she changes back into her normal clothes, and makes sure she's seen by the security cameras when she disembarks at Penn Station. Presto, she's committed a murder in Boston while riding the Amtrak to New York."

Cowley couldn't tell why he had played along with her gag about the mirror, only that he'd been chasing genuine rapport all night and he had finally got it. The game at the moment was congratulation at the scheme, and he was so tired and focused that he couldn't tell how much was real emotion and how much was faked. And he knew she was riding the same wavelength when she met his eyes with a wide smile and said, "Bravo!" Then she dropped her smile like a stone, looked into the mirror with her hard face reflected, and the bottom fell out. "The times don't add up," she said.

"What?"

She looked back at him. "You think you're the first person to come at me with that? Add up the times. Your theory makes no sense. That train gets into New Haven at, what, midnight or something. That's less than half an hour after your murder, and it's at *least* a hundred-mile drive from Hills College. It can't be done. It's ridiculous."

Suddenly the feeling of rapport was gone. Cowley's eyes moved as he made rapid calculations, feeling like he had just made a fool of himself on video. Her voice was cold, as if she had set him up for this, but her tired face was a strange mask: it still contained a germ of encouragement, of *challenge*, and he understood that he hadn't *lost* rapport, she had *switched* it—and he understood this denunciation was for the benefit of the people behind the mirror.

"*Who* suggested that to you?" he asked stupidly.

"And what about the call to my parents I made from the train? How could I make it if I left my cellphone behind on the, on the—"

To his astonishment her sentence quavered upward into a scream and for the first time since he had seen her her eyes were filling with tears. "I mean how many goddamn ridiculous theories are you going to throw at me?" she shrieked. "I'm *sick* of this! I didn't kill Steve Badenhut! I don't know *how* to kill anyone! You and my stupid lawyer who's probably home drunk, you all throw this crazy shit at me because I'm smart! Because I'm smart! None of you would throw stupid James Bond theories at a normal girl. But I write for the newspaper and the dean hates my articles and I'm a strange intellectual feminist and so you're at liberty to invent all this impossible—*I was on the train! I was going home!* Your *times* don't add up!" She buried her face in her arms on the table and her shoulders shook.

Cowley stood stock still in horror. His mind was racing in multiple directions at once. Maybe his theory was ridiculous, his professional reputation ruined—or maybe it wasn't Back Bay—but his gut said this whole performance was for *them*—the people behind the mirror. It was her innocent defense; this was how an innocent person breaks. And it *was* a performance, his whole body told him so, and it would win. He was going to have to give the poor prisoner a break, maybe call the interrogation. He stood tongue-tied. *But he was close, dammit, close to—*

The door of the interrogation room swung wide open without a knock—an extraordinary breach—and into the room walked a man in a steel-grey three-piece suit: none other than Julian Early, the Boston Commissioner of Police. Hard on his heels was McFarrel. At the same moment the lights went on in the room behind the mirror, and there was the sound of many rapid footsteps in the hall.

"Detective Cowley, cease this interrogation and release that girl!" the Commissioner ordered.

What happened next happened so fast that it was almost simultaneous. Cowley, in shock, had started to move forward from the back of the room. Hannah, in her chair with the door behind her, had perked alertly up at the first turn of the doorknob, and as she turned to look her elbow knocked the mug of water, positioned right at the table edge, off the table. As it fell to the floor she slightly moved her left foot—he *saw* it, but wouldn't realize it until later—to intercept the mug and ricochet it under the table. There was a loud clatter, a spray of water almost across the Commissioner's black shoes—the end of his command came together with a startled step back—and instinctively Cowley went into catch mode, ducking under the table for the mug.

Under the table he found himself face to face with Hannah. Clear-faced, smiling, radiant in the dimness, she winked, whispered "Don't give up," and passed the mug from her hand into his with a warm press of her fingers.

The next instant they were both on their feet in a congeries of moving bodies, startled "Whoa!"s, apologies, overriding commands. Scavelli, Racona, and others were in the room. Commissioner Early had a hand on Hannah's shoulder that was at once steadying and displaying as he continued to talk over the minor disruption:

"This girl is innocent, gentlemen. Mr. McFarrel has submitted new evidence that clearly shows she was aboard the train to New York at the time of the murder. This is a DVD he has kindly prepared showing the requisite security camera footage of her, from multiple cameras, at South and Penn stations, and this, Mr. Cowley," he said, handing the thin-boxed disc and a sheet of paper to him together, "is Miss Radhe's cellphone track, which you'll see shows that she was on the train, in Rhode Island, at eleven-thirty when the football player was killed at HC."

Nobody had seen! From the observation room the underside of the table was out of view. If the video camera could see it, his own body would have blocked the shot. His right hand still wore a stunned warmth; his mind reeled; he held the evidence pieces unconsciously together with the empty mug. Hannah was smiling up at the Commissioner in her orange outfit and not failing to send a pointed look across at McFarrel; she wasn't looking at him at all. The Commissioner was. "I don't need to say, gentlemen, that I am not happy with the performance of the division in this..." he began, and as his commentary lighthoused slowly around the room Cowley realized that Hannah *had* used him, picked him and used him from the beginning (and he thought he knew why), and that all through the long waiting hours of this interrogation she had outfenced him at every step. She *wanted* him to know that she was guilty, guilty as fuck, gaily guilty, and now he *did* know it, knew it silenced and alone in a crowded room, and before the practical consequences of that could begin to sink in, what he seemed to hear was her voice, from back at the Peabodys' house, saying: "We can move fast when we have to."

"Mr. McFarrel, I hand the prisoner over to you," the Commissioner said. And to Hannah he said, "Miss Radhe, all charges against you are dropped and you are free to go."

Chapter 13 - Confessed

She still wants a trial.

Cowley lay in bed, still in his wrinkled and sour clothes, less shoes and tie, in the same position where he had fallen upon coming home at 9:00 am. Now it was past 1:00; he had woken to a room floodlit from sun on snow outside, the distant groan of a snowblower. Downstairs he heard soft thumps in the kitchen, a low jangle of digital sound from a video game on the television: Karen and Ricky trying to be quiet.

Well, she's not going to get one.

Am I okay with that?

He understood at last exactly where Hannah stood, and it put him in the most impossible position of his life. Her goal was to get to the public platform of a trial. She had constructed an ingenious alibi that had gotten her released, which was, now, to her, a double-edged sword. He saw at last the nature of her argument with McFarrel: she *had* been on the train when she killed Steve Badenhut (God knows how) and she had all along been willing to go to trial, because she trusted her *evidence* to get her off.

But now she wasn't going to trial—not unless *he*, dogged investigator that he was, kept the heat on her, figured out how she did it, and forced her there. Being released with charges dropped didn't mean she was proven innocent: she was still a suspect in what was now a completely open murder case and could be re-arrested on new evidence at any time. *He* had the power to make

that happen—and only he.   And she—*the damn fool girl!*—she
wanted him to. She was *counting* on him to.

He groaned, a dissonant counterpoint to the snowblower. She
thought that by going to trial, the whole story of the rape would
come out: Badenhut's vicious rant, the transcript of her statement
in New York, even the confessions he had extracted from Chris
Kelly and Reggie Mathis. She *thought* that the prosecution would
need the rape as motive, that they would require her digital audio
recorder to even describe the scene. *That's why she put it on his
naked chest—*

Except he knew it wouldn't happen. Even if Koontz *let* her get
to a trial, what was on that recorder wouldn't come out. The fix
would be in. The audio wouldn't be admitted, the prosecution
would trot out a dozen character witnesses to testify to her opinion of the patriarchy and Hannah Radhe would be sent to prison
for the premeditated murder of Steve Badenhut without bending
a blade of Hills College AstroTurf.

Justice.

He rolled over in bed, coughed, and spat into the wicker basket
filled with tissues. Karen's cold was apparently still with her; was
it time to take her back to the doctor? No—it had actually been
only a few days, hard as that was to believe.

Or he could do nothing.

Let the murder go unsolved. Conviction for pre-med was life.
She had tried in her own way to change a rotten system and failed.
As far as the rest of the world was concerned right now, she was
innocent. *Why not let her go?* And anyway right now he had no
proof that she was the murderer, and no idea how she *could* have
been.

On the bedside table he saw the yellow sticky note covered

with pencil marks, on the folded Amtrak schedule, and groped for it. He remembered that just before falling into bed and oblivion he had worked out train and car times for a rendezvous. He stared at his notes, and growled aloud, this time in harmony with the snowblower. She was right: it didn't add up. It couldn't be done. And yet she did it. She had admitted it. *How? What was he missing?*

And should he care?

On that nonverbal note he got up, peeled off his disgusting clothes, and stamped into the bathroom. He took a very long, very hot shower, shaved, brushed his teeth, and dressed again in a fresh version of his usual slacks and white shirt. He left the tie and his holster on the closet hangers; he had the day off, and he would do his best not to worry about the situation. His stomach growled, in blithe animal disregard for moral dilemmas above. The video game sounds were already at normal volume as he came down the stairs.

It was the first day he had been able to spend at home in a while, and the first since Ricky had come in, but he was preoccupied throughout. Things were uncomfortable with Ricky anyway; the boy had grown the fuzzed head and steroidal body of a soldier without losing his teenage attitude of superiority, and his Navy sneer made silent comment on a father who needed a quiet house to sleep after a night of "talk." The only subject he was willing to discuss with Cowley these days was guns, to which Karen objected listening, so they maneuvered around each other in the small rooms with noncommittal grunts and agreed to go out to a movie. Karen was still pursed-lipped about his unscheduled overnight, and as they had already eaten Cowley made himself a grilled cheese sandwich with jalapenos and a coffee.

She could do it because the train was delayed.

He excused himself from his half-eaten sandwich and stepped upstairs with his cellphone. A call to Amtrak with his badge number confirmed that the 9:30 pm southbound train on December 15, that had been delayed an hour and a half en route, had arrived in New York at 3:45 am, and at the New Haven station at 2:00 am, two and a half hours after Steve was killed. New pencil scribbles on a fresh yellow sticky, and now the math worked. *But how could she know it would?*

And *what* was he was going to say at work tomorrow? Was he or wasn't he going to walk in and say to Koontz, "I still think she's guilty?" Conscience to the side, he saw no happy outcome to that conversation. But at least he could say he'd tried. *Say to whom?* he asked himself. "You might as well go into the office if you're just going to think about your case all day," Karen sniped.

And what would Koontz do now? He hadn't looked at the news but the media must be ripping him and the department a new one every hour on the hour. Had they even put a gag order on Hannah? Was she already giving interviews? He resisted the temptation to call in, or reclaim the TV from Ricky's video games.

Halfway through the dumb superhero movie at the Capitol Theater he got out of his seat and turned his cellphone back on. With a finger in his ear in the lobby he called Amtrak again. What was the *cause* of the train delay, December 15, 9:30 Southbound? A long pause, computer clacks, a barely audible monotone: *Blown transfawma.* And were there any notes as to the cause of the blowout? Feeling now as surreal and implausible as the movie he'd just left. A louder sigh, a longer pause, wider-spaced clacks: *Just blown.* He went back to his seat, shaking his head at himself.

The next morning when he tiptoed down into the kitchen

before dawn in tie and holster he still had no plan for what he was going to do. *I could do nothing. I could let a murderer who I know is guilty go free.* He had spent a miserable night, kept half-awake by Karen's coughing, interspersed with vivid half-dozing dreams of Hannah's smiling face in a bright circle under the table. *I'm going to end by going crazy,* he thought as he unlatched the back door and bent to the brush doormat for the Globe.

Then he was in the kitchen with the paper thrown onto the table under the light, unconscious of noise. His eyes hadn't deceived him. The banner headline read:

BOMBSHELL CONFESSION IN BADENHUT DORM KILLING; HC FENCING COACH BAILEY COMES FORWARD

His eyes zig-zagged down the paragraphs:

> Hills College fencing coach Jacques Bailey yesterday gave a full confession to the sensational fencing sword murder of...standing shoulder-to-shoulder with Police Chief Koontz...friend and mentor to Radhe...believed her false rape accusation against Badenhut...also knew of her hidden recorder...inflamed by her story decided to take vengeance himself...collected Radhe's recorder in a confused attempt to leave a message...unable to bear seeing Radhe accused of his crime at last decided to come forward...Chief Koontz statement...

"Koontz you unbelievable son of a bitch," he said aloud. Then the front door slammed behind him, and his wakened wife and son heard his car slew on the driveway ice and gun away through the dark Arlington neighborhood.

Forty minutes later as he came through the doors of the station his cellphone buzzed in his pocket and he pulled it out. The text was from Hannah Radhe:

> Are you okay with this?

His life was getting more surreal by the second.

> No

he texted back. Four steps across the lobby he stopped and sent another text:

> Confess!

He stood glaring at the screen for half a minute, then shoved the phone in his pocket and continued his march. As he reached the department door it buzzed again:

> I know

A few long seconds later came another:

> Maybe

He suddenly felt as close to her as in that moment under the table. And it occurred to him that this could be the perfect outcome. If Radhe confessed there would be no trial, and she could let McFarrel plea-bargain her down to a light sentence rather than life...

He strode down the hall and into the homicide room; it felt like he hadn't seen his desk in weeks. There were three or four guys in their cubicles under the fluorescent lights; they all looked up. Koontz was in his glassed-in office with the door open.

Cowley left it open and they both started loud. "Koontz there is no way in hell I'm going to let you send an innocent man down for this," he said.

"And how do *you* know he's innocent? He's given a full confession." Koontz rose to his feet behind the desk.

"Yeah and I know exactly the how and why of how *that* happened. Hannah Radhe is the murderer. I am not going to let you send some patsy down in her place."

"Hannah Radhe is innocent, Cowley, or did you miss that? The Commissioner said so himself."

"I can get her to confess."

"You had your chance at that two nights ago and you chose to pussyfoot all around her."

Cowley lowered his voice. "It's different now. She's willing to confess to save Bailey — maybe. Let me — "

"And Bailey's willing to confess to save her! What the fuck is the difference?"

Voices went back up. "Bailey has an iron-clad alibi! I took it myself!"

"Radhe was in fucking Rhode Island! Bailey was a lot closer than that! Cowley you're obsessed and you're about half an inch from an enforced leave!"

"Chief — " Voice lowered again. "If I *can* get Radhe to confess — right now — today — "

"*Cowley* — ! Fuck it — " Koontz shoved around past him and slammed his door, and the two men stood lapel to lapel. It was Koontz' turn to speak in a lowered voice. "If you pulled Hannah Radhe into my office this minute and she confessed, I would reject it as a false confession. I would say that she was trying to save her dear coach and mentor, and I would turn her around and send her home. Bailey is a slam dunk. No fucking *train*, no fucking premed, he's willing to plead heat-of-the-moment and a struggle in the room and do a couple years, and by then the whole thing will have blown over. See? Nobody gets hurt, everybody's happy, problem solved. You wanna get in the way of that? With what? Your girlfriend is innocent, Cowley. Get it through your head."

"She did it," Cowley muttered.

"Oh yeah? How?" Cowley didn't answer, and the chief went on, "You know what? I don't care if she's fucking Spiderman and killed him with X-Ray vision from Rhode Island. This case is over. Done. We have the perp and everything's wrapped up in time for Christmas. Go out to Pete's, have a whiskey or two, and come back to your desk ready to work like a goddamn cop."

He threw open his door.

"I don't like it," Cowley said.

"I don't care."

Cowley returned to his desk and sat down. He wouldn't give Koontz the satisfaction of storming out. He started mechanically organizing his folders without seeing them. After five minutes he pulled out his cellphone and texted:

> No go. They won't accept it anyway.

A few seconds later he added:

> You can stop worrying.

Twenty seconds passed. Then a text came back:

> Have him pick the tree.

Cowley blinked. He knew exactly what she meant.

Her idea was naive, but—there might be a way. He shot a glance at Koontz in his office, then got up and walked out of the room. He picked a deserted spot in the hallway, leaned against the wall, and texted:

> I'll need Det Wilson's map. You'll have to release it. Have her send to me.

According to her statement from New York, Hannah had drawn an exact map for Detective Wilson, meant to guide the police to the specific tree to find the recorder. The statement had been sealed but the map, released to Boston separately, wasn't. If anyone here had it, it would be Detective Solsberger, and Cowley didn't want to go through him.

> OK. What else

Cowley took a deep breath.

> I'll need you. Tonight.

There was a long pause, then a buzz.

> OK

And there followed two more from her:

> I'm at the Peabodys

> I bring my boyfriend too

The last one startled Cowley. What was that about? Did she not trust him? It was true that the last time he drove off with her from the Peabodys' it had been to jail. He rolled his eyes. Well, he had no room to negotiate:

> OK

There followed a few more texts to set up the time, and the email address for Cowley to receive the map. Cowley gave his personal one. Then they signed off.

He hadn't seen Coach Bailey's confession statement, but he had read the same thing in the newspaper that Hannah obviously had: the claim that she had told Bailey about her hidden recorder, and Bailey had gone himself to pick it up. Both of them knew that wasn't true: Bailey had never been told of the recorder's existence and would have no idea where it had been hidden.

A quick question to the desk sergeant confirmed that Bailey was in holding downstairs. *The noble idiot.* All Cowley needed to do was issue a simple request to release a suspect for verification in field; he would pick a few officers he knew to move him. He was in luck that the killer, whoever it was (Cowley chuckled through his teeth), had moved the recorder to Badenhut's room in the dark. That meant Bailey's verification test was best done at night. Hannah, as the person who planted the recorder, would be present to confirm the right tree; since she was no longer in custody she was simply a private citizen requested by the police to assist. There was nothing illegal or improper about the procedure. It would merely all be done behind Koontz' back.

And the findings would be entered in Bailey's record, pretty much exploding his confession.

The day went fast. Cowley had a lot of paperwork left over from other cases that he needed to complete, and he immersed himself in it with a cold, steady focus that kept all his other thoughts at bay. He didn't think about what would happen to the investigation after Bailey was cleared. He wouldn't think about suspicion falling back on Hannah and whether or not he wanted that. He daren't think about the fact that he was embarked on insubordination for the first time in his career. And he couldn't begin to consider the deep problems of an alliance with Hannah over this.

Chapter 14 - The Triangular Park

It was a full house at the Peabodys' big colonial home in Newton, with Hannah's parents settled into the upstairs guest room, Randall put up in the den since Tuesday, and Hannah now in the upstairs small bedroom, and it was perfectly plausible for Hannah and Randall to beg an evening alone to go out to a movie. The rooms and the slightest contacts within them were still ringing with joy and amazement at Hannah's liberation, the tears and champagne toasts, the final handshakes with a rueful McFarrel, the explosion of Christmas decorations (the Peabodys had insisted they stay for the holiday), the ongoing noise and music of the end of her ordeal. Her parents, who had happily signed two pages of release conditions prohibiting Hannah from publicly commenting on the case, were absurdly delighted at the movie idea. Her father pressed forty dollars into her hand saying "Go! Have a wonderful, wonderful, normal night out! God bless you two!"

Five blocks from the house they waited on the corner of Valentine Street in the deserted darkness, heads down in their coats against the 20° wind that carried a brittle glitter of snow particles under the pines in the single streetlight.

"Your father doesn't like me," said Randall.

"Oh, everyone's a little weird right now."

"No, he really doesn't like me. If this ends with you getting arrested again tonight I'm never showing my face around here again. I'm moving to Timbuktu."

It was true that even here there remained an element of the inexplicable to Hannah's relationship with Randall Skokar. At school, that they were an item had confused everyone who knew them; he was as out of place with her toned fencing teammates as she was amid the ill-laundered dark clothes of his role-playing gamer circle. They had met at the beginning of the school year when she took an interest in the male subculture around comic books; someone had pointed him out as having the biggest comic collection on campus, and she had simply knocked on his door and asked if she could read them. For about a week she would show up at his dorm room and sit on the end of his bed flipping through issues and taking notes, while he stood around or sat and answered questions. One night she had looked up. "Are you okay? You seem nervous," she said.

He had sighed, rolled his eyes, shrugged, and finally burst out, "I'm just not used to having really pretty girls hanging out in my room. It makes me act—weird. It's a biological thing."

She had looked at him in a sudden silence. She had never tried to be really pretty. "I'm not immune to it either," she said softly.

She liked Randall. He was smart, completely gentle, and yet not at all shy, striding through the world as if through a half-imaginary place that gave him license to go anywhere and try anything. While he had never thrown a punch in his life he was accompanied by queer appurtenances of warfare and spycraft: he had a display of samurai swords on his wall, was something like a fully-fledged historian of arms and armor, and dabbled to an unknown extent in computer encryption and the Internet hacking community. His gamer world was, first of all, *not* all male, to Hannah's interest, and second quite open-doored; his friends accepted her into their circle as a sort of odd, half-Kryptonian mascot, while *her* friends wanted nothing to do with him. Somehow they made it to the end of the semester together, and to her invitation to come up to New York after Christmas that was such a big step.

This week had been a slightly bigger one.

Publicly he was the hero of the hour, fawned over by Radhes and Peabodys alike, but he was right that their congratulations had a slight undercurrent of something else. He had gone behind their lawyer's back to get the security tapes, and though his risk had paid off gloriously, they did not necessarily evaluate him as the person to have been entrusted with taking it. It would have been useless for Hannah to insist that the risk was hers. As Christmas Day approached, it was beginning to be wondered why Randall was still there.

Worse was that her own attitude to him was tangled in knots. Of course she had to play the liberated innocent game to Randall as well as to everyone else, but the cost was higher. There were two things he was absolutely entitled to receive from her after his triumph, and she could give neither, and she watched with dismay his whip-smart intelligence turn back on itself as increased distance. But then she felt that distance from everything around her. To be back in the Peabody house with its white carpets and cabinets of china figurines was to be back in the world of lies and evasions, agreeing to celebratory stupidities like the stupidity of the Boston police for ever having suspected her. She let the family chalk up her reticence about prison to recovery and treat her with consequent delicacy, while she alone knew that their own world was fragile as a glass bubble. She had raised the hammer herself: she had set Cowley on the hunt. Alone at night, tossing and turning in the little bed under the shelf of old children's books, she was imagining where his wolf-like eyes were turning, what scent he was on, what he would find. The thrift store that sold her the disguises? Eric the Radio Shack clerk? *The fire pump itself?* She wished she could somehow *guide* him, but she couldn't make the slightest peep of guilt, and anyway she had no way to contact him.

In the end she had to accept that she could very well go to trial with the fire pump sitting on the evidence table, and everything that implied. *As long as I get to take my shot*, she whispered to the dark ceiling where only John Brown might hear her. But by day she lived in a suffocating suspense for the moment when the phone would ring and shatter the dream in which she had to participate.

Oddly, her one moment of clarity came when the phone did ring. It was late afternoon on the very day of her release, and she had woken from an uneasy nap to find herself in an animated all-hands discussion in the livingroom about whether she was really going to "return to her plan" by continuing to press charges against the other four rapists next semester. She had forgotten all about that. "After everything you've been through, honey," was her parents' refrain, and as she tried in a strange bewilderment to discern what position Hannah *would* take if Hannah *was* going to have a next semester, Mike Peabody passed the phone to her father and a silence fell over the room at the sight of Mr. Radhe's face.

"Mm-hm. Mm-hm. I see," was all they heard, as Hannah stood rooted to the carpet, and then he extended the receiver to her. "This call is really for you, honey. I think you should listen."

"Hannah?" said the gravelly, familiar male voice. "This is

Dean Haughton, calling from Hills. I want to extend my congratulations at your release. We're all delighted to hear how it turned
out, but let me say that I personally never doubted for a moment
in your innocence. No matter what the papers said about you, I
told everyone, 'That's not the Hannah Radhe of Hills College I
know.'"

"I'm glad to hear it," said Hannah. *Considering you're the likely
author of everything the newspapers said.* She glanced around at everyone staring at her. "What can I do for you, Dean?"

"Well, I've just been speaking with your father. This dreadful
murder has been a terrible shock to Hills, to all of us. The school —
the school is in grief. Next semester is going to be a time for coming together, to mourn and to heal. If you were to intrude on that
with your rape allegations, if that was your intent, well, I'm hoping you agree that such would be tasteless, very tasteless. I'm calling to make sure that that's how you feel."

"I—I don't know how I feel," she said, conscious of her father's
sad eyes on her.

"Let me help you decide." Haughton's tone sharpened.
"Think about this: you have no proof. Your silly plan to get the
boys angry with your audio recorder and your little ambush,
which was a very mean thing to do, failed. The police are holding
that recorder, and they'll continue to, and anyway it has — they've
assured me it has nothing on it but wind in the trees. So you have
nothing."

He's calling to gloat, Hannah realized. *Openly.* Indeed, with the
case unsolved the cops would continue to hold the deadly recorder along with all crime scene evidence, effectively burying it.
To Haughton her release was as good as a life sentence: she was
equally disarmed of her weapon. *He's won — he squelched the rape*

threat and restored the status quo. All that's left is to bully me into shutting up. She licked her lips. "Funny," she said, "it's my impression that there's something quite audible on it. But I guess when they catch Steve's actual murderer we'll both find out, because it will be part of the court case, won't it?"

There was a pause, in which she could almost hear him thinking: *Has she heard it too? How?* He made a dismissive sound in his throat. "Regardless, the important matter for Hills is to put all that behind us. I told your father I'm sending you a letter that retracts all sexual assault allegations you've made, both here and in New York. Sign it, and we'll welcome you back to the community for the rest of your term here. Don't, and we won't. It's that simple. We really can't afford to have any feminist disruptions in our time of grief."

The call had added another pitch of meaningless complexity to the debate with her parents, as well as forced her to say a few words at large about her interrogation with Cowley, which she very much hadn't wanted to do, and even as she stared hypnotically at Haughton's letter with its dandled comfort of returning to a normal life at college, she nursed a core of almost fevered impatience for the trial to come. *Just let me take my shot*, she repeated silently, teeth clenched.

Then her shot was taken away from her in the Globe's banner headline about Coach Bailey.

She looked at Randall's silhouette against the snowy streetlight, his hands in the pockets of his black trench coat. Her reasons for inviting him on this errand were confused, along with everything else. She told him that the police needed her to confirm some campus details of Bailey's statement, and she wanted to do it secretly from the household for fear they would all pile on, but that she needed moral support. She had thus succeeded in the space of a minute in awakening all his suspicions, but he was as game for it as he would have been for an impromptu journey to Pluto, and he was now standing in the freezing cold alongside her with no questions asked.

Headlights swung around the curve and the squad car came to a stop beside them. Cowley was alone, hatless, at the wheel. Hannah and Randall climbed into the back seat and the car moved off.

"This is my boyfriend, Randall Skokar. Randall, this is Detective Cowley, who's been handling the case."

"Nice to meet you, Detective," said Randall. The back of Cowley's head nodded once, above the collar of a black jacket. Hannah was glad that the car was dark, to conceal the hot flush she felt come over her face.

Seeing Cowley again, even from the back against meteoring streetlights, illuminated Chinese restaurant signs, and roving green bus windows, was a shock of physical intimidation. Eight hours of police interrogation had left their mark. Despite the flurry of how it had ended, and their strangely copacetic texts since then, the shape of his head pulled her immediately back into the room with the mirror. A room, a world, of savage power, of fighting for life, where he belonged, where he was her enemy. *As he still is*, she thought dizzily. After all, what was this mutual effort to save Coach Bailey about, if not to clear the decks for their own duel? Not that either of them could mention it.

What has he found so far? What is he going to do? What does he feel?

"And the coach?" she asked, after a moment.

"He'll meet us there," came the curt reply.

No one said another word until they arrived at the bottom of the Hills College campus.

Alongside the little triangular park were already a police van and an unmarked dark car, lights off. A knot of figures in black jackets and black knit hats stood over the snow in a moving jigsaw of multiple flashlights. No one else was around. Cowley made the turn, passed them on his right, and parked some fifty yards further up on the road. Ahead of them the road continued past Edwards and up the hill toward the empty main campus, waiting through winter break for the next semester. They got out. The cold was more aural here, the wind soughing panoramically through the snowy woods on the hill above the single bench, a fresh murmur of waters coming from the reservoir just beyond the foot of the road. The only light was the fitful gloam of the city on the low clouds and bright sloppy pools from the streetlights at the edge of the road. From the knot of cops a couple of flashlights flared in their direction; Hannah saw the gleam of rifle barrels.

"Wait here," Cowley said, and strode off toward the others. In a moment he was huddled with the group by the van, his dark jacket blending with theirs. At a silent hand signal three figures detached and moved quickly without sound to positions around the park, crossing the open snow and vanishing effectively against the shadow of the woods.

Hannah took Randall's hand. Suddenly she didn't want to be here. This was nothing like what she had imagined when agreeing to come: these were professional cops executing a job in the night, and she felt like an unwanted spectator of something illicit, dangerous. She knew they were here secretly, and why, but to see a unit of black-cloaked police working swiftly in the dark with guns and signals was frightening. She didn't know why; ordinarily she would have been interested in the tactics. But she suddenly felt that all sorts of things could go wrong here, and badly. *Was* the campus empty? Where was Coach Bailey — in the van?

Her heart was beating fast. She looked across the snowy field at the bench just under the hill, and another scene repossessed her. The last time she was here she had crossed to that bench, heavy in her disguise with a sharpened sword under her coat, and leaned far over to pick up her audio recorder in its baggie. Then — she glanced left, at where she had collected her Skype "baby monitor." Her heart started thumping harder, and she tore her eyes from that spot. Had Cowley seen her look? Had she given it away? Even from a distance she felt his eyes on her. *No, no, this won't do at all*, she thought, looking hard at the ground. *Whom did he really bring here to test?*

"We should make notes," said Randall. "We're going to need good details of the movie we're supposed to be seeing."

"Yeah," she said weakly.

He squeezed her hand. "Is it hard to be back on campus, after what happened with those guys?"

She looked at him. His voice had a flat, artless sympathy, tracing all the changes in her to the sexual assault, about which he knew only the outlines. And yet he had named something she hadn't known was there. She *wasn't* comfortable being back at Hills College, not yet. It was in this very spot that Steve had boasted to Andrew Keith and perhaps others of his plan to torture and murder her; she had heard him live, then a second time recently, and the hate-filled promises came back to her ears as if still hovering over the cold snow. For all she knew Andrew Keith and the rest of the football team might still be planning to harm her next semester. *They* didn't know why Steve had been killed; all they had was the false narrative of the newspapers; there had been no reform, no greater light, nothing but escalated enmity and re-inforced impunity. Next time would be worse. In fact she could never come back to Hills on these terms. *This is what it means for Haughton to win.* The dark campus seemed to seethe with angry, meaningless violence — some of it her own.

Randall knew nothing of these larger things, and even the out-lines of her sexual assault clearly made him uncomfortable. Yet he was squeezing her hand and offering only warmth.

"Mm-hm," she said, nodding. She realized that she actually *did* need him for moral support. She squeezed back.

"Well just remember, they're probably scared of you," he said. "Finger-breaker."

She shook her head. "No more violence."

"Then we'll have to invent some for our movie. Are you sure? We have all these guns around."

Fifty yards from them the back of the van opened, spilling a yellow light; new figures stepped down in silhouette. Hannah saw the small, jockey-like form of Coach Bailey, held between two large men in black coats with glinting badges. He was bare-headed, wearing a vertically striped prison coat, below the hem of which emerged the orange leggings and soft prison shoes. The group moved from the road up onto the snow and the cops clus-tered around him with flashlights and papers; voices came faintly. Cowley started back toward them, walking across the snow.

Hannah drew a long breath. The expert fencer had looked like a helpless old man. She desperately hoped that no one from the college would come by and see him like this. And she desperately wanted to talk to him.

"All right, we're doing it," Cowley said. She saw his eyes flicker to her hand in Randall's. "Come with me. You, wait here." He led Hannah down the road, leaving Randall by the squad car. To her surprise he was smiling. "It's going well," he said. "They drove him three times around the reservoir and he didn't even know the park. We're going to test him now against the tree."

"Will I get a chance to talk to him?" she asked.

"Probably not. Stop here." They were alongside the un-marked police car, looking over its black hood at the group, which had moved off across the park, feet crunching in the snow. Four cops surrounded Coach Bailey, the two large ones from the van and two thinner men who held flashlights and papers, one sheet of which was presumably her map that she had had Detective Wilson email to Cowley. At least the coach wasn't handcuffed. "Now just stand here and watch what he does," Cowley said. "Look straight ahead, don't indicate in any way which is the cor-rect tree. If he picks a tree just quietly say yes or no."

Hannah shivered. *He could just open the door of this cop car and shove me in*, she thought. She tried to clear her head—*Come on kiddo, hold up.* And she understood wryly that she had created a situation she couldn't handle: she had drawn a target on her back for Cowley to hit, and now she couldn't live with the suspense.

He seemed to be in high spirits. He was in his element and the plan was working. "Where," he asked, "did you get my private cellphone number?"

"I called the station. One of the detectives gave it to me. I'm not supposed to say who."

He glanced down at her briefly. "I'll have to have a word with her about that."

The hardest part was her insane desire to babble to him about everything they both knew. She wanted to tell him about Steve's recorded rant echoing in her head, about how she framed herself specifically to *avoid* someone innocent being sent down like this, about everything. For the first time she felt the vaunted urge of the criminal to confess; it was more powerful than she had dreamed. *If he was wearing a wire and said the right word to me, he could have me in Sing Sing by morning.*

In fact what he said was "Bloody hell."

They were standing in the dim light from the open back door of the van, and Bailey had seen her. "Hannah," he called, and started walking toward them across the snow. His black-coated entourage followed.

"No, no," Cowley muttered, raising his hands ineffectually.

Bailey's round, finely creased face was charged with purpose as it picked up the light. "Hannah," he breathed quickly across the car hood. "Go back to school. Get your degree. Go to Saudi Arabia. I can't teach you any more anyway."

"Mr. Bailey, we have a limited time frame here," Cowley said. "Could you—?" He looked at the officers, who moved in and took his elbows from either side.

"I arranged it with Dean Haughton. Nothing's gonna happen to you. Y'unnerstand? They'll leave you alone. Go back to school. Live your life."

"Coach—" Hannah said. Her greatest fear was that she would look at the tree, and she held her face absolutely still.

"Mr. Bailey, if you want to keep Hannah out of prison I suggest you pick the right goddamn tree," said Cowley.

A car passed on the road behind them in a wave of noise and brilliant light on Hannah's blurred eyelashes; she didn't move her head as the guards turned Bailey away and marched him back across the field. "Aah, I'm pretty sure I found it over there," said the coach...playing a losing strategy...

"Good job," Cowley said appreciatively to her. She felt like her heart would break. "And there—see? He's given it up. He doesn't know. It's official."

Bailey was standing in the center of the snowfield, arms thrown wide. "I don't remember!" he cried. "These trees all look alike!"

"We've saved him," said Cowley, putting a hand briefly on her shoulder. He swung around the front of the black car with a hand on its hood and walked briskly across the field. Figures were trotting back in from the perimeter of the park. "Let's get him back to the van," he called.

Hannah took a deep breath. Someone was yelling in the distance, a faint wavering cry on the wind. She looked up the road and saw Chris Kelly run out of the shadows by Edwards dorm toward where Randall was standing by the squad car. Randall took a step backward onto the snow and Chris tackled him. They both went down and Chris' high screaming never stopped as his fist rose and fell.

"Randall!" Hannah cried; she was running on the road. Cowley blew past a step above her on the snow, coattails flying. He reached them first and she saw him put one hand on Chris' collar and the other somewhere on his lower back, and the next instant he had sprung the big football player upright onto his feet and spun him around. There was a flash of steel as he handcuffed him in a single motion, and a hollow bang as Chris was thrown facedown over the hood of Cowley's car.

He was still yelling as Hannah reached them—Cowley was kicking his legs apart and patting him down—in sobbing shouts with his cheek against the metal: "Fucking pussy! Fucking comic book faggot! You fucked everything up! It's all your fault you dick! Who thinks about me? Who fucking thinks about me? Who cares that my father won't let me come home for Christmas all because of you, you *fuck!* And *you,* you bitch, do you care? You're *gonna* fucking care! You're all gonna get what's coming to you you *dicks* and that goes for you you fucking *bitch!*"

Hannah ran to Randall, who lay moaning, his face and teeth a mass of red in the snow lit by moving flashlights. Other officers knelt around him, leather boots squeaking. "Excuse me Miss." "His nose is broken." "Bring up the car!"

"Christopher Kelly, you are under arrest for assault," came Cowley's voice behind her. "You have the right to remain silent. You —"

The next half hour at the park was a bustle of procedure. Randall was rushed off to the hospital in the unmarked car; Hannah tried to go with him but the cops insisted she stay; she made sure she knew which hospital and promised to visit him tomorrow. As they pulled out another police car slid in by the van with a swallowed siren, into whose caged back seat under flashing lights Chris was eventually pushed, several hands on his head; there followed a long stretch while several different breeds of cops including Hills campus security stood on the flaring pink snow talking and writing on clipboards. Cowley was occupied with those officers, as well as the ones he had brought, and was swallowed in a huddle of shadows and chopped radio syllables.

Hannah was good with the sight of blood, and after Randall and Chris were taken away she felt clear-headed and drained, as if a storm had broken. She wasn't needed for anything and she sat on the bench, across the park from all the activity at the road, not feeling the cold. For the moment she was simply quiet, observant, and blank.

Coach Bailey sat down next to her.

"Everyone's occupied for the moment, and I haven't lost my stealthy tread," he said. "This ridiculous nineteenth-century prison coat is quite good in the shadows. I know what you did for me tonight." His eyes had their clear laser focus back.

"Coach," said Hannah feelingly. "What you were trying to do—it wasn't necessary and I can't believe you would do it. Why?"

"I said my piece about that. That's over. I guess it won't happen now, which means they might go back to looking at you. Uh-huh," he said, seeing her open her mouth. "I thought so. You want it. Well, who knows, I got a long-standing habit of underestimating you." She smiled at him, and he stared away into the night sky. "Sorry about what happened to your boy. I saw him. He'll be all right. You'll have to kiss each other through bandages for a while."

"I can't believe I brought him into all this. And Chris Kelly will probably get a slap on the wrist and probation."

"That's the size of it." He looked back at her. "Now listen up. We don't have much time. You remember our conversation?" When she paused he said, "The one where you didn't tell me nothin' about no audio recorder. You remember that one?"

"I do."

"Hannah, the fix is in. I can't say I know everything they're gonna do, but you're walking into a trap. I been on the inside of this and I seen it. Haughton and the Chief o' Police are like this." He held up two tight fingers. "The press got too close on this one, and if this rape story comes out, everything falls over. Football program's already on shaky ground. They'll spend *anything*, pull *any* strings. Your trial's rigged. They already picked and bought the judge when they thought you were going before. Her name's Clare Miracoli, HC class of '83, happens to be an old college girlfriend of Haughton's. You think your little recorder will be evidence? It's already been ruled out."

"How? It's a recording made in a public park. It's admissible!"

"It's out. I've seen the Motion to Suppress on Haughton's desk. Go ahead, look in my eyes and tell me if I'm an old man exaggerating things."

She didn't say a word.

"You wanna know why you spent seventy-two hours in jail before being arraigned? That's why. You wanna know why your pal Chris Kelly is drunk off his rock every night? 'Cause he's the one blabbed to that reporter about Steve's trophy and your recorder setup, and they snapped their fingers and suddenly he's off the team and on double academic probation and no more scholarship. You wanna know who was leaving the room when I was going in for my little midnight tête-á-tête with Haughton and the police chief? District Attorney Merriweather, class of '85."

"Coach," she said, and couldn't finish her sentence. *Could it be that big?* Now the night, and the wooden bench under her legs, did feel cold.

"I know what you're after, Raider. You wanted the court to tell the truth to the world. Look, I can't beat you on the strip no more, but I've got one more thing to teach you, and this is where you have to grow up fast. You think the courts and the law are like referees, above it all? You think they don't care about money, don't care about a taint on a Massachusetts institution that dates from colonial times and generates a billion dollars a year of revenue? They're part of it, Hannah. They know what you're after, and if your fifteenth point was the rape story coming out, they're gonna splatter you at point six. Now, you got anything solid besides what's on that audio?"

She shook her head.

"Well, then I'll tell you that Andrew Keith, who was smart enough not to say a word to no goddamn cop when they came poking around, has a daddy who's on the State Supreme Court, and there's an injunction on that audio being used for any public purpose whatsoever, justified in the name of 'security for the boys in a hostile campus environment.' That's their little swipe at you and the feminists, you like it? That's why they can say whatever they damn well want to about it in the press. Kid, where you're trying to go—you can't get. At least not that way."

They sat silently on the bench in the faint red and blue flicker of siren light.

Hannah was no stranger to losing fencing matches. She knew how it felt. Coach Bailey had always held her up as a model to the team for *how* to lose, and he didn't mean with grace and dignity. He meant that she never lost the same way twice. She *learned* from every loss. And the least she could do to honor him now, she thought, was learn from this one. Learn the hardest lesson she had ever had to learn.

It *was* that big.

He got to his feet. "I think my animal trainers are coming for me. This damn coat shows too much orange at the bottom."

"Coach—thank you," said Hannah.

"You'll observe that I haven't said a word regarding you and the demise of a certain football player," Bailey said. "But I'll pass this one along from someone else. W— called up to thank Kate and me for our party, and she said, quote, 'I hope she *did* kill him with a fencing sword, the women's movement could use someone with a sense of style.' See you later, kid."

The van's taillights moved away down the campus road, turned at the reservoir and vanished. The other cops were gone and Hannah and Cowley stood alone alongside his squad car. For a moment neither spoke, both still staring at the end of the road. Then he looked at his watch. "Where are you supposed to be?" he asked.

"In a movie."

"You've still got time." For another moment they stood there, looking at each other in the darkness, then Cowley grabbed his own arms. "Jesus, let's get in the car." Hannah nodded rapidly and moved around to the passenger door, and then they were in the front seat with the motor running and the heat roaring, but still he didn't go anywhere. The dashboard threw a faint orange light.

"The car recorder's not on," he said. "If you want to —"

"That doesn't matter," said Hannah. "Thank you for — you know."

"Yeah." To her surprise Cowley ducked his head, a quick movement. "Ah, I don't like being thanked for using force. We have to do it, and I'm glad I was there, but that part's not why I'm a cop."

"You do it well."

"When I *do* have to use force it's about knowing how, so as to use as little as possible."

She nodded. "Kinetic chess. That's what they call fencing."

They looked at each other and there was another pause. His haunted face in the warm light was softened, troubled. In an instant their gaze snowballed into matching questions — *What have you found? / How did you do it?* — that seemed to answer and block each other in a fascinated impossibility of speech. It was too much: they both looked away. Then they spoke together:

"Will you—" "What are you—"

And they both stopped short. Hannah looked out the side window, across the park to the black wooded hill that seemed to breathe in the wind. Her heart was beating hard. He made no move to drive; she didn't want him to.

Cowley exhaled. "Listen, this whole thing—I'm glad we cleared Bailey tonight, that's what we came to do. But I'm sorry for the way it went down. Maybe you didn't even need to be here."

She looked back. "Will you get in trouble?"

He laughed sourly. "That doesn't matter. The department and I, well—"

He met her eyes with a certain intensity, and she knew that the next thing he said was going to reference it. *Her wink. What she said under the table.* Quickly she changed the subject: "I'm glad I was here. I had an interesting conversation just now. It seems no one's going to let my audio evidence be publicized, trial or not. Is that true?"

"Yes," he said. She nodded. "I tried to tell you—"

"During a police interrogation! Not exactly a normal conversation."

"When have we ever had a normal conversation?"

"We can't now either! Now that we've—" She broke off,

waving a hand at the dark road beyond the windshield. *Now that we've opened the case up all over again*, she meant. *While you still suspect me*, she meant. *Which is my fault, which is totally fucked up*, she meant.

"I know," he said, and the remarkable part was that his voice conveyed an understanding of all of that. They held each other's gaze in a strange telepathic frustration across the front seat. The heater was warming up the car rapidly. "The recorder is not on," he insisted softly.

Here we go. "You know the last thing I ever wanted was to see someone I love —" She broke off in time.

"I know that. I saw it, finally, in all that stuff that looked like ego." *Of course he saw it*, she thought wryly, how her whole tactic of framing herself was never about showing off, but about eliminating other suspects. "That's why it had to be Bailey," he said, "for the sake of the sword."

She nodded, looking at him in a different way. His voice had had the sourness of disgust. "You didn't like it either," she said, her voice barely above a whisper.

"It stank, trying to send him down. That's not how I — what you did here tonight was the right thing. Even if —" He broke off in his turn, spreading his hands.

Neither of them could cross it. "It was hard seeing him like that," she said. "Harder than wearing it myself." She turned away and drew a long breath, staring out the side window. "Everything here was hard."

"You did very well."

"Thanks," she whispered, her breath fogging the tableau of snow and darkness. *Don't — compliment me,* she thought.

The rush of the heater diminished, having reached its climate.

He leaned toward her in the quieter sound. "Listen. Bailey was able to plea-bargain down to a couple of years. You should — look at that."

She looked back. "Are you saying —?"

"I'm saying I'd like to help you." She saw the effort in his hard, gaunt face; how all this was difficult for him. "What you did here shows you have a good heart — "

"A good heart? A good heart is not going to help me or anyone else right now!" Something made her turn away from him in her seat; she stared unseeing out the side window into the darkness where the little bench sat under the hill. Her thoughts were whirling; she was too warm.

He said nothing, the hardest prompt of all. *Where is this going? Am I just going to confess to him? He already knows...*

She had overestimated herself; the penalty for encouraging Cowley toward the truth was that in another second she was going to give him everything of her own accord. *And why not?* Where she had been trying to get — she couldn't go.

Not that way.

Learn. Learn from your losses.

After a long moment she faced him again, and her voice was level.

"The world is perfectly satisfied that I'm innocent. My parents were toasting me with champagne the other day. Instead of a plea bargain, how about you just leave it at that and walk away?"

"No," said Cowley.

"Why not?"

"Because you did it," he said quietly.

There it was. She had been right to choose him. Hannah held his eyes through a long steady breath. "So our alliance is over."

"I don't—want it to be." His voice was unexpectedly rough. "Hannah what's the point? You know what's going on now. Your audio of that bastard won't come out in a trial; hell, *we* can't even use it for motive to send you there. You won't—you can't—" He made a gesture up at the night road, vaguely indicating the college, and what she admired most of all was that, whether he knew it or not, the frustrated break in his voice referenced the patriarchy behind it.

She held his eyes, silently acknowledging everything he had revealed. They *were* allies—to that extent. "If I could," she said slowly, "would you support me? Against the cover-up, against your fellow police? Would you?"

He leaned toward her; his voice got lower, more intense, almost whispering. "You know I would. I'm here now. But you can't."

This—is the hardest part. She was trembling. "Then it's the same," she cried softly. "Don't you see? You can't walk away, and I can't plea bargain. That's not who we are. Tonight I've had sympathy and cynicism and I don't want either from you. Between us, let's keep it clean. No more false confessions."

He nodded silently. Their eyes were still locked on each other, she saw his narrow with the accepted challenge, the dare to which she would open. She had used the word "clean;" he had responded strongly to it. Her breath was short. *He understands. He—*

The steady purr of the motor was the only sound. "Hannah," he said in a low voice, shifting—

"*Don't.*" She squeezed her eyes closed. Then: "Turn on the car recorder."

He did, and they drove back to West Newton in silence.

Chapter 15 - Poster Girl

She had never cried the way she did that night, alone in the Peabodys' small bedroom at the end of the upstairs hall. She pressed her face hard to the pillow of the little bed, trying to keep silent and not wake her parents next door, as her body shook and shook. It went on for hours.

In the dawn her reflection in the bathroom mirror looked to her like a different person: red-eyed, gaunter, hair disarrayed around her shoulders, arms looking strangely muscular in her sleeveless light blue shirt. "You still in there, kiddo?" she whispered.

Tiptoeing back into the hall she met her mother, coming toward her in her bluebell nightgown. The house was silent around them. "Oh Hannah," her mother whispered, touching her hair. "All of this has been so hard on you."

She didn't have it in her to lie. "There's more to come, Mom," she whispered back.

Her mother let go of her hair and nodded. "I said I didn't know the blue car when the detective came around with the picture," she said.

Hannah stared goggle-eyed. Her mother had no change of expression, as if she was offering eggs for breakfast.

"Are you sure you don't want some help with makeup this morning?" she continued in a concerned whisper.

"Actually I could really use it," Hannah whispered.

Mike Peabody let her borrow his SUV to run Randall's bag to the hospital, thence to take him to Logan for his flight home. The alarm and concern of last night had settled into a vague sense in which his getting mugged at a movie made it all the more appropriate he return to his own demesnes. "His parents are meeting him at LaGuardia for the drive to New Jersey," Hannah explained, to polite nods for extraneous detail. Mike gave her a thorough tutorial on the BMW's dashboard.

Then she was on the road.

Deep breath, kiddo. Here we go.

She didn't drive to the hospital. Instead at 9:50 am the BMW pulled into the visitor parking loop behind the Neville Place Assisted Living home in Cambridge. The blue Buick was in its usual spot. She walked over to it, retrieved the key from over the right rear wheel, and opened the trunk. She raised the felted cardboard false bottom to reveal the spare tire, used the tire iron to undo the lugnuts, and lifted the tire up lidwise in its well. Underneath, right where she had left it, was her little blue-and-white USB thumb drive.

It contained her own recording of the rapists talking in the park, made from the Skype call between her hidden "baby monitor" and her laptop at Eastern's. She had transferred the audio file to the thumb drive before reformatting her laptop as Amtrak 67 approached Penn Station.

If your fifteenth point is the rape story coming out, they're gonna splatter you at point six.

It was Coach Bailey's phrase that had given her her strategy. *Fine,* she said to herself, *in that case I'll splatter them at point one.*

Her first attempt to publicize the audio had been via the

media's simple reporting of a scandalous crime. That hadn't worked. Her second plan had been to do it via public evidence in a murder trial. Coach Bailey had disabused her of that line of thinking.

Which left one option—broadcast the audio herself. Release Steve's rape confession to the world *in advance* of a trial. *Point fucking one.* Make sure that when her murder trial happened, it would be that of the victim of a brutal attempted gang rape, partly completed, which her venerable school had spared no expense to deny and cover up. That was the trial she wanted, and it was damn well the trial she was going to have.

Until now she hadn't dared use her own copy. Essential to her innocence defense had been that Hannah Radhe never knew what was on her recorder, that she left HC for New York before the rapists even began talking in the park, that only the mystery killer heard it. Now, well, if she was going to go down in flames in her trial like her idol John Brown after all, then it didn't matter; she might as well add to the light.

Nevertheless, she wasn't reckless. Point one wasn't the match, and she was thinking ahead. She wasn't exactly going to release the audio *herself*.

"See, I can't give away that I have this file," she told Randall, in the car on the way to Logan Airport. "All sorts of questions would come up as to how I got it. And it can't come from you either. It has to look like a leak of the original by a well-wisher in the police. Can you post it to the forums while concealing its origin?"

"That part's easy," Randall said. He had his large gaming laptop open on his lap in the passenger seat, the one with the Anonymous mask sticker smiling on the lid, and the file was copying over.

Coach Bailey had been wrong about their having to kiss through bandages, but Randall's mouth was about the only part of his face free of them. He had a Christmas tree of tapes and gauze over his broken nose, the top of his head was swaddled diagonally for a fractured cheekbone, and both eyes were raccooned in puffy purple. "I hope you told your parents all about what happened to the other seven guys," he had said by way of greeting, when his mouth was free.

"There's risk for you in this," Hannah told him again. "If there's the slightest chance of you being identified, don't do it. I'll post it myself and take the consequences. The police will be looking hard at this."

"Boston P.D.? Don't make me smirk, it hurts. The people I'm sending this to have been visited in their homes by the N.S.A and found clean."

He pulled the thumb drive from the laptop and passed it back to her. She was having him post it to three of her favorite feminist forums, in a shortened version tailored for the Internet: only the key section of about four minutes around Steve's rant—his confession.

The Callahan tunnel ramped up into the brightness of an overcast day between cement walls hung with yellow scabs of ice. She replaced the little drive in her shirt pocket. "What did you mean, 'that part is easy?'"

"Well, there are two tricky parts. The first is that your original audio recorder is probably sitting in a tightly-controlled evidence room somewhere. Do you know whether the police ever downloaded the file off it, to a computer?"

She nodded, remembering the little laptop Cowley had carried into the interrogation room. "They did. But I'm sure that's controlled too."

"Doesn't matter. As long as it was downloaded, even if they deleted the copy directly after using it, it's hackable. If it had never been copied, and the recorder wasn't disturbed, they'd come looking for a second copy. That was the biggest thing. The second is that *something's* got to go in the outbound email field. We've got to frame somebody on the police for the leak. Do you have the email of any Boston policemen?"

Hannah had been ready for this, more or less, since last night. Without taking her eyes from the road she handed Randall a strip of notebook paper on which she had written Detective Cowley's private email address, that he had given her to have Detective Wilson relay the map of the park.

Randall looked between the paper and Hannah.

She was framing Cowley for a crime, and not just any crime, but a leak that torpedoed the department's most sensitive cover-up. She couldn't imagine what this would do to him—as she couldn't bear to think that it would seem doubly plausible because of his role in freeing Bailey. The coach had been released that morning; she had seen the article, the Globe practically writhing with the twists and turns of the Badenhut case. Doing this to Cowley, hard on its heels, was the most painful thing she had ever done—and it was why she *knew* she would get a trial. Very soon.

"What I'd like," she said, when she could breathe again, "is for it to somehow be clear, at like a second or third view, that his account was hacked to leak it, that *somebody* framed him, without giving away that it was you. If something like that can be done."

"You're asking for creative amateurism? I will shield you from the nine hundred options you will be offered for how creative and how amateurish."

He continued holding the paper without either typing it in or putting it away.

"My superpowers let you down," she said quietly, eyes on the road.

"That's okay. It's about time I got to show you mine."

She turned a sad smile to him. "I always knew you had them." He bent to type the address in. After a moment she looked at him again. "Why are you willing to do this?" she asked.

Randall answered without looking up. "That one cop, who saved my butt back there? He didn't like me," he said.

Hannah gave a quiet laugh and shook her head as the airport Departure lane rose into view. "No. He didn't," she said.

The news cycle on manhunt stories normally had a duration of a few days at best. It was expected that in short order would come a grande finale of gunfire, suspect death, and sweatily satisfied police officers to provide the climactic headline. The Badenhut Dorm Killing, a/k/a FemiNazi Fatale story, was already guilty of being in excess of its allotted ink, not to mention bad form for causing wrong-girl headline backtracking, and with Christmas almost here and no Hills College students around willing to shiver for their lives on camera the press had been delighted to close its book on Jacques Bailey. It was with great, page-two reluctance that they had to report Bailey's confession being thrown out and charges dropped, whereupon, the case having for the moment nowhere to go, the press was preparing to quietly pass the Badenhut murder over to TV specials on ingenious criminals who got away and say no more about it.

A little-used proviso of the media playbook, however,

specifies that when a case combines (a) celebrity sexual malfeasance, (b) a "viral" Internet event, and (c) a girl, the story can be revived, indefinitely renewed, and elevated to cross-cultural saturation. The leak, to feminist forums, of the sensational "Badenhut Torture Rant" — with its rape confession and lurid plans for worse — triggered this proviso, and touched off a media firestorm that raged unchecked over the dry news timber of the Christmas week. Granted, Steve Badenhut was a celebrity of their own recent creation. But after the Globe threw the first torch with "SLAIN FOOTBALL 'HERO' WAS RAPIST WHO PLANNED MORE," the very fact added vengeful vigor to their illumination of the cover-up, and soon, with Feminist America on the warpath and top Boston figures running for cover, the story became a full-fledged media bonfire:

STUDENT VICTIM'S BRAVE RECORDING CAPTURED CAMPUS RAPE CABAL

HAUGHTON IN HOT SEAT AS HILLS COLLEGE COVER-UP ALLEGATIONS SPREAD

FULL TEXT OF BADENHUT TORTURE RANT - WARNING: EXPLICIT CONTENT

HILLS COLLEGE HAS DATE RAPE HISTORY DATING BACK YEARS

THE TORTURE RANT: A DISEASED SOUL, A DISEASED SOCIETY

DID DEAN HAUGHTON AND POLICE CHIEF KOONTZ MEET TO DISCUSS BADENHUT RAPE COVER-UP?

RESIGNATION OF COACH PRUECASTLE? VOICES MOUNT

MORE WOMEN COME FORWARD WITH BADENHUT ASSAULT ALLE-
GATIONS

FBI: LEAKED BADENHUT AUDIO WAS OUTSIDE HACK OF BOSTON
P.D.

COULD BADENHUT KILLING BE CONSIDERED SELF-DEFENSE BY AS-
SAULT TARGET?

WHO IS HANNAH RADHE? HER FEMINIST WRITINGS REVEALED

Then, about a week in, just when the explosion seemed on the verge of quieting into the pattering fallout of litigations and talk-show sum-ups, came the incendiary Hills College counter-attack, which started the banner headlines all over again in a different direction:

HAUGHTON: CYBER EXPERTS PROVE BADENHUT AUDIO IS HACKER
FAKE

BOSTON POLICE SAY INTERNET RANT AUDIO DOES NOT MATCH
ORIGINAL RECORDING

CAN DIGITAL EVIDENCE BE TRUSTED? WHEN VIRAL MEDIA RE-
PLACES LAW

RUSH TO JUDGE: HOW INTERNET FORUMS AMPLIFY MISINFOR-
MATION

THE FEMINIST WAR AGAINST FOOTBALL: AN ACCOUNTING

SPYWARE TALES: HOW HC TRACKED HACKER ORIGIN

INJUNCTION AGAINST ORIGINAL RECORDER AUDIO PREVENTS

VALIDATION OF TORTURE RANT, CONFUSION GROWS

MEET THE ANGRY WOMEN WHO STILL BELIEVE THE BADENHUT
RANT AUDIO

FEMINISTS IN UPROAR OVER AUDIO EXCLUSION FROM BADENHUT
MURDER TRIAL

OPTIMISTIC MCFARREL CLAIMS 'WITCH-HUNT' ON TRIAL EVE

"WORST CHRISTMAS EVER" FOR HILLS COLLEGE HOLIDAY FUND-
RAISING DUE TO LINGERING RAPE TAINT

Somewhat quietly in the middle of this, Hannah Radhe was arrested again on new evidence, indicted for murder, arraigned with a plea of not guilty, and released on $25,000 bail.

An observer might have expected the nature of the new evidence to cause more stir: State was alleging that Radhe had engineered a complex rendezvous, leaving and rejoining her Amtrak to commit the murder while appearing never to have left the train. But such was the power of the Torture Rant to certify her motive that the press took the FemiNazi Fatale's recapture in stride, and merely footnoted the wily scheme by way of explaining, again, their previous wrong headlines.

As for the Torture Rant, however, those hoping that the trial would resolve the controversy were left disappointed, as the original digital audio recording, which alone could answer the question, was not to be admitted as part of the case.

The trial was set for January 4, in Boston, Judge Clare Miracoli presiding.

Chapter 16 - Racona's Plug

Hannah's re-arrest was the fruit of an emergency three-person meeting, held in Chief Koontz' office at the police station, a few days after the audio first hit the Internet. The chief glowered in silence at Cowley and Lieutenant Racona from a head seemingly pressed down into his shoulders, and the others waited for him to speak. Though it was mid-day, the desks in the homicide room behind the glass wall were empty, and the station was largely quiet around them. Cowley appeared not to have shaved, slept or changed clothes in days; his eyes were black pools; he looked like something dragged up from the bottom of a lake. Professionally this was accurate — everyone in the department knew of his apostasy on the Bailey case and his culpability in the evidence leak that was rocking the force. In his nerveless fingers he held two large photographs. Racona adjusted her tight collar with a long fingernail.

"I hate to fire people the day after Christmas, Cowley, but I swear to God in your case I would make an exception," Koontz began. "The only reason you're standing here is by the grace of God and the CCD people, who say it wasn't you leaked the tape."

"It wasn't," said Cowley.

"Because if it was you, like I *thought* it was, I would have invited your whole family in for Christmas brunch and had them watch as I arrested you for tampering with evidence."

"I know."

"The chain is clean on the evidence room and the FBI agrees it was someone outside. But still, it was *your* idea to use the audio in the interrogation, which is why we had the file on that computer. And somehow it was your email on the leak. It smells, Cowley. And you *did* go behind my back to undo Bailey."

"I did."

Koontz sighed and looked at him sidelong. "Like I said before, I would fire you just for that if I didn't admire your *chutzpah*. That gag was pretty smooth, reminded me of me at your age. Believe it or not there's a reason I keep idealistic cops around. But this leak is something else. Why *was* it your email, Cowley? Do you know who hacked it?"

"No," Cowley lied.

"Cyber says it could have been anyone, chief," said Racona. "Since day one the press has been changing their story about the mystery message on the recorder. Probably got every hacker from here to China going."

"Well, the silver lining is *because* it was a hack it gives us an out. I've spoken with Dean Haughton and Hills' line is gonna be that the hacker faked it. Totally plausible. But there's gonna be a lot of media around this, and if any of you goons is asked anything by the press, just say it doesn't match our recorder audio, that's all."

"Same old line," Racona said evenly.

"Same old line. Cowley, ah, best you not go near any reporters." The chief averted his eyes from Cowley's hollow, focused stare. "Now, much as I hate to say it, the real reason I brought you in on the holiday is I need your goddamn help. The shit is in the fan, everyone's screaming at everyone else, Early has the whole department under scrutiny and meanwhile we're back to goddamn square one on this case. We still have exactly one suspect for killing Badenhut, and she's got camera footage and a cellphone track says she was on the train. You say she did it?"

"She did it," said Cowley.

"You?"

"Yep," said Racona.

"Good. *How?*"

They both looked at Cowley. He cleared his throat and spoke in a monotone. "She disembarked and re-embarked during the journey. She pre-positioned her car at the Providence Amtrak station in the morning and left her murder weapon in the car. At night she got off at Providence, wearing one disguise, drove to HC, put on a second disguise, killed Badenhut, then drove to New Haven in time to get back on the train. Third disguise for that. She then walked off at Penn in her own clothes and made sure she was seen by the cams. She left her cellphone on the train so it followed the train, and she even called her parents from aboard the train before getting off at Providence."

The chief nodded. "And when you laid this on her in the interrogation she burst into tears." He looked at Racona. "You buy this cockamamie story?"

"I do," said Racona. "And those were crocodile tears. Look at her on that Penn Station footage. She puts her bags down and smiles into the camera like a satisfied cat. Show him what you got."

Cowley laid the two photographs on the chief's desk. His monotone didn't vary.

"This is a security camera grab of her Buick Skylark in the parkinglot of the Providence Amtrak station, afternoon of December 15. The camera's on five-minute clicks so we missed it coming or going, but it sits there all afternoon and evening, then vanishes right after her Amtrak arrives."

"Willya look at that," Koontz muttered.

"This is a camera grab from inside the station, these are the passengers disembarking, and *that"*—Cowley's finger forcefully jabbed a woman in a long white coat coming in through the platform doors, her face hidden by a wide-brimmed white hat—"is Radhe. Gomez ran it through his software and it's an absolute match. Much cleaner than the Hills College one."

Koontz grunted. "The damn software again—that's a hard sell. And *three* disguises? Still, it's *something* to give Grand." His finger tapped the car photo, and he looked up. "But there's still a problem with the math, right?"

"Yes. The only reason it worked that night is because the train was delayed. Without that, you couldn't make the rendezvous. The question is, how could she know?"

"Well? How could she? We gotta plug that, or we'll be thrown outta the room."

Cowley spoke shaking his head. "Near as I can figure she must have had an accomplice on the train, someone to hold her bags and cellphone and disembark ahead of her in New York, maybe in her clothes and a hat. Radhe's plan would have been to drive from the murder straight to Penn Station, meet this person outside, the accomplice hands over the bags and cellphone and Radhe goes home to her parents. She'd be quite a bit later than the train but she'll say she had trouble finding a cab at two a.m. and the phone track sitting at Penn will back her up. But that night she gets lucky. After killing Badenhut she finds out somehow that the train was delayed, maybe the accomplice contacts her, it'd have to be on some other phone, anyway she realizes she can make the rendezvous. She makes it, and that's how she smiles into the camera in New York."

Koontz exhaled a weary raspberry. "An accomplice. Who?"

"Nobody. That wasn't her plan. It's—she works alone. But it's the only thing I've got that makes any sense. I'm still looking."

The chief shook his head. "I can't give that to the DA. Especially if it means we have to go track down every fucking person on the train. What else ya got?"

"Nothing," said Cowley. "At the New Haven station there's only one cam and we don't see it. But give me time. I'm going through all the street footage I can find. She reboarded there, I know it. I *will* get her."

Cowley's tone of voice made Racona stare, and even Koontz lifted his eyes briefly before returning them to the photos on his desk.

"I haven't got time, Cowley. You have no idea how hot this is upstairs. Remember when I said people don't want to see Radhe in a trial? Well, things have changed and fuck 'em. Boston P.D. is getting dragged through the wringer for Hills' goddamn cover-up, the whole world now knows that Badenhut wanted to rape and kill her, we've got motive on her with a capital fuck me, *you* say she did it, *I* say the bitch should be in jail, it's right there in the photos—all we need to do is make the math work, right? So gimme a theory!"

Cowley said nothing. There was a pause.

"Maybe we're over-thinking this," said Racona. She looked at Cowley. "How much would she miss the train by, if there wasn't a delay?"

"Ah...the train's normally due at New Haven at twelve-thirty... the blue car leaves HC at eleven-thirtyseven...it's about a two-hour drive, less at night... she'd miss it by at least a half hour, maybe fortyfive minutes. Plus she's got to change her disguise...stop somewhere and dispose of the sword..."

"So look at you, counting on your fingers," Racona said. "Maybe she didn't do the math. Maybe she thought she could make it, and the train delay made her lucky."

"Huh," said Koontz.

"No! Absolutely not," said Cowley.

"Why not?" said Koontz.

"She planned all this—and didn't do the math? It, it's out of character. "

"Who's in character when they're committing murder?" Racona said. "It's pretty close, plus she could speed. Highways are empty at that hour, she could do ninety, maybe she *did* the math and figured she could just make it."

"She *can't* speed," said Cowley. "If anyone stops her and records her not on the train, it's over. She can do at most seventy. I wouldn't—she wouldn't even do that."

"She's hopped up from putting a sword through Badenhut's body. Hell, she's desperate. Badenhut was at that party until eleven-twentyfive, right, so she had to stake him out, her whole timing's off, but hearing that audio drove her berserk and she's not giving up. Afterwards she speeds to New Haven in a blind hope that she can still make her train, not doing any math at all, and broken-down Amtrak makes her lucky."

"I don't like it," said Cowley. "It's—messy."

Chief Koontz had been looking back and forth between them. "All Merriweather has to do is sell it to Grand," he said. "I'm kinda with Cowley that it's out of character, but it plugs the math hole. Everyone's looking at her again anyway."

"Rape-and-revenge," said Racona. "I've said from the beginning that the whole case is easier this way. She's a berserk avenger who doesn't stop to count. *I* wouldn't."

"Cowley?" said the chief.

Cowley made a tight sigh. "You'll get her into court with that. But McFarrel will walk all over it. We'll lose."

The two others looked at him for a moment. His face was set hard. "It's not our ball at that point," Koontz said quietly. Cowley said nothing. "You want more than that?" Koontz prompted. "You want her to go down?" Cowley remained silent. Koontz slammed his hand on the desk with a loud bang. "Then get me the rest of the evidence to do it!" he shouted. "You say she found out in advance about the delay, fine! Prove it. You've got until the trial. Show me how she *really* did it!"

Cowley turned and left the office.

They watched him walk out of the homicide room, then looked at each other with raised eyebrows.

Cowley wasn't used to being hurt. In the world of police work there was enough daily disillusionment to crystallize thick armor, and he had long kept his moral heart in a private place behind it. But *she*—had gotten inside.

Hannah's use of his private email, given in confidence, to frame him for an evidence leak had left him cold in a place that she herself had started to warm. He had escaped the frame job only by the skin of CCD's deep analysis that showed an outside hack, since confirmed by the FBI, but not before a humiliating closed-door session with the Commissioner and other frowning faces, left hanging only by their indecision as to whether to throw him off the force or straight into jail. Had she *intended* to knock him off the force, get him out of the way? Did she *not* want a trial now? After all, she had accomplished her goal — she had released her recording to the world — and walked all over him to do it. He hadn't thought her capable of that. But after all it was perfectly clean and correct for them to be enemies, as she herself had said. *Our alliance is over.*

Well, let them be enemies then. She was going to get a trial whether she wanted it or not.

The worst was that he knew she hadn't done it without pain. There hadn't been a single follow-up text from her. Racona was right about her smile at the cameras at Penn: the girl could gloat when she wanted to. Her silence now was eloquent. But that hurt too much to think about.

In fact he was alone in the department in knowing that Hannah was the outside hacker, and he couldn't broaden that knowledge without incriminating himself. His cellphone with her texts, including the private email address he had sent her, was now a hot property, to be kept close to him both at home and at work. As to *how* she had hacked the department, he didn't know and he didn't care; he suspected the boyfriend, but he wouldn't follow it up. It was *her* betrayal that mattered.

Betrayal? Of what? Nothing, really — the word was inappropriate on every level — but he couldn't stop feeling it. Cowley wasn't used to looking into his feelings and he didn't start now.

His reaction was to stay focused. He turned all the energy of his crippled professional reputation into solving her crime. In the space of nineteen sleepless hours at his desk, including the empty span of Christmas Day, he had found the two photos that pretty much confirmed his rendezvous theory. Now, thanks to Racona, she had been re-arrested (thankfully she wasn't *here*; she was out on bail) with the calendar ticking toward her trial date. And he was still no closer to how she did it.

Cowley wasn't done. He knew damn well that Hannah could *count*. Somehow she had found out about the train delay. Somewhere in the murk between Providence and New Haven her car had changed course, or she had done *something*. She had left *something* behind.

He would find it.

Chapter 17 - Defendant

The thin bare trees bent and fifed in the gusting sleet, flanking the entrance of the John Adams Courthouse under the two straining flags. The men in suits were dark figures hunching quickly up the stone steps, hands to their hats, through a colorful scatter of female protestors keeling their signboards against the wind – for despite the denials the figure of Steve Badenhut was still a locus of anti-rape outrage. On the top floor of the classically handsome old building the courtroom was windowless, crowded, and subdued as the murder trial of Hannah Radhe got under way on January 4.

Hannah sat with McFarrel at the defense table at the front of the long rectangular room. Her rehired lawyer seemed at his ease, dressed in his unvarying pinstriped suit, his bald head perhaps slightly more polished as he scratched behind the earpiece of his wire-rimmed glasses with a gold ballpoint pen. She wore a white turtleneck under a lightblue V-neck sweater with a knee-length cream skirt, her hair in bangs and slightly curled at the shoulders. These details had been selected by McFarrel with as much care as the jurors, to whom they were meant to suggest the good, brave survivor of sexual assault, period. Those twelve arbiters of her fate sat to her right in two tiers of a raised wooden jury box; the faces were mostly middle-class; over half were women. Hannah, who wasn't supposed to look at them, couldn't resist a glance, as at the blank scoreboard before a fencing match, ready to register all the maneuvering below. The scoreboard stared back.

Oddly, the match they were about to witness didn't concern her. That would be the affair of McFarrel and the lawyers of the prosecution, whose table was immediately on her right, between her and the jury: an enclave of three natty men with oiled hair whose job seemed to be to keep a mass of papers in constant motion. McFarrel's pen had singled out from among them Hector E. Rapillo, the State Prosecutor, a stocky man with the shaved, chunky face of a used-car salesman above a red tie. His unenviable task was to sell a murder scheme based on an interstate Amtrak rendezvous that according to the train schedules was physically impossible. Hannah looked at the prosecutor with a touch of secret pride; she had been given to understand that the betting odds were against him.

But then, if her plan worked, she herself would be improving them. Because unbeknownst to everybody, she wasn't here to win the court case.

In truth she was surprised that her re-arrest was on the basis of so *little* evidence. "Nothing!" McFarrel had crowed to the assembled family (she had spent the last several days in a kind of courtroom coaching school in the Peabodys' livingroom). "They've got nothing! They have no proof she left the train, which obviously they can't because we know she never did. All they've got is their stupid blue car, which they still can't tie to her, and they've followed it down the Mass Pike and found it in Providence, and they've got some woman on a train station video that they're going to claim is Hannah on the basis of a *notorious* computer model that last year was proved wrong on appeal by DNA evidence. Most importantly, their crackpot rendezvous theory doesn't add up, and they're going to say she didn't do the math and got lucky because of a train delay. Excuse me, but if she's a cold calculating killer, then she can calculate, right? I'm going to use that line, what do you think? Hannah, pardon my French, but this is going to be a strr-*oll*."

His effusive belittling of their case was his way of apologizing without apologizing for having earlier thought her guilty in the privacy of his heart. She did see, with aching insight, Cowley's hand in the new evidence (even as she kicked herself for not hiding the car better at Providence), and she could almost feel his savage frustration at how they had papered over the gap in the rendezvous math. She also knew he would keep looking—a question to McFarrel confirmed that new evidence could be adduced at any point throughout the trial—which added a random element of uncertainty to the proceedings. *But that's only fair.* She had been prepared to start with the fire pump on the evidence table. In mournful gratitude she thanked him for getting her here, and if her survival chances hung on the last unsolved shred of her alibi against him, she would honor him as she now made the most of it. But what she had to do here, she had to do alone.

For one thing, it would involve breaking the law.

Turning in her seat, she focused on the courtroom behind her, where her parents and the Peabodys sat in the front row of the long gallery that extended to the back of the room. The gallery was full, mostly with young women, and a soft, treble hubbub surged under the ceiling, through which from time to time she caught syllables of her mother's and father's voices. She had had to conceal her real goal from her parents too, of course, and accept their sympathy through the long days when the Hills College counter-attack discredited her recording yet again.

The upshot of that development—the news that the actual

audio recording would be excluded from evidence — had been delivered by a carefully hangdog McFarrel. "I, ah, know you were hoping that your trial would be a kind of platform for the campus rape issue. Admissibility of a public recording actually depends on whether the speaker had a 'reasonable expectation of privacy,' and the judge ruled Steve had that. It's political, of course, but the bright side is it helps your case. Our argument is you're a clear-headed woman who can *count*; taking out the emotions of rape and...*that audio*...makes it a much easier sell. In fact I'll tell you right now that this wrecks their case. So, I know it isn't the trial you envisioned, but all things considered — "

"Oh, it's exactly the trial I envisioned. Don't worry about it."

From under the hangdog face had come a sudden look of suspicion. "What — are you up to now?"

"Nothing! Honest."

Yet.

Even now, at the defense table, McFarrel shot her periodic worried looks, as if, after all the coaching she had received on posture and calmness, she was behaving *too* well. It was with one of those looks that he rose and joined the prosecutor, Rapillo, for a conference at the bench. Their voices were hidden under the general babble. For the moment Hannah was alone at her table.

Or almost so. Behind her right shoulder stood the one person in the courtroom who understood her full purpose here: the figure, visible to her alone, of John Brown, ramrod-straight and silent in a white shirt. She had challenged him, before starting on this adventure, that she could plan it better than he planned his. He too had stood trial for a cause, and he was now come, she knew, at the endgame of their wager to underscore her boast with the freight of pain and the necessity of sacrifice.

I will not fear it, she said silently to him. *As long as I get to take my shot.*

She had prepared the battlefield as best she could. High above the courtroom tussle between McFarrel and Rapillo, her duel with Dean Haughton was entering the final stage.

Hannah had never expected that her own copy of the audio, posted to the Internet, would hold up or accomplish her goal. She no longer underestimated her opponent. Haughton had suppressed the recording when it was on a dead body on his campus; quashing a sourceless forum post of no legal validity would be child's play for him, though she had been amused at what must have been expensive headlines and magazine articles to arrange. No, posting the rant had been only point one, essentially a setup, and his riposte had positioned him just where she wanted: apparently triumphant, but in reality over-extended even further, on the hook for even bigger and more public lies.

It remained only to expose them.

To her left, along the wall before the bench, was the evidence table. On it she could see the stiff, tagged plastic baggie containing her digital audio recorder. As a physical object, integral to the crime scene, it had to be here, though the file on it was verboten.

For her point fifteen all she had to do was get that file, the *true* audio, admitted into evidence—thus publicly, legally, gigantically and irrevocably certifying Haughton as a liar and systematic rape-silencer.

She had a plan to do it. Well, of course *she* couldn't be the one to admit it.

Judge Miracoli would.

She looked straight forward.

In front, the long bare box of the courtroom broke out in a

modernist blossom of reddish wood, with tiered stages, railed steps, half-columns and bas-relief fronds, at the high pistil of which the head of Judge Clare Miracoli rose over her black robe. "As tough as they come," McFarrel had said. As the judge stepped forward to confer with the lawyers Hannah stared at the strong, hard face under short steel-grey hair, its expression as impassive as her own.

Hills College Class of '93, friend of Alistair Haughton, widow, conservative Boston Catholic judge, implacable record on the bench in defense of wealthy institutions, stickler for protocol, identified by Coach Bailey as being in on the fix.

The judge was the lynchpin of her plan. She had excluded the audio, and she would admit it. Not yet — Hannah had to wait for one more thing. She was working on it now; it was happening out of sight, but she would know the moment when it came.

And at that point everything would hang on the judge, who now sent sharp bangs of the gavel through the courtroom. In the jerky, shelving quiet the robed figure stood to deliver her opening remarks. Hannah studied her carefully.

Who are you, Clare Miracoli? Talk to me.

"This trial takes place, unfortunately, in an atmosphere of media hoopla," the scratchy, surprisingly deep voice began. "It is being held here in Boston because, given the nature of modern media, also unfortunate, things would have been the same anywhere. That puts an onus on you, the jury. Now, some or all of you may have heard, or heard of, the audio recording making the rounds of the Internet that the papers are calling the Torture Rant, which purports to contain the voice of Steve Badenhut and purports to relate, among other things, to the rape of the defendant at her school. (Cries from the gallery: "It does!" Raps of the gavel.)

That audio is *not* part of this trial. Whether it's genuine or not, is not part of this trial. Whether or not a rape occurred at the defendant's school, is not part of this trial. So you, the jury, are not to consider that audio one way or the other, up down or sideways. You are here to determine the innocence or guilt of Hannah Radhe on the single charge of premeditated murder. Did she do it or not? Nothing else. The State will present their evidence to that charge only, and you, the jury, are to base your finding on that evidence only. Whatever you may feel, or think, or have experienced about rape on college campuses, you must now put aside. All right? Put it aside, people. The trial is now in session."

You are bought and paid for, Hannah thought, *and I think it shows.*

Cowley stretched backward in his desk chair, the springs squeaking, and looked at his watch; he had to rub his eyes and look again. He resisted the urge to groan. It was after 7:00 pm, and he had promised Karen that there wouldn't be another late night. But the highway video disks he'd requested hadn't come in until late afternoon, and there had been an overflowing cardboard box of them. He sent another glance at the silenced TV in the corner of the homicide room, whose news crawl was again reporting on the trial; across town they had concluded their second day, dominated by McFarrel's devastating cross-examinations. The State's case was falling apart, as he had known it would. *She* must be expecting pretty confidently to walk free.

He had watched with a strange, fatalistic detachment the Hills College debunking of her audio that Koontz had promised, and seen how with the judge in their pocket they had excluded the real audio, as he had known they would. So she had all but destroyed his career for nothing; the system had silenced her regardless.

There was an uncomfortable moral in there somewhere, that Cowley didn't want to look at. *All she has left is the desire to walk,* he thought, and at some angry unspoken level it was the thought of the future into which she would that drove him to nail her.

He was back from a New Years trip to Cape Cod: Karen had insisted on it, and he'd been in no position to refuse; the agencies he was querying were closed for the holiday anyway. But he had lost precious time, and he still had *nothing* —

A couple of other detectives were in the office; from the far corner Scavelli had glanced over at his movement, then quickly back down. Everyone knew what he was looking for; everyone knew to leave him alone.

Somewhere you slipped up. Somewhere you left a trace.

He was still chasing the blue car. He knew its route, or thought he did: it goes from Providence north to HC, then south to New Haven, where she reboards. Okay. But *then* where did it go? New Haven cops had long since confirmed that it wasn't physically still there. Assuming she borrowed it from someone in or near Boston, she presumably returned it soon thereafter, so he had been scanning through Mass Pike tollbooth footage *northbound* for the day after the murder...and the next day...and the next day...and the next and the next. There was no sign of the blue Buick on 84 from New Haven to Boston.

Did she drop it in the sea? Where did it go? What am I missing?

He rubbed his eyes. He knew he should head home, face Karen's wrath, pick it up again in the morning. He blinked around at the office, suddenly realizing how hungry he was. He hadn't eaten since breakfast. His Italian sub from yesterday was, he remembered, still in the fridge in the lounge.

With stiff, uncertain movements, not quite knowing where he

was going, he slung his jacket over his shoulder and left the office.

He was walking down the hall to the lounge when he heard his own name pronounced in a man's voice he didn't know, from behind a closed door. He paused instinctively, then, when he heard Chief Koontz's response, drew closer to the door.

"Yeah, it was his name on the leak, but it *wasn't* him. And there's no way—"

"So threaten him into it, Koontz, I don't care. She *sent* him the texts! They'll be on his phone, ask him. It *had* to be her."

"Fine, but with all due respect, Dean, asking a cop to lie on the stand—"

"Koontz it's the smallest thing. It's just one last—it *has* to be done—these feminists—nobody's believing our—don't you see, we have to bury this damn thing once and for all. He doesn't have to accuse her outright, Rapillo will do that. We just need him to say—"

"You don't know Cowley! He won't—"

Cowley pulled open the door. "Won't what?" He held out his cellphone to the chief.

The other man in the small office, recoiling into the leather furniture with a look of childish fear in his eyes under dark curls, was Dean Haughton, though somewhat reduced from when Cowley had seen him last, on campus the day the body was found.

"You heard?" said Koontz, taking the phone. "Close the door." As Cowley complied the chief looked briefly down at the cellphone screen. "Did you send Hannah Radhe your private email address?"

"For Bailey. Nice to see you, Dean. Chief, I had nothing to do with the hack."

"Lemme ask you this: do you suspect Hannah Radhe for it?"

Oddly Cowley was more protective of the boyfriend. "I do."

"You see?" Dean Haughton said with soft emphasis, as if trying to prompt Koontz into his suggested threat without admitting that he had suggested it.

Koontz sighed and rolled his eyes, handing the phone back to Cowley. "Rapillo's on board?" he asked the Dean.

"And Miracoli. They'll add it tomorrow."

Koontz looked at Cowley. "What they're gonna do is tack on a defamation charge saying Radhe was the one who fabricated the rant audio and posted it. They got her phone when she went through security at John Adams and they can show she had your email to use on the posting. For the rest they're gonna trot out a tech expert to stand up and say the audio's fake, plus show some data that supposedly points to Radhe's location for the posting, right? Though from what I understand—"

"It's Logan Airport!" Haughton spat. "It's close enough. And getting it wasn't cheap."

"All they need is a cop to swear that the Internet rant doesn't match the audio on the actual recorder. It's the same line we've given before, just on the stand. You don't need to describe what *is* on our recorder, or answer a single cross question about *how* it's different. Just say yes it is."

"Chief, I won't lie under oath," said Cowley.

"Dammit, Detective, you already suspect her of the hack. Plus you had this evidence in your possession and never told me and your name is gonna come up in court and I could easily let you burn. Or I could ask for your badge right now."

Cowley didn't care that the performance was for Dean Haughton's benefit. He reached into his coat pocket and withdrew his badge. "I will never lie under oath. And what you're doing stinks," he said, transferring his hard stare to Haughton. "I know you've heard the real audio."

The Dean emitted a theatrical sigh, as if above explaining the interests involved to the naive. He was clearly feeling better.

"There ya go," Koontz said to him. "Keep your badge, Cowley. I can get someone else. Do me a favor on your way back and send Scavelli in here. And Cowley? Don't breathe a fucking word of this." This time the chief's eyes were dead serious; Cowley knew the difference.

He marched back into the homicide office and threw his coat at the chair hard enough to roll it. "Chief wants to see you in the VIP room," he said to Scavelli's surprised eyes. As the soon-to-be-promoted detective wandered curiously into the hall Cowley stared at the cardboard box of disarranged DVD cases, and suddenly gave it a vicious kick. *This is the price of my failure*, he thought. Because he couldn't cleanly solve Hannah's crime, they were going to bury her in garbage. Not only had they blocked her recording from the trial but now they were going to drag her down for inventing it. It occurred to Cowley that the Internet release had made Haughton desperate; Hannah had unleashed the "patriarchy" at its ugliest—and most dangerous. He sighed. *And I've always tried to stay out of politics.* He sagged back down into his chair and stared at the screen, where the image of the last empty Mass Pike tollbooth had sprung up from black at the movement. For a moment he couldn't remember what he had been looking for—

"I'm on the wrong track," he suddenly said aloud.

He'd been obsessing over the car, trying to find more physical proof of the rendezvous. But that had nothing to do with the real question: how she had made the rendezvous work in the first place. It *couldn't* have been luck. That wasn't Hannah. No, she had done the impossible: she had made a complex plan, a day in advance, to meet a train that no one could meet. She had a faster means of travel. Or—or she had *known* the train would be delayed.

Blown transfawma.

Blown how?

Just blown.

Since when do transformers just blow?

She'd been out and about in the car since pre-dawn on the day of the murder, to be at Mayden School. Where else might she have gone that morning?

In a strange fascination Cowley picked up his phone and dialed Amtrak, like he had before, only this time he asked for the maintenance department. He felt something settle inside himself; a sort of fever disappeared leaving him steady and dogged. Patiently, relentlessly, calmly explaining himself over and over again, he made one person transfer him to another, and on to another, and look up a number, and thumb through a thick dirty log book hanging by a corner on a wall, until finally he was talking to crew chief Don Evans, who had serviced the blown transformer on the night of December 15.

"Yeah, that was weird. There was nothing on the lines. It's like it just blew. But it was a new unit, less than a year old. And man, was it shot to hell inside. It's like whatever shorted it out went on for a while. But we didn't find anything up or down the track to explain it. So I just put 'blown transformer' in the log, 'cause that's all we had. What's that? It was in East Greenwich, East Greenwich Rhode Island. Right where the tracks go along the Bay."

Chapter 18 - Defamed

It was a warm afternoon, archipelagos of green lawn showing through the snow before the seaside colonial homes. Cowley strolled through the quaint little town of East Greenwich, hands in his trench coat pockets. The shops and cafes still had wreaths in their windows and colored lights along the lintels, lit even in daylight, and something of a festive population was abroad in defiance of the hunkered-down New England winter. At the Main Street Coffeehouse locals rose from their stools—elderly couples in windbreakers, teenagers in denim jackets—to tell him about the night of the blown transformer, with the godawful explosions and the flashing lights like nothing they'd ever seen before. "Just up the Post Road from here, near Bayview, by the Ocean Point condos."

He had a strange smile on his face as he parked his squad car along the nondescript shabbiness of Route 1 and walked the road in the freshness of sea air. There was a high likelihood that he was on a fool's errand, the kind that, if it didn't pan out, he could never tell anyone about. The fact made him feel oddly alone with Hannah. It was purely him versus her here, and he had the sense of closing in on the final secret of the smartest criminal he had ever known.

His motive, openly acknowledged now, was to save her from death by garbage. They had crushed her dreams of reform; he wasn't going to let the bastards send her down on false defamation charges and insulting implications that she couldn't count. *Keep it clean.* He no longer knew whether he was out to nail her or honor her—if she did what he *thought* she did it was worth a hell of a salute—but either way he would uncover the truth.

The tracks of the Eastern Corridor paralleled the road here, back behind the waterfront homes atop an old stone aqueduct that effectively blocked the homes' water view. At the given location he was able to look up at the line from both sides, first from a condominium parkinglot, then, after ducking through a pedestrian archway, from a narrow strip of land along the water. He saw no signs of trespass or damage up there. He even scrambled a little way up the incline of loose rocks and black gravel for a closer look at the catenary wires, but he still saw nothing amiss. From the base of the incline he turned and looked out at the Bay: a grey blanket under soft clouds, extending in a gentle scintillation out to a border of low land half a mile away. A weathered lobster boat hovered in the offing. It was a pleasant spot to stand.

And yet this was where the short circuit had occurred. He had exact notes from Dan Evans, confirmed by the locals. Returning to the parkinglot of the condominium he talked to a short, white-haired lady in a bucket hat whose eyes widened excitedly behind her large glasses. "I couldn't see it from my window, but it was right over there, right over there. I saw the light. This blue light. It lit up everything. Then finally it went dark."

"Did you notice anything unusual about it, or anyone unusual in the area, or out on the water?"

"Well, there was a sound. I mean, there was an awful noise of buzzing and popping like the wires were going to blow up, but I also heard a, a motorboat or something running."

"A motorboat?"

"When I opened the window and leaned out to try and see. I could hear it. I thought it sounded like a motorboat, from out on the water, maybe close off shore. I didn't see it, I just heard it."

He entered the condominium with the lady and spent a half hour or so knocking on doors and interviewing other residents, but no one had seen anything suspicious, and no else had heard the "motorboat."

Earlier he had noted the single traffic cam overlooking Main Street in town. Back at the same coffeehouse he ordered a tall coffee, then walked the few blocks to the police station. The cleancut young cop on duty went into a back room and ran his finger along a shelf of old-school videotape boxes, talking about the big semi-truck accident back in '88 that had led to them putting in the camera. From a shelf at floor level he dragged out a dusty VCR with a dangling cable, and back at his desk set it down atop a pile of papers and plugged it into his computer. He tapped a few buttons to launch a connection program, and passed Cowley two videos. "I have to head out for an hour; you're welcome to sit here."

Five minutes later Cowley hit the pause key, carefully set his coffee cup down on the desk, and sucked a long breath in through his teeth.

There was his car.

There was no mistaking it. It was the blue Buick, seen from above as it made the left turn from Division Street onto Route 1 towards the condominiums, at roughly 9:00 am on the morning of the murder.

She did it. Holy fuck. I don't know how, but she caused the train delay.

She blew up Amtrak. That's *how she made her math work.*

He burst into laughter.

Three hours later the VHS tape in its white sleeve was sitting on the table of his booth, alongside a lobster roll and a beer at a blandly generic seafood joint whose windows overlooked industrial arc lights shimmering in the narrow black waters of Apponaug Cove. In Boston they would be wrapping up the day's work, the last day of State's Evidence; he had lost another day of the trial, though new evidence could be admitted throughout.

He had gotten no further in his investigation. And he was okay with that.

Oh, he had gone up and down the Bay, talking to marina owners and lobstermen and rental agencies in search of the "motorboat," with no luck. It was pure diligence; he knew he wouldn't find anything. A boat implied an accomplice, some arrangement in the morning for an action at night, and he knew that Hannah worked alone. Whatever she had done that morning, she had done herself. She had set something up at the tracks: she had gotten up on the aqueduct and climbed onto the catenary and attached something to the transformer with a timer or remote trigger on it. And Dan Evans' crew had found no trace of it.

Just like the dorm room. Just like the Mayden School.

There would be no fingerprints on the fence. There would be no DNA on the mangled transformer when they dragged it out of the pile. There would be no wire to a battery on the condominium roof. He was in the presence of one last secret, and he had to find it alone, if he could.

Maybe he wouldn't find it. Maybe he could admit that.

Veils were falling inside him. She was likely to win her case. It had been another day of McFarrel walking all over State's sorry-ass argument; he was one of the best in town in a courtroom. She might actually get away with it. Live to fight for her cause another day. *Is that so bad?* The alternative — what he was pursuing — was life in prison, for daring to take on a rotten system. Yes, murder was the wrong way to do it, but still: *Is that what I wanted?*

He looked out at the dark water. *Maybe I'll just sit on this one.*

A big reflection crossed the glass and a shadow fell across his table. He looked up in time to meet Chief Koontz' eyes as his bulk slid into the booth opposite Cowley. The chief was in street clothes, something Cowley had rarely seen, a beat-up jacket over a check hunting shirt, bareheaded with a greying crewcut. He put a podgy hand on the videotape.

"So the other part of being an idealistic cop," he said, "is that you're a damn good one. I light a fire under you, I watch what happens. *I* know where we are relative to what happened to that nine-thirty train. You got a theory to maybe beat Racona's, make us all look good?"

Cowley looked at the videotape. He drained the last of his beer.

"I think you should have CSI go over the tracks and the catenaries around here," he said.

Hannah had been in a sort of terror that they would bring Cowley in to testify regarding the crime scene, which during the two days of State's Evidence Rapillo went over in lovingly malicious detail. *How can I face him? Where would I look?* But they used the CSI guy exclusively. So far he hadn't appeared. *Where is he?* She said a silent prayer that no new evidence had come in: she was still waiting for one thing to happen before she made her move, and the ambiguous status of the case gave her decided advantages.

In the meantime she watched with detachment McFarrel's superb performance on cross-examination. He got Gomez, the police computer expert, to admit that his pattern identification software had sent an innocent man to prison. He brought poor Tom Corcoran, the teenager, to tears on the stand as he extracted that on the day Tom identified the missing weapon from the foot-locker he was high, had run from the cops, and had made a deal with Detective Cowley that he would not be charged for pos-session if he cooperated. Head shakes and *tsks* from the jury rewarded him on that one. More important was his reduction of the CSI man Bannister to a broken record regarding forensics in the dorm room: on the rug, *no*, on the door, *no*, on the bed, *no*, on the desk, *no, no, no*...

She paid far more attention to the progress of two other things: the news, dominated now by the banner-headline denials of the Internet audio, and the feminist protests outside the John Adams courthouse, which were growing bigger. That morning when she and McFarrel entered through the back door they moved in an escort of four policemen through a cheering throng of dozens of young women (and several men), waving signs saying "Truth," "We Believe," "Stop Rape Now!"

In both those venues she had become "famous," a sudden tran-sition that bewildered her parents when she got to see them. Her father, the TV producer, would pat her on the back, in his general happiness at McFarrel's coming victory, and say, "Don't worry, honey, all this will evaporate as fast as it came on." To which her mother would say, "Darling, she *wants* to be a spokesman for them." To Hannah, isolated in her courtroom bubble, the news and protests were only weathervanes, by which she measured the growing pressure on Dean Haughton.

Almost. Let him make one more stupid move. He has to.

The old courthouse was at the best of times ill-suited to the human corralling used in modern trials. The upstairs rooms all gave onto a single curved hall, lined with six-foot paintings of the Founders, that at breaks filled up indiscriminately with participants. It was here that she could meet briefly with her parents and the Peabodys. And it was here, on the third day of the trial, in the noisy hubbub with everyone going down to the atrium dome for coffee amid green-uniformed guards standing watch, that McFarrel stood with the family to inform them of the sudden new defamation charge to be added on. Groans of outraged disbelief rose from her family.

"Fabricate an audio track?" her father cried, hands at his head. "How is she supposed to have done that? That takes *studio technology!*"

"They have evidence tying the initial post to her location," McFarrel hastily explained, "and unfortunately they have her phone which they say shows the police email used for the post. They're going to trot in an audio expert to say it's artificial, and a detective from the homicide department who's heard the real recording to vouch for the Internet version being different."

He wouldn't, Hannah thought in horror, which gave her father and Mike Peabody time to bombard McFarrel with questions about the penalties involved in a defamation charge as added to or, hopefully, surviving alone after, a murder charge —

"Plead guilty to it," Hannah said.

"Hannah honey, slow down," said her father, "You don't want to be cleared of murder only to face, what, how many years of — "

"And it's a vicious lie," said her mother. "You'd be putting your name to having falsified your own sexual assault. And with all these girls looking to you—shouldn't you at least fight it?"

"I am fighting it," she said. "None of this will matter when the real audio comes out."

"Well, ah, *that's* not—it's already been—" McFarrel spluttered, before his desire to agree with a guilty plea took control. "Folks, the good news here is this takes the Torture Rant off the table for good. It's a strange case in that everyone knows about the rape but no one can talk about it. Rapillo's been dancing around it— his whole argument is going to be based on the rant making Hannah too berserk to count. He's waiting for his closing speech where he can say whatever he wants and he'll drag it out front and center despite Miracoli. Now he can't do that. A guilty plea here is good: let's keep our focus on the main thing, the murder charge."

And so, back at the defense table, Hannah watched as the new charge was read out, to ripples of shocked, re-evaluating murmurs through the gallery. She had been coached to keep a steady, emotionless demeanor as the various experts testified, but she couldn't help shaking her head and narrowing her eyes at Captain Scavelli when he delivered his one-line confirmation from the witness box, consigning to fantasyland the rape confession he himself had heard, in the interrogation booth if not elsewhere. She didn't think she imagined the blush somewhere between his crew cut and necktie.

She paid more attention to Judge Miracoli. *Does she know?* The true audio file was sitting right there on the evidence table, despite her ruling it inadmissible. *Has she heard it? Did she peek? Does she know this charge is false, or does she believe my guilty plea?* A lot hung on that question and Hannah tried to read the answer in the way the judge looked at her.

The gavel rapped and the strong deep voice rang out. "The defendant has pleaded guilty to the supplementary charge of defamation against the Hills College Kingfishers. We may now return, if Mr. Rapillo is ready, to State's Evidence on the primary charge of murder. Mr. Rapillo? We are still living in hope of finishing by five o'clock today, if that is all right with you."

Miracoli had a good poker face.

So did Hannah.

This was the moment she had been waiting for. *This* was Dean Haughton's stupid move—and it was stupider than she had dared hope. But she had known he would do something, because she had forced him into it. Forced him—with the Internet.

When she posted Steve's rant to the forums she knew it would be easy to deny. But it nevertheless served a purpose: to start a conversation. It was the same purpose Hannah had intended long ago, but amplified a hundredfold by the murder trial and media frenzy. And that impassioned conversation, spreading throughout these weeks, impervious to reason or counter-attack like anything online, fed in speculation by Haughton's own injunction prohibiting a check on the true recorder, swollen with the outrage of the anonymous abused in their seething thousands, was *un*deniable, was *un*stoppable—all of it putting pressure on the Hills College football program. At a certain point Haughton would *have* to act. And because he could do nothing against *it*, he would have to come after either the original, or *her*. And both of them were here.

He had done both. And in the process he had done nothing less than formally put the lie about her recorder audio, in Hills College's name, on the record, in court. And she would bet the farm that he had walked all over Judge Miracoli to do it.

This was a bald-faced intervention in her carefully isolated murder case; it *did* tilt the case against the prosecution (McFarrel was right); Miracoli was a stickler for formality and this was a hi-jacking of her courtroom for political and even personal reasons. She could practically hear Haughton (or someone from Hills) leaning on the judge with the in-for-a-penny argument to do it, and looking hard into the judge's eyes—which interestingly enough were staring hard right back—she thought she saw re-sentment.

Now. Tonight. He's forced her hand. Now it's my turn.

That night she would undertake the biggest risk of her life. She would get Judge Clare Miracoli to break ranks and admit the true recorder audio as legal evidence.

How?

She would talk her into it.

Chapter 19 - Housebreaker

As a defendant, Hannah was not permitted to have the slightest private interaction with her judge. But she wasn't in jail. And what would a judge do if a defendant simply — knocked on her door at night?

That evening at the Peabodys' diningroom table Hannah took only a few bites of the chicken alfredo dinner, then pushed her chair back and asked Mike if she could borrow his car. "I just need some private time. I have to go clear my head," she said. "I shouldn't be long."

"Don't leave the State!" her father commanded, his mouth full.

"Honey, that's not funny," said her mother.

With a long eye-to-eye pause communicating that his BMW had better not appear on tollbooth photographs in court, Mike handed her the keys. Throughout the week there had been a fine line in the household between unanimous consent that she was innocent and unconditional support if she was not, and she knew on which side Mike fell. "Thanks Mike," she said. "I promise I won't go far."

On her way out the door she grabbed the day's Boston Globe from the hall table, where she had made sure to leave it that morning. Its latest headline would help her in her attempt to talk Judge Miracoli around.

This was the most desperate thing she had ever done.

As she drove, heart pounding, she thanked her lucky stars that

State's Evidence had ended without any sudden new additions from Rapillo. She had been almost surprised: she had *felt* Cowley still out there. But somehow that last slender thread of her alibi still held and, true to her vow, she would honor him by putting it to good use.

Judge Clarabell D. Miracoli's private residence was on a tony side street near Harvard Square, a trim two-story Cape Cod house with gabled windows and a pillared entry from the porch, set back across a dark garden. Hannah found parking a block away and walked back, leaving clear sneakerprints in the thin snow on the buckled brick sidewalk. She stood at the iron fence, hands tucked into the pockets of her white parka. Overhead the moon sailed between icebergs of cloud. Lights were on in the curtained windows both downstairs and upstairs, but she knew Miracoli lived alone since being widowed seven years ago. She had done her research.

For a long moment she stood there, looking at the house. Her heart thumped in her throat. Somehow knocking on that door was a scarier prospect than committing murder. That, in the end, had been a job for Hannah the fencer. Now she had to bring to bear the full persuasive power of her intellect in the righteousness of her cause against a wall of hardened prejudice. As she saw it, Haughton had given her a big push that day; she should already be leaning. It was up to her to complete the job. As weapons she had the Globe tucked under her arm and, warm in her clenched fist in her pocket, her blue-and-white USB thumb drive with the audio recording on it. These things would be her lever to move power.

The problem was that power would likely slam the door in her face before she could get a word of her rehearsed speech out. She had come up with a plan to prevent that: she would confess. As soon as the door opened she would hold out the USB drive and tell the judge the truth: that it was the recording she made the night she killed Steve. *That* should create just enough of a pause for her to begin talking.

It really wasn't a very good plan.

Still, there was nothing for it.

She pushed the iron gate open and started toward the house. It seemed a long walk down the path to the porch steps, and though she knew it would make more sense to stomp noisily up them she found herself slinking onto the porch as silent as a shadow. Then she was in the pillared entryway before the strong wooden door with a little curtained window of frosted glass.

Fundamentally, beyond all the legal and strategic arguments she had marshalled, she was there to appeal to Judge Miracoli as a woman in the cause against rape. "*For sisterhood*," she whispered, and knocked.

A pause that seemed an eternity. Then came the judge's deep, muffled voice: "Who is it?"

The question caught Hannah stupidly unprepared. On the spur of the moment she decided that the best policy was to say nothing. Then she heard a latch slide and the door opened inward a bright half foot.

"*You?*" Judge Miracoli said in simple out-of-context shock. She was in a maroon blouse and pearl necklace; her shoulder-length steel-grey hair was loose; firelight moved behind her. "Are you—" her darting eyes made the word *alone* unnecessary; immediately her comprehending face was hard. "You *cannot*—"

Hannah stuck out the USB drive. "Judge, you've been misled. This is the real audio of Steve Badenhut. I can guarantee that, because I recorded it myself the night I—"

She was interrupted by a voice from inside the house: a man called, "Who's there? What's going—*her?*" And over Miracoli's shoulder the eyes of Dean Haughton met Hannah's. He was standing in the middle of the room, craning for a better view. "What—what is this—who's there?" he barked, waving his head to try to see more of the porch.

Miracoli's eyes never left Hannah, and her voice was a strong hiss. "Do you understand that by being here you invalidate the entire trial, that I'll have to recuse myself and—" Her eyes flickered three times between the extended USB drive and Hannah's set face, and her voice lowered. "Look—*please* go home, and please—"

Hannah spoke in a lowered voice too. "I'm here to ask you to admit the audio. I can't confess until you do."

"You're here to *confess*—?" The voice, down to a whisper, carried the stress of being caught between ridiculous teenage melodrama on one hand and something else on the other.

"No. I can't, not until you admit—"

"For God's sake, Clare, let her in and close the goddamn door!" Dean Haughton called. "Someone else might see!"

"Oh for Heaven's sake," Judge Miracoli breathed, and her eyes scanned the street behind Hannah to see whether the Dean's own shout had drawn attention to Hannah under the porch light. In a deep fatalistic moan she said, "Come in."

Then Hannah was standing in the firelit warmth of a small livingroom with an Oriental rug, mullioned side windows, a mantelpiece full of photographs, and Dean Haughton cleverly angling himself so as not to be seen through the door that was already closed.

The judge turned from sliding the lock. "Now, I will not for a *moment* entertain—"

"Young lady, you stand right there and listen to me very closely," Dean Haughton shouted, pointing a finger from his full height before the fireplace. "You're a defendant in a murder case and nothing you say will be listened to by anyone, but *nevertheless*, if you breathe a word that you saw me here, I swear to God Hills College will, will expel you in absentia—will blacken—we'll file suit against your parents—we'll—"

"What, am I interrupting a payoff or something?" Hannah asked Judge Miracoli. The game was on, in an unexpected form but on regardless, and she was immediately in total, graceful focus. She made up her mind on the spot that her best move was to speak only to the judge. Miracoli rolled her eyes and opened her mouth.

"Whatever you saw is no concern of yours!" Haughton said. "And you'll forget you saw it if you know what's good—"

"Al!" Miracoli barked, silencing the dean. For a moment the fluttering of the fire was the only sound as she stood with her fingers at her pained forehead. Then, without removing them, she looked at Hannah. "*What*—do you want? Or did you come to murder us too?"

"I'm unarmed," said Hannah evenly. "Your Honor, I'm here to prevail on you to admit the rapist audio in court. The time has come."

"The audio that's just been pronounced a forgery and a slander? And you're here to offer me your original homemade version of the forgery?"

Hannah looked at the USB drive in her own fingers, and at the judge with an appreciative smile. With a few words she had taken

control of the situation in her home instantly. Hannah laid the
USB drive on the coffeetable next to a porcelain ashtray. "It could
be. But what I released to the Internet was only a little bit at the
end around Steve's rant. This is my copy of the full eight-hour
recording as the boys were stalking the park getting ready for me.
Why would I fabricate the voices of Chris Kelly, Andrew Keith,
Reggie Mathis, and others and not release them? Why would Andrew Keith's father put an injunction on the recorder audio if it
wasn't real? Listen to it yourself. Or you can just ask him—I'm
pretty sure he's heard the original."

She was merely trying to play hard and fast in a crazy situation. To her surprise she was convincing, or at any rate she saw
the judge turn an inquiring look upon Haughton.

The latter, at the back of the room, had turned to the fireplace
while Hannah spoke and, as if recovered from his apparent initial
shock at being caught red-handed paying off a judge, was lei-
surely stirring the fire. With his normal poise he leaned the poker
against the inner hearth and turned back, pretending to notice
Miracoli's look for the first time.

"The original audio? Yes, I've heard it," he said. "But be careful what you say, Miss Radhe. You see, if you *didn't* fabricate it,
then either you're the hacker of the police department, which is a
far worse crime than defamation, or it's your own copy and
you've just confessed to being the killer. Are you sure you want
to keep talking?"

The dean smiled smugly at his trap. Hannah met it with a
smile of her own that, to him, could stand as a confirmation of
either or both while, to Miracoli, could have been gratitude for the
giveaway. After an instant the dean's widening eyes told Hannah
that his part had been received clearly.

The judge looked at Hannah, and spoke sharply. "You pled guilty to fabricating it. The police verified under oath that the Internet audio did not match theirs."

I was right. She didn't know. And I'm still here because she wants to.

"They lied," she said gently. "Captain Scavelli personally knew it was real. He was observing the interrogation room when they played my actual recorder audio, to test whether I'd heard it before. As for pleading guilty to the false audio," she shrugged, "if my mission here fails, it doesn't matter, and if it succeeds, it *really* won't matter."

Miracoli didn't smile, but her eyes narrowed with a glint of the same appreciation, tempered by the cold condition that she hadn't succeeded. Hannah had to proceed very carefully here: Haughton's presence made everything different and she had no time to strategize, or even wonder if her plan was still possible. Her main argument, intended to break her from Haughton, was now an issue between *them,* making her peripheral. Sure enough, after her searching look the judge turned abruptly to him. "Is it true?"

Haughton spread his hands. "Clare, this maniac was threatening to bring the whole college down around our ears. You understood the circumstances. She's a murderer and a, a fucking cultural arsonist. I don't need to explain again—"

"You told *me* it was a fake. You—"

"I have already apologized for how I behaved. You hadn't heard it and I needed it to go through. I did what I had to."

There was the barest pause, eloquent of what made further apology unnecessary. Miracoli said, "That included paying the police to lie in my courtroom?"

He gave a chuckle, as if they were over the hard part. "Lord, if you only knew the extent of the budget that goes to —"

"Stop." Her raised hand silenced him as she turned back to Hannah with a sigh. "You're a brave girl, Miss Radhe. And if *this* is real then I'm sorry for what you went through at Hills. But I can't release the audio. I want the two of you to walk out my back door, now, and tomorrow I will recuse myself from this case. Unfortunately *you* will now spend another year as a defendant while they arrange —"

"Not the whole college," Hannah said. "Down around your ears. Just him." She took from under her arm the Boston Globe and turned it to show the banner headline. In the fact that the judge stopped talking Hannah knew that she had already seen, and understood, it too. It was the one that read:

"WORST CHRISTMAS EVER" FOR HILLS COLLEGE HOLIDAY FUND-
RAISING DUE TO LINGERING RAPE TAINT

"This is why you should switch sides. It's over for Dean Haughton. The money's gone against him. You should get clear now, because he can't save himself from this."

And this was not at *all* how Hannah had imagined making her pitch. But if she had to get Miracoli to turn against Haughton with Haughton in the room, then she might as well widen the rift she had just created. "He tried everything to silence the rape story and the college has thrown a lot of money after him, but it isn't silenced, it's louder than ever. Look at the headline: he's failed. He's now a liability; his day is done. Step clear of the wreck."

Again she spoke to the judge alone, as if the dean wasn't present, and again she was rewarded with the judge turning to Haughton, this time with raised eyebrows and an amused smile. "How about it, Dean? Am I a rat on a sinking ship?"

I'm still here. She wants this fight — through me. How can I — ?

"*That?*'" said Dean Haughton, raising his nose at the paper. "Pff. Miss Radhe, don't be dense. Weren't you in court today? The rape taint is over—I took care of it. There *was* no rape. If you're trying sophomorically to gloat over my downfall you'd do better to look to yourself. Anyway, that—*that*—is a typical headline exaggeration. I realize you're a newspaper writer, but you overestimate the power of the media."

Miracoli had a look on her face almost of entertainment. "Go on," she said, clearly indicating Hannah. "I'm sure you have more." She seemed to have accepted Hannah in the house, albeit conditionally. "And by the way I have never seen anyone get under his skin like you have. I'd love to know how much money you've spent on her, Al."

The air in the room thickened.

With such encouragement Hannah could at last begin her prepared arguments, but all of it had to be reevaluated on the spot. She was now Miracoli's mouthpiece in a jab at Haughton—wherever that would end—though her real target was Miracoli herself. Still, she stuck to her rule and addressed herself entirely to the judge.

"I don't overestimate the newspapers, Your Honor. The reason it's come to this for the dean is precisely because they're no match today for social media. I have a feeling you don't approve"—a quick eye movement by the judge confirmed it—"and it's true there's a lot of garbage on the Internet." She took a risk and transferred her look to Haughton. "But it's also true that when social media is backed by tens of thousands of college girls who've been abused and raped and silenced and know the truth when they hear it, then there would be no stopping the force."

"A large percentage of those feminist rape numbers are hearsay based on false accusations," Haughton stated. "Like yours." Too late he remembered that the audio was here genuine, and his waxen face reddened in anger.

Hannah continued to stare at him but talk to Miracoli. "I knew the dean would try for a legal fix; it's his only card to play, and he plays it well. But it's too late. *Hills* has to pay attention to the popular reality. High school girls are questioning their safety at HC. Even if you and Dean Haughton bury the evidence forever, the college would *still* have to act." *Now* she turned to Miracoli. "There's going to be a very public housecleaning gesture coming, to show the alumni that they take campus rape seriously. Three guesses whom it will target. Your Honor, you're on the wrong side of it. Now is the moment to do the right thing. Step clear. Change your mind."

The judge had been relentlessly staring at Haughton, referring the attack to him, but at the last phrase she turned back with a warning look. Hannah understood that she had heard an implied "Or else" based on her having caught the two of them together. She shook her head. "I'm not here to threaten you. I can't. In fact if you do agree to admit the audio, then obviously I was never here. We never spoke. And *I* can keep a secret, trust me."

She got what she wanted: a glint of *Did she?* in the judge's eyes. She wasn't prepared, however, for how Haughton interpreted that attention.

"Oh, the audio, the audio!" he cried in a mock falsetto. "You're still trying! Even now you're still out to prove to the world that Steve Badenhut raped you. Yes, he raped you, and yes, you got him to admit it on tape, brava!" He pointed at the USB drive on the coffee table. "Do you honestly think that Hills College is going to jeopardize a hundred million dollar football program and the revenue from five thousand Kingfisher alumni to *tell the truth* about him? Give it up! He's dead! You *got* your revenge, and McFarrel might even get you off for it, so for God's sake call it a day in Oh-I-was-raped-world and grow up!" He ameliorated the beat of shocked silence in the livingroom by going still further: "I mean, seriously, Hannah, leaving the recorder on the boy's dead body didn't work, did you really think coming to Clare Miracoli's house in the middle of the night and pleading would?"

She broke her rule. "Yes," she said.

"Not gonna happen," was his immediate riposte, complete with a roundhouse point down the hall toward the back door.

"Did you really kill him by sneaking off and on the train—and if so, *how?*" Clare Miracoli asked Hannah.

In the completely appropriate change of subject Hannah saw many things, not least permission to stay in the room. She licked her lips. "I can't confess. To do so would end the trial and I need the trial to continue so the audio can be admitted. That's all I care about, exposing the truth, about Steve yes but also about the whole damn Boston-wide cover-up of ongoing rape. If I'm convicted after that, which is likely, then we'll all find out the details together. And by the way the request for the audio is a perfectly legal one from McFarrel; he intends to show that the simple *volume* of Steve's rant would suffice to attract a stranger to the park and find the recorder."

The judge blinked out of a different, deeper expression. "*McFarrel* sent you?"

"No, he has no idea I'm here. But the request has to come from somewhere, and I'll arrange it with him." Miracoli again turned raised eyebrows to Haughton—with a different emphasis that caused an immediate warning frown on the dean's face—and Hannah continued, pulling random arguments out of her mental grab-bag: "Your Honor, I obviously don't know what the gesture from Hills will be. I think they'll fire him for taking risks with the college's name that didn't pay off, but he might survive to silence other girls. But don't you see, if *you* release the audio tomorrow, *you* expose his cover-up. Then he's the perfect scapegoat for their reform. It'll be faster and less damaging for Hills as well as being a real reform. And by doing it *now*, at exactly the right time, not only will you be on the right side but Hills will *hail* you as the courageous judge who stood up to corruption and blew the whistle against campus rape." She drew a fast deep breath. "I know you suppressed my audio to protect the school. But this way Hills will only lose Haughton, and I guarantee that *you'll* be making commencement speeches there for years to come as a heroine for women's rights."

That was her ultimate broadside—*choose me or him*—and she knew it was premature. *But what happens now?* All she could do was keep pushing and see.

Miracoli whistled through her teeth. "She does paint a compelling picture," she said. "I think someday *you'll* be making commencement speeches." Then the amusement left her voice and it got hard. "She's right about one thing, Al: I hold your fate in my hands. Tell me, why shouldn't I release the audio tomorrow? What's *your* argument? Come on, now, what do *you* have to say?" Her strong voice and straight look were those that had met many an errant lawyer in her courtroom.

Haughton spread his hands and looked at her from under his brows. "I'd say it's a little late to be rediscovering your idealism, Clare. —Seriously?" he added, after a beat. "You're angling for more? Is this a conversation you want to have?" His eyes flicked back and forth from her to Hannah. "Is this because of—shit, do I need to call you tomorrow morning or—" He broke off as Miracoli bent to pick the USB drive off the coffee table and put it in the pocket of her slacks, still holding him in her gaze. Hannah watched carefully; she knew this was payback for his crass comments and she wouldn't break faith for it. He didn't.

"Clare, come on—look, what do you want to do about this?" He gestured at Hannah. "If you want I'll take her out the back door and drive her home and you can resume tomorrow. Or if you want to recuse yourself I'll vouch for whatever you want to say to do it. It's your call. I'm a fixer and I'm at your service."

Something in Haughton's tone, beyond the half-scared quasi-apology, gave Hannah another clue: that Miracoli had *already* been thinking of recusing herself, and perhaps even talking about it when interrupted. *It's why she welcomed me in.* And she understood her reasons—but the insight came too late.

"May I keep this?" the judge asked Hannah.

"Of course..."

"Now just a *minute*—" Haughton began.

"Miss Radhe, I am not going to undo the Motion to Suppress on the audio." As Haughton let out a breath of exasperated relief she turned to Hannah. "Even if I *did* think it was the right thing, which I don't necessarily, the sad fact is I can't. The audio has a prior injunction on it."

Hannah nodded and spoke carefully. Her coat was still on and she was sweating in the firelight. "Yes. I've looked into that. The injunction is in the name of security for the boys on a hostile campus. It was imposed by Andrew Keith's father and is intended for Andrew. It doesn't apply to Steve. Security is no longer a concern of his. I'm not asking you to release the whole tape or anyone else's voice. Just Steve's—just the confession."

She watched the judge's face closely, very much wishing that they were alone, and saw two reactions in rapid succession: in the grey eyes a single bright flash of legal possibility, then an eye roll and long inhalation as she groped for another out. "Granted. But even so—"

She struck hard on the insight she had had. "Your Honor, forgive me, but this case could be the capstone of your career and instead they've made it a travesty. You don't like media circuses so you agreed to keep the rape audio out, but the result is that everyone's dancing around the rape issue and walking all over you. You know how Rapillo's going to close, don't you? He's going to reference the Torture Rant despite you and thumb his nose at you, because the *people* still believe it, and he's trying to sell the jury on the bullshit argument that sexual assault makes a woman too berserk to count. *Do you think I can't count?*" That, in a suddenly loud voice, looking directly into her eyes, was as close as she could come. One of the things she had seen was that Miracoli was *curious*, curious about the *murder*. Hannah had a window and she didn't mind breaking glass. "*That's* what going to happen to you in the public eye, and you know it. But Your Honor if you admit the audio it puts the circus *behind* you, it *resolves* it. It ought to have been there for motive and after tomorrow it becomes just motive. Then Rapillo and McFarrel can fight it out openly about whether I could or couldn't have killed Steve and *how*. I think I can guarantee you," she added through gritted teeth, "that there are a few surprises remaining." She made a mental apology for bluffing up McFarrel when she meant Cowley, and drew another breath, she didn't know for what. "I read the commencement speech you gave at Stamford in 2003 where you said—"

"Al," said Miracoli. "Do me a favor and leave by the back door."

There was a moment of complete silence in the house. *Point fucking fifteen*, thought Hannah, drenched under her parka.

"I—will—do—no such thing," Dean Haughton said in a tone of hard horror. "Clare, I'm warning you—come to your senses or—"

"Or what? You *will* leave when I tell you to, and I'm telling you to. I've changed my mind."

"Well you can damn well un-change—"

"Leave us please. This is my house and you are no longer—"

"Oh *your* house? Really? And what do you think paid for it all th—"

"Just for that! You get out of my house just for that! You—*you* have presumed on a college friendship for too long. I'm sorry it has to—you know what? I'm not. She's right. Just *go*." She pointed an imperious finger down the back hall.

It was at that point that Hannah, in the habit of staying as alert as possible to everything, was not looking diplomatically at the floor as Haughton's eyes swept the room, and they met hers. Whatever remained in hers had an immediate effect, and he lunged from his position at the fireplace, put a hand on her chest, and shoved her hard. She fell against the edge of an armchair and a torchiere lamp toppled over her. Miracoli screamed.

His voice roared. "Are you going to let this crazy bitch destroy—"

"Yes! Go! Get out!" the judge shrieked.

He took a step toward her. "So that's it, huh? Fine, I'll go, but

I am damn sure taking my —"

"Here then! Take it," spat Miracoli, backed to the front door, and made to throw a white envelope at him; he, however, was close enough to snatch it from her hand.

"Good. And the audio too."

"Don't be stupid! It's just a copy — it's not the —"

"It's a copy I can use. Against you and your puerile attempt to stab me in the back. I don't get stabbed. Hand it over." He held out one hand and made a fist with the other. "It's bloody ridiculous that it's come to this but sometimes it has to. And I swear I wouldn't mind. *Give* it to me."

"I will not."

"Don't," said Hannah, moving to her side. "It's mine and it's not for him."

Haughton looked from one to the other. "An old woman and a teenage girl," he said conversationally, "are not going to do this to Hills College, *or* to me." Abruptly he turned on his heel, took two steps back to reach into the fireplace, and turned forward holding the iron fire poker that had been left braced in the coals. Its tip glowed a dull red. "Get out! Help!" Miracoli screamed. "Apologies for ungentlemanly behavior," he said, walking toward them, "but the beauty of this is that neither of you can run, because you're both in far too compromised a position. *Don't try it,*" he said with a fast step toward Hannah, who was circling around him, causing her to stumble over the fallen lamp. Miracoli was backing the other way, toward the stairs, and he advanced on her with the poker. As he went he swung it whistling over the cupboard shelf, scattering smashed photographs and teapots, then aimed it back at her. "Come on, Clare, use your legal mind. In this spot I have nothing to lose, do I? I'm quite willing to get as ugly as you. Give me the drive."

"I told you, it's mine," said Hannah, coming sideways out of the red light of the hearth with another fire poker in her hand.

Haughton whirled, and in a blur of motion made for her. They met in the middle of the room, Haughton swinging his poker downward like a club. Miracoli made a high gasp. But it was really one of the easiest moves to defend against, and even with a weapon that didn't have a helpful hook on the side Hannah would have been able to deflect his stroke, catch it in a quick circle that exerted immense lateral force, and disarm him. Haughton's poker sailed across the room to crash against the cupboard, and even while he was staring dumbly at his stunned hand his feet were backpedaling instinctively from her implacable forward thrust that brought the tip of her poker with a hard push against the exact center of his heart. As he fell backwards near Miracoli's feet his eyes met Hannah's, and what he saw *then* made him shriek aloud.

"Look!" he screamed from the floor. "She *did* kill him! Did you see? She did! She's the murderer!"

"Alistair, you're babbling," said Miracoli, holding the finally unlatched front door open to the winter night. "Now for the last time — *go away.*"

And he went, as fast as his knees, wrists, and finally legs could carry him. The judge slammed the door and locked it. A silent beat later, a painting fell from the wall.

"Would you like a cup of tea," Miracoli said, turning.

"No, thank you. I, um, can't stay. I'm supposed to be on a short drive to clear my head."

They both exhaled a single breath of a shared giggle, then both stopped. Miracoli looked away to her smashed livingroom.

"Seems clear enough to me," she said drily.

"I'm sorry," said Hannah, following her eyes. "I'd stay to help clean up—"

"No, no. How can you? You were never here."

"I wasn't. *Thank* you, Your Honor."

"Oh, call me that tomorrow." She unlatched the front door again, but held her hand on the knob and didn't open it. She was looking at Hannah appraisingly. "I'm not sure you *should* thank me. You're right about Rapillo's argument, and having the real audio as motive will give him more advantage against you, not less. But you know that, don't you, and you don't care." Hannah held her gaze steadily and Miracoli slowly nodded. There was a strange pause, as if the judge was reflecting on something. "I'd…like to ask you one thing. You obviously had a lot of smart arguments up your sleeve to 'swing' me, that you must have prepared well in advance."

"I did."

"Well, if you don't mind, beyond the general lunacy of it, what on Earth made you think I could be 'swung?' Last I looked, I had a well-deserved reputation as a hard-ass."

"I might have tried anyway. But I noticed something in your opening remarks to the jury, when you were talking about excluding the audio, that made me think I could really do it." Now Hannah did look diplomatically at the floor. "When you talked about whether I was raped or not, and whether a rape did or didn't happen …you always said 'at her school.' Not once did you sat 'at Hills.'"

For a long moment the only sound in the room was the faint flutter and hiss of the fire. "It was Stamford," Miracoli said at last. "My daughter." As she opened the door to the porch her eyebrows went up. "I didn't realize I had a tell."

"I can keep a secret," said Hannah.

Chapter 20 - Reformer

Getting McFarrel on board was almost the hardest part of Hannah's triumph. He was summoned to a midnight conference at the Peabodys' to receive his new commands, and whether it was his forced appearance without a suit — he wore a blue Lacoste shirt — or general principles regarding mid-trial client mutinies he threw a proper stink, stalking the livingroom and threating to resign unless Hannah told him exactly *who* her mystery court go-between was that had carried a proposal in *his* name to Judge Miracoli in chambers. He only accepted that such a proposal existed when, at Hannah's urging, he checked his voicemail and found a message from the judge agreeing to his request and asking him to please have the Evidence Submission Form on her desk by 7:00 am. Even then he balked, marshalling all his arguments about how the audio would undermine Hannah's case, until Hannah's mother unexpectedly spoke up.

"Mr. McFarrel, I don't care. I raised my daughter to take a stand on matters of principle, and that's what this is. Exposing this rapist and his protectors is the right thing to do, and you *will* do it."

And so, the next morning, as the opening move in the Defense Evidence phase, the Torture Rant from Hannah's physical audio recorder was played out loud and entered into the court record.

It was every bit the sensation she had imagined. At its announcement — "The segment you are about to hear *is* the message,

exactly as dialed up for police to find, that the killer of Steve Badenhut left on his corpse" — a breathless vacuum filled the gallery,
and as the very first words sounded that proved the Internet version genuine such a cacophony of shrieks and cheers shook the
walls that the gallery had to be cleared — in a confused crush with
reporters running both out and in — and the audio restarted. For
the jury, selected as much as possible from those who had not
heard the Internet release, the as-yet-unencountered voice of
Steve Badenhut affected them so strongly that a fifteen-minute recess had to be called for them to file out to their quarters and re-
cover themselves. It then took almost another hour of legal
wrangling by the lawyers of both sides at the bench to dissect the
appropriate pieces of perjury out of the court record and render
the defamation charge finally nolle prosequi.

Throughout it Hannah sat at the defense table in her demure
outfit, holding herself as still as possible, unsuspected as agent of
the change and receiving only the ambiguous reward of a grim
smile on the face of John Brown behind her shoulder.

She and Judge Miracoli were very careful not to meet each
other's eyes.

Her spectral escort remained, fully stoic again and with emerg-
ing reason, through the two days of Defense Evidence that followed, in which the tide of the case swung palpably against her.

McFarrel had been right: with the Torture Rant on exhibit as
motive, the case was finally a clear rape-and-revenge narrative
and Rapillo, though limited to cross-examination, was lethal.
Hannah was no longer the clear-headed college student who, if
she *was* going to commit murder, would be able to *count*; she was
now officially the girl who had been abused, hunted, and named
for violent death in a recording that would drive *anyone* berserk.

Even McFarrel's own argument boiled down to someone *else* finding the recorder in the park and, yes, being driven to murder by the rant alone. With every expert he summoned to testify to highway driving times and rendezvous math, the jury seemed less convinced.

Hannah sat quiet, erect, calm, as that scoreboard accumulated its total in the wrong direction. *I took my shot.*

In the evenings at the Peabodys' she watched the news and saw the ripples spread. The Boston Police Department was under Federal investigation and several officers had been suspended, including Captain Scavelli; at Hills College the headmaster had announced a sweeping new program of sexual safety and rape awareness; the Rose Bowl featured a moment of silence before the game to condemn rape in athletic programs. A great satisfaction enhanced her feeling of ready resolve. One headline, however, on the computer upstairs, sent her thundering down the carpeted steps with a war whoop that shattered the nervous silence of the house to slosh wine on the tablecloth as she poured herself a glass:

BELEAGUERED HAUGHTON RESIGNS AS HC DEAN OF STUDENTS

On the morning of Rapillo's closing statement she saw Cowley at the courthouse.

She was standing with her parents in the usual crowded hallway before the session, with the usual escort of green-uniformed guards protecting them from, mainly, curious well-wishers peeking in from other cases. For once the Peabodys weren't there—"I can't bear to listen to it," Pam had said—and the Radhe family stood making nervous small talk about the advantage McFarrel would have closing second, tomorrow. Suddenly, at the far end of the curved hall she caught sight of a trench coat and dark hair.

A second look confirmed that this time it really was Cowley.

She froze. He was in conversation with Rapillo and another man, a big policeman in uniform who held in his podgy hand a white box the size of a VHS tape. They were too far away for her to hear over the echoing hubbub, but he was gesturing with the box as Cowley stood alongside. Bodies occluded her view for a moment, and when they cleared Rapillo was clapping his hands — she heard the sound — and laughing delightedly. Her heart pounded. *Did he do it — did he find it?* She licked her lips; she didn't know whether she was frightened or excited. And at that moment Cowley looked up and met her eyes.

He gave her a sad, strange smile — then her view was blocked again and when it cleared he was gone. She had a brief glimpse of the backs of Rapillo and the policeman as they went their separate ways in the crowd; the chimes were sounding. She stood rooted. She had no idea what that look meant — it somehow reminded her of the texts they had exchanged — but she could only assume that she was to be totally exposed. *Miracoli will finally get her surprise,* she thought dully. Her parents were talking to her; she stared suddenly at them, wondering for the first time how their lives would be altered by her disappearance into prison for life. "Be strong," her father was saying, as the guards moved to separate them. "Remember, McFarrel gets the last word."

"I, I hope so," she said.

She spent the whole of Rapillo's closing speech in a speculative daze, barely listening to his preliminaries as she waited for the sudden bombshell. Only slowly did it sink in that he was *not* going to reveal the fire pump, *not* pull out new evidence, that he was making his same old argument that she couldn't count and got miraculously lucky thanks to a random Amtrak delay. He had no new information. *Then what did Cowley show him? What did he say?* It was inexplicable. But it was a reprieve.

In this state she largely missed what was universally acknowledged as a home run by Rapillo on close. Liberated by Steve's villainy he hit new heights of rhetoric. "Folks, as soon as she hears that, that *thing* on her recorder, all thoughts of *timing* go out the window. She goes crazy — as anyone would! Right? Right? The hell with whatever clock she's on — she *has* to kill this bastard! Her life depends on it! *Then*, guess what, he's not in his room. He's at a party until eleven-twentyfive. She has to stake him out! Her timing's shot but who cares? Would you care — after hearing that, with your name on it? No! *I* sure wouldn't," etc. etc.

She looked at the jury. Their faces were riveted on Rapillo, nodding at every word.

Now she understood Cowley's sad smile. There had been no reprieve. The Torture Rant she had released had done its work and she would go down after all, the last piece of her saving alibi overridden by her own evidence. She drew and released a long breath, in exact company with the white shirt of John Brown.

Across the homicide office John Scavelli, dressed in jeans and a red flannel shirt, set the last of the cardboard boxes down on his desk and smiled. "Well, it was a short life with my own office. Now when I come back in three months I expect everything in this box to still be here. I'm looking at you, Racona. And keep the chief's paws out of it too."

"In three months the chief won't be here," Racona said. "And who knows, *I* might have the office. I think I'm the only one to come out of this smelling good. Ask Cowley."

"Cowley? You'll keep an eye on my box?"

It was 11:00 pm and they were the only ones in the office. Cowley, tie loosened and shirt wrinkled, glared slowly over from his chair. "Get your sorry ass out of here," he said.

"What's the matter with you?" Racona asked when Scavelli was gone. "You still burned because of the defamation charge? *You* didn't lie under oath. Granted, it does suck that the one part of it left is you emailing your girlfriend for the hack. When's your date with the inquest?"

Cowley looked up at her innocent, needling eyes. "I was wrong about you, Racona. Looks like your solution to the train problem is going to work after all. '*She was too berserk to count.*' Be proud."

His vicious falsetto on the quote took the smile out of her eyes, and they moved to his desk, where a large overhead photo of the blue car at Greenwich Bay lay creased. "You still think she caused the train delay herself? 'Cause CSI—"

"I know. And they won't. It doesn't matter."

"I'd be careful with that at the inquest. Pulling manpower down there on that theory helped get Koontz retired. I know you never wanted the Captain's office, but you don't want crazy either."

"Go home, Racona," he said.

From the doorway she looked back. "You got her, Cowley. It was your work that roped her back in, and now she'll go to jail. Things are never as clean as you want."

When she was gone he sat alone in the homicide office thinking about that. Racona was right: she *was* guilty, and Rapillo's argument would probably win; he had watched the closing, standing at the back of the courtroom, and had seen its deadly effectiveness on the jury. So why wasn't he happy?

The ventilator hummed under the fluorescent lights. Dull sounds of chaotic noise came through the walls from the main lobby; another busy night in Boston. He had no reason to still be here.

Was it because Rapillo had laughed in his and Koontz' face that morning in the hall when, in a last act of due diligence, they had presented their theory apropos of a postponement? Koontz had taken the brunt of that, and anyway Rapillo had crowed happily that he didn't need it.

He was right.

Things are never as clean as you want.

Everything had certainly turned out differently from what he had expected — as by now he should be used to, with that girl. He had gone to Greenwich Bay thinking her rapist evidence forever silenced but that McFarrel would at least get her off. Instead she had gotten her real audio *admitted* — no one else had any idea how that had happened, but Cowley knew at once that converting Clare goddamn Miracoli to feminism was something only Hannah Radhe could do, and with a little private detective work he had confirmed it, to his immense relish. And now, as if in recompense, she would probably go to prison on garbage.

But that was her choice. For her — cause.

He had seen the headlines, including the one about Dean Haughton's ouster. And her victory was getting bigger, spreading farther, day by day. She had started to change the world. Now she was going to pay for it. Those things happened, he saw dimly, in a region far above his own of law.

Well, McFarrel still has his closing statement tomorrow. Do I — want him to pull it out? Can he?

He growled. One thing *he* would pull out against Rapillo's

impenetrably bush-league argument was that Hannah *wasn't* driven berserk by the Torture Rant. She took that evil thing in stride when she encountered it in the park and stuck coolly to her plan: her sword didn't waver an inch. That wasn't exactly a legal defense, but *that's* who Hannah Radhe was.

It still bugged him, though, that her plan involved leaving the train and driving all the way back to HC before she finds out what's on her recorder. He had always felt something wrong there. The whole thing depends on Steve confessing, and she leaves the train without knowing if he's said anything at all? Was that foolish confidence?

Oh, give it up. Probably she just knew Steve Badenhut that well. *As we all do, now.* Strangely, despite the whole trial in his name, it had been a long time since he'd thought about Steve himself, the man. The monster. *Hell, if ever murder was justified –*

No. Stop. Don't go down that road.

He rubbed his eyes and looked around the empty office. Why was he still here? He should go home to bed and stop worrying about justice and virtue and things that never did a cop any good.

He reached for his computer to turn it off, but instead found himself navigating to the folder for the electronic evidence archive.

No, no, no – this won't help her. This won't help anybody.

He entered his password, and descended through subfolders until he reached the one marked "Steve Badenhut Audio." Again he paused and looked around the office, then quickly fished his headphones out of the drawer and plugged them in. He opened the folder and double-clicked a file.

He had heard Steve's murderous rant only twice: the first time in company with the other detectives on the case, then again in the interrogation room when he had played it for Hannah. Both times had been for a purpose. Now he was doing what a wise cop should never do: look closely into evil. *This doesn't justify – it can't justify – hell,* she *didn't even do it for vengeance –*

Steve Badenhut's living intent took close possession of his ears. To kidnap Hannah to a remote cabin. To hold her there for months. To beat, torture, and rape her. To finally —

Suddenly Cowley frowned. He lowered his head and closed his eyes, listening hard. Then he opened his eyes wide and looked at the folder contents.

There were two files in the locked folder: the original from the digital audio recorder, that had been copied over for the interrogation, and a download of the infamous Internet version. The department cops had long known them to be the same. He had clicked the second one.

They *weren't* the same.

He stopped the recording, double-clicked the other file, and listened to the same beginning of Steve's rant. Then he stopped that recording, pulled off his headphones, and leaned back in his chair with a squeak and a smile.

He got it. Scavelli had been right on the witness stand after all, though he hadn't known it. The Internet version *didn't* match the recorder's, exactly. It was the same content, but slightly different in tone, a subtle but clear variance. It meant there had been *two* recorders going in the park that night. One was her digital audio recorder to be put on the body, the other was likely a live feed over wi-fi to her laptop as she sat at Eastern's. He remembered the deposition of the waitress, Kimberly Atkins, that Hannah had sat there for hours at her computer listening on her headphones. *That's it — that's how she knew.*

He was nodding with an appreciative smile — and suddenly he gasped.

It meant more than that.

It meant the department had never been hacked. The copy she posted to the Internet was the second file — *her own copy*. She had it all along. She had posted her own file to the forums, and the only "hack" was to route it *through* the department using his email — the only cop's email she had — to disguise her possession of the copy. *Therefore* — if she was framing the department for an evidence leak of their file that never actually happened — it meant the "outside hacker" was her work too.

She planted my save. She planted the "hack" exoneration, for CCD and the FBI to find. Or, of course, got her boyfriend to.

He shook his head slowly, smiling. *Damn, she's good*, he thought, and he didn't know which sense of the word he was using. With a stinging in his eyes he felt the last of his anger disappear.

A muffled group of loud voices went brawling past in the hall and faded. He looked at the clock. 1:00 am.

It was already tomorrow.

Chapter 21 - The Verdict

Hannah and McFarrel arrived early at the back entrance of the John Adams courthouse—there were no protestors now—and went through the security screening together. As they handed over their cellphones to the clerk for the day Hannah checked her iPhone one more time for text messages, as she had regularly done since her glimpse of Cowley, but there were none. She didn't know why she was expecting one. They rode the wood-paneled elevator to the top floor, he in his suit, she in a conservative white blouse and dark-blue skirt under her parka. A few other court functionaries rode with them and snuck looks at her.

She was quiet. It had come down to McFarrel's closing speech, the last act of the trial, and she tried to face evenly whatever might come. And she too, perhaps, thought about justice and its mysterious workings, for she had the calm that comes from knowing the outcome was no longer in her hands.

I took my shot.

Up ahead in the big curved hallway Cowley was leaning against the wall on the right, opposite the portraits. He was in his normal outfit of trench coat and tie, and was by himself. His eyes met her wide ones from a distance, and for a strong second she drank in a look full of inexplicable forgiveness and sympathy. Then he looked away.

She *had* to talk to him. In private, somehow, somewhere. She licked her lips. She and McFarrel were approaching him amid an escort of three uniformed guards, who wouldn't allow it; other guards were present, observing: *everyone* was watching her as she came. She looked rapidly around the hall. She was mere steps from him.

As they passed she turned to McFarrel and said loudly, "I love the architecture here. I particularly like those big windows in the restrooms; they open and close as smooth as butter. Speaking of which, I'll be right back," and with a bright smile she turned right and pushed through the ladies' room door.

The high-ceilinged, handsome restroom had a broad expanse of maroon floor between the cream-colored sinks on her right and the line of stalls on her left. A woman passed her adjusting her business dress under the recessed lighting and exited. Hannah was alone.

She crossed rapidly to the back wall. The five-foot windows of frosted glass were sunk in deep insets, their bottoms as high as her waist. She went for the one on the right. She had to climb up over the gold-faced heater grille and half-lie on the sill with her feet off the floor, but it did lift easy on smooth counterweights, and in a second her head was outdoors.

A short moment later the window to her right rolled up, and Cowley stuck his head out and looked at her. He smiled. And there they were in the gold light of the winter sunrise, high above the streets of Boston with their hair stirring in the wind off the Inner Harbor, seven feet apart and perfectly alone.

"Be careful—you don't want to muss up your clothes for court," he said. They looked at each other for a moment. "You look great," he said.

"I, I needed to say I'm sorry," she said. "For the leak. I'm so sorry. I'm so—"

"It's all right! I understand. I know you had your own copy now, from Eastern's. Thank *you!* For adding the, the underlying —" He gave her a look full of unsaid information.

She nodded. *Then he knew.* "When I saw you yesterday I thought —" She paused. He was looking down and to the side. How much could she say — of everything she wanted to? "I thought you'd caught me."

He looked up. "I got to Greenwich Bay." He licked his lips; he seemed to be weighing the same question. They held each other's eyes. "CSI's been climbing all over the catenary down there," he prompted.

She smiled. "That's nice," she confirmed, and saw his eyes narrow in delicious frustration. A swirl of Atlantic wind through the stone channels of Pemberton Square brought the long moan of a boat horn in a silence full of truths known, mysteries that must remain unspoken, if only for a few more hours.

They both spoke at once. "Will you —" "I wanted to —" And fell silent again.

"Congratulations on getting your audio released," he said. He gave her a mischievous smile, communicating that he knew it was her work, and her breath caught. *He's the only one who will ever say that. But how —* Her eyes must have widened, because he added, "I looked at your cellphone track; we still have access while the case is on. Don't worry, I won't tell. Whatever the hell you did in there, it was the right thing, to get that audio out. I mean, it wasn't right to —" he trailed off with a pained look, and she knew he was referencing her first method of trying to publicize it.

"I know! I know. If, if I —" She didn't know what she was trying to say.

He did. "I hope it doesn't count against you too much, in

there."

She nodded. "That Rapillo is a good prosecutor."

"I'd like to put him in cement overshoes," Cowley said, and she laughed. "Hey. Do you remember the day we met, when you said you would bring down Steve Badenhut and more than him? I didn't take you seriously. I do now."

Again their eyes locked. "Remember I said you shouldn't flatter yourself?" She saw, rather than heard, his soft chuckle. "I lied. You should." Her cheeks were burning.

"Hannah, I—" This time what passed between their interlocked eyes was a single thought. He freed an arm through his window and stretched out his hand; she did the same, sliding her belly forward on the windowsill. From window to window across the high stone facade their fingertips just touched, and held at the first joint. Her body was dangerously unbalanced on the sill but she had strong legs and they held her as she felt the warm strength of his hand. There were rustlings in the rest room behind her; she didn't have much time. Their arms fell and she recovered her balance. The traffic sounds rose up between them.

That — that was our —

"They're going to start soon," she said.

Cowley looked hard at her, unsmiling; his eyes had never looked more deeply sunk in their dark sockets. His farewell words came as if pulled out of him, stating the obvious in anguished regret: "You know if they convict you it will be for malice prepense—first degree—it's the worst kind of murder."

She gave him a brave smile. "Funny," she said, "my opinion of this Badenhut case is that it was the best kind of murder."

She watched the tip of his tongue play over his lower lip as a smile worked his mouth. "Oh hell, mine too!" he cried.

Her parents and the Peabodys were in their usual spot in the front row; when she turned she saw their faces full of tension and faith. The gallery was full as always but less solidly female: her supporters were still there, stretching their necks at the unexpected view of her face, but the trial had also accumulated the generally curious since Judge Miracoli's electric stand against corruption.

At the back of the room she saw Cowley come in and lean against the wall.

The gavel rapped, and Hannah faced front as the room quieted like a switch. Miracoli's new standing had translated into an added gravitas, and in her purple-draped robe she now ruled her sensation trial with a word.

"Mr. McFarrel, at this time you may begin the defense closing."

McFarrel pushed back his chair and stood. Hannah felt a visitor arrive behind her right shoulder. She sat straight and breathed deeply.

At first she could make no sense of McFarrel's speech, and wondered whether she was concentrating so hard on his words as to turn them to gibberish. But no — he hadn't yet made a single reference to train schedules, to rendezvous math, to Rapillo's argument. He was rambling on — apparently forever — about other things entirely, like the streetlights in the triangular park, the presence of several shouting boys calling attention to the area. "But most importantly, ladies and gentlemen, that recorder finished recording at seven-oh-four p.m. Steve Badenhut was murdered at eleven-thirty p.m., and that is a precise clock time. Ladies and gentlemen, that is four and a half hours. Four and a half hours.

"In contrast, and I say this again, this is based on clock times meticulously established by the prosecution, the blue car of the killer, which they have not proved to be connected in any way to Hannah, this blue car arrives at the lower parkinglot of the HC campus at eleven-oh-three p.m. That is twenty-seven minutes before the murder. Twenty-seven minutes."

And Hannah saw what he was doing. He wasn't *going* to talk about the train math. Rapillo had overridden it with his Torture Rant argument and there was no getting it back. Instead he was using the little fact that the Torture Rant had been dialed up when left on the corpse.

"Ladies and gentlemen, don't forget that this vivid, appalling, enraging speech takes up one minute and thirty-three seconds out of an eight-hour tape. And yet Steve Badenhut's killer *found* that tiny segment, and *evaluated* it as the best part, meaning he compared it to the rest, and *selected* it, correctly, as the point to set the recorder when he put it on the body. Ladies and gentlemen, who had the time to search that eight-hour tape? Well, the person who finds it *four and a half hours* before the murder — *that* person has time. In contrast, let's look at the prosecution's strange theory of the killer being Hannah Radhe, fresh from a train, in a hurry, on the clock, in a heavy disguise, grabbing that recorder from the park, let's talk about her *twenty-seven minutes* to sit somewhere and listen and find and evaluate…"

Hannah listened in a kind of numb wonder. Rapillo had firmly established, in the jury's mind, that hearing the Torture Rant drives the killer "berserk" — so McFarrel was simply exempting Hannah from those who could have heard it. It was logical legerdemain, but it was *working*: she saw it not only in the jurors' faces but in Rapillo's, whose olive complexion had turned an un-dersea shade of green.

She had the odd sensation of watching the last piece of her alibi, for the sake of which she had brought Amtrak's Northeast Corridor shuddering to a halt, dismissed, made irrelevant, replaced with an abstract ping-pong game of competing fictions. This, then, was Law, and she sensed John Brown's nose lifted as if suspecting that she would win their bet on a cheat. And she *might* win, she saw, simply because, for quite different reasons, she had put her "baby monitor" in the park and listened to it at Eastern's. And so she had known where the rant was.

When McFarrel was done there was a genuine sensation-trial sensation. Everyone recognized that he had made a stunning defense and that the momentum of the case had shifted, and when the judge granted Rapillo's request for a break the room erupted in talk and the newsmen crowded each other out the doors in their haste to make their reports. Hannah looked at her family: Mike Peabody's forehead ridge was drawn in deeper relief and he wagged his forefinger at McFarrel; her parents looked bloodless with the tension of suppressed hope. McFarrel himself, discreetly aglow, gave Hannah a tight, confident smile.

The gavel rapped; the spectators returned to their seats, the jury filed back into their box. A moment later Rapillo came back to his table from a conference at the bar.

"Do I understand that State wants a rebuttal?" the judge asked.

"We do," said Rapillo, "and we move to add new evidence, as is our right if and when such evidence bears directly upon the closing argument."

"And what evidence is that?" asked Miracoli, and for the first time Hannah heard a faint pitch of entertainment in her voice.

The surprises were finally coming in.

"Your Honor, we wish to question one witness on one issue. It relates to the audio recording that was at the center of Defense's argument. Your Honor, we have reason to ask whether Hannah Radhe had prior knowledge of the contents of that recording by the time she arrived on campus. We have reason to ask whether she was listening to it, long distance, as it was being made."

Uneasy murmurs rippled through the courtroom. A cold spike went through Hannah's stomach—and Miracoli picked that moment to meet her eyes. The judge's eyes perceptibly widened with curiosity.

The next instant Hannah's widened further.

"Your Honor, the State calls Detective Alan Cowley to the stand."

Cowley walked down the center aisle of the gallery as if in a dream. He took his stand in the box, put his hand on the Bible, and was sworn in. In front of him the sea of faces swam away in blurring colors to the back of the room; in the foreground were Hannah's eyes, round and staring under her brown bangs. He knew he mustn't meet them.

His mind whirled. How had they known? Had *they* noticed the slight difference between the recorder audio and the Internet version? But how had they known to pick *him*? He remembered hearing someone hastily leaving the restroom behind him, that morning; he hadn't thought anything of it. *What had he said?*

He steadied himself. It didn't matter. They *had* picked him, and he was being sworn in. He was under oath. They took the Bible away and he looked at the veins of his hand as if his body had acted on its own to betray him.

Rapillo's chunky face with its slicked-back hair became a closer foreground. The chunks seemed a little out of focus, and Cowley realized it wasn't his own eyesight: the prosecutor looked desperate. Cowley knew the look. This was a man unsure of himself, taking a last shot. *Whatever it is, let it miss*, he thought.

"Detective Cowley, this is Exhibit Thirtyfive, the testimony of Kimberly Atkins, where she says that Hannah Radhe spent hours at Eastern's with her laptop open and her headphones in. Is that correct?"

"Yes."

"Uh-huh, and this is Exhibit Fourteen, your own deposition, sir, concerning your analysis of Hannah Radhe's laptop, which showed that her laptop had been erased, reformatted, thus removing all record of what programs she had on it, including audio programs to which she might have been listening during those hours with those headphones. Is that correct?"

"Yes." *It was getting closer.*

"And if a recording device in that park had wi-fi, connected to the Hills College network, then its pickup could be received live by a device that was also connected to a network, such as the free wi-fi network that's available at Eastern's Bar, is that so?"

"That is so."

"Now, Detective Cowley, I want to talk about that audio. There's been a lot of unusual activity surrounding that audio lately, hasn't there? Not long ago, a lot of perjured statements were removed from the record about it, because it turned out to be the actual original, leaked from police custody with your name, Detective Cowley, as the leaker. Detective, did you leak the audio?"

"No, sir."

"You didn't. And in fact, the FBI determined that it was an outside hack of the police department. We have also seen sworn statements from the police that the evidence room was undisturbed. Do you have any reason to doubt those sworn statements or the FBI findings?"

"No." Cowley understood that Rapillo had picked him to answer these questions because presumably he would lie if necessary to cover his own ass. Cowley despised him.

"Therefore, Detective, if the evidence room was undisturbed, then logic tells us a simple thing: Hannah Radhe's audio recorder was hacked electronically, over wi-fi. Thus we know it had the *capability* of broadcasting to Hannah Radhe on the night of the murder. Now, I'm not saying that's what happened. I am merely raising the possibility, before the court and the jury, that it *could* have happened. It *might* have happened. And you know, it does seem to me that among those earlier statements was a finding that the Internet posting matched Hannah Radhe's location. The jury, of course, may not consider those statements, but gosh, it would match what they *must* consider, the possibility that she had her own copy from that live, wi-fi broadcast from the Hills College wi-fi to Eastern's wi-fi. And, Detective, you can oblige me by taking a look at this, Exhibit One, which is Hannah Radhe's digital audio recorder. Will you please confirm for the court that this model has wi-fi capabilities."

Do not smile, Cowley ordered himself. Yet it was with immense personal pleasure that he answered, "Sir, this model does not have wi-fi capabilities."

"What?" Rapillo said.

Cowley repeated himself.

"Are — you sure?"

"Objection," said McFarrel. "Witness has already answered the question."

"Sustained."

Cowley had the even greater pleasure of watching Rapillo's face collapse from within as his last argument folded impossibly in on itself. He almost heard the *whoosh* as the intended dart sailed past his ear, and he risked the briefest eye contact with Hannah. He saw that she had heard it too.

God bless you and your second recorder, he thought. *It was worth having my name on the leak for this.*

Judge Miracoli cleared her throat. "Do you have any further questions for the witness, Mr. Rapillo?"

"No further questions, Your Honor." Rapillo turned a mournful back to the bench and retreated into his uncertain future. "The State rests..."

With a certain deflated weariness the judge asked, "Defense? Do you wish to cross-examine?"

McFarrel got to his feet. "We-el, just to confirm for the record the clear meaning of that bizarre exchange, Detective Cowley, do you say positively before the jury that there is no way, to the best of your knowledge, that Hannah Radhe had any knowledge of what was on her audio recorder that night?"

Cowley paused.

A long silence fell over the courtroom.

A thousand eyes stared at him in confusion. The Bible seemed to throb on its wooden platform to his right. The walls of the very building seemed to stoop in upon him.

"Detective? Did you hear the question?" the judge asked.

In the whole room one pair of eyes looked straight into his with the calm of complete readiness. The world shrunk to a small circle of light.

And he lied.

"Thank you, Detective," said McFarrel. "Your Honor, the defense rests."

After a little less than an hour's deliberation, the jury pronounced Hannah Radhe innocent.

From halfway through the two words of the verdict a great tumult arose in the courtroom behind her; she heard her father's voice cry "Yes!" and a shriek from her mother. She turned in her chair to see them, and for a fraction of second her passing eyes met McFarrel's close up in a glance of keenly conditional gratitude—a glance so full of information that it had the power to awaken him in the still watches of the night years later—and then she was buried in her parents' arms, pounded by her father's hands, covered in her mothers' tears and Pam's kisses, and she was struggling to pull free enough to look—through the sudden absence of a white shirt—toward the far back of the gallery.

Cowley was gone.

From his resumed position standing at the back of the room Cowley had a quick sight of the family members embracing, and heard their shrieks, before his view was blocked by the great saltation of the gallery to its feet in a clamor that defied the little pops of Miracoli's gavel. He turned and was one of the first through the doors. He had seen Hannah's eyes when descending from the stand; he needed no further reward.

He was alone in the elevator that descended slowly to the garage where his squad car waited—if he would be getting into it.

The verdict had sent a spear of pure delight through him, but somehow in his turn and exit and brief passage to the elevator it had changed into a surge of bitter anger: anger at himself, anger at Rapillo's stupid sandbag setup, anger at the whole filthy court system that had waylaid him into betraying his sworn oath. It was sudden feeling of disgust that made him, as the empty cab descended, want to pull out his badge and hurl it on the floor. Cowley was no good at the best of times when it came to looking at his emotions, and all he knew now was that he was in tumultuous trouble.

He had crossed a line, somehow much bigger than lying under oath, though that stood out as a stark symbol. Because he *would* do it again—every time, in that situation. *What did that mean?* Something in him had violently changed—he seemed to be operating from some new, rebellious place, taking a stand with Hannah against the garbagy nonsense of courts and maybe law itself. Was that him? And if so why was he so—angry about it? He knew he had to come to terms with it before he could open the door to his car.

He was unequivocally glad that Hannah was free. He was fine with that, even happy. What was infuriating was that he would now have to defend himself against the charge of ulterior motive—for "his girlfriend," Racona would tease—a clever play so that now he could—so that they—no! That was completely off base! That had nothing to do with it.

And it was then that he understood he was never going to see Hannah again.

Well, what are you going to do, he asked himself scathingly, *visit her in her dorm at HC?* Their—interaction—whatever you could call it—existed for and within the case, and the case was done. There would be, there could be, nothing more.

The elevator doors opened and he started across the underground garage.

He very much hadn't wanted her to go to prison. That was what slowed his steps toward his squad car. That was the part he could never explain to, for example, the department shrink. He had helped a murderess evade justice because he wanted her to be free.

To kill again? Do I think she will? Probably not.

Is she a dangerous woman, dangerous to society? Oh yes. Even more so now. This was just the beginning of the Hannah Radhe story.

He stood at his car, hand resting on the roof, and smiled as he imagined it. Because that's exactly where it *wasn't* a small lie to help her go free. In a way he had aided and abetted whatever she would do next. Which, as that girl grew up, could be a lot, he thought.

But that's why she couldn't be in prison. Because I agree with what she's going to do. Even if I myself don't do it.

He leaned back against the car with his arms folded, and took a deep breath. The garage with its grimy square pillars rematerialized to his sight. He was okay now. He would stay the cop, within the dirt and mess of the law. Let her be the reformer, and change the system. She was right: some of it needed changing. In his own way, and despite himself, carried out of his comfort zone on the best case of his life, he had helped something happen at that other level. He could never regret it—and he knew it would never happen again.

He pulled out his cellphone. It had been mere minutes since the verdict; she wouldn't be getting her own phone back from security for a while yet. This wouldn't be to start a dialogue; this text would be a farewell message.

He scrolled to the end of their brief, luminous conversation and added a new line. He wrote:

> Do Good

and pressed Send.

Then he unlocked his car and got in, and brought the motor to life with a growl that echoed under the grey roof. For a terrible minute he was tempted to send a second text, and ask how she did it. How she delayed that train. She was innocent now; it was safe; it would be double jeopardy to — but no. He shook his head, and left his phone in his pocket. It was over. He would let his last message stand.

As his squad car came up the ramp onto Pemberton Street his radio came to life and he picked up the mic. "Car fifteen, coming on patrol."

The radio squawked.   "Fifteen, we have a 10-35 in Chelsea, officers at the scene. Can you report?"

"On my way."

"Fifteen — sorry, Cowley, is that you? Are you on duty?"

"I am," he said.

Epilogue

On the night of her return to Hills College Hannah opened the safe in the offices of the Vista and replaced the stolen money with cash from her own account. It was never missed.

The murder of Steve Badenhut was never solved: the spotlight was left on an empty stage. This gave Hannah a certain suppositional notoriety on campus during the Spring semester. There were recurring jokes on the fencing team about not pissing her off when she had a sword in her hand, which made her roll her eyes, and she did have to intervene when a group of earnest freshmen wanted to start a women's literary magazine called FemiNazi Fatale, which turned into a bit of a spat, but by and large she was able to mature into the receipt of a weightier attention befitting her new celebrity. She did interviews, and accepted lecture invitations at the Ivy League (her article for the Vista had attracted new notice), received book offers (for which she had no time) and the inevitable requests for television appearances ("Don't go near television!" her father, the NBC producer, commanded). Her name was rising within the women's movement, with a slightly maverick, action-oriented halo that she liked, and she began to learn how to leverage it in a manner of her choosing. In all this she found she was merely entering a fuller self.

It was with a little of that fuller self, and a lot of that notoriety, that she walked into the Kingfishers' clubhouse on her second day back. She stood before the team, that included Davey Coleman,

Reggie Mathis and Andrew Keith amongst a lot of wide-eyed
boys who never had or would hurt a woman, and explained what
she had actually said in her newspaper article, that she hadn't intended to malign ("or injure") anyone individually, nor the team,
and she hoped they were square. If there was a subtext of "If not,
look to your own" that contributed to their rapid handshaking
agreement all around, she didn't mind. She had no further trouble with the football club.

A final note is necessary about Andrew Keith. True to his pre-
diction, his career ended its football phase with graduation, and
some short years later it found him ensconced in a corporate vice
presidency, plump, comfortably married and father of three teenagers. The one moment in which his evil tendencies arose to the
call of a leader past, he never again tried or really wanted to abuse
a woman.

Normal college life materialized at full velocity around
Hannah as if from a roller coaster car shot out of a tunnel. She
started the semester two weeks late and had to catch up in her
classes, plus rush back into condition for the big fencing meet with
Harvard, and in between she was dreadfully behind in studying
Arabic for her rapidly approaching summer program. (June Anders had somehow communicated, through diplomatic elisions in
her emails, that whatever brouhaha had lately troubled the Boston
media left no impression in Washington.) It wasn't until almost a
month had passed in the ebb and flux of classrooms, cafeterias,
fencing practices at the echoing Enleike Center, meetings with the
rape-awareness group established by Amy Enlaw, the new Dean
of Students, and too occasional movie dates with Randall, that she
noticed the great background relief attending her every move:

The threat of violence was gone.

The thought came to her suddenly at 2:00 in the morning as she bent over her "Problems in American History" textbook. She paused, listening to the calm, breathing silence of the Fitzhenry dorm around her, weighing the lightness of that huge, simple absence and its meaning. She thought of that winter night at the triangular park when she had helped clear Coach Bailey, when in darkness and ignorance everything seemed imbued with rage and sexual predation. She had changed that feeling, not only for herself but for others — for the boys on the football team, for so many safer and happier girls, for the whole campus — and in fact made it better than it was. She had brought the light.

And she had done it by murdering Steve.

The moment of realizing it was the moment of cascading complications. She turned and looked at the framed photograph on her wall, to which the spirit of John Brown had returned to take its silent place among her other heroes. She had grown since the night she had pointed a summoning finger at it. His firm clean chin and lips compressed for action still told the truth that violent acts are not merely *acceptable* in a good cause, but sometimes *indispensable* to it. And yet his eyes now seemed to hold a strange salute with a different meaning. She had won her bet — she had both changed the world and survived to live in it — she was now in a realm he had never entered. What behavior is appropriate in that better world? More violence? He, her hero, seemed now to look to her for the answer, and it was no.

Though her life and rebel intelligence were still, and always would be, dedicated in full to the cause of liberation, of changing a system, and though in that combat she would be unafraid to draw her sword when necessary, never again would she willingly choose murder as a means.

She turned from the photo and picked up her cellphone, and gazed again at her last text from Cowley:

Do Good

Will I ever see him again? Somehow she knew she wouldn't. The world that had brought them almost together had ended, leaving them both, she knew, changed, and neither able to return.

In silence she felt again her obligation and reaffirmed over the glowing words her vow.

In the first warm week of April, Karen Cowley had the upstairs windows open as she was vacuuming the bedrooms, bent and sweating with a bandana over her hair. The unending groan of the machine, like a person undergoing monotonous torture, mingled with the soft rush of the lilac tree just outside the curtains and the muffled declamations of the TV news downstairs, and it was only because it was the last thing she wanted to hear at that moment that she caught the sound of the doorbell.

She turned off the vacuum, straightened and drew an annoyed breath to call downstairs, but Alan's voice came up first: "I'll get it!" She went to the window and looked down; at the curb was a UPS truck. She heard the rustle of packaging being opened, and started descending the stairs, curious.

She never knew why Alan cried out, in a voice that filled the house, "Motorboat!"

It seemed to have nothing to do with the strange, messy object in her livingroom atop a flower of cardboard panels: a damaged, half-rusted, portable red fire pump, covered in — she was sure — strips of dried seaweed.

Cowley looked up at her and spread his arms with a grin. "Motorboat!" he crowed again.

Made in the USA
Middletown, DE
03 June 2022

66626482R00186